GHOST S'
FOR
CHRISTMAS
Volume Two

A Kikui
Christmas Classic

GHOST STORIES
FOR
CHRISTMAS
Volume Two

Edited by

Andi Brooks

KIKUI PRESS
TOKYO

Ghost Stories for Christmas
Volume Two

Compiled, edited and introduced by Andi Brooks
Published by Kikui Press © 2023
Compilation, organization, editing and design of this
anthology, introduction and notes copyright © 2023
Andi Brooks

All inquiries should be directed to Kikui Press at
kikuipress@gmail.com

ISBN: 9798857591666

Cover design by
designmanjapan
www.designmanjapan.com

For
ARNOLD PETIT
A fellow haunter of the dark

INTRODUCTION

For this second volume of *Ghost Stories For Christmas*, I have selected twenty-six stories from the golden age of the festive ghost story. Spanning the years 1858-1929, the majority of these stories were originally published in British, American and Canadian magazines and newspapers. Although some were later revised by their authors for publication in book form, I have once again chosen to go back to those original versions to present the stories as they first appeared. One exception is the chilling story *Afterward* by Edith Wharton. A very noticeable lapse in continuity in the original version of the story published in the January 1910 edition of *The Century Magazine* was corrected in the slightly revised version published in Wharton's October 1910 collection *Tales of Men and Ghosts*. It is this revised version which I have included in this anthology.

Other than the correction of obvious typographical errors, all of the stories are reproduced as originally published, complete with their archaic spelling, punctuation, and sometimes offensive vocabulary. While some modern-day publishers choose to edit or rewrite past writing containing language expressing once prevalent and socially accepted prejudices, the sanitizing of historical literature to avoid discomfort or offence can only serve to promote ignorance, fertile ground upon which to sow the seeds of hatred and prejudice. With this in mind, the reader is forewarned that *Mustapha* by Sabine Baring-Gould contains strong racial slurs.

The Christmas ghost story is a rich and varied genre which has evolved through the years. In each volume of this series, it is my aim to reflect the full range of the genre by including examples of stories sentimental, comical, and, of course, truly terrifying for your seasonal delectation. Although it is my sincere hope that the reading of these anthologies will become a regular part of your Christmas, please don't leave them to languish upon your bookshelf throughout the rest of the year least the ghosts contained within their pages, growing resentful at your neglect, decide to...well, you have been warned!

Andi Brooks, Tokyo, 2023.

CONTENTS

NOTES

The Dead Man's Story by James Hain Friswell (May 8, 1825–March 12, 1878) was published in Friswell's *Ghost Stories and Phantom Fancies* in1858.

Horror: A True Tale by John Berwick Harwood (1828–February 15, 1899) appeared in the January 1861 edition of *Blackwood's Edinburgh Magazine.*

A Goblin Ditty by George Manville Fenn (January 3, 1831–August 26, 1909) was published in Fenn's *Christmas Penny Readings, Original Sketches for the Season* in October 1867.

The Ghost. A Christmas Story by William Douglas O'Connor (January 2, 1832–May 9, 1889) was published in the January 1856 edition of *Putnam's Monthly Magazine of American Literature, Science and Art.* When revised and republished by G. P. Putnam & Son in 1867, the story was accompanied by two illustrations by Thomas Nast (September 26, 1840–December 7, 1902). For this anthology, I have included those illustrations with the original 1856 version of the story.

A Strange Christmas Game by Charlotte Riddell (September 30, 1832–September 24, 1906) was published in *The Broadway Annual* in 1867. During her lifetime, Charlotte Riddell published her work under the name of Mrs J. H. Riddell.

The Ghost's Summons by Ada Buisson (March 26, 1839–December 27, 1866) was published posthumously in the January 1868 issue of the *Belgravia* monthly magazine.

The Christmas Club, A Ghost Story by Edward Eggleston (December 10, 1837–September 3, 1902) was published in the January 1873 edition of *Scribner's Monthly, an Illustrated Magazine for the People.*

The Ghost of Charlotte Cray by Florence Marryat (July 9, 1833–October 27, 1899) was published in 1878 in *Judy's Annual* for 1879.

The Wraith of Barnjum by F. Ansty, the pen name of Thomas Anstey Guthrie (August 8, 1856–March 10, 1934), was published in the March 1879 edition of *Temple Bar*.

The Open Door by Margaret O. Wilson Oliphant (April 4, 1828–June 20, 1897) was published in the January 1882 edition of *Blackwood's Edinburgh Magazine*.

A Christmas Ghost. A Story of Christmas-Tide—A Lively Experience and a Very Happy Result by an uncredited author was published in the Canadian newspaper the *Daily British Whig* on Saturday, December 23, 1882.

What Was He? by Theo Gift, the pen name of Dorothy Henrietta Boulger (May 30, 1847–July 22, 1923), was published in *All the Year Round* i
n November 1883.

The Beeston Ghost; or Forty Years Ago. A Norfolk Tale edited by the Reverend John Swaffield Orton, Rector of Beeston-next-Mileham (June 17, 1837–February 24, 1895) was published in 1884 to raise funds for the restoration of Beeston Church in the village of Beeston in Norfolk, England.

The Christmas Shadrach by Frank Richard Stockton (April 5, 1834–April 20, 1902) was published in the December 1891 edition of *The Century Monthly Magazine* with an illustration by Albert Beck Wenzell (1864–March 4, 1917).

The Wicked Editor's Christmas Dream by Alice Mary Vince (Dates of birth and death unknown) was published in the supplement to the English newspaper *The Tamworth Herald* on Saturday December 23, 1893.

Mustapha by Sabine Baring-Gould (January 28, 1834–January 2, 1924) was first published in the *Western Weekly Mercury* in 1894. When revised and republished in Baring-Gould's *A Book of Ghosts* in October 1904, it was illustrated by David Murray Smith (July 4,1865–May 29,1952). For this anthology, I have included that illustration with the original 1894 version of the story.

A Christmas Ghost Story by Percy Andreae (October 31, 1858–May 3, 1924) was published in the 1895 Christmas edition of *The Woman at Home, Annie S. Swan's Magazine* with illustrations by Charles H. Heydemann.

The Old Portrait by Hume Nisbet, born James Hume Nisbet, (August 8, 1849 –June 4, 1923) was published in the February 1896 edition of *The Penny Illustrated Paper and Illustrated Times*.

Wolverden Tower by Grant Allen (February 24, 1848–October 25, 1899) was published in the 1896 Christmas number of the *Illustrated London News*.

The Blue Room by Lettice Galbraith, the pen name of Lizzie Susan Gibson (January 27, 1859–July 8, 1932), was published in the October 1897 edition of *Macmillan's Magazine*. The true identity of Lettice Galbraith remained a mystery until revealed by the writer and anthologist Alastair Gunn in 2023. The result of five years research, Gunn's complete biography of the writer, along with a comprehensive bibliography, can be found in *The Blue Room & Other Tales, the Ghost Stories of Lettice Galbraith* (Wimbourne Books 2023).

Ghosts Who Became Famous by Carolyn Wells (June 18, 1862–March 26, 1942) was published in the December 1900 edition of the *Century Illustrated Magazine* with an illustration by Bernard Jacob Rosenmeyer (1870–1943).

A Ghost Child by Bernard Edward Joseph Capes (August 30, 1854–November 2, 1918) was published in the January 1906 edition of the *Pall Mall Magazine*.

Afterward by Edith Wharton (January 24, 1862–August 11, 1937) was published in the January 1910 edition of *The Century Magazine* with illustrations by Ernest Leonard Blumenschein (May 26, 1874–June 6, 1960). The version presented in this anthology is taken from Wharton's October 1910 collection *Tales* *of Men and Ghosts*, which corrected a lapse in continuity in the original. In 1921, Edith Wharton became the first woman to be awarded the Pulitzer Prize for Fiction for her 1920 novel *The Age of Innocence*.

Bone To Bone by Edmund Gill Swain (February 19, 1861–January 29, 1938) was published in Swain's *The Stoneground Ghost Tales: Compiled from the Recollections of the Reverend Roland Batchel, Vicar of the Parish* in 1912. Swain was a friend and colleague of the renowned English ghost story writer M. R. James, to whom he dedicated *The Stoneground Ghost Tales*.

A Ghost Story by Alice Hegan Rice (January 11, 1870–February 10, 1942) was published in *Stories About The Other Child*, a supplement to *The Child Labor Bulletin, Vol. II No. 3* for December 1913.

The Snow by Hugh Walpole (March 13, 1884–June 1, 1941) was originally published in 1929 in *Shudders*, an anthology edited by Cynthia Asquith (September 27, 1887–March 31, 1960).

BALLADE OF CHRISTMAS GHOSTS

by
Andrew Lang
(March 31, 1844–July 20, 1912)

BETWEEN the moonlight and the fire
In winter twilights long ago,
What ghosts we raised for your desire
To make your merry blood run slow!
How old, how grave, how wise we grow!
No Christmas ghost can make us chill,
Save those that troop in mournful row,
The ghosts we all can raise at will!

The beasts can talk in barn and byre
On Christmas Eve, old legends know,
As year by year the years retire,
We men fall silent then I trow,
Such sights hath Memory to show,
Such voices from the silence thrill,
Such shapes return with Christmas snow,—
The ghosts we all can raise at will.

Oh, children of the village choir,
Your carols on the midnight throw,
Oh bright across the mist and mire
Ye ruddy hearths of Christmas glow!
Beat back the dread, beat down the woe,
Let's cheerily descend the hill;
Be welcome all, to come or go,
The ghosts we all can raise at will!

ENVOY.

Friend, sursum corda, soon or slow
We part, like guests who've joyed their fill;
Forget them not, nor mourn them so,
The ghosts we all can raise at will!

From *Ballades & Rhymes* (1911)

THE DEAD MAN'S STORY
by
James Hain Friswell
1858

On a dreary night in December, three gentlemen were seated in a painter's studio. The night was intensely dark and cold, and a slight hail beat against the window with a monotonous and ceaseless noise.

The studio was immense and gloomy, the sole light within it proceeding from a stove, around which the three were seated. Although they were bold, and of the age when men are most jovial, the conversation had taken, in spite of their efforts to the contrary, a reflection from the dull weather without, and their jokes and, frivolity were soon exhausted.

In addition to the light which issued from the crannies in the stove, there was another emitted from a bowl of spirits, which was ceaselessly stirred by one of the young men, as he poured from an antique silver ladle some of the flaming spirit into the quaint old glasses from which the students drank. The blue flame of the spirit lighted up in a wild and fantastic manner the surrounding objects in the room, so that the heads of old prophets, of satyrs, or Madonnas, clothed in the same ghastly hue, seemed to move and to dance along the walls like a fantastic procession of the dead; and the vast room, which in the day-time sparkled with the creations of genius, seemed now, in its alternate darkness and sulphuric light, to be peopled with its dreams.

Each time also that the silver spoon agitated the liquid, strange shadows traced themselves along the walls, hideous and of fantastic form. Unearthly tints spread also upon the hangings of the studio, from the old bearded prophet of Michael Angelo to those eccentric caricatures which the artist had scrawled upon his walls, and which resembled an army of demons that one sees in a dream, or such as Goya has painted; whilst the lull and rise of the tempest without but added to the fantastic and nervous feeling which pervaded those within.

Besides this, to add to the terror which was creeping over the three occupants of the room, each time that they looked at each other they appeared with faces of a blue tone, with eyes fixed and glittering like live embers, and with pale lips and sunken cheeks; but the most fearful object of all was that of a plaster mask taken from the face of an intimate friend but lately dead, which, hanging near the window, let the light from the spirit fall upon its face, turned three parts towards them, which gave it a strange, vivid, and mocking expression.

All people have felt the influence of large and dark rooms, such as Hoffman has portrayed and Rembrandt has painted; and all the world has experienced those wild and unaccountable terrors— panics without a cause—which seize on one like a spontaneous fever, at the sight of objects to which a stray glimpse of the moon or a feeble ray from a lamp give a mysterious form; nay, all, we should imagine, have at some period of their lives found themselves by the side of a friend, in a dark and dismal chamber, listening to some wild story, which so enchains them, that although the mere lighting of a candle could put an end to their terror, they would not do so; so much need has the human heart of emotions, whether they be true or false.

So it was upon the evening mentioned. The conversation of the three companions never took a direct line, but followed all the phases of their thoughts; sometimes it was light as the smoke which curled from their cigars, then for a moment fantastic as the flame of the burning spirit, and then again dark, lurid, and sombre as the smile which lit up the mask from their dead friend's face.

At last the conversation ceased altogether, and the respiration of the smokers was the only sound heard; and their cigars glowed in the dark, like Will-of-the-wisps brooding o'er a stagnant pool.

It was evident to them all, that the first who should break the silence, even if he spoke in jest, would cause in the hearts of the others a start and tremor, for each felt that he had almost unwittingly plunged into a ghastly reverie.

"Henry," at last said one, again dipping the spoon into the flaming spirit, "hast thou read Hoffman?"

"I should think so," said Henry.

"What think you of him?"

"Why, that he writes admirably; and, moreover, what is more admirable—in such a manner that you see at once he almost believes that which he relates. As for me, I know very well that when I read him of a dark night, I am obliged to creep to bed without shutting my book, and without daring to look behind me."

"Indeed; then you love the terrible and fantastic?"

"I do," said Henry.

"And what do *you* think of such romances?" said the questioner, addressing the third.

"I like them much," was the answer.

"Good; then I will tell you a strange story which happened to myself."

"I presumed as much," said Henry.

"An adventure in which you are the hero?" said the third.

"Yes, I myself. I must again before I commence assure you that I am the hero of this strange adventure."

"Go on, then; we will listen."

The silver spoon fell from his fingers into the bowl; the flame of the spirit, not enlivened by agitation, faded out little by little, and in a few moments they were in almost complete darkness, a warm light only being thrown upon their legs by the fire in the stove.

He began his story:—

"One mid-winter evening, it might be about a year ago, the weather was just as it is now—the same cold, the same sleet and hail, the same dulness. You know my profession is that of a surgeon, and on that day I had a great many cases to attend; so that after having made my last visit, instead of going, as sometimes I did, to the theatre, I made haste home. I then dwelt in one of the most deserted streets of the Faubourg Saint Germain. I was very tired and I quickly got to bed. I extinguished the lamp and amused myself with gazing at my fire, watching the great shadows which each little flame made dance upon my bed-curtains; then at last my eyes shut, and I fell asleep.

"It might have been an hour after I first closed my eyes, when I felt some person shaking me roughly. I woke with a start, and in not the very best temper, and stared with some surprise at my nocturnal visitor. It was my man-servant.

"'Sir,' said he, 'rise at once; you are sent for to a young lady who is dying.'

"'Where does she live?' said I.

"'Nearly opposite; but there is a messenger down stairs who will take you to her.'

"I rose, and thinking that at such a moment my toilet was of little consequence, dressed myself in haste. I took my instrument-case, and followed the man who had come for me.

"It rained in torrents. Happily, however, I had only the street to cross; and I was almost immediately at the house of the person who required my assistance. She dwelt in a large and aristocratic hotel. I had to cross a wide court-yard, and to ascend a stone staircase which ran up outside the building: then, passing a vestibule, wherein some servants were waiting to show me upstairs, I was at once conducted to the chamber of the sick lady. It was a very large room, furnished throughout with oaken furniture very ancient and beautifully carved. A maid-servant showed me into the chamber, and then left me. I went at once to the bedside, carved like the rest of the furniture, with tall pillars running up to some height, supporting a canopy of rich arras, and upon which, pressing a snowy pillow, lay a head more ravishing than ever Raphael dreamed of when he painted his finest Madonna. Locks, bright and golden as a wave of Pactolus, floated round her face. Her eyes were nearly closed, and her mouth partly open, discovering a row of teeth beautifully even and as white as pearls. Her neck surpassed the lily in whiteness; and when I took her hand I saw so fine an arm, that it recalled to me those which Homer has assigned to Juno.

"I remained there, forgetful of the cause for which I came, gazing at her, and recalling nothing like her in my recollections or my dreams; when she turned towards me, and opening her large blue eyes, said to me, 'I suffer much.'

"Still there was, I found, little the matter with her. I took my lancet, but at the moment of touching an arm so beautiful and white, my hand trembled. However, the feelings of the doctor triumphed over those of the man; I opened a vein—there came from her blood pure and bright as melted coral—she fainted.

"I did not wish to quit her. I remained with her. I felt a secret happiness in holding, as it were, the life of so beautiful a being in my hands. I stanched the blood; she opened her eyes by degrees, carried the hand she had free to her bosom, turned towards me, and fixed upon me a grateful look. 'Thank you,' she said, 'I suffer less.'

"She had about her such beauty that I felt rooted to my place, counting each pulsation of my heart against each throb of her pulse; listening to her respiration, which each time grew less feverish, and thinking to myself that if ever there existed a heaven upon earth, it must be in the love of such a woman as I saw before me.

"She slept!"

"I remained, almost kneeling by the side of her bed. A lamp of alabaster, suspended from the ceiling, threw its golden light upon all the room. The woman who had come with me had gone away to announce that her mistress was better, and had no farther need of any of the servants. I was alone; and there she lay, calm and beautiful as an angel who has fallen asleep in the midst of a prayer! As for me—I was madly in love.

"However, I felt that I could no longer remain there; I retired, therefore, without making a noise, so as not to waken her. I ordered some little things to be given her when she woke, and I left word that I would return the next day.

"When I reached my home, I could no longer sleep. I lay awake, thinking of her. I felt that the love of such a woman would be an eternal enchantment, made up of reverie and delight. With these thoughts of her, I passed away the night; and when the day came, I was still madly in love; madly—I was a maniac!

"However, after these follies of a night so agitated, came morning's reflections. I remembered that an unfathomable abyss separated me from the loved object; that she was too beautiful *not* to have long had some one who loved and would be united to her; that she would love him so tenderly, so devotedly, that she could not forget, or be faithless to him: so I set myself to hate him without knowing who he was—this man, to whom I thought, in my mad way, that Providence had given in this world such exquisite felicity that he could submit to suffer in the next an eternity of pain without a murmur.

"I waited impatiently the hour when I could again visit her—each moment seemed an age; but at last the time came, and I set forth.

"When I arrived, I was shown into a boudoir furnished with the most exquisite taste, and altogether with a lavish luxury, which was shown in every article of furniture. She was alone, reading; a large robe of black velvet covered her from head to foot so completely that, like one of Perugino's angels, only her face and hands could be seen. She held coquettishly, in a scarf, the arm from which I had bled her, and was holding to the fire her two pretty little feet, which did not seem formed for our earth; and there she sat, looking so pure and beautiful that I thought her an ideal of one of the angels! She held out her hand, and bade me sit down beside her.

"'So soon up, madam,' said I: 'you are surely imprudent.'

"'No,' she said, 'I am quite strong;' she smiled sweetly as she said it; 'besides, I have slept well, and am, moreover, not very ill.'

"'You said, however, that you suffered.'

"'More in mind than body,' said she, with a sigh.

"'You are sad, madam!'

"'Oh! deeply so,' she returned; 'but happily Providence is also a physician, and has found for grief a universal panacea—forgetfulness!'

"'But,' said I, 'there are some griefs which kill.'

"'True,' she said; 'but the grave and forgetfulness, are they not the same? One is the tomb of the body, the other that of the heart. There is no other difference.'

"'But you, madam, how can you suffer grief? You are too high to be touched by it; sorrow should pass beneath you like clouds pass under the feet of angels; to us come storms and lightning—to you the blue serenity of heaven.'

"'Ah!' she said, ''tis there you deceive yourself; there all your science ends; your knowledge does not reach the heart.'

"'Well,' said I, 'try at least, madam, to forget. God sometimes permits a joy to succeed grief, and a smile to follow on our tears; and 'tis also true that when the heart of one He tries is too wide to refill of itself, and when the wound is too deep to heal without succour. He sends across the path of such a one a soul which can comprehend and know it; for He knows that we suffer less in suffering together, and that a moment must come when the desolate heart must leap again with joy, and when the deadly wound must heal.'

"'And what is the prescription, doctor,' said she, 'by which you would heal such a wound?'

"'That must be according to the patient,' I returned; 'to some I should counsel faith; to others, love!'

"'You are right,' she answered; 'they are the two sisters of charity who visit the soul.'

"Then ensued a long silence, during which I fixed my eyes upon that sweet countenance, on which the light which peeped through the silken curtains cast such a charming tint; upon those beautiful tresses, which now no longer floated over her face like a veil, but which were banded on her temples, and were drawn behind her ears. The conversation had taken from the beginning a sad cast; but by this, the beautiful being before me seemed more radiant than before, diademed as she was with the triple crown of beauty, love, and grief.

"Thus I remained gazing at her, not so mad as I was on the first evening, but the more collected by her quietude. If that moment had made her mine, I should have fallen at her feet, I should have taken her hands, I should have wept with her as a sister; and whilst I reverenced her as an angel, should have consoled her as a woman.

"But I was yet ignorant what grief it was which she should forget, or what had caused the deep wound still unhealed; and this was what I had to find out, for between the physician and patient there was not as yet sufficient confidence for her to own her sorrow, although there had been enough for her to confess the cause. Nothing, however, that I could divine gave me the clue; no one had called at the hotel to inquire for her—none appeared to trouble themselves, as lovers would, about her. Her grief, then, must lay in the past, and must be reflected alone in the present.

"'Doctor,' said she to me, suddenly awakening from her reverie, 'can I soon dance?'

"'Yes, madam,' I answered, astonished at the question.

"'Because you must know that I must give a ball which I have promised for some long time; you must come—will you not? You will have very little opinion of my illness, which, making me dream all day, does not hinder me from dancing all night. My grief, however, is one of those which must be concealed in the depth of one's heart, so that the world may learn nothing there are tortures which must be masked with a smile, lest any one should guess them; mine I wish to keep to myself, as closely as some would conceal a hidden joy. The world around me envies me as beautiful and happy—it is a deception of which I do not wish to rob them. That is why I appear gay, and dance; surely do I weep on the morrow, but I weep alone.'

"As she said these words, she threw upon me a glance inexpressibly sweet and confiding, and added—

"'You will come—come soon, will you not?'

"I carried her hand to my lips, and I retired.

"When I got home, I seemed in a dream. My windows looked upon hers; I remained all the day looking at them, and all the day they were closed and dark. I forgot everything for this woman; I slept not, I eat nothing. That evening I fell into a fever, the next morning I was delirious, and the next evening I was DEAD!"

"*Dead!*" cried his hearers.

"Dead!" answered the narrator, with a conviction in his voice which words alone cannot give; "dead as Fabian, the cast of whose dead face hangs from that wall!"

"Go on," whispered the others, holding their breath. The hail still rattled against the windows, and the fire had so nearly died out, that they threw more wood on the feeble flame which penetrated the darkness of the studio and cast a faint light upon the pale face of him who told the story.

He resumed:—

"From that moment I felt nothing but a numbing chill, and a slight but still freezing motion. The latter was doubtless that of being put into the grave. I had been buried for some time—I do not exactly know how long, for there is no time-keeping in the grave—when I heard some one calling my name. I shook with cold and fear, without being able to answer. After a lapse of some moments, I was again called. I made an effort to speak, and then felt the bandage which wrapped me from head to foot. It was my shroud. At last, I managed feebly to articulate, 'Who calls?'

"''Tis I!' said a voice.

"'Who art thou?'

"'I! I! I!' was the answer; and the voice grew weaker, as if it was lost in the distance; or as if it was but the icy rustle of the trees.

"A third time my name sounded on my ears; but now it seemed to run from tree to tree, as if it whistled in each dead branch; so that the entire cemetery repeated it with a dull sound. Then I heard a noise of wings, as if my name, pronounced in the silence, had suddenly awakened a troop of night-birds. My hands, as if by some mysterious power, sought my face. In silence I undid the shroud which bound me, and tried to see. It seemed as if I had awakened from a long sleep. I was cold.

"I then recalled the dread fear which oppressed me, and the mournful images by which I was surrounded. The trees had no longer any leaves upon them, and seemed to stretch forth their bare branches like huge spectres! A single ray of moonlight which shone forth, showed me a long row of tombs, forming an horizon around me, and seeming like the steps which might lead to Heaven. All the vague voices of the night, which seemed to preside at my awakening, were full of terror.

"I turned my head, and sought for him who called me. He was seated at my side, watching me, his head leaning on his hands, and his face pregnant with a terrible look, and clothed with a horrible smile. Fear ran like an electric shock through me. 'Who art thou?' said I, with an endeavour to gather up all my strength; 'and why dost thou awaken me?'

"'To render you a service,' he answered.

"'Where am I?'

"'In the grave-yard.'

"'Who art thou?'

"'A friend.'

"'Leave me to my sleep,' said I.

"'Listen!' cried he to me; 'dost thou remember aught of the earth?'

"'No.'

"'Dost thou regret anything?'

"'No.'

"'How long hast thou been asleep?'

"'I know not.'

"'I will tell you,' he said: 'Thou hast been dead two days; and the last word you uttered was the name of a woman, instead of that of the Lord. Therefore, if Satan wished to possess it, your soul belongs to him. Dost understand me?'

"'Yes,' I answered.

"'And dost thou wish to live?'

"'Who art thou who offerest me life?—art thou Satan?'

"'Satan, or not,' was the answer; 'will you live?'

"'Alone?'

"'No. You shall see *her*.'

"'When?'

"'This very night; and at her own house.'

"'I accept it,' cried I, trying to rise; 'what are thy conditions?'

"'I make none,' said the speaker, with a lurid smile. 'Do you believe that, from time to time, I am not capable of doing good? This very night *she* gives a ball: I will take you thither.'

"'Let us set out.'

"'Good!' cried Satan. He held forth his hand and dragged me from the place.

"'You imagine that what I say was impossible. All that *I* say is, that I felt a penetrating cold, which froze all my limbs.

"'Now,' cried the fiend, 'follow me! You must understand that I cannot get out by the great gate—the porter will not suffer that. Once here, there is no retreat. Follow me, therefore: we will just go to your house, where you shall dress yourself; for you can hardly go to a ball in your present costume—especially as it is not a *bal masqué*. Mind and wrap yourself well up in your winding-sheet, for the nights are cold, and you may feel unpleasantly touched by it.'

"As he said this, Satan laughed malignantly; and I continued silently to walk after him.

"'I am sure,' continued he, 'that, in spite of the service I am doing you, you do not yet like me. You are always thus, you men—ungrateful to your friends. Not that I blame ingratitude; it is a vice upon which I pride myself, since I invented it myself; and I must say, that it is one most in vogue. But I do wish to see you a little more merry—it is the only thing I ask of you.'

"I answered not, but still followed my guide, white as a statue, and as cold. I was silent; but, at the pauses in the fiend's voice, I could hear my teeth chatter against each other, and my bones rattle in my body.

"'Shall we soon arrive?' said I, with effort.

"'Still impatient,' said my guide, sardonically. 'You must think her very beautiful?'

"'As an angel!' I cried.

"'Ah! my friend,' said he, with a laugh, 'one must confess that you have a want of delicacy in your answers. How can you talk to me of angels, knowing I have been one: in fact, I have done for you to-day somewhat more than an angel could have done. I excuse you, however; one must excuse a good deal to a man who has been dead upwards of two days. Besides, I am, as I have told you, very good-tempered to-day. There has happened in the world a few things which please me very much. I *did* think that men were degenerate; I absolutely fancied that they were getting virtuous. But, no; they are always the same—just the same as when first created. Well! to-day has been a rare day for me: I have seldom found things succeed so well as to-day. I have counted, since yesterday evening, six hundred and twenty-two suicides in France alone! Among them, there has, however, been more young men than old fellows, which is a pity, because they die without children, and are therefore a loss to me. Two thousand four hundred and forty-three in the whole of Europe. The other parts of the world I do not count; *there*, I am like rich capitalists, who cannot count their gains. Twelve hundred judges, who have given false judgment: ordinarily I have more than this latter number. There are also twenty-seven cases of atheism—cases which gave me greater pleasure than all the rest put together. With these and others, you will find that they make together a rough aggregate of nearly three million souls in Europe alone! I have not reckoned petty crimes, such as theft, forgery, &c.; these are merely the farthings in the gross account. So you can easily calculate in what space of time the whole world will fall into my hands, at three millions of souls per day! I really fancy that I shall be obliged to enlarge my place of accommodation.'

"'I understand your triumph,' I muttered to myself, as I hastened onwards.

"'Indeed!' said Satan, with a sombre and melancholy air; 'do you fear me, then, since you see me face to face?—am I so repulsive? Let us reason a little: What would become of your world without me? It would die of spleen. It is I who invented gold-gambling! 'Tis I love! Business—'tis I! Thinking of these things, I cannot, for the life of me, understand the spite which you men seem to bear against me. Your poets, for instance, who keep talking of an ideal love, cannot understand that, in raving of the

love which exalts, they point out the way to that which debases—
that in seeking a Diana they manage to find an Aphrodite. Now
look for instance to yourself; you have just arisen from the dead;
you are yet as cold as a corpse; and yet you seek the embraces
of love. You see evil survives death, and that a man who has lived
a wicked life, would, if he were put to the proof, prefer an eternity
of his own passions to an eternity of pure and heavenly happiness.'

"I interrupted him with—'Shall we soon get there?' for the
horizon seemed to grow lighter every moment, and still we did not
seem to advance an inch.

"'How impatient you are,' ejaculated the fiend, querulously:
'you must know that over the great gate of the cemetery there is a
cross, and that that cross is a kind of barrier or custom-house to
me. As I generally travel about for purposes which the cross
forbids, I should be obliged to make the sign of it upon my
forehead to pass it. Now, I am willing enough to carry on my own
little peccadilloes, but the fiend himself revolts at sacrilege: so, as I
have told you before, we can't pass there. But never mind that—
follow me. I have promised to conduct you to a ball; and I will
keep my word. *My* word,' added he, sardonically, 'is well known
to be as good as my bond.'

"There was, in all this irony of the fiend, something so fatal,
cold, and devilish, that almost each word which dropped from his
mouth seemed to freeze me. Still, what I tell you I heard with these
ears! I could not drag myself away from my strange companion.

"We continued to walk for some hundred feet, when we came to
a wall, before which an accumulation of tombstones formed a kind
of flight of steps. Satan placed his foot upon the first, and, without
any remorse, strode upon the sacred memorials till he reached the
top of the wall.

"I hesitated; I was afraid to follow him: but he held out his hand
to me, saying, 'There is not the slightest danger—you can step
upon these paving-stones. They are those of some acquaintances of
mine.'

"When I had reached the place where he stood, he suddenly
asked me, 'Whether he should show me the town?' But I
answered, 'No, no! let us move forward,' We therefore leapt down
from the wall upon the ground.

"The moon seemed to veil herself before the bold looks of Satan. The night was cold. All the doors were closed, all the windows darkened, and the streets deserted. From their appearance, one would have imagined that, for a long time past no foot had traversed those silent streets. Everything around us bore a death-like aspect. It seemed as if, when day came, no one would open their doors; that no head, of woman or of child, would look out of those dark, dull windows; that no step would break the silence which fell, like a pall, upon all around. I seemed to be walking in a city which had been buried some ages. In truth, the town seemed to have been depopulated, and the cemetery to have grown full.

"Still we went forward, without hearing a murmur, or meeting even with a shadow. The street stretched for a long way across this fearful city of silence and repose. At last we reached my house.

"'You remember it?' said the fiend.

"'Yes,' replied I, sullenly, 'let us enter.'

"'First,' said he, 'we must open the door. It is I, by the way, who invented the science of opening doors without breaking them in. In fact, I have a second key to all doors and gates—with one exception—that of Paradise!'

"We entered. The calm without continued within. It was horrible!

"I felt as in a dream: I did not breathe nor move. Imagine, if you can, yourselves entering your chambers, after having been dead for two days—finding everything in the same position in which it was during your illness, but wrapped in that dark gloom which death alone can give, and seeing all the objects arranged, never again to be disturbed by you! The only thing which seemed to have any motion in it which I had seen since I arose from the tomb, was a large clock, by the side of which a human being had ceased to exist, and which now ticked slowly on, counting the hours of my eternity, as it had the minutes of my life.

"I went to the mantel-shelf; I lighted a wax candle to assure myself of the existence of everything; for all which surrounded me appeared so strange that I could not believe my senses. Every object was real: I saw before me the portrait of my mother, with the same smile upon her lips—smiling on me now in death—as it had before in life. I opened the books which I had read only some few days before my death; everything was the same. The only alteration was that the linen had been removed from the bed, and that on each chest and drawer there was a seal. As for Satan, he was sitting down upon the tester of the bed, reading attentively the "Lives of the Saints,"

"I passed before a cheval glass, and I saw myself from head to foot in my strange costume, wrapped in my winding-sheet, my face pale, my eyes heavy and dull; I began to doubt this life which an unknown power had returned to me. I placed my hand upon my heart, it did not beat—I carried my hand to my brow, my brow was cold as ice; so also was my chest: my pulse was, of course, as motionless as my heart. However, memory lived within me, and I could move about; the thought was horrible, my eyes and my brain were alone really alive.

"What was yet more horrible was, that I could not detach my eyes from the glass, which gave back my figure, cold, pale, and frozen. Each movement of my lips was reflected by a ghastly and sinister smile. I could not quit my place, and I had no power to cry out.

"The time-piece gave out that dull sound which warns us that it will soon strike; then it struck two o'clock. A few seconds after, the neighbouring church clock struck also, then another, and another, and all was again silent. By the reflection of the glass, I saw that the fiend had fallen comfortably to sleep over the volume he had tried to read.

"I turned round, and caught my reflection in another glass with that pale clearness which a single wax candle in a vast chamber gives; I seemed haunted by myself; fear reached its culminating point, and I cried out aloud. Satan awoke.

"'Look.' said he, not regarding my fear, 'how you men try to instil virtue into others. Here is this book, absolutely so nonsensical and dull, that I, who have not been to sleep for nearly six thousand years, am obliged to take a nap over it. How is this? Are you not yet ready?'

"'Look at me,' said I, mechanically.

"'Come, come.' answered my companion, 'break the seals, take your clothes, and plenty of gold— aplenty of gold. To-morrow, when it is found out, justice will step in and condemn some poor devil for the robbery, and,' continued he, condescending for a moment to be vulgar, for the devil is always a gentleman, '*that will be a little bit of fat for me.*'

"I dressed myself in haste, but noticed every time that I touched my forehead or my bosom that they were still cold as ice. When ready, I looked at Satan.

"Shall we see *her*?' said I.

"'In five minutes.'

"'And to-morrow, what then?'

"'To-morrow,' said he, 'you may take yourself to your ordinary pursuits and to your common life. I do not do things by halves.'

"'Without conditions!'

"'Without any.'

"'Let us set out then,' I returned.

"We did so; in a few minutes we were before the house at which I had called some few days previously.

"'Let us go upstairs,' said my conductor. He did so. I recognized the grand staircase, the vestibule, the ante-chamber. The entrance of the saloon was crowded with people; the party was brilliant, the rooms seemed to glitter as it were with light, flowers, jewels, and beautiful women.

"When we entered they were dancing. I cannot tell how I felt, seeing all these things, and with yet the presence of the grave about me. I took Satan aside, and whispered to him, 'Where is *she*?'

"'In her boudoir,' he answered. I waited till the dance was finished; I then crossed the saloon. The huge mirrors, by the light of the chandeliers, reflected my pale and sombre figure, and I recognized that deathlike smile which had so frozen me. But *here* at least I was safe—*here* was no solitude, but a crowd of joyous people; no cemetery, but a ball-room—no tomb, but beauty, ravishing beauty. For one moment, dreaming of her for whom I came, I forgot *whence* I came.

"Arrived at the door of the boudoir, I glanced in, and saw her; there she sat, more beautiful than Beauty's self—chaste as a statue of Diana. I stopped for an instant in an ecstasy: she was clothed in a dress of dazzling whiteness, with bare arms and shoulders; I thought I saw upon one of her arms the little red point where I had bled her; perhaps, however, this was more fancy than anything else. When I appeared she was surrounded by hand-some young men, to whose vapid talk she did not, however, seem to listen;

raising her beautiful eyes mechanically, she saw me, seemed to hesitate for a moment, and then, with a sweet smile, she quitted the rest and came to me.

"'You see,' said she, 'I am quite strong.' As she said this the orchestra again struck up; she continued, 'And you can make proof of it if you wish; let us waltz together.' She then added some words to some one at her side; I looked towards him—it was Satan.

"'You have kept your word,' said I; 'I thank you for it, but this woman must become mine this very night.'

"'Thou shalt have her,' he said, coldly; 'but wipe your face before you dance, there is a worm crawling upon your cheek;' so saying he departed, leaving me more cold and ghastly than before. To restore my feelings, I pressed the arm of her for whom I had come from the grave, and thus I entered the ball-room with her.

"It was one of those delicious entrancing waltzes where all those who surround us seem to disappear, and we see none but ourselves; so we waltzed with our eyes fixed on each other, till they seemed to make a language of their own. Hers seemed to say, 'I am young and beautiful, and to him who possesses me all the beauties of my heart and soul will be revealed.'

"Still the waltz went on; the measure ceased at last, and we were alone. She leaned upon my arm, and turned her fine eyes upon me with a look which seemed to say, 'I love you.'

"I led her back into the saloon—it was deserted; she sat down, reclining on an ottoman, and turned her eyes to me, half closed, as if with love rather than fatigue. I leaned towards her: 'Ah,' said I, 'if you only knew how I love you.'

"'I know it,' she answered; 'I love you equally as well.'

"'I would give ray soul,' said I, earnestly, 'to possess you as my bride.'

"The eyes of the lady lit up with a fire which resembled those of the fiend—their light seemed to enter into my soul, 'Listen,' she said, anxiously; 'in a few moments we shall be alone; that door leads to my chamber; wait till all are gone, and we will ratify the compact.'

"The door opened silently, and then shut upon me. I was alone in the chamber where first I had seen her: there was the same mysterious perfume, which one cannot describe. I glanced in the mirror, I was still as pale as ever; I heard the carriages which took up the guests, and departed one by one, until the last had disappeared, and the silence again became dreadful and mournful; I felt, little by little, step by step, my terrors return, upon me. I dared not recall my former thoughts. I was astonished that my mistress never came. I counted the minutes till they seemed hours. I sat down and rested my elbows on my knees.

"Then I began to think of my mother, who at that moment was weeping for me—my mother to whom I had been *all* in life—to whom, alas, I had given but little, too little thought. Then came back the days of my childhood: I remembered that I had never had a moment's grief but that my mother had consoled it; and now, perhaps, when I was about to prepare for a crime, she was passing a vigil of tears and prayers in remembrance of me. The thought was fearful; I felt full of remorse—tears came into my eyes. I rose and looked at myself again in the glass: my eyes, before dull, seemed to brighten with resolution. I prayed within myself, and determined to rush from the present danger. I saw behind me a pale and motionless figure, it was my mistress; she had just entered the room. I rushed past her, through the half-opened door, and before I thought of anything else, I regained my own home. In the sanctity of that I remained in meditation and prayer; I was safe from the intrusion of the fiend who tempted me. Not so, however, were my thoughts. In the morning, which slowly dawned, the beauty to which I had so blindly bowed myself seemed to have regained its power. I forgot my good resolutions—I threw behind me my prayers—I again gave myself up to the passions which devoured me. I determined again to seek her. It was broad daylight when I went out of my room, but by the door-post a figure, formed, it seemed to me, of a dark vapour, stood and looked at me sardonically. I *felt* that it was the fiend, and I knew his power over me, and that he followed upon my steps.

"The day was dark, dull, and cold; I walked carelessly, and, heedless of anything but of the purpose I had before me, I at last arrived.

"At the moment I placed my foot upon the step, I saw an old man, pale and feeble, who was about to descend the flight of stairs which ran up to the door.

"'Who do you want, sir?' said the porter.

"'Madame P——,' I replied.

"'*Madame P——*,' returned he, with a look of astonishment, pointing out the old man at the time; 'that gentleman now inhabits this hotel; Madame P—— died three months ago.'

"I gave a loud cry, and fell forward senseless."

A silence fell upon the party who listened to this strange story: none dared for a few moments to break it. At last, one asked, "What further happened?" No one answered, and when they looked through the increasing gloom of the studio, they found that the narrator of the strange story had departed—none knew how, or when; nor did either of us ever again meet with the hero of the DEAD MAN'S STORY.

HORROR: A TRUE TALE
by
John Berwick Harwood
1861

I was but nineteen years of age when the incident occurred which has thrown a shadow over my life; and, ah me! how many and many a weary year has dragged by since then! Young, happy, and beloved, I was in those long-departed days. They said that I was beautiful. The mirror now reflects a haggard old woman, with ashen lips and face of deadly pallor. But do not fancy that you are listening to a mere puling lament. It is not the flight of years that has brought me to be this wreck of my former self: had it been so, I could have borne the loss cheerfully, patiently, as the common lot of all; but it was no natural progress of decay which has robbed me of bloom, of youth, of the hopes and joys that belong to youth, snapped the link that bound my heart to another's, and doomed me to a lone old age. I try to be patient, but my cross has been heavy, and my heart is empty and weary, and I long for the death that comes so slowly to those who pray to die. I will try and relate, exactly as it happened, the event which blighted my life. Though it occurred many years ago, there is no fear that I should have forgotten any of the minutest circumstances: they were stamped on my brain too clearly and burningly, like the brand of a red-hot iron. I see them written in the wrinkles of my brow, in the dead whiteness of my hair, which was a glossy brown once, and has known no gradual change from dark to grey, from grey to white, as with those happy ones who were the companions of my girlhood, and whose honoured age is soothed by the love of children and grandchildren. But I must not envy them. I only meant to say that the difficulty of my task has no connection with want of memory—I remember but too well. But as I take the pen, my hand trembles, my head swims, the old rushing faintness and Horror comes over me again, and the well-remembered fear is upon me. Yet I will go on. This, briefly, is my story: I was a great heiress, I believe, though I cared little for the fact, but so it was. My father had great possessions, and no son to inherit after him. His three daughters, of whom I was the youngest, were to share the broad acres among them. I have said, and truly, that I cared little for this circumstance; and, indeed, I was so rich then in health and youth and love, that I felt myself quite indifferent to all else. The possession of all the treasures of earth could never have made up for what I then had—and lost, as I am about to relate. Of course, we girls knew that we were heiresses, but I do not think Lucy and Minnie were any the prouder or the happier on that account. I know I was not. Reginald did not court me for my money. Of *that* I felt assured. He proved it, Heaven be praised! when he shrank from my side after the change. Yes, in all my lonely age, I can still be thankful that he did not keep his word, as some would have done, did not clasp at the altar a hand he had learned to loathe and shudder at, because it was full of gold—much gold! At least, he spared me that. And I know that I was loved, and the knowledge has kept me from going mad through many a weary day and restless night, when my hot eyeballs had not a tear to shed and even to weep was a luxury denied me. Our house was an old Tudor mansion. My father was very particular in keeping the smallest peculiarities of his home unaltered. Thus the many peaks and gables, the numerous turrets, and the mullioned windows with their quaint lozenge panes set in lead, remained very nearly as they had been three centuries back. Over and above the quaint melancholy of our dwelling, with the deep woods of its park and the sullen waters of the mere, our neighbourhood was thinly peopled and primitive, and the people round us were ignorant, and tenacious of ancient ideas and traditions. Thus it was a superstitious atmosphere that we children were reared in, and we heard, from our infancy, countless tales of horror, some mere fables doubtless, others legends of dark deeds of the olden time exaggerated by credulity and the love of the marvellous. Our mother had died when we were young, and our other parent being, though a kind father, much absorbed in affairs of various kinds, as an active magistrate and landlord, there was no one to check the unwholesome stream of tradition with which our plastic minds were inundated in the company of nurses and servants. As years went on, however, the old ghostly tales partially lost their effects, and our undisciplined minds were turned more towards balls, dresses, and partners, and other matters airy and trivial, more welcome to our riper age. It was at a county assembly that Reginald and I first met—met and loved. Yes, I am sure that he loved me with all his heart. It was not as deep a heart as some, I have thought in my grief and anger; but I never doubted its truth and honesty. Reginald's father and mine approved of our growing attachment; and as for myself, I know I was so happy then, that I look back upon those fleeting moments as on some delicious dream. I now come to the change. I have lingered on my childish reminiscences, my bright and happy youth, and now I must tell the rest—the blight and the sorrow. It was Christmas, always a joyful and a hospitable time in the country, especially in such an old hall as our home, where quaint customs and frolics were much clung to, as part and parcel of the very dwelling itself. The hall was full of guests—so full, indeed, that there was great difficulty in providing sleeping accommodation for all. Several narrow and dark chambers in the turrets—mere pigeon-holes, as we irreverently called what had been thought good enough for the stately gentlemen of Elizabeth's reign—were now allotted to bachelor visitors, after having been empty for a century. All the spare rooms in the body and wings of the hall were occupied, of course; and the servants who had been brought down were lodged at the farm and at the keeper's, so great was the demand for space. At last the unexpected arrival of an elderly relative, who had been asked months before, but scarcely expected, caused great commotion. My aunts went about wringing their hands distractedly. Lady Speldhurst was a personage of some consequence; she was a distant cousin, and had been for years on cool terms with us all, on account of some fancied affront or slight when she had paid her *last* visit, about the time of my christening. She was seventy years old; she was infirm, rich, and testy; moreover, she was my godmother, though I had forgotten the fact, but it seems that though I had formed no expectations of a legacy in my favour, my aunts had done so for me. Aunt Margaret was especially eloquent on the subject. "There isn't a room left," she said; "was ever anything so unfortunate? We cannot put Lady Speldhurst into the turrets, and yet where is she to sleep? And Rosa's godmother, too! poor dear child! how dreadful! After all these years of estrangement, and with a hundred thousand in the funds, and no comfortable warm room at her own unlimited disposal—and Christmas, of all times in the year!" What *was* to be done? My aunts could not resign their own chambers to Lady Speldhurst, because they had already given them up to some of the married guests. My father was the most hospitable of men, but he was rheumatic, gouty, and methodical. His sisters-in-law dared not propose to shift his quarters, and indeed he would have far sooner dined on prison fare than have been translated to a strange bed. The matter ended in my giving up my room. I had a strange reluctance to making the offer, which surprised myself. Was it a boding of evil to come? I cannot say. We are strangely and wonderfully made. It *may* have been. At any rate, I do not think it was any selfish unwillingness to make an old and infirm lady comfortable by a trifling sacrifice. I was perfectly healthy and strong. The weather was not cold for the time of year. It was a dark moist Yule—not a snowy one, though snow brooded overhead in the darkling clouds. I *did* make the offer, which became me, I said with a laugh, as youngest. My sisters laughed too, and made a jest of my evident wish to propitiate my godmother. "She is a fairy godmother, Rosa," said Minnie; "and you know she was affronted at your christening, and went away muttering vengeance. Here she is coming back to see you; I hope she brings golden gifts with her." I thought little of Lady Speldhurst and her possible golden gifts. I cared nothing for the wonderful fortune in the funds that my aunts whispered and nodded about so mysteriously. But, since then, I have wondered whether, had I then shown myself peevish or obstinate, had I refused to give up my room for the expected kinswoman, it would not have altered the whole of my life? But then Lucy or Minnie would have offered in my stead, and been sacrificed—what do I say?—better that the blow should have fallen as it did, than on those dear ones. The chamber to which I removed was a dim little triangular room in the western wing, and was only to be reached by traversing the picture-gallery, or by mounting a little flight of stone stairs which led directly upwards from the low-browed arch of a door that opened into the garden. There was one more room on the same landing-place, and this was a mere receptacle for broken furniture, shattered toys, and all the lumber that *will* accumulate in a country-house. The room I was to inhabit for a few nights was a tapestry-hung apartment, with faded green curtains of some costly stuff, contrasting oddly with a new carpet and the bright fresh hangings of the bed, which had been hurriedly erected. The furniture was half old, half new, and on the dressing-table stood a very quaint oval mirror, in a frame of black wood—unpolished ebony, I think. I can remember the very pattern of the carpet, the number of chairs, the situation of the bed, the figures on the tapestry. Nay, I can recollect not only the colour of the dress I wore on that fatal evening, but the arrangement of every scrap of lace and ribbon, of every flower, every jewel, with a memory but too perfect. Scarcely had my maid finished spreading out my various articles of attire for the evening (when there was to be a great dinner-party), when the rumble of a carriage announced that Lady Speldhurst had arrived. The short winter's day drew to a close, and a large number of guests were gathered together in the ample drawing-room, around the blaze of the wood fire, after dinner. My father, I recollect, was not with us at first. There were some squires of the old hard-riding, hard-drinking stamp still lingering over their port in the dining-room, and the host, of course, could not leave them. But the ladies and all the younger gentlemen—both those who slept under our roof, and those who would have a dozen miles of fog and mire to encounter on their road home—were all together. Need I say that Reginald was there?

He sat near me—my accepted lover, my plighted future husband. We were to be married in the spring. My sisters were not far off; they, too, had found eyes that sparkled and softened in meeting theirs, had found hearts that beat responsive to their own. And, in their cases, no rude frost nipped the blossom ere it became the fruit; there was no canker in their flowerets of young hope, no cloud in their sky. Innocent and loving, they were beloved by men worthy their esteem.

The room, a large and lofty one, with an arched roof, had somewhat of a sombre character from being wainscoted and ceiled with polished black oak of a great age. There were mirrors, and there were pictures on the walls, and handsome furniture, and marble chimney-pieces, and a gay Tournay carpet; but these merely appeared as bright spots on the dark background of the Elizabethan woodwork. Many lights were burning, but the blackness of the walls and roof seemed absolutely to swallow up their rays, like the mouth of a cavern. A hundred candles could not have given that apartment the cheerful lightness of a modern drawing-room. But the gloomy richness of the panels matched well with the ruddy gleam from the enormous wood fire, in which, crackling and glowing, now lay the mighty Yule log. Quite a blood-red lustre poured forth from the fire, and quivered on the walls and the groined roof. We had gathered round the vast antique hearth in a wide circle. The quivering light of the fire and candles fell upon us all, but not equally, for some were in shadow. I remember still how tall and manly and handsome Reginald looked that night, taller by the head than any there, and full of high spirits and gaiety. I, too, was in the highest spirits; never had my bosom felt lighter, and I believe it was my mirth which gradually gained the rest, for I recollect what a blithe, joyous company we seemed. All save one. Lady Speldhurst, dressed in grey silk and wearing a quaint head-dress, sat in her armchair, facing the fire, very silent, with her hands and her sharp chin propped on a sort of ivory-handled crutch that she walked with (for she was lame), peering at me with half-shut eyes. She was a little spare old woman, with very keen delicate features of the French type. Her grey silk dress, her spotless lace, old-fashioned jewels, and prim neatness of array, were well suited to the intelligence of her face, with its thin lips, and eyes of a piercing black, undimmed by age. Those eyes made me uncomfortable, in spite of my gaiety, as they followed my every movement with curious scrutiny. Still I was very merry and gay; my sisters even wondered at my ever-ready mirth, which was almost wild in its excess. I have heard since then of the Scottish belief that those doomed to some great calamity become *fey*, and are never so disposed for merriment and laughter as just before the blow falls. If ever mortal was *fey*, then, I was so on that evening. Still, though I strove to shake it off, the pertinacious observation of old Lady Speldhurst's eyes *did* make an impression on me of a vaguely disagreeable nature. Others, too, noticed her scrutiny of me, but set it down as a mere eccentricity of a person always reputed whimsical, to say the least of it.

However, this disagreeable sensation lasted but a few moments. After a short pause my aunt took her part in the conversation, and we found ourselves listening to a weird legend which the old lady told exceedingly well. One tale led to another. Every one was called on in turn to contribute to the public entertainment, and story after story, always relating to demonology and witchcraft, succeeded. It was Christmas, the season for such tales; and the old room, with its dusky walls and pictures, and vaulted roof, drinking up the light so greedily, seemed just fitted to give effect to such legendary lore. The huge logs crackled and burnt with glowing warmth; the blood-red glare of the Yule log flashed on the faces of the listeners and narrator, on the portraits, and the holly wreathed about their frames, and the upright old dame in her antiquated dress and trinkets, like one of the originals of the pictures stepped from the canvas to join our circle. It threw a shimmering lustre of an ominously ruddy hue upon the oaken panels. No wonder that the ghost and goblin stories had a new zest. No wonder that the blood of the more timid grew chill and curdled, that their flesh crept, and their hearts beat irregularly, and the girls peeped fearfully over their shoulders, and huddled close together like frightened sheep, and half-fancied they beheld some impish and malignant face gibbering at them from the darkling corners of the old room. By degrees my high spirits died out, and I felt the childish tremors, long latent, long forgotten, coming over me. I followed each story with painful interest; I did not ask myself if I believed the dismal tales. I listened, and fear grew upon me—the blind, irrational fear of our nursery days. I am sure most of the other ladies present, young or middle-aged, were affected by the circumstances under which these traditions were heard, no less than by the wild and fantastic character of them. But with them the impression would die out next morning, when the bright sun should shine on the frosted boughs, and the rime on the grass, and the scarlet berries and green spikelets of the holly; and with me— but, ah! what was to happen ere another day dawn? Before we had made an end of this talk, my father and the other squires came in, and we ceased our ghost stories, ashamed to speak of such matters before these newcomers—hard-headed, unimaginative men, who had no sympathy with idle legends. There was now a stir and bustle.

Servants were handing round tea and coffee, and other refreshments. Then there was a little music and singing. I sang a duet with Reginald, who had a fine voice and good musical skill. I remember that my singing was much praised, and indeed I was surprised at the power and pathos of my own voice, doubtless due to my excited nerves and mind. Then I heard some one say to another that I was by far the cleverest of the Squire's daughters, as well as the prettiest. It did not make me vain. I had no rivalry with Lucy and Minnie. But Reginald whispered some soft fond words in my ear, a little before he mounted his horse to set off homewards, which *did* make me happy and proud. And to think that the next time we met—but I forgave him long ago. Poor Reginald! And now shawls and cloaks were in request, and carriages rolled up to the porch, and the guests gradually departed. At last no one was left but those visitors staying in the house. Then my father, who had been called out to speak with the bailiff of the estate, came back with a look of annoyance on his face. "A strange story I have just been told," said he; "here has been my bailiff to inform me of the loss of four of the choicest ewes out of that little flock of Southdowns I set such store by, and which arrived in the north but two months since. And the poor creatures have been destroyed in so strange a manner, for their carcasses are horribly mangled." Most of us uttered some expression of pity or surprise, and some suggested that a vicious dog was probably the culprit. "It would seem so," said my father; "it certainly seems the work of a dog; and yet all the men agree that no dog of such habits exists near us, where, indeed, dogs are scarce, excepting the shepherds' collies and the sporting dogs secured in yards. Yet the sheep are gnawed and bitten, for they show the marks of teeth. Something has done this, and has torn their bodies wolfishly; but apparently it has been only to suck the blood, for little or no flesh is gone." "How strange!" cried several voices. Then some of the gentlemen remembered to have heard of cases when dogs addicted to sheep-killing had destroyed whole flocks, as if in sheer wantonness, scarcely deigning to taste a morsel of each slain wether. My father shook his head. "I have heard of such cases, too?" he said; "but in this instance I am tempted to think the malice of some unknown enemy has been at work. The teeth of a dog have been busy no doubt, but the poor sheep have been mutilated in a fantastic manner, as strange as horrible; their hearts, in especial, have been torn out, and left at some paces off, half-gnawed. Also, the men persist that they found the print of a naked human foot in the soft mud of the ditch, and near it—this." And he held up what seemed a broken link of a rusted iron chain. Many were the ejaculations of wonder and alarm, and many and shrewd the conjectures, but none seemed exactly to suit the bearings of the case. And when my father went on to say that two lambs of the same valuable breed had perished in the same singular manner three days previously, and that they also were found mangled and gore-stained, the amazement reached a higher pitch. Old Lady Speldhurst listened with calm intelligent attention, but joined in none of our exclamations. At length she said to my father, "Try and recollect—have you no enemy among your neighbours?" My father started, and knit his brows. "Not one that I know of," he replied; and indeed he was a popular man and a kind landlord. "The more lucky you," said the old dame, with one of her grim smiles. It was now late, and we retired to rest before long. One by one the guests dropped off. I was the member of the family selected to escort old Lady Speldhurst to her room—the room I had vacated in her favour. I did not much like the office. I felt a remarkable repugnance to my godmother, but my worthy aunts insisted so much that I should ingratiate myself with one who had so much to leave, that I could not but comply. The visitor hobbled up the broad oaken stairs actively enough, propped on my arm and her ivory crutch. The room never had looked more genial and pretty, with its brisk fire, modern furniture, and the gay French paper on the walls. "A nice room, my dear, and I ought to be much obliged to you for it, since my maid tells me it is yours," said her ladyship; "but I am pretty sure you repent your generosity to me, after all those ghost stories, and tremble to think of a strange bed and chamber, eh?" I made some commonplace reply. The old lady arched her eyebrows. "Where have they put you, child?" she asked; "in some cockloft of the turrets, eh? or in a lumber-room—a regular ghost-trap? I can hear your heart beating with fear this moment. You are not fit to be alone." I tried to call up my pride, and laugh off the accusation against my courage, all the more, perhaps, because I felt its truth. "Do you want anything more that I can get you, Lady Speldhurst?" I asked, trying to feign a yawn of sleepiness. The old dame's keen eyes were upon me. "I rather like you, my dear," she said, "and I liked your mamma well enough before she treated me so shamefully about the christening dinner. Now, I know you are frightened and fearful, and if an owl should but flap your window tonight, it might drive you into fits. There is a nice little sofa-bed in this dressing-closet—call your maid to arrange it for you, and you can sleep there snugly, under the old witch's protection, and then no goblin dare harm you, and nobody will be a bit the wiser, or quiz you for being afraid." How little I knew what hung in the balance of my refusal or acceptance of that trivial proffer! Had the veil of the future been lifted for one instant! but that veil is impenetrable to our gaze. Yet, perhaps, *she* had a glimpse of the dim vista beyond, *she* who made the offer; for when I declined, with an affected laugh, she said, in a thoughtful, half abstracted manner, "Well, well! we must all take our own way through life. Good night, child—pleasant dreams!" And I softly closed the door. As I did so, she looked round at me rapidly, with a glance I have never forgotten, half malicious, half sad, as if she had divined the yawning gulf that was to devour my young hopes. It may have been mere eccentricity, the odd phantasy of a crooked mind, the whimsical conduct of a cynical person, triumphant in the power of affrighting youth and beauty. Or, I have since thought, it *may* have been that this singular guest possessed some such gift as the Highland "second-sight," a gift vague, sad, and useless to the possessor, but still sufficient to convey a dim sense of coming evil and boding doom. And yet, had she really known *what* was in store for me, *what* lurked behind the veil of the future, not even that arid heart could have remained impassive to the cry of humanity. She would, she *must* have snatched me back, even from the edge of the black pit of misery. But, doubtless, she had not the power. Doubtless she had but a shadowy presentiment, at any rate of some harm to happen, and could not see, save darkly, into the viewless void where the wisest stumble. I left her door. As I crossed the landing a bright gleam came from another room, whose door was left ajar; it (the light) fell like a bar of golden sheen across my path. As I approached, the door opened, and my sister Lucy who had been watching for me came out. She was already in a white cashmere wrapper, over which her loosened hair hung darkly and heavily, like tangles of silk. "Rosa, love," she whispered, "Minnie and I can't bear the idea of your sleeping out there, all alone, in that solitary room—the very room, too, nurse Sherrard used to talk about! So, as you know Minnie has given up her room, and come to sleep in mine, still we should so wish you to stop with us tonight at any rate, and I could make up a bed on the sofa for myself, or you—and—" I stopped Lucy's mouth with a kiss. I declined her offer. I would not listen to it. In fact, my pride was up in arms, and I felt I would rather pass the night in the churchyard itself than accept a proposal dictated, I felt sure, by the notion that my nerves were shaken by the ghostly lore we had been raking up, that I was a weak, superstitious creature, unable to pass a night in a strange chamber. So I would not listen to Lucy, but kissed her, bade her good night, and went on my way laughing, to show my light heart. Yet, as I looked back in the dark corridor, and saw the friendly door still ajar, the yellow bar of light still crossing from wall to wall, the sweet kind face still peering after me from amid its clustering curls, I felt a thrill of sympathy, a wish to return, a yearning after human love and companionship. False shame was strongest, and conquered. I waved a gay adieu. I turned the corner, and, peeping over my shoulder, I saw the door close; the bar of yellow light was there no longer in the darkness of the passage. I thought, at that instant, that I heard a heavy sigh. I looked sharply round. No one was there. No door was open, yet I fancied, and fancied with a wonderful vividness, that I did hear an actual sigh breathed not far off, and plainly distinguishable from the groan of the sycamore branches, as the wind tossed them to and fro in the outer blackness. If ever a mortal's good angel had cause to sigh for sorrow, not sin, mine had cause to mourn that night. But imagination plays us strange tricks, and my nervous system was not over-composed, or very fitted for judicial analysis. I had to go through the picture-gallery. I had never entered this apartment by candle-light before, and I was struck by the gloomy array of the tall portraits, gazing moodily from the canvas on the lozenge-paned or painted windows, which rattled to the blast as it swept howling by. Many of the faces looked stern, and very different from their daylight expression. In others, a furtive flickering smile seemed to mock me, as my candle illumined them; and in all, the eyes, as usual with artistic portraits, seemed to follow my motions with a scrutiny and an interest the more marked for the apathetic immovability of the other features. I felt ill at ease under this stony gaze, though conscious how absurd were my apprehensions, and I called up a smile and an air of mirth, more as if acting a part under the eyes of human beings, than of their mere shadows on the wall. I even laughed as I confronted them. No echo had my short-lived laughter but from the hollow armour and arching roof, and I continued on my way in silence. I have spoken of the armour. Indeed, there was a fine collection of plate and mail, for my father was an enthusiastic antiquary, In especial there were two suits of black armour, erect, and surmounted by helmets with closed visors, which stood as if two mailed champions were guarding the gallery and its treasures. I had often seen these, of course, but never by night, and never when my whole organization was so overwrought and tremulous as it then was. As I approached the Black Knights, as we had dubbed them, a wild notion seized on me that the figures moved, that men were concealed in the hollow shells which had once been borne in battle and tourney. I knew the idea was childish, yet I approached in irrational alarm, and fancied I absolutely beheld eyes glaring on me from the eyelet-holes in the visors. I passed them by, and then my excited fancy told me that the figures were following me with stealthy strides. I heard a clatter of steel, caused, I am sure, by some more violent gust of wind sweeping the gallery through the crevices of the old windows, and with a smothered shriek I rushed to the door, opened it, darted out, and clapped it to with a bang that re-echoed through the whole wing of the house. Then by a sudden and not uncommon revulsion of feeling, I shook off my aimless terrors, blushed at my weakness, and sought my chamber only too glad that I had been the only witness of my late tremors. As I entered my chamber, I thought I heard some thing stir in the neglected lumber-room, which was the only neighbouring apartment. But I was determined to have no more panics, and resolutely shut my ears to this slight and transient noise, which had nothing unnatural in it; for surely, between rats and wind, an old manor-house on a stormy night needs no sprites to disturb it. So I entered my room, and rang for my maid. As I did so, I looked around me, and a most unaccountable repugnance to my temporary abode came over me, in spite of my efforts. It was no more to be shaken off than a chill is to be shaken off when we enter some damp cave. And, rely upon it, the feeling of dislike and apprehension with which we regard, at first sight, certain places and people, was not implanted in us without some wholesome purpose. I grant it is irrational—mere animal instinct—but is not instinct God's gift, and is it for us to despise it? It is by instinct that children know their friends from their enemies—that they distinguish with such unerring accuracy between those who like them and those who only flatter and hate them. Dogs do the same; they will fawn on one person, they slink snarling from another. Show me a man whom children and dogs shrink from, and I will show you a false, bad man—lies on his lips, and murder at his heart. No, let none despise the heaven-sent gift of innate antipathy, which makes the horse quail when the lion crouches in the thicket—which makes the cattle scent the shambles from afar, and low in terror and disgust as their nostrils snuff the blood-polluted air. I felt this antipathy strongly as I looked around me in my new sleeping-room, and yet I could find no reasonable pretext for my dislike. A very good room it was, after all, now that the green damask curtains were drawn, the fire burning bright and clear, candles burning on the mantelpiece, and the various familiar articles of toilet arranged as usual. The bed, too, looked peaceful and inviting—a pretty little white bed, not at all the gaunt funereal sort of couch which haunted apartments generally contain. My maid entered, and assisted me to lay aside the dress and ornaments I had worn, and arranged my hair, as usual, prattling the while, in Abigail fashion. I seldom cared to converse with servants; but on that night a sort of dread of being left alone—a longing to keep some human being near me—possessed me, and I encouraged the girl to gossip, so that her duties took her half an hour longer to get through than usual. At last, however, she had done all that could be done, and all my questions were answered, and my orders for the morrow reiterated and vowed obedience to, and the clock on the turret struck one. Then Mary, yawning little, asked if I wanted anything more, and I was obliged to answer No, for very shame's sake; and she went. The shutting of the door, gently as it was closed, affected me unpleasantly. I took a dislike to the curtains, the tapestry, the dingy pictures—everything. I hated the room. I felt a temptation to put on a cloak, run, half-dressed, to my sisters' chamber, and say I had changed my mind, and come for shelter. But they must be asleep, I thought, and I could not be so unkind as to wake them. I said my prayers with unusual earnestness and a heavy heart. I extinguished the candles, and was just about to lay my head on my pillow, when the idea seized me that I would fasten the door. The candles were extinguished, but the fire-light was amply sufficient to guide me. I gained the door. There was a lock, but it was rusty or hampered; my utmost strength could not turn the key. The bolt was broken and worthless. Baulked of my intention, I consoled myself by remembering that I had never had need of fastenings yet, and returned to my bed. I lay awake for a good while, watching the red glow of the burning coals in the grate. I was quiet now, and more composed. Even the light gossip of the maid, full of petty human cares and joys, had done me good—diverted my thoughts from brooding. I was on the point

of dropping asleep, when I was twice disturbed. Once, by an owl, hooting in the ivy outside—no unaccustomed sound, but harsh and melancholy; once, by a long and mournful howling set up by the mastiff, chained in the yard beyond the wing I occupied. A long-drawn lugubrious howling, was this latter, and much such a note as the vulgar declare to herald a death in the family. This was a fancy I had never shared; but yet I could not help feeling that the dog's mournful moans were sad, and expressive of terror, not at all like his fierce, honest bark of anger, but rather as if something evil and unwonted were abroad. But soon I fell asleep. How long I slept, I never knew. I awoke at once, with that abrupt start which we all know well and which carries us in a second from utter unconsciousness to the full use of our faculties. The fire was still burning but was very low, and half the room or more was in deep shadow. I knew, I felt, that some person or thing was in the room, although nothing unusual was to be seen by the feeble light. Yet it was a sense of danger that had aroused me from slumber. I experienced, while yet asleep, the chill and shock of sudden alarm, and I knew, even in the act of throwing off sleep like a mantle, why I awoke, and that some intruder was present. Yet, though I listened intently, no sound was audible, except the faint murmur of the fire,—the dropping of a cinder from the bars—the loud irregular beatings of my own heart. Notwithstanding this silence, by some intuition I knew that I had not been deceived by a dream, and felt certain that I was not alone. I waited. My heart beat on; quicker, more sudden grew its pulsations, as a bird in a cage might flutter in presence of the hawk. And then I heard a sound, faint, but quite distinct, the clank of iron, the rattling of a chain! I ventured to lift my head from the pillow. Dim and uncertain as the light was, I saw the curtains of my bed shake, and caught a glimpse of something beyond, a darker spot in the darkness. This confirmation of my fears did not surprise me so much as it shocked me. I strove to cry aloud, but could not utter a word. The chain rattled again, and this time the noise was louder and clearer. But though I strained my eyes, they could not penetrate the obscurity that shrouded the other end of the chamber, whence came the sullen clanking. In a moment several distinct trains of thought, like many-coloured strands of thread twining into one, became palpable to my mental vision. Was it a robber? could it be a supernatural visitant? or was I the victim of a cruel trick, such as I had heard of, and which some thoughtless persons love to practise on the timid, reckless of its dangerous results? And then a new idea, with some ray of comfort in it, suggested itself. There was a fine young dog of the Newfoundland breed, a favourite of my father's, which was usually chained by night in an outhouse. Neptune might have broken loose, found his way to my room, and, finding the door imperfectly closed, have pushed it open and entered. I breathed more freely as this harmless interpretation of the noise forced itself upon me. It was—it must be—the dog, and I was distressing myself uselessly. I resolved to call to him; I strove to utter his name—"Neptune, Neptune!" but a secret apprehension restrained me, and I was mute. Then the chain clanked nearer and nearer to the bed, and presently I saw a dusky shapeless mass appear between the curtains on the opposite side to where I was lying. How I longed to hear the whine of the poor animal that I hoped might be the cause of my alarm. But no; I heard no sound save the rustle of the curtains and the clash of the iron chain. Just then the dying flame of the fire leaped up, and with one sweeping hurried glance I saw that the door was shut, and, horror! it is not the dog! it is the semblance of a human form that now throws itself heavily on the bed, outside the clothes, and lies there, huge and swart, in the red gleam that treacherously dies away after showing so much to affright, and sinks into dull darkness. There was now no light left, though the red cinders yet glowed with a ruddy gleam, like the eyes of wild beasts. The chain rattled no more. I tried to speak, to scream wildly for help; my mouth was parched, my tongue refused to obey. I could not utter a cry, and indeed, who could have heard me, alone as I was in that solitary chamber, with no living neighbour, and the picture-gallery between me and any aid that even the loudest, most piercing shriek could summon. And the storm that howled without would have drowned my voice, even if help had been at hand. To call aloud—to demand who was there—alas! how useless, how perilous! If the intruder were a robber, my outcries would but goad him to fury; but what robber would act thus? As for a trick, that seemed impossible. And yet, *what* lay by my side, now wholly unseen? I strove to pray aloud, as there rushed on my memory a flood of weird legends—the dreaded yet fascinating lore of my childhood. I had heard and read of the spirits of wicked men forced to revisit the scenes of their earthly crimes—of demons that lurked in certain accursed spots—of the ghoul and vampire of the East, stealing amid the graves they rifled for their ghostly banquets; and I shuddered as I gazed on the blank darkness where I knew it lay. It stirred—it moaned hoarsely; and again I heard the chain clank close beside me—so close that it must almost have touched me. I drew myself from it, shrinking away in loathing and terror of the evil thing—what, I knew not, but felt that something malignant was near. And yet, in the extremity of my fear, I dared not speak; I was strangely cautious to be silent, even in moving farther off; for I had a wild hope that it—the phantom, the creature, whichever it was—had not discovered my presence in the room. And then I remembered all the events of the night—Lady Speldhurst's ill-omened vaticinations, her half-warnings, her singular look as we parted, my sister's persuasions, my terror in the gallery, the remark that "this was the room nurse Sherrard used to talk of." And then memory stimulated by fear, recalled the long forgotten past, the ill-repute of this disused chamber, the sins it had witnessed, the blood spilled, the poison administered by unnatural hate within its walls, and the tradition which called it haunted. The green room—I remembered now how fearfully the servants avoided it—how it was mentioned rarely, and in whispers, when we were children, and how we had regarded it as a mysterious region, unfit for mortal habitation. Was It—the dark form with the chain—a creature of this world, or a spectre? And again—more dreadful still—could it be that the corpses of wicked men were forced to rise, and haunt in the body the places when they had wrought their evil deeds? And was such as these my grisly neighbour? The chain faintly rattled. My hair bristled; my eyeballs seemed starting from their sockets; the damps of a great anguish were on my brow. My heart laboured as if I were crushed beneath some vast weight. Sometimes it appeared to stop its frenzied beatings, sometimes its pulsations were fierce and hurried; my breath came short and with extreme difficulty, and I shivered as if with cold; yet I feared to stir. *It* moved, it moaned, its fetters clanked dismally, the couch creaked and shook. This was no phantom, then—no air-drawn spectre. But its very solidity, its palpable presence, were a thousand times more terrible. I felt that I was in the very grasp of what could not only affright, but harm; of something whose contact sickened the soul with deathly fear. I made a desperate resolve: I glided from the bed, I seized a warm wrapper, threw it around me, and tried to grope, with extended hands, my way to the door. My heart beat high at the hope of escape. But I had scarcely taken one step, before the moaning was renewed, it changed into a threatening growl that would have suited a wolf's throat, and a hand clutched at my sleeve. I stood motionless. The muttering growl sank to a moan again, the chain sounded no more, but still the hand held its grip of my garment, and I feared to move. It knew of my presence, then. My brain reeled, the blood boiled in my ears, and my knees lost all strength, while my heart panted like that of a deer in the wolf's jaws. I sank

back, and the benumbing influence of excessive terror reduced me
to a state of stupor. When my full consciousness returned, I was
sitting on the edge of the bed, shivering with cold, and bare-footed.
All was silent, but I felt that my sleeve was still clutched by my
unearthly visitant. The silence lasted a long time. Then followed
achuckling laugh, that froze my very marrow, and the gnashing
of teeth as in demoniac frenzy; and then a wailing moan, and this
was succeeded by silence. Hours may have passed—nay, though
the tumult of my own heart prevented my hearing the clock strike,
must have passed—but they seemed ages to me. And how were
they spent? Hideous visions passed before the aching eyes that I
dared not close, but which gazed ever into the dumb darkness
where It lay—my dread companion through the watches of the
night. I pictured It in every abhorrent form which an excited fancy
could summon up: now as a skeleton, with hollow eye-holes and
grinning fleshless jaws; now as a vampire, with livid face and
bloated form, and dripping mouth wet with blood. Would it never
be light! And yet, when day should dawn, I should be forced to see
It face to face. I had heard that spectre and fiend are compelled to
fade as morning brightened, but this creature was too real, too foul
a thing of earth, to vanish at cock-crow. No! I should see it—the
horror—face to face! And then the cold prevailed, and my teeth
chattered, and shiverings ran through me, and yet there was the
damp of agony on my bursting brow. Some instinct made me
snatch at a shawl or cloak that lay on a chair within reach, and
wrap it round me. The moan was renewed, and the chain just
stirred. Then I sank into apathy, like an Indian at the stake, in the
intervals of torture. Hours fled by, and I remained like a statue of
ice, rigid and mute. I even slept, for I remember that I started to
find the cold grey light of an early winter's day was on my face,
and stealing around the room from between the heavy curtains of
the window. Shuddering, but urged by the impulse that rivets the
gaze of the bird upon the snake, I turned to see the Horror of the
night. Yes, it was no fevered dream, no hallucination of sickness,
no airy phantom unable to face the dawn. In the sickly light I saw
it lying on the bed, with its grim head on the pillow. A man? Or a
corpse arisen from its unhallowed grave, and awaiting the demon
that animated it? There it lay—a gaunt gigantic form, wasted to a
skeleton, half clad, foul with dust and clotted gore, its huge limbs

flung upon the couch as if at random, its shaggy hair streaming over the pillows like a lion's mane. Its face was towards me. Oh, the wild hideousness of that face, even in sleep! In features it was human, even through its horrid mask of mud and half-dried bloody gouts, but the expression was brutish and savagely fierce; the white teeth were visible between the parted lips, in a malignant grin; the tangled hair and beard were mixed in leonine confusion, and there were scars disfiguring the brow. Round the creature's waist was a ring of iron, to which was attached a heavy but broken chain—the chain I had heard clanking. With a second glance I noted that part of the chain was wrapped in straw, to prevent its galling the wearer. The creature—I cannot call it a man—had the marks of fetters on its wrists, the bony arm that protruded through one tattered sleeve was scarred and bruised, the feet were bare, and lacerated by pebbles and briers, and one of them was wounded, and wrapped in a morsel of rag. And the lean hands, one of which held my sleeve, were armed with talons like an eagle's. In an instant the horrid truth flashed upon me—I was in the grasp of a madman. Better the phantom that scares the sight than the wild beast that rends and tears the quivering flesh—the pitiless human brute that has no heart to be softened, no reason at whose bar to plead, no compassion, nought of man save the form and the cunning. I gasped in terror. Ah! the mystery of those ensanguined fingers, those gory wolfish jaws! that face, all besmeared with blackening blood, is revealed!

The slain sheep, so mangled and rent—the fantastic butchery—the print of the naked foot—all, all were explained; and the chain the broken link of which was found near the slaughtered animals—it came from *his* broken chain—the chain he had snapped, doubtless, in his escape from the asylum where his raging frenzy had been fettered and bound. In vain! in vain! Ah, me! how had this grisly Samson broken manacles and prison bars—how had he eluded guardian and keeper and a hostile world, and come hither on his wild way, hunted like a beast of prey, and snatching his hideous banquet like a beast of prey, too? Yet, through the tatters of his mean and ragged garb I could see the marks of the severities, cruel and foolish, with which men in that time tried to tame the might of madness. The scourge—its marks were there; and the scars of the hard iron fetters, and many a cicatrice and welt, that told a dismal tale of harsh usage. But now he was loose, free to play the brute—the baited, tortured brute that they had made him—now without the cage, and ready to gloat over the victims his strength should overpower. Horror! Horror! I was the prey—the victim—already in the tiger's clutch; and a deadly sickness came over me, and the iron entered into my soul, and I longed to scream, and was dumb! I died a thousand deaths as that awful morning wore on. I *dared not* faint. But words cannot paint what I suffered as I waited—waited till the moment when he should open his eyes and be aware of my presence; for I was assured he knew it not. He had entered the chamber as a lair, when weary and gorged with his horrid orgie; and he had flung himself down to sleep without a suspicion that he was not alone. Even his grasping my sleeve was doubtless an act done betwixt sleeping and waking, like his unconscious moans and laughter, in some frightful dream. Hours went on; then I trembled as I thought that soon the house would be astir, that my maid would come to call me as usual, and awake that ghastly sleeper. And might he not have time to tear me, as he tore the sheep, before any aid could arrive? At last what I dreaded came to pass—a light footstep on the landing—there is a tap at the door. A pause succeeds, and then the tapping is renewed, and this time more loudly. Then the madman stretched his limbs and uttered his moaning cry, and his eyes slowly opened—very slowly opened, and met mine. The girl waited awhile ere she knocked for the third time. I trembled lest she should open the door unbidden—see that grim thing, and by her idle screams and terror bring about the worst. Long before strong men could arrive I knew that I should be dead—and what a death! The maid waited, no doubt surprised at my unusually sound slumbers, for I was in general a light sleeper and an early riser, but reluctant to deviate from habit by entering without permission. I was still alone with the thing in man's shape, but he was awake now. I saw the wondering surprise in his haggard bloodshot eyes; I saw him stare at me half vacantly, then with a crafty yet wondering look; and then I saw the devil of murder begin to peep forth from those hideous eyes, and the lips to part as in a sneer, and the wolfish teeth to bare themselves. But I was not what I had been. Fear gave me a new and a desperate composure—a courage foreign to my nature. I had heard of the best method of managing the insane; I could but try; I did try.

Calmly, wondering at my own feigned calm, I fronted the glare of those terrible eyes. Steady and undaunted was my gaze— motionless my attitude. I marvelled at myself, but in that agony of sickening terror I was *outwardly* firm. They sink, they quail abashed, those dreadful eyes, before the gaze of a helpless girl; and the shame that is never absent from insanity bears down the pride of strength, the bloody cravings of the wild beast. The lunatic moaned and drooped his shaggy head between his gaunt squalid hands. I lost not an instant. I rose, and with one spring reached the door, tore it open, and, with a shriek, rushed through, caught the wondering girl by the arm, and, crying to her to run for her life, rushed like the wind along the gallery, down the corridor, down the stairs. Mary's screams filled the house as she fled beside me. I heard a long-drawn, raging cry, the roar of a wild animal mocked of its prey, and I knew what was behind me. I never turned my head—I flew rather than ran. I was in the hall already; there was a rush of many feet, an outcry of many voices, a sound of scuffling feet, and brutal yells, and oaths, and heavy blows, and I fell to the ground, crying, "Save me!" and lay in a swoon. I awoke from a delirious trance. Kind faces were around my bed, loving looks were bent on me by all, by my dear father and dear sisters, but I scarcely saw them before I swooned again.

When I recovered from that long illness, through which I had been nursed so tenderly, the pitying looks I met made me tremble. I asked for a looking-glass. It was long denied me, but my importunity prevailed at last—a mirror was brought. My youth was gone at one fell swoop. The glass showed me a livid and haggard face, blanched and bloodless as of one who sees a spectre; and in the ashen lips, and wrinkled brow, and dim eyes, I could trace nothing of my old self. The hair, too, jetty and rich before, was now as white as snow, and in one night the ravages of half a century had passed over my face. Nor have my nerves ever recovered their tone after that dire shock. Can you wonder that my life was blighted, that my lover shrank from me, so sad a wreck was I? I am old now—old and alone. My sisters would have had me to live with them, but I chose not to sadden their genial homes with my phantom face and dead eyes. Reginald married another. He has been dead many years. I never ceased to pray for him, though he left me when I was bereft of all. The sad weird is nearly over now. I am old, and near the end, and wishful for it. I have not been bitter or hard, but I cannot bear to see many people, and am best alone. I try to do what good I can with the worthless wealth Lady Speldhurst left me, for at my wish my portion was shared between my sisters. What need had I of inheritances?—I, the shattered wreck made by that one night of horror!

A GOBLIN DITTY
by
George Manville Fenn
1867

"You don't believe in ghostsh?"

"No, I don't believe in ghostsh."

"Nor yet in goblinsh?"

"No, nor yet in goblinsh, nor witches, nor nothing of the kind, I don't," cried Sandy Brown, talking all the while to himself as he was making his way home from the village alehouse on Christmas-eve. "I'm the right short I am, and I ain't 'fraid o' nothin', nor I don't care for nothin', an' I'm aw' right, and rule Britannia never shall be slaves. I'm a Hinglishman, I am, an' I'm a goin' crosh the churchyard home, and I'll knock the wind outer any ghosht— azh—azh—azh—you know—ghosht, and who shaysh it ain't all right? I never shee a ghosht yet azh could get the better o' me, for I'm a man, I am, a true born Briton if I am a tailor. And when I getsh to the head of affairsh I'll do it p'litically, and put a shtop to ghoshts, and all the whole lot of 'em, and my namesh Brown, and I'm a-going home through churchyard I am."

And a very nice man was Sandy Brown, the true born Briton, as he went rolling along the path that gloriously bright Christmas-eve, when there were myriads of stars in the East, and the whole heavens above seemed singing their wondrous eternal chorus—

"The hand that made us is Divine."

The moon shone; the sky was of a deep blue; the stars gemmed the vast arch like diamonds; ay, and, like the most lustrous of jewels, shone again the snow and frost from the pure white earth, while from far away came the northern breeze humming over woodland, down, and lea, turning everything to ice with its freezing breath, so that river and brook forgot to flow, and every chimney sent up its incense-like smoke, rising higher and higher in the frosty air.

The bells had been ringing, and the ringers had shut up the belfry-door. The curate's and rector's daughters had finished their task, so that the inside of the church was one great wreath of bright evergreens; while many a busy housewife was hard at work yet, even though past twelve, to finish dressing the goose or stoning the plums.

And what a breeze that was that came singing over the hills, sharp, keen, and blood dancing. Why, it was no use to try and resist it, for it seemed to make your very heart glow, so that you wanted to hug everybody and wish them a merry Christmas. Late, yes, it was late, but there were glaring lights in many a window, and even bright sparks dancing out of the tops of chimneys, for wasn't it Christmas-eve, and was not the elder wine simmering in the little warmer, while many a rosy face grew rosier through making the toast? And there, too, when you stood by Rudby churchyard and looked at the venerable pile, glittering with snow and ice in the moonlight, while the smooth, round hillocks lay covered as it were with white fur for warmth, the scene brought then no saddening thoughts, for you seemed only gazing upon the happy, peaceful resting-place of those who enjoyed Christmas in the days of the past.

For it's of no use, you can't help it, it's in the bells, or the wind, or the time, or something, you must feel jolly at Christmas, whether you will or no, and though you may set up your back and resist, and all that sort of thing, it's of no avail, so you may just as well yield with a good grace, and in making others enjoy themselves, enjoy yourself too. Selfishness! Bah, it's madness, folly: why, the real—the true enjoyment of life is making other people happy, but Sandy Brown thought that making himself the receptacle for more beer than was good for him was being happy; and Sandy Brown was wrong. And perhaps you'll say, too, that you don't believe in ghosts, goblins, and spirits? Hold your tongue, for they're out by the thousand this Christmas-time, putting noble and bright inspirations into people's hearts, showing us the sufferings of the poor, and teaching us of the good that there is room to do in this wicked world of ours. But there, fie! fie! fie! to call it this wicked world—this great, wondrous, glorious, beautiful world, if we did not mar its beauty. But there, it's Christmas-time, when we all think of the coming year, and hopefully gird up our loins for the new struggle.

Sandy Brown had left his wife and child at home, while he went out to enjoy himself after his fashion, which was to drink till he grew so quarrelsome that the landlord turned him out, when he would go home, beat his wife, and then lay upon the bed and swear.

Ah, he was a nice man, was Sandy, just the fellow to have had in a glass case to show as a specimen of a free-born Briton—of the man who never would be a slave—to anything but his own vile passions.

It was very bleak at Sandy's cottage that night, for the coals were done, and there was no wood. Little Polly could not sleep for the cold, and her mother sat shivering over the fire trying to warm the little thing, who cried piteously, as did its mother. There were no preparations for spending a happy Christmas there, but poor Mrs Brown, pale, young, and of the trusting heart, sat watching and waiting till her lord and master should choose to return.

"There," said Sandy, blundering through the swing-gate and standing in the churchyard. "Who'sh afraid? Where'sh yer ghosh—eh?"

"Hallo!" said a voice at his elbow, while it seemed that a cold, icy, chilling breath swept over his cheek.

"Where'sh yer ghosh?" cried Sandy, startled and half sober already.

"Don't make such a noise, man, we're all here," said the voice, "come along."

"Eh?" cried Sandy, now quite sober and all of a shiver, for a cold breath seemed to have gone right through him, and he looked behind him on each side and then in front, but there was nothing visible but the glittering snow—covered graves and tombstones sparkling in the brilliant moonlight.

"Bah!" cried Sandy, "I don't believe—"

"Yes, you do," said the same voice, and again the cold breath seemed to go through Sandy and amongst his hair, so that it lifted his hat, already half off, and it fell to the ground.

"N-n-no, I don't," cried Sandy, trying to start off in a run, but he stopped short, for just in front of him stood a bright, glittering, white figure, apparently made of snow, only that it had jolly rosy cheeks, and a pair of the keenest eyes ever seen.

"Yes, you do, Sandy Brown," said the same voice, "and so don't contradict. Bring him along."

In a moment, before he could turn himself, there came a rushing sound like when the wintry breeze plunges into a heap of leaves, and whirls and rustles them away, when Sandy felt himself turned in a moment as it were to ice, and then rising higher and higher as he was borne round and round for some distance; when in the midst of myriads of tiny, glittering, snow-like figures, he was carried all at once right over the church; while like a beam of light the figures swept on after him as now rising, now falling, then circling, he was at last wafted round and round the old church, till he was placed upon the tower top, and like a swarm of bees in summer, the tiny figures came clustering and humming round him till they were all settled.

"Let me go home, please," cried Sandy, as soon as he could speak, but before the last word was well said, the first figure he had seen clapped its hand upon his mouth, when the tailor's jaw seemed to freeze stiff, so that he could not move his jaw.

"How dare you?" cried the spirit angrily.

"Dare I what?" Sandy said with his eyes.

"Profane good words," cried the spirit, in answer. "How dare you talk about home, when you have murdered it, and cast the guardian spirit out? Freeze him. But there, stop a bit."

Hundreds of the little fellows round had been about to make a dash at Sandy, but they fell back once more, and the tailor sat immoveable.

"There, look there," said the cold voice; "that's what you have spoilt." And Sandy began to weep bitterly, so that his tears froze and fell in little hard pellets of ice on to the snow before him, for he was looking upon the happy little home he had once had before he took to drinking, and watching in the humble but comfortable spot the busy wife preparing for the next day's Christmas feast, while he, busy and active, was finishing some work to take back.

"Now, look," cried the cold voice, and in an instant the scene had changed from light to darkness, for he could see his own dissipated, ragged self standing in the open door of his cottage, with the moonlight casting his shadow across the figure of his wife, lying cold and pale, with her child clasped to her breast. The black shadow—his shadow—the gloomy shade of her life cast upon her; and in speechless agony Sandy tried to shriek, for it seemed that she was dead—that they were dead, frozen in the bitter night while waiting for him.

The poor wretch looked imploringly at the figure before him, but there was only a grim smile upon its countenance as it nodded its head; and then, as if in the midst of a storm of snow flakes, Sandy was borne away and away, freezing as he went, now higher, now lower; now close up to some bright window, where he could see merry faces clustering round the fire; now by the humblest cottage, now by the lordly mansion; but see what he would, there was still the black shadow of himself cast upon those two cold figures, and he turned his eyes imploringly from tiny face to tiny face, till all at once he found that they were sailing once more round and round, now higher, now lower, till from sailing round the church the tiny spirits began to settle slowly down more and more in the churchyard, till they left Sandy, stiff and cold, lying between two graves, with the one tall ghostly figure glittering above him. And now began something more wondrous than ever, for the bright figure glittering in the moonlight began to hover and quiver its long arms and legs above the tailor, and as it shook itself it seemed to fall all away in innumerable other figures, each one its own counterpart, till there was nothing left but the face, which stayed staring right in front.

The old clock struck four, when, groaning with pain and trembling with fear and cold, Sandy Brown slowly raised himself, keeping his eyes fixed upon a stony-faced cherub powdered with snow, which sat upon a tombstone in front, and returned the stare with its stony eyes till Sandy slowly and painfully made his way across the churchyard, leaving his track in the newly fallen snow; while, after an hour or two's overclouding, the heavens were once more bright and clear, so that when Sandy stood shuddering at his own door he feared to raise the latch, for the moon shone brightly behind him, and he trembled and paused in dread, for he knew where his black shadow would fall.

But in an agony of fear he at length slowly and carefully raised the latch, gazed upon his shadow falling across his wife and child, and then, in the revulsion of feeling to find that they only slept, he staggered for a moment, and as his frightened wife shrieked, he fell to the ground, as if stricken by some mighty blow.

But joy don't kill, especially at Christmas-time, and when Mrs. Brown rose rather late that morning, she could not make out why Sandy was gone out so soon, for his usual custom was to lie half the day in bed after a drinking bout. But Sandy had gone to see about the day's dinner, and—

But there, Sandy's home a year after showed the effect of his meeting with the Christmas spirits, for it was well-furnished, and his wife looked happy, plump, and rosy—another woman, in fact; while as to people saying that Sandy fell down drunk in the churchyard, and that it was the little snow storm that he saw, why that's all nonsense; the story must be true, for a man picked up Sandy's old hat just by the swing-gate, where it fell off when he felt the spirit's breath. And as to there being no spirits out at Christmas-time, why I could name no end of them, such as love, gratitude, kindness, gentleness, good humour, and scores more with names, besides all those nameless spirits that cluster round every good, true, and loving heart at Christmas; ay, and at all times. While among those who have listened to this story and thought of its moral, surely there is at this moment that most gracious of spirits—Forbearance.

THE GHOST.
A CHRISTMAS STORY
by
William D. O'Connor
1867

Illustrated by Thomas Nast

At the West End of Boston is a quarter of some fifty streets, more or less, commonly known as Beacon Hill.

It is a rich and respectable quarter, and everybody knows it. The very houses have become sentient of its prevailing character of riches and respectability; and, when the twilight deepens on the place, or at high noon, if your vision is gifted, you may see them as long rows of our first giants, with very corpulent or very broad fronts—with solid-set feet of sidewalk, ending in square-toed curb-stone—with an air about them as if they had thrust their hard hands into their wealthy pockets forever—with a character of arctic reserve, and portly dignity, and a well-dressed, full-fed, self-satisfied, opulent, stony, repellent

aspect to each, which says plainly: "I belong to a rich family, of the very highest respectability."

History, having much to say of Beacon Hill generally, has, on the present occasion, something to say particularly, of a certain street which bends over the eminence, sloping steeply down to its base. It is an old street—quaint, quiet, and somewhat picturesque. It was young once, though—having been born before the Revolution, and was then given to the city by its father, Mr. Middlecott, who died without heirs, and did this much for posterity. Posterity has not been grateful to Mr. Middlecott. The street bore his name till he was dust, and then got the more aristocratic epithet of Bowdoin. Posterity has paid him by effacing what would have been his noblest epitaph. We may expect, after this, to see Faneuil Hall robbed of its name, and called Smith Hall! Republics are proverbially ungrateful. What safer claim to public remembrance has the old Huguenot, Peter Faneuil, than the old Englishman, Mr. Middlecott? Ghosts, it is said, have risen from the grave to reveal wrongs done them by the living; but it needs no ghost from the grave to prove the proverb about republics.

Bowdoin-street only differs from its kindred, in a certain shady, grave, old-fogy, fossil aspect, just touched with a pensive solemnity, as if it thought to itself, "I'm getting old but I'm highly respectable; that's a comfort." It has, moreover, a dejected, injured air, as if it brooded solemnly on the wrong done to it by taking away its original name, and calling it Bowdoin: but as if, being a very conservative street, it was resolved to keep a cautious silence on the subject, lest the Union should go to pieces. Sometimes it wears a profound and mysterious look, as if it could tell something if it had a mind to, but thought it best not. Something of the ghost of its father—it was the only child he ever had!—walking there all the night, pausing at the corners to look up at the signs, which bear a strange name, and wringing his ghostly hands in lamentation at the wrong done his memory! Rumor told it in a whisper, many years ago. Perhaps it was believed by a few of the oldest inhabitants of the city; but the highly respectable quarter never heard of it; and, if it had, would not have been bribed to believe it, by any sum. Some one had said that some very old person had seen a phantom there. Nobody knew who some one was. Nobody knew who the very old person was. Nobody knew who had seen it; nor when; nor how. The very rumor was spectral.

All this was many years ago. Since then it has been reported that a ghost was seen there one bitter Christmas eve, two or three years back. The twilight was already in the street; but the evening lamps were not yet lighted in the windows—and the roofs and chimney-tops were still distinct in the last clear light of the dropping day. It was light enough, however, for one to read, easily, from the opposite sidewalk, "Dr. C. Renton," in black letters, on the silver plate of a door, not far from the gothic portal of the Swedenborgian church. Near this door stood a misty figure, whose sad, spectral eyes floated on vacancy, and whose long, shadowy white hair, lifted like an airy weft in the streaming wind. That was the ghost! It stood near the door a long time, without any other than a shuddering motion, as though it felt the searching blast, which swept furiously from the north up the declivity of the street, rattling the shutters in its headlong passage. Once or twice, when a passer-by, muffled warmly from the bitter air, hurried past, the phantom shrank closer to the wall, till he was gone. Its vague, mournful face seemed to watch for some one. The twilight darkened, gradually; but it did not flit away. Patiently it kept its piteous look fixed in one direction—watching—watching; and, while the howling wind swept frantically through the chill air, it still seemed to shudder in the piercing cold.

A light suddenly kindled in an opposite window. As if touched by a gleam from the lamp, or as if by some subtle interior illumination, the spectre became faintly luminous, and a thin smile seemed to quiver over its features. At the same moment, a strong, energetic figure—Dr. Renton, himself—came in sight, striding down the slope of the pavement to his own door, his over-coat thrown back, as if the icy air were a tropical warmth to him—his hat set on the back of his head, and the loose ends of a 'kerchief about his throat, streaming in the nor'-wester. The wind set up a howl the moment he came in sight, and swept upon him; and a curious agitation began on the part of the phantom. It glided rapidly to and fro, and moved in circles, and then, with the same swift, silent motion, sailed toward him, as if blown thither by the gale. Its long, thin arms, with something like a pale flame spiring from the tips of the slender fingers, were stretched out, as in greeting, while the wan smile played over its face; and when he rushed by, unheedingly, it made a futile effort to grasp the swinging arms with which he appeared to buffet back the buffeting gale. Then it glided on by his side, looking earnestly into his countenance, and moving its pallid lips with agonized rapidity, as if it said: "Look at me—speak to me—speak to me—see me!" But he kept his course with unconscious eyes, and a vexed frown on his bold, white forehead, betokening an irritated mind. The light that had shone in the figure of the phantom, darkened slowly, till the form was only a pale shadow. The wind had suddenly lulled, and no longer lifted its white hair. It still glided on with him, its head drooping on its breast, and its long arms hanging by its side; but when he reached the door, it suddenly sprang before him, gazing fixedly into his eyes, while a convulsive motion flashed over its grief-worn features, as if it had shrieked out a word. He had his foot on the step at the moment. With a start, he put his gloved hand to his forehead, while the vexed look went out quickly on his face. The ghost watched him breathlessly. But the irritated expression came back to his countenance more resolutely than before, and he began to fumble in his pocket for a latch-key, muttering petulantly, "What the devil is the matter with me now!" It seemed to him that a voice had cried, clearly, yet as from afar, "Charles Renton!"—his own name. He had heard it in his startled mind; but, then, he knew he was in a highly wrought state of nervous excitement, and his medical science, with that knowledge for a basis, could have reared a formidable fortress of explanation against any phenomenon, were it even more wonderful than this.

He entered the house; kicked the door to; pulled off his over-coat; wrenched off his outer 'kerchief; slammed them on a branch of the clothes-tree; banged his hat on top of them; wheeled about; pushed in the door of his library; strode in, and, leaving the door ajar, threw himself into an easy chair, and sat there in the fire-reddened dusk, with his white brows knit, and his arms tightly locked on his breast. The ghost had followed him, sadly, and now stood motionless in a corner of the room, its spectral hands crossed on its bosom, and its white locks drooping down.

It was evident Dr. Renton was in a bad humor. The very library caught contagion from him, and became grouty and sombre. The furniture was grim, and sullen, and sulky; it made ugly shadows on the carpet and on the wall, in allopathic quantity; it took the red gleams from the fire on its polished surfaces, in homœopathic globules, and got no good from them. The fire itself peered out sulkily from the black bars of the grate, and seemed resolved not to burn the fresh deposit of black coals at the top, but to take this as a good time to remember that those coals had been bought in the summer at five dollars a ton—under price, mind you—when poor people, who cannot buy at advantage, but must get their firing in the winter, would then have given nine or ten dollars for them. And so (glowered the fire), I am determined to think of that outrage, and not to light them, but to go out myself, directly! And the fire got into such a spasm of glowing indignation over the injury, that it lit a whole tier of black coals with a series of little explosions, before it could cool down, and sent a crimson gleam over the moody figure of its owner in the easy chair, and over the solemn furniture, and into the shadowy corner filled by the ghost.

It did not move when Dr. Renton arose and lit the chandelier. It stood there, still and gray, in the flood of mellow light. The curtains were drawn, and the twilight without had deepened into darkness. The fire was now burning in despite of itself, fanned by the wintry gusts, which found their way down the chimney. Dr. Renton stood with his back to it—his hands behind him; his bold white forehead shaded by a careless lock of black hair, and knit sternly; and the same frown in his handsome, open, searching dark eyes. Tall and strong—with an erect port, and broad, firm shoulders—high, resolute features—a commanding figure garbed in aristocratic black, and not yet verging into the proportions of obesity—take him for all in all, a very fine and favorable specimen of the solid men of Boston. And seen in contrast (O, could he but have known it!) with the attenuated figure of the poor, dim ghost!

Hark! A very light foot on the stairs—a rich rustle of silks. Every-
thing still again—Dr. Renton looking fixedly, with great sternness, at the half-open door, from whence a faint, delicious perfume floats into the library. Somebody there, for certain. Somebody peeping in with very bright, arch eyes. Dr. Renton knew it, and prepared to maintain his ill humor against the invader. His face became triply armed with severity for the encounter. That's Netty, I know, he thought. His daughter. So it was. In she bounded. Bright little Netty! Gay little Netty! A dear and sweet little creature, to be sure, with a delicate and pleasant beauty of face and figure, it needed no costly silks to grace or heighten. There she stood. Not a word from her merry lips, but a smile which stole over all the solitary grimness of the library, and made everything better, and brighter, and fairer, in a minute. It floated down into the cavernous humor of Dr. Renton, and the gloom began to lighten directly—though he would not own it, nor relax a single feature. But the wan ghost in the corner lifted its head to look at her, and slowly brightened as to something worthy a spirit's love, and a dim phantom's smiles. Now then, Dr. Renton! the lines are drawn, and the foe is coming. Be martial, sir, as when you stand in the ranks of the cadets on training-days! Steady, and stand the charge! So he did. He kept an inflexible front as she glided toward him, softly, slowly—with her bright eyes smiling into his, and doing dreadful execution. Then she put her white arms around his neck, laid her dear, fair head on his breast, and peered up archly into his stern visage. Spite of himself, he could not keep the fixed lines on his face from breaking confusedly into a faint smile. Somehow or other, his hands came from behind him, and rested on her head. There! That's all. Dr. Renton surrendered at discretion! One of the solid men of Boston was taken after a desperate struggle—internal, of course—for he kissed her, and said, "Dear little Netty!" And so she was.

The phantom watched her with a smile, and wavered and brightened as if about to glide to her; but it grew still, and remained.

"Pa's in the sulks to-night?" she asked, in the most winning, playful, silvery voice.

"Pa's a fool," he answered in his deep chest-tones, with a vexed good humor; "and you know it."

"What's the matter with pa? What makes him be a great bear? Papa-sy, dear," she continued, stroking his face with her little hands, and patting him, very much as Beauty might have patted the Beast after she fell in love with him—or, as if he were a great baby. In fact, he began to look then as if he were.

"Matter? O, everything's the matter, little Netty. The world goes round too fast. My boots pinch. Somebody stole my umbrella last year. And I've got a headache." He concluded this fanciful abstract of his grievances by putting his arms around her, and kissing her again. Then he sat down in the easy-chair, and took her fondly on his knee.

"Pa's got a headache! It is t-o-o bad, so it is," she continued in the same soothing, winning way, caressing his bold, white brow with her tiny hands. "It's a horrid shame, so it is! P-o-o-r pa. Where does it ache, papa-sy, dear? In the forehead? Cerebrum or cerebellum, papa-sy? Occiput or sinciput, deary?"

"Bah! you little quiz," he replied, laughing and pinching her cheek, "none of your nonsense! And what are you dressed up in this way for, to-night? Silks, and laces, and essences, and what not! Where are you going, fairy?"

"Going out with mother for the evening, Dr. Renton," she replied briskly; "Mrs. Larrabee's party, papa-sy. Christmas eve, you know. And what are you going to give me for a present, to-morrow, pa-sy?"

"To-morrow will tell, little Netty."

"Good! And what are you going to give me, so that I can make *my* presents, Beary?"

"Ugh!" but he growled it in fun, and had a pocket-book out from his breast-pocket directly after. Fives—tens—twenties—fifties—all crisp, and nice, and new bank-notes.

"Will that be enough, Netty?" He held up a twenty. The smiling face nodded assent, and the bright eyes twinkled.

"No, it won't. But *that* will," he continued, giving her a fifty.

"Fifty dollars, Kilby Bank, Boston!" exclaimed Netty, making great eyes at him. "But we must take all we can get, pa-sy; mustn't we? It's too much, though. Thank you all the same, pa-sy, nevertheless." And she kissed him, and put the bill in a little bit of a porte-monnaie with a gay laugh.

"Well done, I declare!" he said, smilingly. "But you're going to the party?"

"Pretty soon, pa."

He made no answer; but sat smiling at her. The phantom watched them, silently.

"What made pa so cross and grim, to-night? Tell Netty—do," she pleaded.

"O—because;—everything went wrong with me, to-day. There." And he looked as sulky, at that moment, as he ever did in his life.

"No, no, pa-sy; that won't do. I want the particulars," continued Netty, shaking her head, smilingly.

"Particulars! Well, then, Miss Nathalie Renton," he began, with mock gravity, "your professional father is losing some of his oldest patients. Everybody is in ruinous good health; and the grass is growing in the graveyards."

"In the winter-time, papa?—smart grass!"

"Not that I want practice," he went on, getting into soliloquy; "or patients, either. A rich man who took to the profession simply for the love of it, can't complain on that score. But to have an interloping she-doctor take a family I've attended ten years, out of my hands, and to hear the hodge-podge gabble about physiological laws, and woman's rights, and no taxation without representation, they learn from her—well, it's too bad!"

"Is that all, pa-sy? Seems to me, *I'd* like to vote, too," was Netty's piquant rejoinder.

"Hoh! I'll warrant," growled her father. "Hope you'll vote the Whig ticket, Netty, when you get your rights."

"Will the Union be dissolved, then, pa-sy—when the Whigs are beaten?"

"Bah! you little plague," he growled, with a laugh. "But, then, you women don't know anything about politics. So, there. As I was saying, everything went wrong with me to-day. I've been speculating in railroad stock, and singed my fingers. Then, old Tom Hollis outbid me, to-day, at Leonard's on a rare medical work, I had set my eyes upon having. Confound him! Then, again, two of my houses are tenantless, and there are folks in two others that won't pay their rent, and I can't get them out. Out they'll go, though, or I'll know why. And, to crown all—um-m. And I wish the devil had him! as he will."

"Had who, Beary-papa?"

"Him. I'll tell you. The street floor of one of my houses in Hanover street lets for an oyster-room. They keep a bar there, and sell liquor. Last night they had a grand row—a drunken fight, and one man was stabbed, it's thought fatally."

"O, father!" Netty's bright eyes dilated with horror.

"Yes. I hope he won't die. At any rate, there's likely to be a stir about the matter, and my name will be called into question, then, as I'm the landlord. And folks will make a handle of it, and there'll be the deuce to pay, generally."

He got back the stern, vexed frown, to his face, with the anticipation, and beat the carpet with his foot. The ghost still watched from the angle of the room, and seemed to darken, while its features looked troubled.

"But, father," said Netty, a little tremulously, "I wouldn't let my houses to such people. It's not right; is it? Why, it's horrid to think of men getting drunk, and killing each other!"

Dr. Renton rubbed his hair into disorder, with vexation, and then subsided into solemnity.

"I know it's not exactly right, Netty; but I can't help it. As I said before, I wish the devil had that bar-keeper. I ought to have ordered him out long ago, and then this wouldn't have happened. I've increased his rent twice, hoping to get rid of him so; but he pays without a murmur; and what am I to do? You see, he was an occupant when the building came into my hands, and I let him stay. He pays me a good, round rent; and, apart from his cursed traffic, he's a good tenant. What can I do? It's a good thing for him, and it's a good thing for me, pecuniarily. Confound him. Here's a nice rumpus brewing!"

"Dear pa, I'm afraid it's not a good thing for you," said Netty, caressing him, and smoothing his tumbled hair. "Nor for him either. I wouldn't mind the rent he pays you. I'd order him out. It's bad money. There's blood on it."

She had grown pale, and her voice quivered. The phantom glided over to them, and laid its spectral hand upon her forehead. The shadowy eyes looked from under the misty hair into the doctor's face, and the pale lips moved as if speaking the words heard only in the silence of his heart—"hear her, hear her!"

"I must think of it," resumed Dr. Renton, coldly. "I'm resolved, at all events, to warn him that if anything of this kind occurs again, he must quit at once. I dislike to lose a profitable tenant; for no other business would bring me the sum his does. Hang it, everybody does the best he can with his property—why shouldn't I?"

The ghost, standing near them, drooped its head again on its breast, and crossed its arms. Netty was silent. Dr. Renton continued, petulantly:—

"A precious set of people I manage to get into my premises. There's a woman hires a couple of rooms for a dwelling, overhead, in that same building, and for three months I haven't got a cent from her. I know these people's tricks. Her month's notice expires to-morrow, and out she goes."

"Poor creature!" sighed Netty.

He knit his brow, and beat the carpet with his foot, in vexation.

"Perhaps she can't pay you, pa," trembled the sweet, silvery voice. "You wouldn't turn her out in this cold winter, when she can't pay you—would you, pa?"

"Why don't she get another house, and swindle some one else?" he replied, testily; "there's plenty of rooms to let."

"Perhaps she can't find one, pa," answered Netty.

"Humbug!" retorted her father; "I know better."

"Pa, dear, if I were you, I'd turn out that rum-seller, and let the poor woman stay a little longer; just a little, pa."

"Shan't do it. Hah! that would be scattering money out of both pockets. Shan't do it. Out she shall go; and as for him—well, he'd better turn over a new leaf. There, let us leave the subject, darling. It vexes me. How did we contrive to get into this train. Bah!"

He drew her closer to him, and kissed her forehead. She sat quietly, with her head on his shoulder, thinking very gravely.

"I feel queerly, to-day, little Netty," he began, after a short pause. "My nerves are all high-strung with the turn matters have taken."

"How is it, papa? The headache?" she answered.

"Ye-s—n-o—not exactly; I don't know," he said dubiously; then, in an absent way, "it was that letter set me to think of him all day, I suppose."

"Why, pa, I declare," cried Netty, starting up, "if I didn't forget all about it, and I came down expressly to give it to you! Where is it? O, here it is."

She drew from her pocket an old letter, faded to a pale yellow, and gave it to him. The ghost started suddenly.

"Why, bless my soul! it's the very letter! Where did you get that, Nathalie?" asked Dr. Renton.

"I found it on the stairs after dinner, pa."

"Yes, I do remember taking it up with me; I must have dropped it," he answered, musingly, gazing at the superscription. The ghost was gazing at it, too, with startled interest.

"What beautiful writing it is, pa," murmured the young girl. "Who wrote it to you? It looks yellow enough to have been written a long time since."

"Fifteen years ago, Netty. When you were a baby. And the hand that wrote it has been cold for all that time."

He spoke with a solemn sadness, as if memory lingered with the heart of fifteen years ago, on an old grave. The dim figure by his side had bowed its head, and all was still.

"It is strange," he resumed, speaking vacantly and slowly, "I have not thought of him for so long a time, and to-day—especially this evening—I have felt as if he were constantly near me. It is a singular feeling."

He put his left hand to his forehead, and mused—his right clasped his daughter's shoulder. The phantom slowly raised its head, and gazed at him with a look of unutterable tenderness.

"Who was he, father?" she asked with a hushed voice.

"A young man—an author—a poet. He had been my dearest friend, when we were boys; and, though I lost sight of him for years—he led an erratic life—we were friends when he died. Poor, poor fellow! Well, he is at peace."

The stern voice had saddened, and was almost tremulous. The spectral form was still.

"How did he die, father?"

"A long story, darling," he replied gravely, "and a sad one. He was very poor and proud. He was a genius—that is, a person without an atom of practical talent. His parents died, the last, his mother, when he was near manhood. I was in college then. Thrown upon the world, he picked up a scanty subsistence with his pen, for a time. I could have got him a place in the counting-house, but he would not take it; in fact, he wasn't fit for it. You can't harness Pegasus to the cart, you know. Besides, he despised mercantile life—without reason, of course; but he was always notional. His love of literature was one of the rocks he foundered on. He wasn't successful; his best compositions were too delicate—fanciful—to please the popular taste; and then he was full of the radical and fanatical notions which infected so many people at that time in New England, and infect them now, for that matter; and his sublimated, impracticable ideas and principles, which he kept till his dying day, and which, I confess, alienated me from him, always staved off his chances of success. Consequently, he never rose above the drudgery of some employment on newspapers. Then he was terribly passionate, not without cause, I allow; but it wasn't wise. What I mean is this: if he saw, or if he fancied he saw, any wrong or injury done to any one, it was enough to throw him into a frenzy; he would get black in the face and absolutely shriek out his denunciations of the wrongdoer. I do believe he would have visited his own brother with the most unsparing invective, if that brother had laid a harming finger on a street-beggar, or a colored man, or a poor person of any kind. I don't blame the feeling; though with a man like him, it was very apt to be a false or mistaken one; but, at any rate, its exhibition wasn't sensible. Well, as I was saying, he buffeted about in this world a long time, poorly paid, fed, and clad; taking more care of other people than he did of himself. Then mental suffering, physical exposure, and want killed him."

The stern voice had grown softer than a child's. The same look of unutterable tenderness brooded on the mournful face of the phantom by his side; but its thin, shining hand was laid upon his head, and its countenance had undergone a change. The form was still undefined; but the features had become distinct. They were those of a young man, beautiful and wan, and marked with great suffering.

A pause had fallen on the conversation, in which the father and daughter heard the solemn sighing of the wintry wind around the dwelling. The silence seemed scarcely broken by the voice of the young girl.

"Dear father, this was very sad. Did you say he died of want?"

"Of want, my child, of hunger and cold. I don't doubt it. He had wandered about, as I gather, houseless for a couple of days and nights. It was in December, too. Some one found him, on a rainy night, lying in the street, drenched and burning with fever, and had him taken to the hospital. It appears that he had always cherished a strange affection for me, though I had grown away from him; and in his wild ravings he constantly mentioned my name, and they sent for me. That was our first meeting after two years. I found him in the hospital—dying. He was delirious, and never recognized me. And, Nathalie, his hair—it had been coal-black, and he wore it very long, he wouldn't let them cut it either; and as they knew no skill could save him, they let him have his way—his hair was then as white as snow! God alone knows what that brain must have suffered to blanch hair which had been as black as the wing of a raven!"

He covered his eyes with his hand, and sat silently. The fingers of the phantom still shone dimly on his head, and its white locks drooped above him, like a weft of light.

"What was his name, father?" asked the pitying girl.

"George Feval. The very name sounds like fever. He died on Christmas eve, fifteen years ago this night. It was on his death-bed, while his mind was tossing on a sea of delirious fancies, that he wrote me this long letter—for to the last, I was uppermost in his thoughts. It is a wild, incoherent thing, of course—a strange mixture of sense and madness. But I have kept it as a memorial of him. I have not looked at it for years; but this morning I found it among my papers, and somehow it has been in my mind all day."

He slowly unfolded the faded sheets, and sadly gazed at the writing. His daughter had risen from her half-recumbent posture, and now bent her graceful head over the leaves. The phantom covered its face with its hands.

"What a beautiful manuscript it is, father!" she exclaimed. "The writing is faultless."

"It is, indeed," he replied. "Would he had written his life as fairly!"

"Read it, father," said Nathalie.

"No—but I'll read you a detached passage here and there," he answered, after a pause. "The rest you may read yourself some time, if you wish. It is painful to me. Here's the beginning:

"*'My Dear Charles Renton:—Adieu, and adieu. It is Christmas eve, and I am going home. I am soon to exhale from my flesh, like the spirit of a broken flower. Exultemus forever!'*

"It is very wild. His mind was in a fever-craze. Here is a passage that seems to refer to his own experience of life:

"*'Your friendship was dear to me. I give you true love. Stocks and returns. You are rich, but I did not wish to be your bounty's pauper. Could I beg? I had my work to do for the world, but oh! the world has no place for souls that can only love and suffer. How many miles to Babylon? Three score and ten. Not so far—not near so far! Ask starvelings—they know.*
I wanted to do the world good and the world has killed me, Charles.'"

"It frightens me," said Nathalie, as he paused.

"We will read no more," he replied sombrely. "It belongs to the psychology of madness. To me, who knew him, there are gleams of sense in it, and passages where the delirium of the language is only a transparent veil on the meaning. All the remainder is devoted to what he thought important advice to me. But it's all wild and vague. Poor—poor George!"

The phantom still hid its face in its hands, as the doctor slowly turned over the pages of the letter. Nathalie, bending over the leaves, laid her finger on the last, and asked—"What are those closing sentences, father? Read them."

"O, that is what he called his 'last counsel' to me. It's as wild as the rest—tinctured with the prevailing ideas of his career. First he says, '*Farewell—farewell*;' then he bids me take his '*counsel into memory on Christmas day*;' then, after enumerating all the wretched classes he can think of in the country, he says, '*These are your sisters and your brothers—love them all.*' Here he says, '*O friend, strong in wealth for so much good, take my last counsel. In the name of the Saviour, I charge you be true and tender to mankind.'* He goes on to bid me *'live and labor for the fallen, the neglected, the suffering, and the poor;'* and finally ends, by advising me to help upset any, or all, institutions, laws, and so forth, that bear hardly on the fag-ends of society; and tells me that what he calls 'a service to humanity' is worth more to the doer than a service to anything else, or than anything we can gain from the world. Ah, well! poor George."

"But isn't all that true, father?"—said Netty; "it seems so."

"H'm," he murmured through his closed lips. Then, with a vague smile, folding up the letter, meanwhile, he said, "Wild words, Netty, wild words. I've no objection to charity, judiciously given; but poor George's notions are not mine. Every man for himself, is a good general rule. Every man for humanity, as George has it, and in his acceptation of the principle, would send us all to the alms-house pretty soon. The greatest good of the greatest number—that's my rule of action. There are plenty of good institutions for the distressed, and I'm willing to help support 'em, and do. But as for making a martyr of one's self, or tilting against the necessary evils of society, or turning philanthropist at large, or any quixotism of that sort, I don't believe in it. We didn't make the world, and we can't mend it. Poor George. Well—he's at rest. The world wasn't the place for him."

They grew silent. The spectre glided slowly to the wall, and stood as if it were thinking what, with Dr. Renton's rule of action, was to become of the greatest good of the smallest number. Nathalie sat on her father's knee, thinking only of George Feval, and of his having been starved and grieved to death.

"Father," said Nathalie, softly, "I felt, while you were reading the letter, as if he were near us. Didn't you? The room was so light and still, and the wind sighed so."

"Netty, dear, I've felt that all day, I believe," he replied—"hark! there is the door-bell. Off goes the spirit-world, and here comes the actual. Confound it! Some one to see me, I'll warrant, and I'm not in the mood."

He got into a fret at once. Netty was not the Netty of an hour ago, or she would have coaxed him out of it. But she did not notice it now in her abstraction. She had risen at the tinkle of the bell, and seated herself in a chair. Presently a nose, with a great pimple on the end of it, appeared at the edge of the door, and a weak, piping voice said, reckless of the proper tense, "there was a woman wanted to see you, sir."

"Who is it, James?—no matter, show her in."

He got up with the vexed scowl on his face, and walked the room. In a minute the library door opened again, and a pale, thin, rigid, frozen-looking little woman, scantily clad, the weather being considered, entered, and dropped a curt, awkward bow to Dr. Renton.

"O—Mrs. Miller. Good evening, ma'am. Sit down," he said, with a cold, constrained civility.

The little woman faintly said, "Good evening, Dr. Renton," and sat down stiffly, with her hands crossed before her, in the chair nearest the wall. This was the obdurate tenant, who had paid no rent for three months, and had a notice to quit, expiring to-morrow.

"Cold evening, ma'am," remarked Dr. Renton, in his hard way.

"Yes, sir, it is," was the cowed, awkward answer.

"Won't you sit near the fire, ma'am," said Netty, gently; "you look cold."

"No, miss, thank you. I'm not cold," was the faint reply. She was cold, though, as well she might be with her poor, thin shawl, and open bonnet, in such a bitter night as it was outside. And there was a rigid, sharp, suffering look in her pinched features that betokened she might have been hungry, too.

"Poor people don't mind the cold weather, miss," she said, with a weak smile, her voice getting a little stronger. "They have to bear it, and they get used to it."

She had not evidently borne it long enough to effect the point of indifference. Netty looked at her with a tender pity. Dr. Renton thought to himself—Hoh!—blazoning her poverty—manufacturing sympathy already—the old trick—and steeled himself against any attacks of that kind, looking jealously, meanwhile, at Netty.

"Well, Mrs. Miller," he said, "what is it this evening? I suppose you've brought me my rent."

The little woman grew paler, and her voice seemed to fail on her quivering lips. Netty cast a quick, beseeching look at her father.

"Nathalie, please to leave the room." We'll have no nonsense carried on here, he thought, triumphantly, as Netty rose, and obeyed the stern, decisive order, leaving the door ajar behind her.

He seated himself in his chair, and resolutely put his right leg up to rest on his left knee. He did not look at his tenant's face, determined that her piteous expressions (got up for the occasion, of course) should be wasted on him.

"Well, Mrs. Miller," he said again.

"Dr. Renton," she began, faintly gathering her voice as she proceeded, "I have come to see you about the rent. I am very sorry, sir, to have made you wait, but we have been unfortunate."

"Sorry, ma'am," he replied, knowing what was coming; "but your misfortunes are not my affair. We all have misfortunes, ma'am. But we must pay our debts, you know."

"I expected to have got money from my husband before this, sir," she resumed, "and I wrote to him. I got a letter from him to-day, sir, and it said that he sent me fifty dollars a month ago, in a letter; and it appears that the post-office is to blame, or somebody, for I never got it. It was nearly three months' wages, sir, and it is very hard to lose it. If it hadn't been for that, your rent would have been paid long ago, sir."

"Don't believe a word of *that* story," thought Dr. Renton, sententiously.

"I thought, sir," she continued, emboldened by his silence, "that if you would be willing to wait a little longer, we would manage to pay you soon, and not let it occur again. It has been a hard winter with us, sir; firing is high, and provisions, and everything; and we're only poor people, you know, and it's difficult to get along."

The doctor made no reply.

"My husband was unfortunate, sir, in not being able to get employment here," she resumed; "his being out of work, in the autumn, threw us all back, and we've got nothing to depend on but his earnings. The family that he's in now, sir, don't give him very good pay—only twenty dollars a month, and his board—but it was the best chance he could get, and it was either go to Baltimore with them, or stay at home and starve, and so he went, sir. It's been a hard time with us, and one of the children is sick, now, with a fever, and we don't hardly know how to make out a living. And so, sir, I have come here this evening, leaving the children alone, to ask you if you wouldn't be kind enough to wait a little longer, and we'll hope to make it right with you in the end."

"Mrs. Miller," said Dr. Renton, with stern composure, "I have no wish to question the truth of any statement you may make; but I must tell you plainly, that I can't afford to let my houses for nothing. I told you a month ago, that if you couldn't pay me my rent, you must vacate the premises. You know very well that there are plenty of tenants who are able and willing to pay when the money comes due. You *know* that."

He paused as he said this, and, glancing at her, saw her pale lips falter. It shook the cruelty of his purpose a little, and he had a vague feeling that he was doing wrong. Not without a proud struggle, during which no word was spoken, could he beat it down. Meanwhile, the phantom had advanced a pace toward the centre of the room.

"That is the state of the matter, ma'am," he resumed, coldly. "People who will not pay me my rent must not live in my tenements. You must move out. I have no more to say."

"Dr. Renton," she said faintly, "I have a sick child—how can I move now? O, sir, it's Christmas eve—don't be hard with us!"

Instead of touching him, this speech irritated him beyond measure. Passing all considerations of her difficult position involved in her piteous statement, his anger flashed at once on her implication that he was unjust and unkind. So violent was his excitement that it whirled away the words that rushed to his lips, and only fanned the fury that sparkled from the whiteness of his face in his eyes.

"Be patient with us, sir," she continued; "we are poor, but we mean to pay you; and we can't move now in this cold weather; please, don't be hard with us, sir."

The fury now burst out on his face in a red and angry glow, and the words came.

"Now, attend to me!" He rose to his feet. "I will not hear any more from you. I know nothing of your poverty, nor of the condition of your family. All I know is that you owe me three months' rent, and that you can't or won't pay me. I say, therefore, leave the premises to people who can and will. You have had your legal notice; quit my house to-morrow; if you don't, your furniture shall be put in the street. Mark me—to-morrow!"

The phantom had rushed into the centre of the room. Standing, face to face with him—dilating—blackening—its whole form shuddering with a fury to which his own was tame; the semblance of a shriek upon its flashing lips, and on its writhing features, and an unearthly anger streaming from its bright and terrible eyes; it seemed to throw down, with its tossing arms, mountains of hate and malediction on the head of him whose words had smitten poverty and suffering, and whose heavy hand was breaking up the barriers of a home.

Dr. Renton sank again into his chair. His tenant—not a woman!—not a sister, but only his tenant; she sat crushed and frightened by the wall. He knew it vaguely. Conscience was battling in his heart with the stubborn devils that had entered there. The phantom stood before him, like a dark cloud in the image of a man. But its darkness was lightening slowly, and its ghostly anger had passed away.

Mrs. Miller, paler than before, had sat mute and trembling, with all her hopes ruined. Yet her desperation forbade her to abandon the chances of his mercy, and she now said:

"Dr. Renton, you surely don't mean what you have told me. Won't you bear with me a little longer, and we will yet make it all right with you?"

"I have given you my answer," he returned, coldly; "I have no more to add. I never take back anything I say—never!"

It was true. He never did—never! She half rose from her seat as if to go; but weak and sickened with the bitter result of her visit, she sunk down again with her head bowed. There was a pause. Then, solemnly gliding across the lighted room, the phantom stole to her side with a glory of compassion on its wasted features. Tenderly, as a son to a mother, it bent over her; its spectral hands of light rested upon her in caressing and benediction; its shadowy fall of hair, once blanched by the anguish of living and loving, floated on her throbbing brow.

The stern and sullen mood from which had dropped but one fierce flash of anger, still hung above the heat of his mind, like a dark rack of thunder-cloud. It would have burst anew into a fury of rebuke, had he but known his daughter was listening at the door, while the colloquy went on. It might have flamed violently, had his tenant made any further attempt to change his purpose. She had not. She had left the room meekly, with the same curt, awkward bow that marked her entrance. He recalled her manner very indistinctly; for a feeling, like a mist, began to gather in his mind, and make the occurrences of moments before uncertain.

Alone, now, he was yet oppressed with a sensation that something was near him. Was it a spiritual instinct? for the phantom stood by his side. It stood silently, with one hand raised above his head, from which a pale flame seemed to flow downward to his brain; its other hand pointed movelessly to the open letter on the table beside him.

Dr. Renton took the sheets from the table, thinking, at the moment, only of George Feval; but the first line on which his eye rested was, "In the name of the Saviour, I charge you, be true and tender to all men!" and the words touched him like a low voice from the grave. Their penetrant reproach pierced the hardness of his heart. He tossed the letter back on the table. The very manner of the act accused him of an insult to the dead. In a moment he took up the faded sheets more reverently, but only to lay them down again.

He had thrown himself on a sofa, still striving to be rid of his remorseful visitations, when the library door opened, and the inside man appeared, with his hand held bashfully over his nose. It flashed on him at once, that his tenant's husband was the servant of a family like this fellow; and, irritated that the whole matter should be thus broadly forced upon him in another way, he harshly asked him what he wanted. The man only came in to say that Mrs. Renton and the young lady had gone out for the evening, but that tea was laid for him in the dining-room. He did not want any tea, and if anybody called, he was not at home. With this charge, the man left the room, closing the door behind him.

Rising from the sofa, he turned the lights of the chandelier low, and screened the fire. The room was still. The ghost stood, faintly radiant, in a remote corner. Dr. Renton lay down again, but not to repose. Things he had forgotten of his dead friend, now started up again in remembrance, fresh from the grave of many years; and not one of them but linked itself by some mysterious bond to something connected with his tenant, and became an accusation.

He had lain thus for more than an hour, his mental excitement fast becoming intolerable, when he heard a low strain of music, from the Swedenborgian chapel, hard by. Its first impression was one of solemnity and rest, and its first sense, in his mind, was of relief. Perhaps it was the music of an evening meeting; or it might be that the organist and choir had met for practice. Whatever its purpose, it breathed through his heated fancy like a cool and fragrant wind. Low and sad at first, he heard it swell and rise to a mournful dirge, but so subdued, that it touched him with awe. Gradually the fires in his brain sank down, and all yielded to a sense of coolness and repose.

Gradually sinking, also, the music failed. A pause, and then it rose again, blended with the solemn voices of the choir. It rose from pathos into wild despair; and swelling upward in an agony of supplication, sank, and died in a low and wailing sigh.

Yielding now with a sense in his spirit like despair, the tears streamed down the listener's face; and the low chant sighed above him, and died away. Dr. Renton slept. All light had gone from the spectral form. It knelt beside him, mutely, as in prayer. Once it gazed at his quiet face with a mournful tenderness, and its shadowy hands caressed his forehead. Then it resumed its former attitude, and the slow hours crept by.

At last it rose and glided to the table, on which lay the open letter. It seemed to try to lift the sheets with its misty hands—but vainly. Next it essayed the lifting of a pen which lay there—but failed. It was a piteous sight, to see its idle efforts on these shapes of grosser matter, which, to its strengthless essence, had now but the existence of illusions. Wandering about the shadowy room, it wrung its phantom hands as in despair.

Presently it grew still. Then it passed quickly to his side, and stood before him. He slept calmly. It placed one ghostly hand above his forehead, and, with the other pointed to the open letter. In this attitude its shape grew momentarily more distinct. It began to kindle into brightness. The pale flame again flowed from its hand, streaming downward to his brain. A look of trouble darkened the sleeping face. Stronger—stronger; brighter—brighter; until, at last, it stood before him, a glorious shape of light, with an awful look of commanding love in its shining features—and the sleeper sprang to his feet with a cry!

The phantom had vanished. He saw nothing. His first impression was, not that he had dreamed, but that, awaking in the familiar room, he had seen the spirit of his dead friend, bright and awful by his side, and that it had gone! In the flash of that quick change, from sleeping to waking, he had detected, he thought, the unearthly being that, he now felt, watched him from behind the air, and it had vanished! The library was the same as in the moment of that supernatural revealing; the open letter lay upon the table still; only *that* was gone which had made these common aspects terrible. Then, all the hard, strong skepticism of his nature, which had been driven backward by the shock of his first conviction, recoiled, and rushed within him, violently struggling for its former vantage ground; till, at length, it achieved the foothold for a doubt. Could he have dreamed? The ghost, invisible, still watched him. Yes—a dream—only a dream; but, how vivid—how strange! With a slow thrill creeping through his veins—the blood curdling at his heart— a cold sweat starting on his forehead, he stared through the dimness of the room.

In a moment, remembering the letter to which the phantom of his dream had pointed, he turned and took it from the table. The last page lay upward, and every word of the solemn counsel at the end seemed to dilate on the paper, and all its mighty meaning rushed upon his soul. Trembling in his own despite, he laid it down and moved away. A physician—he remembered that he was in a state of violent nervous excitement, and thought that when he grew calmer its effects would pass from him. But the hand that had touched him had gone down deeper than the physician, and reached what God had made.

He strove in vain. The very room, in its light and silence, and the lurking sentiment of something watching him, became terrible. He could not endure it. The devils in his heart, grown pusillanimous, cowered beneath the flashing strokes of his aroused and terrible conscience. He could not endure it. He must go out. He will walk the streets. It is not late—it is but ten o'clock. He will go.

The air of his dream still hung heavily about him. He was in the street—he hardly remembered how he had got there, or when; but there he was, wrapped up from the searching cold, thinking, with a quiet horror in his mind, of the darkened room he had left behind, and haunted by the sense that something was groping about there in the darkness, searching for him. The night was still and cold.

The full moon was in the zenith. Its icy splendor lay on the bare streets, and on the walls of the dwellings. The lighted oblong squares of curtained windows, here and there, seemed dim and waxen in the frigid glory. The familiar aspect of the quarter had passed away, leaving behind only a corpse-like neighborhood, whose huge, dead features, staring rigidly through the thin, white shroud of moonlight that covered all, left no breath upon the stainless skies. Through the vast silence of the night he passed along; the very sound of his footfalls was remote to his muffled sense.

Gradually, as he reached the first corner, he had an uneasy feeling that a thing—a formless, unimaginable thing—was dogging him. He had thought of going down to his club-room; but he now shrank from entering, with this thing near him, the lighted rooms where his set were busy with cards and billiards, over their liquors and cigars, and where the heated air was full of their idle faces and careless chatter, lest some one should bawl out that he was pale, and ask him what was the matter, and he should answer, tremblingly, that something was following him, and was near him then! He must get rid of it first; he must walk quickly, and baffle its pursuit by turning sharp corners, and plunging into devious streets and crooked lanes, and so lose it!

It was difficult to reach through memory to the crazy chaos of his mind on that night, and recall the route he took while haunted by this feeling; but he afterwards remembered that, without any other purpose than to baffle his imaginary pursuer, he traversed at a rapid pace a large portion of the moonlit city; always (he knew not why) avoiding the more populous thoroughfares, and choosing unfrequented and tortuous byways, but never ridding himself of that horrible confusion of mind in which the faces of his dead friend and the pale woman were strangely blended, nor of the fancy that he was followed. Once, as he passed the hospital where Feval died, a faint hint seemed to flash and vanish from the clouds of his lunacy, and almost identify the dogging goblin with the figure of his dream; but the conception instantly mixed with a disconnected remembrance that this was Christmas eve, and then slipped from him, and was lost. He did not pause there, but strode on. At last he was haunted with a gathering sense that his journey was coming to an end. And suddenly, thank God! The goblin was gone. He was free. He stood panting, like one just roused from some terrific dream, wiping the reeking perspiration from his forehead. He felt he had wandered a long distance from his house, but had no distinct perception of his whereabouts. He only knew he was in some thinly-peopled street, whose familiar aspect seemed lost to him in the magical disguise the superb moonlight had thrown over all. Suddenly a film seemed to drop from his eyes, as they became riveted on a lighted window, on the opposite side of the way. He started, and a secret terror crept over him, vaguely mixed with the memory of the shock he had felt as he turned the last corner, and his distinct, awful feeling that something invisible had passed him. At the same instant he felt, and thrilled to feel, a touch, as of a light finger, on his cheek. He was in Hanover street. Before him was the house—the oyster-room staring at him through the lighted transparencies of its two windows, like two square eyes, below; and his tenant's light in a chamber above! The added shock which this discovery gave to the heaving of his heart, made him gasp for breath. Could it be? Did he still dream? While he stood panting, and staring at the building, the city clocks began to strike. Eleven o'clock; it was ten when he came away; how he must have driven! His thoughts caught up the word. Driven—by what? Driven from his house in horror, through street and lane, over half the city—driven—hunted in terror, and smitten by a shock here! Driven—driven! He could not rid his mind of the word, nor of the meaning it suggested. The pavements about him began to ring and echo with the tramp of many feet, and the cold, brittle air was shivered with the noisy voices that had roared and bawled applause and laughter at the National Theatre all the evening, and were now singing and howling homeward. Groups of rude men, and ruder boys, their breaths steaming in the icy air, began to tramp by, jostling him as they passed, till he was forced to draw back to the wall, and give them the sidewalk. Dazzled and giddy, in cold fear, and with the returning sense of something near him, he stood and watched the groups that pushed and tumbled in through the entrance of the oyster-room, whistling and chattering as they went, and banging the door behind them. He noticed that some came out presently, banging the door harder, and went, smoking and shouting, down the street. Still they poured in and out, while the street was startled with their riot, and the bar-room within echoed their trampling feet and hoarse voices. Then, as his glance wandered upward to his tenant's window, he thought of the sick child, mixing this hideous discord in the dreams of fever. The word brought up the name and the thought of his dead friend. "In the name of the Saviour, I charge you be true and tender to men!" The memory of these words seemed to ring clearly, as if a voice had spoken them, above the roar that suddenly rose in his mind. In that moment he felt himself a wretched and most guilty man. He felt that his cruel words had entered that humble home, to make desperate poverty more desperate, to sicken sickness, and to sadden sorrow. Before him was the dram-shop, let and licensed to nourish the worst and most brutal appetites and instincts of human natures, at the sacrifice of all their highest and holiest tendencies. The throng of tipplers and drunkards was swarming through its hopeless door, to gulp the fiery liquor whose fumes give all shames, vices, miseries, and crimes, a lawless strength and life, and change the man into the pig or tiger. Murder was done, or nearly done, within those walls last night. Within those walls no good was ever done; but, daily, unmitigated evil, whose results were reaching on to torture unborn generations. He had consented to it all! He could not falter, or equivocate, or evade, or excuse. His dead friend's words rang in his conscience like the trump of the judgment angel.

With this he was conquered, and then the world, sadder than before, but sweeter than before, seemed to come back to him. A great feeling of relief flowed upon his mind. Pale and trembling still, he crossed the street with a quick, unsteady step, entered a yard at the side of the house, and, brushing by a host of white, rattling spectres of frozen clothes, which dangled from lines in the inclosure, mounted some wooden steps, and rang the bell. In a minute he heard footsteps within, and saw the gleam of a lamp. His heart palpitated violently as he heard the lock turning, lest the answerer of his summons might be his tenant. The door opened, and, to his relief, he stood before a rather decent-looking Irishman, bending forward in his stocking feet, with one boot and a lamp in his hand. The man stared at him from a wild head of tumbled red hair, with a half smile round his loose open mouth, and said, "Begorra!" This was a second floor tenant.

Dr. Renton was relieved at the sight of him; but he rather failed in an attempt at his rent-day suavity of manner, when he said:

"Good evening, Mr. Flanagan. Do you think I can see Mrs. Miller to-night?"

"She's up *there*, docther, anyway." Mr. Flanagan made a sudden start for the stairs, with the boot and lamp at arm's length before him, and stopped as suddenly. "Yull go up?—or wud she come down to ye?" There was as much anxious indecision in Mr. Flanagan's general aspect, pending the reply, as if he had to answer the question himself.

"I'll go up, Mr. Flanagan," returned Dr. Renton, stepping in, after a pause, and shutting the door. "But I'm afraid she's in bed."
"Naw—she's not, sur." Mr. Flanagan made another feint with the boot and lamp at the stairs, but stopped again in curious bewilderment, and rubbed his head. Then, with another inspiration, and speaking with such velocity that his words ran into each other, pell-mell, he continued: "Th' small girl's sick, sur. Begorra, I wor just pullin' on th' boots tuh gaw for the docther, in th' nixt streth, an' summons him to her relehf, for it's bad she is. A'id betther be goan." Another start, and a movement to put on the boot instantly, baffled by his getting the lamp into the leg of it, and involving himself in difficulties in trying to get it out again without dropping either, and stopped finally by Dr. Renton.

"You needn't go, Mr. Flanagan. I'll see to the child. Don't go."

He stepped slowly up the stairs, followed by the bewildered Flanagan. All this time Dr. Renton was listening to the racket from the bar-room. Clinking of glasses, rattling of dishes, trampling of feet, oaths and laughter, and a confused din of coarse voices, mingling with boisterous calls for oysters and drink, came, hardly deadened by the partition walls, from the haunt below, and echoed through the corridors. Loud enough within—louder in the street without, where the oysters and drink were reeling and roaring off to brutal dreams. People trying to sleep here; a sick child up stairs. Listen!

"Two stew! One roast! Four ale! Hurry 'em up! Three stew! In number six! One fancy—two roast! One sling! Three brandy—hot Two stew! One whisk' skin! Hurry 'em up! What yeh 'bout! Three brand' punch—hot! Four stew! What-ye-e-h 'BOUT! Two gin-cock

-t'il! One stew! Hu-r-r-y 'em up!" Clashing, rattling, cursing, swearing, laughing, shouting, trampling, stumbling, driving, slamming, of doors. "Hu-r-ry 'em UP."

"Flanagan," said Dr. Renton, stopping at the first landing, "do you have this noise every night?"

"Naise? Hoo! Divil a night, docther, but I'm wehked out ov me bed wid 'em, Sundays an' all. Sure didn't they murdher wan of 'em, out an' out, last night!"

"Is the man dead?"

"Dead? Troth he is. An' cowld."

"H'm"—through his compressed lips. "Flanagan, you needn't come up. I know the door. Just hold the light for me here. There, that'll do. Thank you." He whispered the last words from the top of the second flight.

"Are ye there, docther?" Flanagan anxious to the last, and trying to peer up at him with the lamp-light in his eyes.

"Yes. That'll do. Thank you!" in the same whisper. Before he could tap at the door, then darkening in the receding light, it opened suddenly, and a big Irish woman bounced out, and then whisked in again, calling to some one in an inner room: "Here he is, Mrs. Mill'r," and then bounced out again, with a "Walk royt in, if *you* plaze; here's the choild"—and whisked in again, with a "Sure an' Jehms was quick;" never once looking at him, and utterly unconscious of the presence of her landlord. He had hardly stepped into the room and taken off his hat, when Mrs. Miller came from the inner chamber with a lamp in her hand. How she started! With her pale face grown suddenly paler, and her hand on her bosom, she could only exclaim: "Why, it's Dr. Renton!" and stand, still and dumb, gazing with a frightened look at his face, whiter than her own. Whereupon Mrs. Flanagan came bolting out again, with wild eyes and a sort of stupefied horror in her good, coarse, Irish features; and then, with some uncouth ejaculation, ran back, and was heard to tumble over something within, and tumble something else over in her fall, and gather herself up with a subdued howl, and subside.

"Mrs. Miller," began Dr. Renton, in a low, husky voice, glancing at her frightened face, "I hope you'll be composed. I spoke to you very harshly and rudely to-night; but I really was not myself—I was in anger—and I ask your pardon. Please to overlook it all, and—but I will speak of this presently; now—I am a physician; will you let me look now at your sick child?"

He spoke hurriedly, but with evident sincerity. For a moment her lips faltered; then a slow flush came up, with a quick change of expression on her thin, worn face, and, reddening to painful scarlet, died away in a deeper pallor.

"Dr. Renton," she said, hastily, "I have no ill-feeling for you, sir, and I know you were hurt and vexed—and I know you have tried to make it up to me again, sir—secretly. I know who it was, now; but I can't take it, sir. You must take it back. You know it was you sent it, sir?"

"Mrs. Miller," he replied, puzzled beyond measure, "I don't understand you. What do you mean?"

"Don't deny it, sir. Please not to," she said imploringly, the tears starting to her eyes. "I am very grateful—indeed I am. But I can't accept it. Do take it again."

"Mrs. Miller," he replied, in a hasty voice, "what do you mean? I have sent you nothing—nothing at all. I have, therefore, nothing to receive again."

She looked at him fixedly, evidently impressed by the fervor of his denial.

"You sent me nothing to-night, sir?" she asked, doubtfully.

"Nothing at any time—nothing," he answered, firmly.

It would have been folly to have disbelieved the truthful look of his wondering face, and she turned away in amazement and confusion. There was a long pause.

"I hope, Mrs. Miller, you will not refuse any assistance I can render to your child," he said, at length.

She started, and replied, tremblingly and confusedly, "No, sir; we shall be grateful to you, if you can save her"—and went quickly, with a strange abstraction on her white face, into the inner room. He followed her at once, and, hardly glancing at Mrs. Flanagan, who sat there in stupefaction, with her apron over her head and face, he laid his hat on a table, went to the bedside of the little girl, and felt her head and pulse. He soon satisfied himself that the little sufferer was in no danger, under proper remedies, and now dashed down a prescription on a leaf from his pocket-book. Mrs. Flanagan, who had come out from the retirement of her apron, to stare stupidly at him during the examination, suddenly bobbed up on her legs, with enlightened alacrity, when he asked if there was any one that could go out to the apothecary's, and said, "sure I wull!" He had a little trouble to make her understand that the prescription, which she took by the corner, holding it away from her, as if it were going to explode presently, and staring at it upside down—was to be left—"*left*, mind you, Mrs. Flanagan— with the apothecary—Mr. Flint—at the nearest corner—and he will give you some things, which you are to bring here." But she had shuffled off at last with a confident, "yis, sur—aw, I knoo," her head nodding satisfied assent, and her big thumb covering the line on the margin, "charge to Dr. C. Renton, Bowdoin-street," (which *I* know, could not keep it from the eyes of the angels!) and he sat down to await her return.

"Mrs. Miller," he said, kindly, "don't be alarmed about your child. She is doing well; and, after you have given her the medicine Mrs. Flanagan will bring, you'll find her much better, to-morrow. She must be kept cool and quiet, you know, and she'll be all right soon."

"O, Dr. Renton, I am very grateful," was the tremulous reply; "and we will follow all directions, sir. It is hard to keep her quiet, sir; we keep as still as we can, and the other children are very still; but the street is very noisy all the daytime and evening, sir, and—"

"I know it, Mrs. Miller. And I'm afraid those people down-stairs disturb you somewhat."

"They make some stir in the evening, sir; and it's rather loud in the street sometimes, at night. The folks on the lower floors are troubled a good deal, they say."

Well they may be. Listen to the bawling outside, now, cold as it is. Hark! A hoarse group on the opposite sidewalk beginning a song. "Ro-o-l on, sil-ver mo-o-n"—. The silver moon ceases to roll in a sudden explosion of yells and laughter, sending up broken fragments of curses, ribald jeers, whoopings, and cat-calls, high into the night air. "Ga-l-a-ng! Hi-hi! What ye-e-h *'bout!"*

"This is outrageous, Mrs. Miller. Where's the watchman?"

She smiled faintly. "He takes one of them off occasionally, sir; but he's afraid; they beat him sometimes." A long pause.

"Isn't your room rather cold, Mrs. Miller?" He glanced at the black stove, dimly seen in the outer room. "It is necessary to keep the rooms cool just now, but this air seems to me cold."

Receiving no answer, he looked at her, and saw the sad truth in her averted face.

"I beg your pardon," he said quickly, flushing to the roots of his hair. "I might have known, after what you said to me this evening."

"We had a little fire here to-day, sir," she said, struggling with the pride and shame of poverty; "but we have been out of firing for two or three days, and we owe the wharfman something now. The two boys picked up a few chips; but the poor children find it hard to get them, sir. Times are very hard with us, sir; indeed they are. We'd have got along better, if my husband's money had come, and your rent would have been paid—"

"Never mind the rent!—don't speak of that!" he broke in, with his face all aglow. "Mrs. Miller, I haven't done right by you—I know it. Be frank with me. Are you in want of—have you—need of—food?"

No need of answer to that faintly stammered question. The thin, rigid face was covered from his sight by the worn, wan hands, and all the pride and shame of poverty, and all the frigid truth of cold, hunger, anxiety, and sickened sorrow they had concealed, had given way at last in a rush of tears. He could not speak. With a smitten heart, he knew it all now. Ah! Dr. Renton, you know these people's tricks? you know their lying blazon of poverty, to gather sympathy?

"Mrs. Miller"—she had ceased weeping, and as he spoke, she looked at him, with the tear-stains still on her agitated face, half ashamed that he had seen her—"Mrs. Miller, I am sorry. This shall be remedied. Don't tell me it shan't! Don't! I say it shall! Mrs. Miller, I'm—I'm ashamed of myself. I am, indeed."

"I am very grateful, sir, I'm sure," said she; "but we don't like to take charity though we need help; but we can get along now, sir—for, I suppose I must keep it, as you say you didn't send it, and use it for the children's sake, and thank God for his good mercy—since I don't know, and never shall, where it came from, now."

"Mrs. Miller," he said quickly, "you spoke in this way before; and I don't know what you refer to. What do you mean by—*it?*"

"O, I forgot sir: it puzzles me so. You see, sir, I was sitting here after I got home from your house, thinking what I should do, when Mrs. Flanagan came up-stairs with a letter for me, that she said a strange man left at the door for Mrs. Miller; and Mrs. Flanagan couldn't describe him well, or understandingly; and it had no direction at all, only the man inquired who was the landlord, and if Mrs. Miller had a sick child, and then said the letter was for me; and there was no writing inside the letter, but there was fifty dollars. That's all, sir. It gave me a great shock, sir; and I couldn't think who sent it, only when you came to-night, I thought it was you; but you said it wasn't, and I never shall know who it was, now. It seems as if the hand of God was in it, sir, for it came when everything was darkest, and I was in despair."

"Why, Mrs. Miller," he slowly answered, "this is very mysterious. The man inquired if I was the owner of the house—oh, no—he only inquired who was—but then he knew I was the—O bother! I'm getting nowhere. Let's see. Why, it must be some one you know, or that knows your circumstances."

"But there's no one knows them but yourself; and I told you," she replied; "no one else but the people in the house. It must have been some rich person, for the letter was a gilt-edge sheet, and there was perfume in it, sir."

"Strange," he murmured. "Well, I give it up. All is, I advise you to keep it, and I'm very glad some one did his duty by you in your hour of need, though I'm sorry it was not myself. Here's Mrs. Flanagan."

There was a good deal done, and a great burden lifted off an humble heart—nay, two! before Dr. Renton thought of going home. There was a patient gained, likely to do Dr. Renton more good than any patient he had lost. There was a kettle singing on the stove, and blowing off a happier steam than any engine ever blew on that railroad, whose unmarketable stock had singed Dr. Renton's fingers. There was a yellow gleam flickering from the blazing fire on the sober binding of a good old Book upon a shelf with others, a rarer medical work than ever slipped at auction from Dr. Renton's hands, since it kept the sacred lore of Him who healed the sick, and fed the hungry, and comforted the poor, and who was also the Physician of souls.

And there were other offices performed, of lesser range than these, before he rose to go. There were cooling mixtures blended for the sick child; medicines arranged; directions given; and all the items of her tendance orderly foreseen, and put in pigeon-holes of When and How, for service.

At last he rose to go. "And now, Mrs. Miller," he said, "I'll come here at ten in the morning, and see to our patient. She'll be nicely by that time. And—(listen to those brutes in the street!—twelve o'clock, too—ah! there's the bell),—as I was saying, my offence to you being occasioned by your debt to me, I feel my receipt for your debt should commence my reparation to you; and I'll bring it to-morrow. Mrs. Miller—you don't quite come at me—what I mean is—you owe me, under a notice to quit, three months' rent. Consider that paid in full. I never will take a cent of it from you—not a copper. And I take back the notice. Stay in my house as long as you like; the longer the better. But, up to this date, your rent's paid. There. I hope you'll have as happy a Christmas as circumstances will allow, and I mean you shall."

A flush of astonishment—of indefinable emotion, overspread her face.

"Dr. Renton, stop, sir!" He was moving to the door. "Please, sir, *do* hear me! You are very good—but I can't allow you to—Dr. Renton, we are able to pay you the rent, and we *will*, and we *must*—here—now. O, sir, my gratefulness will never fail to you—but here—here—be fair with me, sir, and *do* take it!"

She had hurried to a chest of drawers, and came back with the letter which she had rustled apart with eager, trembling hands, and now, unfolding the single bank-note it had contained, she thrust it into his fingers as they closed.

"Here, Mrs. Miller"—she had drawn back with her arms locked on her bosom, and he stepped forward—"no, no. This shan't be. Come, come, you must take it back. Good heavens!" he spoke low, but his eyes blazed in the red glow which broke out on his face, and the crisp note in his extended hand shook violently at her—"Sooner than take this money from you, I would perish in the street! What! Do you think I will rob you of the gift sent you by some one who had a human heart for the distresses I was aggravating? Sooner than—here, take it! O, my God! what's this?"

The red glow on his face went out, with this exclamation, in a pallor like marble, and he jerked back the note to his starting eyes; Kilby Bank—Boston—Fifty Dollars. For a minute he gazed at the motionless bill in his hand. Then, with his hueless lips compressed, he seized the blank letter from his astonished tenant, and looked at it, turning it over and over. Grained letter-paper—gilt-edged—with a favorite perfume in it. Where's Mrs. Flanagan? Outside the door, sitting on the top of the stairs, with her apron over her head, crying. Mrs. Flanagan! Here! In she tumbled, her big feet kicking her skirts before her, and her eyes and face as red as a beet.

"Mrs. Flanagan, what kind of a looking man gave you this letter at the door to-night?"

"A-w, Docther Rinton, dawn't ax me!—Bother, an' all, an' sure an' I cudn't see him wud his fur-r hat, an' he a-ll boondled oop wud his co-at oop on his e-ars, an' his big han'kershuf smotherin' thuh mouth uv him, an' sorra a bit uv him tuh be looked at, sehvin' thuh poomple on thuh ind uv his naws."

"The *what* on the end of his nose?"

"Thuh poomple, sur."

"What does she mean, Mrs. Miller?" said the puzzled questioner, turning to his tenant.

"I don't know, sir, indeed," was the reply; "she said that to me, and I couldn't understand her."

"It's thuh poomple, docther. Dawn't ye knoo? Thuh big, flehmin poomple oop there." She indicated the locality, by flattening the rude tip of her own nose with her broad forefinger.

"O-h, the pimple! I have it." So he had. Netty, Netty!

He said nothing, but sat down in a chair, with his bold, white brow knitted, and the warm tears in his dark eyes.

"You know who sent it, sir, don't you?" asked his wondering tenant, catching the meaning of all this.

"Mrs. Miller, I do. But I cannot tell you. Take it, now, and use it. It is doubly yours. There. Thank you."

She had taken it with an emotion in her face that gave a quicker motion to his throbbing heart. He rose to his feet, hat in hand, and turned away. The noise of a passing group of roysterers in the street without, came strangely loud into the silence of that room.

"Good night, Mrs. Miller. I'll be here in the morning. Good night."

"Good night, sir. God bless you, sir!"

He turned around quickly. The warm tears in his dark eyes had flowed on his face, which was pale; and his firm lip quivered.

"I hope He will, Mrs. Miller—I hope He will. It should have been said oftener."

He was on the outer threshold. Mrs. Flanagan had, somehow, got there before him, with a lamp, and he followed her down through the dancing shadows, with blurred eyes. On the lower landing he stopped to hear the jar of some noisy wrangle, thick with oaths, from the bar-room. He listened for a moment, and then turned to the staring stupor of Mrs. Flanagan's rugged visage.

"Sure, they're at ut, docther, wud a wull," she said, smiling.

"Yes. Mrs. Flanagan, you'll stay up with Mrs. Miller to-night, won't you?"

"Dade an' I wull, sur."

"That's right. Do. And make her try and sleep, for she must be tired. Keep up a fire—not too warm, you understand. There'll be wood and coal coming to-morrow, and she'll pay you back."

"A-w, docther, dawn't noo!"

"Well, well. And—look here; have you got anything to eat in the house? Yes; well; take it up-stairs. Wake up those two boys, and give them something to eat. Don't let Mrs. Miller stop you. Make her eat something. Tell her I said she must. And, first of all, get your bonnet, and go to that apothecary's—Flint's—for a bottle of port wine, for Mrs. Miller. Hold on. There's the order." (He had a leaf out of his pocket-book in a minute, and wrote it down.) "Go with this, the first thing. Ring Flint's bell, and he'll wake up. And here's something for your own Christmas dinner, to-morrow." Out of the roll of bills, he drew one of the tens—Kilby Bank—Boston—and gave it to Mrs. Flanagan.

"A-w, dawn't noo, docther."

"Bother! It's for yourself, mind. Take it. There. And now unlock the door. That's it. Good night, Mrs. Flanagan."

"An' meh thuh Hawly Vurgin hape blessn's on ye, Docther Rinton, wud a-ll thuh compliments uv thuh sehzin, for yur thuh—"

He lost the end of Mrs. Flanagan's parting benedictions in the moonlit street. He did not pause till he was at the door of the oyster-room. He paused then, to make way for a tipsy company of four, who reeled out—the gaslight from the bar-room on the edges of their sodden, distorted faces—giving three shouts and a yell, as they slammed the door behind them.

He pushed after a party that was just entering. They went at once for drink to the upper end of the room, where a rowdy crew, with cigars in their mouths, and liquor in their hands, stood before the bar, in a knotty wrangle concerning some one who was killed. Where is the keeper? Om there he is, mixing hot brandy punch for two. Here, you, sir, go up quietly, and tell Mr. Rollins Dr. Renton wants to see him. The waiter came back presently to say Mr. Rollins would be right along. Twenty-five minutes past twelve. Oyster trade nearly over. Gaudy-curtained booths on the left all empty but two. Oyster-openers and waiters—three of them in all—nearly done for the night, and two of them sparring and scuffling behind a pile of oysters on the trough, with the colored print of the great prize fight between Tom Hyer and Yankee Sullivan, in a veneered frame above them on the wall. Blower up from the fire opposite the bar, and stewpans and griddles empty and idle on the bench beside it, among the unwashed bowls and dishes. Oyster trade nearly over. Bar still busy.

Here comes Rollins in his shirt sleeves, with an apron on. Thick-set, muscular man—frizzled head, low forehead, sharp, black eyes, flabby face, with a false, greasy smile on it now, oiling over a curious, stealthy expression of mingled surprise and inquiry, as he sees his landlord here at this unusual hour.

"Come in here, Mr. Rollins; I want to speak to you."

"Yes, sir. Jim" (to the waiter), "go and tend bar." They sat down in one of the booths, and lowered the curtain. Dr. Renton, at one side of the table within, looking at Rollins, sitting leaning on his folded arms, at the other side.

"Mr. Rollins, I am told the man who was stabbed here last night is dead. Is that so?"

"Well, he is, Dr. Renton. Died this afternoon."

"Mr. Rollins, this is a serious matter; what are you going to do about it?"

"Can't help it, sir. Who's a-goin' to touch *me*? Called in a watchman. Whole mess of 'em had cut. Who knows 'em? Nobody knows 'em. Man that was stuck never see the fellers as stuck him in all his life till then. Didn't know which one of 'em did it. Didn't know nothing. Don't now, an' never will, 'nless he meets 'em in hell. That's all. Feller's dead, an' who's a-goin' to touch *me*? Can't do it. Ca-n-'t do it."

"Mr. Rollins," said Dr. Renton, thoroughly disgusted with this man's brutal indifference, "your lease expires in three days."

"Well, it does. Hope to make a renewal with you, Dr. Renton. Trade's good here. Shouldn't mind more rent on, if you insist—hope you won't—if it's anything in reason. Promise sollum, I shan't have no more fightin' in here. Couldn't help this. Accidents *will* happen, yo' know."

"Mr. Rollins, the case is this: if you didn't sell liquor here, you'd have no murder done in your place—murder, sir. That man was murdered. It's your fault, and it's mine, too. I ought not to have let you the place for your business. It *is* a cursed traffic, and you and I ought to have found it out long ago. *I* have. I hope *you* will. Now, I advise you, as a friend, to give up selling rum for the future: you see what it comes to—don't you? At any rate, I will not be responsible for the outrages that are perpetrated in my building any more—I will not have liquor sold here. I refuse to renew your lease. In three days you must move."

"Dr Renton, you hurt my feelin's. Now, how would you—"

"Mr. Rollins, I have spoken to you as a friend, and you have no cause for pain. You must quit these premises when your lease expires. I'm sorry I can't make you go before that. Make no appeals to me, if you please. I am fixed. Now, sir, good-night."

The curtain was pulled up, and Rollins rolled over to his beloved bar, soothing his lacerated feelings by swearing like a pirate, while Dr. Renton strode to the door, and went into the street, homeward.

He walked fast through the magical moonlight, with a strange feeling of sternness, and tenderness, and weariness, in his mind. In this mood, the sensation of spiritual and physical fatigue gaming on him, but a quiet moonlight in all his reveries, he reached his house. He was just putting his latch-key in the door, when it was opened by James, who stared at him for a second, and then dropped his eyes, and put his hand before his nose. Dr. Renton compressed his lips on an involuntary smile.

"Ah! James, you're up late. It's near one."

"I sat up for Mrs. Renton and the young lady, sir. They're just come, and gone up stairs."

"All right, James. Take your lamp and come in here. I've got something to say to you." The man followed him into the library at once, with some wonder on his sleepy face.

"First, put some coal on that fire, and light the chandelier. I shall not go up stairs to-night." The man obeyed. "Now, James, sit down in that chair." He did so, beginning to look frightened at Dr. Renton's grave manner.

"James"—a long pause—"I want you to tell me the truth. Where did you go to-night? Come, I have found you out. Speak."

The man turned as white as a sheet, and looked wretched with the whites of his bulging eyes, and the great pimple on his nose awfully distinct in the livid hue of his features. He was a rather slavish fellow, and thought he was going to lose his situation. Please not to blame him, for he, too, was one of the poor.

"O, Dr. Renton, excuse me, sir; I didn't mean doing any harm."

"James, my daughter gave you an undirected letter this evening; you carried it to one of my houses in Hanover street. Is that true?"

"Ye-yes, sir. I couldn't help it. I only did what she told me, sir."

"James, if my daughter told you to set fire to this house, what would you do?"

"I wouldn't do it, sir," he stammered, after some hesitation.

"You wouldn't? James, if my daughter ever tells you to set fire to this house, do it, sir! Do it. At once. Do whatever she tells you. Promptly. And I'll back you."

The man stared wildly at him, as he received this astonishing command. Dr. Renton was perfectly grave, and had spoken slowly and seriously. The man was at his wits' end.

"You'll do it James—will you?"

"Ye-yes, sir, certainly."

"That's right. James, you're a good fellow. James, you've got a family—a wife and children—hav'n't you?"

"Yes, sir, I have; living in the country, sir. In Chelsea, over the ferry. For cheapness, sir."

"For cheapness, eh? Hard times, James? How is it?"

"Pretty hard, sir. Close, but toler'ble comfortable. Rub and go, sir."

"Rub and go. Ve-r-y well. Rub and go. James, I'm going to raise your wages—to-morrow. Generally, because you're a good servant. Principally, because you carried that letter to-night, when my daughter asked you. I shan't forget it. To-morrow, mind. And if I can do anything for you, James, at any time, just tell me. That's all. Now, you'd better go to bed. And a happy Christmas to you!"

"Much obliged to you, sir. Same to you and many of 'em. Good-night, sir." And with Dr. Renton's "good-night" he stole up to bed, thoroughly happy, and determined to obey Miss Renton's future instructions to the letter. The shower of golden light which had been raining for the last two hours, had fallen, even on him. It would fall all day to-morrow in many places, and the day after, and for long years to come. Would that it could broaden and increase to a general deluge, and submerge the world!

Now the whole house was still, and its master was weary. He sat there, quietly musing, feeling the sweet and tranquil presence near him. Now the fire was screened, the lights were out, save one dim glimmer, and he had lain down on the couch with the letter in his hand, and slept the dreamless sleep of a child.

He slept until the gray dawn of Christmas day stole into the room, and showed him the figure of his friend, a shape of glorious light, standing by his side, and gazing at him with large and tender eyes! He had no fear. All was deep, serene, and happy with the happiness of heaven. Looking up into that beautiful, wan face—so tranquil—so radiant; watching, with a child-like awe, the star-fire in those shadowy eyes; smiling faintly, with a great, unutterable love thrilling slowly through his frame, in answer to the smile of light that shone upon the phantom countenance; so he passed a space of time which seemed a calm eternity, till, at last, the communion of spirit with spirit—of ancient love with love immortal—was perfected, and the shining hands were laid on his forehead, as with a touch of air. Then the phantom smiled, and, as its shining hands were withdrawn, the thought of his daughter mingled in the vision. She was bending over him! The dawn—the room, were the same. But the ghost of Feval had gone out from earth, away to its own land!

"Father, dear father! Your eyes were open, and they did not look at me. There is a light on your face, and your features are changed! What is it—what have you seen?"

"Hush, darling: here—kneel by me, for a little while, and be still. I have seen the dead."

She knelt by him, burying her awe-struck face in his bosom, and clung to him with all the fervor of her soul. He clasped her to his breast, and for minutes all was still.

"My dear—my good child!"

The voice was tremulous and low. She lifted her fair, bright countenance, now convulsed with a secret trouble, and dimmed with streaming tears, to his, and gazed on him. His eyes were shining; but his pallid cheeks, like hers, were wet with tears. How still the room was! How like a thought of solemn tenderness, the pale gray dawn! The world was far away, and his soul still wandered in the peaceful awe of his dream. The world was coming back to him—but oh! how changed!—in the trouble of his daughter's face.

"Darling, what is it? Why are you here? Why are you weeping? Dear child, the friend of my better days—of the boyhood when I had noble aims, and life was beautiful before me—he has been here! I have seen him. He has been with me—oh! for a good I cannot tell!"

"Father, dear father!"—he had risen, and sat upon the couch, but she still knelt before him, weeping, and clasped his hands in hers—"I thought of you and of this letter, all the time. All last night till I slept, and then I dreamed you were tearing it to pieces, and trampling on it. I awoke, and lay thinking of you, and of ——. And I thought I heard you come down-stairs, and I came here to find you. But you were lying here so quietly, with your eyes open, and so strange a light on your face. And I knew—I knew you were dreaming of him, and that you saw him, for the letter lay beside you. O father! forgive me, but do hear me! In the name of this day—it's Christmas day, father—in the name of the time when we must both die—in the name of that time, father, hear me! That poor woman last night—O father! forgive me, but don't tear that letter in pieces and trample it under foot! You know what I mean—you know—you know. Don't tear it, and tread it under foot!"

She clung to him, sobbing violently, her face buried in his hands.

"Hush, hush! It's all well—it's all well. Here, sit by me. So. I have"—his voice failed him, and he paused. But sitting by him—

clinging to him—her face hidden in his bosom—she heard the strong beating of his disenchanted heart!

"My child, I know your meaning. I will not tear the letter to pieces and trample it under foot. God forgive me my life's slight to those words. But I learned their value last night, in the house where your blank letter had entered before me."

She started, and looked into his face steadfastly, while a bright scarlet shot into her own.

"I know all, Netty—all. Your secret was well kept, but it is yours and mine now. It was well done, darling—well done. O, I have been through strange mysteries of thought and life since that starving woman sat here! Well—thank God!"

"Father, what have you done?" The flush had failed, but a glad color still brightened her face, while the tears stood trembling in her eyes.

"Netty," he answered, "I have done what you wished yesterday. Mrs. Miller is to stay—forever, if she likes. The liquor-seller is to go, and he will have no successor."

"O, father!"—She stopped. The bright scarlet shot again into her face, but with an April shower of tears, and the rainbow of a smile.

"Listen to me, Netty, and I will tell you, and only you, what I have done." Then, while she mutely listened, sitting by his side, and the dawn of Christmas broadened into Christmas-day, he told her all.

And when he had told all, he read to his daughter the lesson of the day and of his life, the words of George Feval's letter:— *"Farewell—farewell! But, oh! take my counsel into memory on Christmas Day, and forever. Once again, the ancient prophecy of peace and good-will shines on a world of wars and wrongs and woes. Its soft ray shines into the darkness of a land wherein swarm slaves, poor laborers, social pariahs, weeping women, homeless exiles, hunted fugitives, despised aliens, drunkards, convicts, wicked children, and Magdalens unredeemed. These are but the ghastliest figures in that sad army of humanity which advances, by a dreadful road, to the Golden Age of the poets' dream. These are your sisters and your brothers. Love them all. Beware of wronging one of them by word or deed. O friend! strong in wealth for so much good—take my last counsel. In the name of the Saviour, I charge you, be true and tender to all men! Come out from Babylon into manhood, and live and labor for the fallen, the neglected, the suffering, and the poor. Lover of arts, customs, laws, institutions, and forms of society, love these things only as they help mankind! With stern love, overturn them, or help to overturn them, when they become cruel to a single—the humblest—human being. In the world's scale, social position, influence, public power, the applause of majorities, heaps of funded gold, services rendered to creeds, codes, sects, parties, or federations—they weigh weight; but in God's scale— remember!—on the day of hope, remember!—your least service to Humanity, outweighs them all!"*

A STRANGE CHRISTMAS GAME
by
Charlotte Riddell
1867

When, through the death of a distant relative, I, John Lester, succeeded to the Martingdale Estate, there could not have been found in the length and breadth of England a happier pair than myself and my only sister Clare.

We were not such utter hypocrites as to affect sorrow for the loss of our kinsman, Paul Lester, a man whom we had never seen, of whom we had heard but little, and that little unfavourable, at whose hands we had never received a single benefit—who was, in short, as great a stranger to us as the then Prime Minister, the Emperor of Russia, or any other human being utterly removed from our extremely humble sphere of life.

His loss was very certainly our gain. His death represented to us, not a dreary parting from one long loved and highly honoured, but the accession of lands, houses, consideration, wealth, to myself—John Lester, artist and second-floor lodger at 32, Great Smith Street, Bloomsbury.

Not that Martingdale was much of an estate as country properties go. The Lesters who had succeeded to that domain from time to time during the course of a few hundred years, could by no stretch of courtesy have been called prudent men. In regard of their posterity they were, indeed, scarcely honest, for they parted with manors and farms, with common rights and advowsons, in a manner at once so baronial and so unbusiness-like, that Martingdale at length in the hands of Jeremy Lester, the last resident owner, melted to a mere little dot in the map of Bedfordshire.

Concerning this Jeremy Lester there was a mystery. No man could say what had become of him. He was in the oak parlour at Martingdale one Christmas Eve, and before the next morning he had disappeared—to reappear in the flesh no more.

Over night, one Mr. Wharley, a great friend and boon companion of Jeremy's, had sat playing cards with him until after twelve o'clock chimes, then he took leave of his host and rode home under the moonlight. After that no person, as far as could be ascertained, ever saw Jeremy Lester alive.

His ways of life had not been either the most regular, or the most respectable, and it was not until a new year had come in without any tidings of his whereabouts reaching the house, that his servants became seriously alarmed concerning his absence.

Then enquiries were set on foot concerning him—enquiries which grew more urgent as weeks and months passed by without the slightest clue being obtained as to his whereabouts. Rewards were offered, advertisements inserted, but still Jeremy made no sign; and so in course of time the heir-at-law, Paul Lester, took possession of the house, and went down to spend the summer months at Martingdale with his rich wife, and her four children by a first husband. Paul Lester was a barrister—an over-worked barrister, who everyone supposed would be glad enough to leave the bar and settle at Martingdale, where his wife's money and the fortune he had accumulated could not have failed to give him a good standing even among the neighbouring country families; and perhaps it was with such intention that he went down into Bedfordshire.

If this were so, however, he speedily changed his mind, for with the January snows he returned to London, let off the land surrounding the house, shut up the Hall, put in a caretaker, and never troubled himself further about his ancestral seat.

Time went on, and people began to say the house was haunted, that Paul Lester had "seen something", and so forth—all which stories were duly repeated for our benefit when, forty-one years after the disappearance of Jeremy Lester, Clare and I went down to inspect our inheritance.

I say "our", because Clare had stuck bravely to me in poverty—grinding poverty, and prosperity was not going to part us now. What was mine was hers, and that she knew, God bless her, without my needing to tell her so.

The transition from rigid economy to comparative wealth was in our case the more delightful also, because we had not in the least degree anticipated it. We never expected Paul Lester's shoes to come to us, and accordingly it was not upon our consciences that we had ever in our dreariest moods wished him dead.

Had he made a will, no doubt we never should have gone to Martingdale, and I, consequently, never written this story; but, luckily for us, he died intestate, and the Bedfordshire property came to me.

As for the fortune, he had spent it in travelling, and in giving great entertainments at his grand house in Portman Square. Concerning his effects, Mrs. Lester and I came to a very amicable arrangement, and she did me the honour of inviting me to call upon her occasionally, and, as I heard, spoke of me as a very worthy and presentable young man "for my station", which, of course, coming from so good an authority, was gratifying. Moreover, she asked me if I intended residing at Martingdale, and on my replying in the affirmative, hoped I should like it.

It struck me at the time that there was a certain significance in her tone, and when I went down to Martingdale and heard the absurd stories which were afloat concerning the house being haunted, I felt confident that if Mrs. Lester had hoped much, she had feared more.

People said Mr. Jeremy "walked" at Martingdale. He had been seen, it was averred, by poachers, by gamekeepers, by children who had come to use the park as a near cut to school, by lovers who kept their tryst under the elms and beeches.

As for the caretaker and his wife, the third in residence since Jeremy Lester's disappearance, the man gravely shook his head when questioned, while the woman stated that wild horses, or even wealth untold, should not draw her into the red bedroom, nor into the oak parlour, after dark.

"I have heard my mother tell, sir—it was her as followed old Mrs. Reynolds, the first caretaker—how there were things went on in these self same rooms as might make any Christian's hair stand on end. Such stamping, and swearing, and knocking about on furniture; and then tramp, tramp, up the great staircase; and along the corridor and so into the red bedroom, and then bang, and tramp, tramp again. They do say, sir, Mr. Paul Lester met him once, and from that time the oak parlour has never been opened. I never was inside it myself."

Upon hearing which fact, the first thing I did was to proceed to the oak parlour, open the shutters, and let the August sun stream in upon the haunted chamber. It was an old-fashioned, plainly furnished apartment, with a large table in the centre, a smaller in a recess by the fire-place, chairs ranged against the walls, and a dusty moth-eaten carpet upon the floor. There were dogs on the hearth, broken and rusty; there was a brass fender, tarnished and battered; a picture of some sea-fight over the mantel-piece, while another work of art about equal in merit hung between the windows. Altogether, an utterly prosaic and yet not uncheerful apartment, from out of which the ghosts flitted as soon as daylight was let into it, and which I proposed, as soon as I "felt my feet", to redecorate, refurnish, and convert into a pleasant morning-room. I was still under thirty, but I had learned prudence in that very good school, Necessity; and it was not my intention to spend much money until I had ascertained for certain what were the actual revenues derivable from the lands still belonging to the Martingdale estates, and the charges upon them. In fact, I wanted to know what I was worth before committing myself to any great extravagances, and the place had for so long been neglected, that I experienced some difficulty in arriving at the state of my real income.

But in the meanwhile, Clare and I found great enjoyment in exploring every nook and corner of our domain, in turning over the contents of old chests and cupboards, in examining the faces of our ancestors looking down on us from the walls, in walking through the neglected gardens, full of weeds, overgrown with shrubs and birdweed, where the boxwood was eighteen feet high, and the shoots of the rosetrees yards long. I have put the place in order since then; there is no grass on the paths, there are no trailing brambles over the ground, the hedges have been cut and trimmed, and the trees pruned and the boxwood clipped. But I often say nowadays that in spite of all my improvements, or rather, in consequence of them, Martingdale does not look one half so pretty as it did in its pristine state of uncivilised picturesqueness.

Although I determined not to commence repairing and decorating the house till better informed concerning the rental of Martingdale, still the state of my finances was so far satisfactory that Clare and I decided on going abroad to take our long-talked-of holiday before the fine weather was past. We could not tell what a year might bring forth, as Clare sagely remarked; it was wise to take our pleasure while we could; and accordingly, before the end of August arrived we were wandering about the continent, loitering at Rouen, visiting the galleries at Paris, and talking of extending our one month of enjoyment into three. What decided me on this course was the circumstance of our becoming acquainted with an

English family who intended wintering in Rome. We met accidentally, but discovering that we were near neighbours in England—in fact that Mr. Cronson's property lay close beside Martingdale—the slight acquaintance soon ripened into intimacy, and ere long we were travelling in company.

From the first, Clare did not much like this arrangement. There was "a little girl" in England she wanted me to marry, and Mr. Cronson had a daughter who certainly was both handsome and attractive. The little girl had not despised John Lester, artist, while Miss Cronson indisputably set her cap at John Lester of Martingdale, and would have turned away her pretty face from a poor man's admiring glance—all this I can see plainly enough now, but I was blind then and should have proposed for Maybel— that was her name—before the winter was over, had news not suddenly arrived of the illness of Mrs. Cronson, senior. In a moment the programme was changed; our pleasant days of foreign travel were at an end. The Cronsons packed up and departed, while Clare and I returned more slowly to England, a little out of humour, it must be confessed, with each other.

It was the middle of November when we arrived at Martingdale, and found the place anything but romantic or pleasant. The walks were wet and sodden, the trees were leafless, there were no flowers save a few late pink roses blooming in the garden. It had been a wet season, and the place looked miserable. Clare would not ask Alice down to keep her company in the winter months, as she had intended; and for myself, the Cronsons were still absent in Norfolk, where they meant to spend Christmas with old Mrs. Cronson, now recovered.

Altogether, Martingdale seemed dreary enough, and the ghost stories we had laughed at while sunshine flooded the room, became less unreal, when we had nothing but blazing fires and wax candles to dispel the gloom. They became more real also when servant after servant left us to seek situations elsewhere; when "noises" grew frequent in the house; when we ourselves, Clare and I, with our own ears heard the tramp, tramp, the banging and the chattering which had been described to us.

My dear reader, you doubtless are free from superstitious fancies. You pooh-pooh the existence of ghosts, and "only wish you could find a haunted house in which to spend a night," which is all very brave and praiseworthy, but wait till you are left in a dreary, desolate old country mansion, filled with the most unaccountable sounds, without a servant, with none save an old care-taker and his wife, who, living at the extremest end of the building, heard nothing of the tramp, tramp, bang, bang, going on at all hours of the night.

At first I imagined the noises were produced by some evil-disposed persons, who wished, for purposes of their own, to keep the house uninhabited; but by degrees Clare and I came to the conclusion the visitation must be supernatural, and Martingdale by consequence untenantable.

Still being practical people, and unlike our predecessors, not having money to live where and how we liked, we decided to watch and see whether we could trace any human influence in the matter. If not, it was agreed we were to pull down the right wing of the house and the principal staircase.

For nights and nights we sat up till two or three o'clock in the morning, Clare engaged in needlework, I reading, with a revolver lying on the table beside me; but nothing, neither sound nor appearance rewarded our vigil. This confirmed my first ideas that the sounds were not supernatural; but just to test the matter, I determined on Christmas-eve, the anniversary of Mr. Jeremy Lester's disappearance, to keep watch myself in the red bed-chamber. Even to Clare I never mentioned my intention.

About ten, tired out with our previous vigils, we each retired to rest. Somewhat ostentatiously, perhaps, I noisily shut the door of my room, and when I opened it half an hour afterwards, no mouse could have pursued its way along the corridor with greater silence and caution than myself. Quite in the dark I sat in the red room. For over an hour I might as well have been in my grave for anything I could see in the apartment; but at the end of that time the moon rose and cast strange lights across the floor and upon the wall of the haunted chamber.

Hitherto I had kept my watch opposite the window; now I changed my place to a corner near the door, where I was shaded from observation by the heavy hangings of the bed, and an antique wardrobe.

Still I sat on, but still no sound broke the silence. I was weary with many nights' watching; and tired of my solitary vigil, I dropped at last into a slumber from which I wakened by hearing the door softly opened.

"John," said my sister, almost in a whisper; "John, are you here?"

"Yes, Clare," I answered; "but what are you doing up at this hour?"

"Come downstairs," she replied; "they are in the oak parlor."

I did not need any explanation as to whom she meant, but crept downstairs after her, warned by an uplifted hand of the necessity for silence and caution.

By the door—by the open door of the oak parlor, she paused, and we both looked in.

There was the room we left in darkness overnight, with a bright wood fire blazing on the hearth, candles on the chimney-piece, the small table pulled out from its accustomed corner, and two men seated beside it, playing at cribbage.

We could see the face of the younger player; it was that of a man about five-and-twenty, of a man who had lived hard and wickedly; who had wasted his substance and his health; who had been while in the flesh Jeremy Lester. It would be difficult for me to say how I knew this, how in a moment I identified the features of the player with those of the man who had been missing for forty-one years—forty-one years that very night. He was dressed in the costume of a bygone period; his hair was powdered, and round his wrists there were ruffles of lace.

He looked like one who, having come from some great party, had sat down after his return home to play cards with an intimate friend. On his little finger there sparkled a ring, in the front of his shirt there gleamed a valuable diamond. There were diamond buckles in his shoes, and, according to the fashion of his time, he wore knee breeches and silk stockings, which showed off advantageously the shape of a remarkably good leg and ankle.

He sat opposite the door, but never once lifted his eyes to it. His attention seemed concentrated on the cards.

For a time there was utter silence in the room, broken only by the momentous counting of the game. In the doorway we stood, holding our breath, terrified and yet fascinated by the scene which was being acted before us.

The ashes dropped on the hearth softly and like the snow; we could hear the rustle of the cards as they were dealt out and fell upon the table; we listened to the count—fifteen-one, fifteen-two, and so forth—but there was no other word spoken till at length the player whose face we could not see, exclaimed, "I win; the game is mine."

Then his opponent took up the cards, sorted them over negligently in his hand, put them close together, and flung the whole pack in his guest's face, exclaiming, "Cheat; liar; take that!"

There was a bustle and confusion—a flinging over of chairs, and fierce gesticulation, and such a noise of passionate voices mingling, that we could not hear a sentence which was uttered. All at once, however, Jeremy Lester strode out of the room in so great a hurry that he almost touched us where we stood; out of the room, and tramp, tramp up the staircase to the red room, whence he descended in a few minutes with a couple of rapiers under his arm.

When he re-entered the room he gave, as it seemed to us, the other man his choice of the weapons, and then he flung open the window, and after ceremoniously giving place for his opponent to pass out first, he walked forth into the night air, Clare and I following.

We went through the garden and down a narrow winding walk to a smooth piece of turf, sheltered from the north by a plantation of young fir trees. It was a bright moonlight night by this time, and we could distinctly see Jeremy Lester measuring off the ground.

"When you say 'three,'" he said at last to the man whose back was still towards us. They had drawn lots for the ground, and the lot had fallen against Mr. Lester. He stood thus with the moonbeams falling upon him, and a handsomer fellow I would never desire to behold.

"One," began the other; "two," and before our kinsman had the slightest suspicion of his design, he was upon him, and his rapier through Jeremy Lester's breast.

At the sight of that cowardly treachery, Clare screamed aloud. In a moment the combatants had disappeared, the moon was obscured behind a cloud, and we were standing in the shadow of the fir-plantation, shivering with cold and terror. But we knew at last what had become of the late owner of Martingdale, that he had fallen, not in fair fight, but foully murdered by a false friend.

When late on Christmas morning I awoke, it was to see a white world, to behold the ground, and trees, and shrubs all laden and covered with snow. There was snow everywhere, such snow as no person could remember having fallen for forty-one years.

"It was on just such a Christmas as this that Mr. Jeremy disappeared," remarked the old sexton to my sister, who had insisted on dragging me through the snow to church, whereupon Clare fainted away and was carried into the vestry, where I made a full confession to the Vicar of all we had beheld the previous night.

At first that worthy individual rather inclined to treat the matter lightly, but when a fortnight after, the snow melted away and the fir-plantation came to be examined, he confessed there might be more things in heaven and earth than his limited philosophy had dreamed of.

In a little clear space just within the plantation, Jeremy Lester's body was found. We knew it by the ring and the diamond buckles, and the sparkling breastpin; and Mr. Cronson, who in his capacity as magistrate came over to inspect these relics, was visibly perturbed at my narrative.

"Pray, Mr. Lester, did you in your dream see the face of—of the gentleman—your kinsman's opponent?"

"No," I answered, "he sat and stood with his back to us all the time."

"There is nothing more, of course, to be done in the matter," observed Mr. Cronson.

"Nothing," I replied; and there the affair would doubtless have terminated, but that a few days afterwards, when we were dining at Cronson Park, Clare all of a sudden dropped the glass of water she was carrying to her lips, and exclaiming, "Look, John, there he is!" rose from her seat, and with a face as white as the table cloth, pointed to a portrait hanging on the wall. "I saw him for an instant when he turned his head towards the door as Jeremy Lester left it," she explained; "that is he."

Of what followed after this identification I have only the vaguest recollection. Servants rushed hither and thither; Mrs. Cronson dropped off her chair into hysterics; the young ladies gathered round their mamma; Mr. Cronson, trembling like one in an ague fit, attempted some kind of an explanation, while Clare kept praying to be taken away—only to be taken away.

I took her away, not merely from Cronson Park but from Martingdale. Before we left the latter place, however, I had an interview with Mr. Cronson, who said the portrait Clare had identified was that of his wife's father, the last person who saw Jeremy Lester alive.

"He is an old man now," finished Mr. Cronson, "a man of over eighty, who has confessed everything to me. You won't bring further sorrow and disgrace upon us by making this matter public?"

I promised him I would keep silence, but the story gradually oozed out, and the Cronsons left the country.

My sister never returned to Martingdale; she married and is living in London. Though I assure her there are no strange noises in my house, she will not visit Bedfordshire, where the "little girl" she wanted me so long ago to "think of seriously," is now my wife and the mother of my children.

THE GHOST'S SUMMONS
by
Ada Buisson
1868

"Wanted, sir—a patient."

It was in the early days of my professional career, when patients were scarce and fees scarcer; and though I was in the act of sitting down to my chop, and had promised myself a glass of steaming punch afterwards, in honour of the Christmas season, I hurried instantly into my surgery.

I entered briskly; but no sooner did I catch sight of the figure standing leaning against the counter than I started back with a strange feeling of horror which for the life of me I could not comprehend.

Never shall I forget the ghastliness of that face—the white horror stamped upon every feature—the agony which seemed to sink the very eyes beneath the contracted brows; it was awful to me to behold, accustomed as I was to scenes of terror.

"You seek advice," I began, with some hesitation.

"No; I am not ill."

"You require then—"

"Hush!" he interrupted, approaching more nearly, and dropping his already low murmur to a mere whisper. "I believe you are not rich. Would you be willing to earn a thousand pounds?"

A thousand pounds! His words seemed to burn my very ears.

"I should be thankful, if I could do so honestly," I replied with dignity. "What is the service required of me?"

A peculiar look of intense horror passed over the white face before me; but the blue-black lips answered firmly, "To attend a death-bed."

"A thousand pounds to attend a death-bed! Where am I to go, then?—whose is it?"

"*Mine.*"

The voice in which this was said sounded so hollow and distant, that involuntarily I shrank back. "Yours! What nonsense! You are not a dying man. You are pale, but you appear perfectly healthy. You—"

"Hush!" he interrupted; "I know all this. You cannot be more convinced of my physical health than I am myself; yet I know that before the clock tolls the first hour after midnight I shall be a dead man."

"But—"

He shuddered slightly; but stretching out his hand commandingly, motioned me to be silent. "I am but too well informed of what I affirm," he said quietly; "I have received a mysterious summons from the dead. No mortal aid can avail me. I am as doomed as the wretch on whom the judge has passed sentence. I do not come either to seek your advice or to argue the matter with you, but simply to buy your services. I offer you a thousand pounds to pass the night in my chamber, and witness the scene which takes place. The sum may appear to you extravagant. But I have no further need to count the cost of any gratification; and the spectacle you will have to witness is no common sight of horror."

The words, strange as they were, were spoken calmly enough; but as the last sentence dropped slowly from the livid lips, an expression of such wild horror again passed over the stranger's face, that, in spite of the immense fee, I hesitated to answer.

"You fear to trust to the promise of a dead man! See here, and be convinced," he exclaimed eagerly; and the next instant, on the counter between us lay a parchment document; and following the indication of that white muscular hand, I read the words, "And to Mr. Frederick Read

, of 14 High-street, Alton, I bequeath the sum of one thousand pounds for certain services rendered to me."

"I have had that will drawn up within the last twenty-four hours, and I signed it an hour ago, in the presence of competent witnesses. I am prepared, you see. Now, do you accept my offer, or not?"

My answer was to walk across the room and take down my hat, and then lock the door of the surgery communicating with the house.

It was a dark, icy-cold night, and somehow the courage and determination which the sight of my own name in connection with a thousand pounds had given me, flagged considerably as I found myself hurried along through the silent darkness by a man whose death-bed I was about to attend.

He was grimly silent; but as his hand touched mine, in spite of the frost, it felt like a burning coal.

On we went—tramp, tramp, through the snow—on, on, till even I grew weary, and at length on my appalled ear struck the chimes of a church-clock; whilst close at hand I distinguished the snowy hillocks of a churchyard.

Heavens! was this awful scene of which I was to be the witness to take place veritably amongst the dead?

"Eleven," groaned the doomed man. "Gracious God! but two hours more, and that ghostly messenger will bring the summons. Come, come; for mercy's sake, let us hasten."

There was but a short road separating us now from a wall which surrounded a large mansion, and along this we hastened until we reached a small door.

Passing through this, in a few minutes we were stealthily ascending the private staircase to a splendidly-furnished apartment, which left no doubt of the wealth of its owner.

All was intensely silent, however, through the house; and about this room in particular there was a stillness that, as I gazed around, struck me as almost ghastly.

My companion glanced at the clock on the mantelshelf, and sank into a large chair by the side of the fire with a shudder. "Only an hour and a half longer," he muttered. "Great heaven! I thought I had more fortitude. This horror unmans me." Then, in a fiercer tone, and clutching my arm, he added, "Ha! you mock me, you think me mad; but wait till you see—wait till you see!"

I put my hand on his wrist; for there was now a fever in his sunken eyes which checked the superstitious chill which had been gathering over me, and made me hope that, after all, my first suspicion was correct, and that my patient was but the victim of some fearful hallucination.

"Mock you!" I answered soothingly. "Far from it; I sympathise intensely with you, and would do much to aid you. You require sleep. Lie down, and leave me to watch."

He groaned, but rose, and began throwing off his clothes; and, watching my opportunity, I slipped a sleeping-powder, which I had managed to put in my pocket before leaving the surgery, into the tumbler of claret that stood beside him.

The more I saw, the more I felt convinced that it was the nervous system of my patient which required my attention; and it was with sincere satisfaction I saw him drink the wine, and then stretch himself on the luxurious bed.

"Ha," thought I, as the clock struck twelve, and instead of a groan, the deep breathing of the sleeper sounded through the room; "you won't receive any summons to-night, and I may make myself comfortable."

Noiselessly, therefore, I replenished the fire, poured myself out a large glass of wine, and drawing the curtain so that the firelight should not disturb the sleeper, I put myself in a position to follow his example.

How long I slept I know not, but suddenly I aroused with a start and as ghostly a thrill of horror as ever I remember to have felt in my life.

Something—what, I knew not—seemed near, something nameless, but unutterably awful.

I gazed round.

The fire emitted a faint blue glow, just sufficient to enable me to see that the room was exactly the same as when I fell asleep, but that the long hand of the clock wanted but five minutes of the mysterious hour which was to be the death-moment of the "summoned" man!

Was there anything in it, then?—any truth in the strange story he had told?

The silence was intense.

I could not even hear a breath from the bed; and I was about to rise and approach, when again that awful horror seized me, and at the same moment my eye fell upon the mirror opposite the door, and I saw—

Great heaven! that awful Shape—that ghastly mockery of what had been humanity—was it really a messenger from the buried, quiet dead?

It stood there in visible death-clothes; but the awful face was ghastly with corruption, and the sunken eyes gleamed forth a green glassy glare which seemed a veritable blast from the infernal fires below.

To move or utter a sound in that hideous presence was impossible; and like a statue I sat and saw that horrid Shape move slowly towards the bed.

What was the awful scene enacted there, I know not. I heard nothing, except a low stifled agonised groan; and I saw the shadow of that ghastly messenger bending over the bed.

Whether it was some dreadful but wordless sentence its breathless lips conveyed as it stood there, I know not; but for an instant the shadow of a claw-like hand, from which the third finger was missing, appeared extended over the doomed man's head; and then, as the clock struck one clear silvery stroke, it fell, and a wild shriek rang through the room—a death-shriek.

I am not given to fainting, but I certainly confess that the next ten minutes of my existence was a cold blank; and even when I did manage to stagger to my feet, I gazed round, vainly endeavouring to understand the chilly horror which still possessed me.

Thank God! the room was rid of that awful presence—I saw that; so, gulping down some wine, I lighted a wax-taper and staggered towards the bed. Ah, how I prayed that, after all, I might have been dreaming, and that my own excited imagination had but conjured up some hideous memory of the dissecting-room!

But one glance was sufficient to answer that.

No! The summons had indeed been given and answered.

I flashed the light over the dead face, swollen, convulsed still with the death-agony; but suddenly I shrank back.

Even as I gazed, the expression of the face seemed to change: the blackness faded into a deathly whiteness; the convulsed features relaxed, and, even as if the victim of that dread apparition still lived, a sad solemn smile stole over the pale lips.

I was intensely horrified, but still I retained sufficient self-consciousness to be struck professionally by such a phenomenon.

Surely there was something more than supernatural agency in all this?

Again I scrutinised the dead face, and even the throat and chest; but, with the exception of a tiny pimple on one temple beneath a cluster of hair, not a mark appeared. To look at the corpse, one would have believed that this man had indeed died by the visitation of God, peacefully, whilst sleeping.

How long I stood there I know not, but time enough to gather my scattered senses and to reflect that, all things considered, my own position would be very unpleasant if I was found thus unexpectedly in the room of the mysteriously dead man.

So, as noiselessly as I could, I made my way out of the house. No one met me on the private staircase; the little door opening into the road was easily unfastened; and thankful indeed was I to feel again the fresh wintry air as I hurried along that road by the churchyard.

There was a magnificent funeral soon in that church; and it was said that the young widow of the buried man was inconsolable; and then rumours got abroad of a horrible apparition which had been seen on the night of the death; and it was whispered the young widow was terrified, and insisted upon leaving her splendid mansion.

I was too mystified with the whole affair to risk my reputation by saying what I knew, and I should have allowed my share in it to remain for ever buried in oblivion, had I not suddenly heard that the widow, objecting to many of the legacies in the last will of her husband, intended to dispute it on the score of insanity, and then there gradually arose the rumour of his belief in having received a mysterious summons.

On this I went to the lawyer, and sent a message to the lady, that, as the *last person* who had attended her husband, I undertook to prove his sanity; and I besought her to grant me an interview, in which I would relate as strange and horrible a story as ear had ever heard. The same evening I received an invitation to go to the mansion. I was ushered immediately into a splendid room, and there, standing before the fire, was the most dazzlingly beautiful young creature I had ever seen.

She was very small, but exquisitely made; had it not been for the dignity of her carriage, I should have believed her a mere child.

With a stately bow she advanced, but did not speak.

"I come on a strange and painful errand," I began, and then I started, for I happened to glance full into her eyes, and from them down to the small right hand grasping the chair. The *wedding-ring* was on that hand!

"I conclude you are the Mr. Read who requested permission to tell me some absurd ghost-story, and whom my late husband mentions here." And as she spoke she stretched out her left hand towards something—but what I knew not, for my eyes were fixed on that hand.

Horror! White and delicate it might be, but it was shaped like a claw, and the third finger was missing!

One sentence was enough after that. "Madam, all I can tell you is, that the ghost who summoned your husband was marked by a singular deformity. The third finger of the left hand was missing," I said sternly; and the next instant I had left that beautiful sinful presence.

That will was never disputed. The next morning, too, I received a check for a thousand pounds; and the next news I heard of the widow was, that she had herself seen that awful apparition, and had left the mansion immediately.

THE CHRISTMAS CLUB: A GHOST STORY
by
Edward Eggleston
1873

I.

"The Dickens!"

That was just what Charley Vanderhuyn said that Christmas Eve, and as a faithful historian I give the exact words. It sounded like swearing, though why we should regard it profane to make free with the devil's name, or even his nickname, I never could see. Can you? Besides, there was some ambiguity about Charley's use of the word under the circumstances, and he himself couldn't tell whether his exclamation had reference to the Author of Evils or only to the Author of Novels. The circumstances were calculated to suggest equally thoughts of the Great Teller of Stories and of the Great Story-teller, and I have a mind to amuse you at this Christmas season by telling you the circumstances, and letting you decide, if you can, which Dickens it was that Charles Vanderhuyn intended.

Charley Vanderhuyn was one of those young men that could grow nowhere on this continent except in New York. He had none of the severe dignity that belongs to a young man of wealth who has passed his life in sight of long rows of red brick houses with clean doorsteps and white wooden shutters. Something of the venerableness of Independence Hall, the dignity of Girard College, and the air of financial importance that belongs to the Mint, gets into the blood of a Philadelphian. Charley had none of that. Neither did he have that air of profound thought, that Adams-Hancock-Quincy-Webster-Emerson-Sumner look that is the inevitable mark of Beacon Street. When you see such a young man you know that he has grown part of Faneuil Hall, and the Common, and the Pond, and the historic elm. He has lived where the very trees are learned and carry their Latin names about with them. Charley had none of the "vim" and dash that belongs to a Westerner. He was of the metropolis–metropolitan. He had good blood in him, else he could never have founded the Christmas Club, for you can not get more out of a man than there is in his blood. Charley Vanderhuyn bore a good old Dutch name–I have heard that the Van der Huyns were a famous and noble family; his Dutch blood was mingled with other good strains, and the whole was mellowed into generousness and geniality in generations of prosperous ancestors; for the richest and choicest fruit (and the rankest weeds as well!) can be produced only in the sunlight. And a very choice fruit of a very choice stock was and is our Charley Vanderhuyn. That everybody knows who knows him now, and that we all felt who knew him earlier in the days of the Hasheesh Club.

You remember the Hasheesh Club, doubtless. In its day it numbered the choicest spirits in New York, and the very center of all of them was this same Charley Vanderhuyn, whose face, the boys used to say, was like the British Empire—for on it the sun never set. His unflagging spirits, his keen love for society, his quick sympathy with everybody, his fine appreciation of every man's good points, whatever they might be, made Charley a prince wherever he went. I said he was the center of the circle of young men about the Hasheesh Club ten years ago; and so he was, though, to tell the truth, he was then but about twenty-one years of age. They had a great time at the club, I remember, when he came of age and came into possession of his patrimony—a trifle of half a million, I believe. He gave a dinner, and there was such a time as the Hasheesh Club never saw before nor since. I fear there was overmuch wine-drinking, and I am sure there was a fearful amount of punch drunk. Charley never drank to excess, never lost his self-control for a moment under any temptation. But there was many another young man, of different temperament, to whom the rooms of the club were what candles are to moths. One poor fellow, who always burned his wings, was a blue-eyed, golden-haired young magazine writer of that day. We all thought of his ability and promise—his name was John Perdue, but you will doubtless remember him by his *nom de plume* of "Baron Bertram." Poor fellow! he loved Charley passionately, and always drank himself drunk at the club. He wasted all he had and all he made; his clothes grew shabby, he borrowed of Charley, who was always open-handed, until his pride would allow him to borrow no more. He had just married, too, and he was so ashamed of his own wreck that he completed his ruin by drinking to forget it. I am not writing a story with a temperance moral; temperance tales are always stupid and always useless. The world is brimful of walking morals on that subject, and if one will not read the lesson of the life of his next-door neighbor, what use of bringing Lazarus from the dead to warn him of a perdition that glares at him out of the eyes of so many men?

I mentioned John Perdue—poor golden-haired "Baron Bertram"—only because he had something to do with the circumstances which led Charley Vanderhuyn to use that ambiguous interjection about "the Dickens!" Perdue, as I said, dropped away from the Hasheesh Club, lost his employment as literary editor of the *Luminary*, fell out of good society, and at last earned barely enough to keep him and his wife and his child in bread, and to supply himself with whiskey, by writing sensation stories for the "penny dreadfuls." We all suspected that he would not have received half so much for his articles had they been paid for on their merits or at the standard price for hack writing. But Charley Vanderhuyn had something to do with it. He sent Henry Vail—he always sent Henry Vail on his missions of mercy—to find out where Perdue sold his articles, and I have no doubt the price of each article was doubled, at Vanderhuyn's expense.

And that mention of Henry Vail reminds me that I can not tell this story rightly unless I let you know who he was. A distant relation of Charley's, I believe. He was a studious fellow from the country, and quite awkward in company. The contrast between him and Charley was marked. Vanderhuyn was absolutely *au fait* in all the usages of society; he knew by instinct how a thing ought to be done, and his example was law. He had a genius for it, everybody said. Vail was afraid of his shadow; did not know just what was proper to do in any new circumstances. His manners hung about him loosely; Vanderhuyn's were part of himself. When Vail came to the Hasheesh Club for the first time it was on the occasion of Charley's majority dinner. Vail consulted Vanderhuyn about his costume, and was told that he must wear evening dress; and, never having seen anything but provincial society, he went with perfect assurance to a tailor's and ordered a new frock coat and a white vest. When he saw that the other gentlemen present wore dress coats, and that most of them had black vests, he was in some consternation. He even debated whether he should not go out and hire a dress coat for the evening. He drew Charley aside, and asked him why he did not tell him that those sparrow-tail things had come into fashion again!

But he never took kindly to the club life; he soon saw that however harmless it might be to some men, it was destruction to others. After attending a few times, Henry Vail, who was something of a Puritan and much of a philanthropist, declared his opposition to what he called an English dissipation.

Henry Vail was a scholarly fellow, of real genius, and had studied for the ministry; but he had original notions, and about the time he was to have taken deacon's orders in the Episcopal Church he drew back. He said that orders would do for some men, but he did not intend to build a wall between himself and his fellows. He could do more by remaining a man of like passions with other men than he could by casing himself in a clerical "strait-jacket," as he called it. Having a little income of his own, he set up on his own account in the dingiest part of that dingy street called Huckleberry Street—the name, with all its suggestions of fresh fields and pure air and liberty, is a dreary mockery. Just where Greenfield Court—the dirtiest of New York alleys—runs out of Huckleberry Street, he set up shop, to use his own expression. He was a kind of independent lay clergyman, ministering to the physical and spiritual wants of his neighbors, climbing to garrets and penetrating to cellars, now talking to a woman who owned a candy and gingerbread stall, and now helping to bury a drunken sailor. Such a life for a scholar! But he always declared that digging out Greek and Hebrew roots was not half so fascinating a work as digging out human souls from the filth of Huckleberry Street.

Of course he did not want for money to carry on his operations. Charley Vanderhuyn's investments brought large returns, and Charley knew how to give. When Vail would begin a pathetic story, Vanderhuyn would draw out his check book, and say: "How much shall it be, Harry?—never mind the story. It's handy to have you to give away my money for me. I should never take the trouble to see that it went to the people that need. One dollar given by you is worth ten that I bestow on Tom, Dick, and Harry; so I prefer to let Tom and Dick go without, and give it all to Harry." In fact Vanderhuyn had been the prey of so many impostors that he adopted the plan of sending all of his applicants to Vail, with a note to him, which generally ran thus, "Please investigate." The tramps soon ceased to trouble him, and then he took to entrusting to Vail each month a sum equal to what he had been in the habit of giving away loosely.

It was about the first of December, four years ago, that Harry Vail, grown younger and fresher in two years of toil among the poor—glorified he seemed by the tenderness of his sympathies and the nobleness of his aims—it was four years ago that Harry came into Charley Vanderhuyn's rooms for his regular monthly allotment. Vail generally came in the evening, and Charley generally managed to be disengaged for that evening. The two old friends whose paths diverged so widely were fond of each other's company, and Vail declared that he needed one evening in the month with Vanderhuyn; he liked to carry away some of Charley's sunshine to the darkness of Huckleberry Street and Greenfield Court. And Charley said that Harry brought more sunlight than he took. I believe he was right. Charley, like all men who live without a purpose, was growing less refined and charming than he had been, his cheeks were just a trifle graver than those of the young Charley had been. But he talked magnificently as ever. Vail said that he himself was an explorer in a barbarous desert, and that Charles Vanderhuyn was the one civilized man he could meet.

It is a curious thing that Vail had never urged Charley to a different life from the self-indulgent one that he led, but it was a peculiarity of Henry's that he was slow to attack a man directly. I have heard that it was one great secret of his success among the poor, that he would meet an intemperate man twenty times, perhaps, before he attacked his vice. Then, when the man had ceased to stand guard, Vail would suddenly find an entrance to him by an unwatched gate. It was remarkable, too, that when he did seize on a man he never for an instant relaxed his grasp. I have often looked at his aquiline nose, and wondered if it were not an index to this eagle-like swoop at the right moment, and this unwavering firmness of hold.

On this evening, about the first of December, four years ago, he sat in Charley's cozy bedroom and listened to Vanderhuyn's stories of a life antipodal to the life he was accustomed to see—for the antipodes do not live round the world, but round the first street corner—he listened and laughed at the graphic and eloquent and grotesque pictures that Charley drew for him till nearly midnight, and then got ready to go back to his home, among the noisy saloons of Huckleberry Street. Charley drew out his check book and wrote and tore off the check, and handed it to Vail.

"I want more, Charley, this time," said Vail in his quiet, earnest way, with gray eyes fixed on his friend's blue ones.

"Got more widows without coal than usual, eh, old fellow? How much shall it be? Double? Ask anything. I can't refuse the half of my fortune to such a good angel as you are, Vail. I don't spend any money that pays so well as what I give you. I go to the clubs and to parties. I sit at the opera and listen to Signora Scracchioli, and say to myself, 'Well, there's Vail using my money to help some poor devil in trouble.' I tell you I get a comfortable conscience by an easy system of commutation. Here, exchange with me; this is for double the amount, and I am glad you mentioned it."

"But I want more than that this time," and Vail fixed his eyes on Charley in a way that made the latter feel just a little ill at ease, a sensation very new to him.

"Well, how much, Harry? Don't be afraid to ask. I told you you should have half my kingdom, old fellow!" And Vanderhuyn took his pen and began to date another check.

"But, Charley, I am almost afraid to ask. I want more than half you have–I want something worth more than all you have."

"Why, you make me curious. Never saw you in that vein before, Vail," and Charley twisted a piece of paper, lighted it in the gas jet, and held it gracefully in his fingers while he set his cigar going, hoping to hide his restlessness under the wistful gaze of his friend by this occupation of his attention.

But however nervous Henry Vail might be in the performance of little acts that were mere matters of convention, there was no lack of quiet self-possession in matters that called out his earnestness of spirit. And now he sat gazing steadily at Charley until the cigar had been gracefully lighted, the bit of paper tossed on the grate, and until Charley had watched his cigar a moment. When the latter reluctantly brought his eyes back into range with the dead-earnest ones that had never ceased to look on him with that strange wistful expression, then Henry Vail proceeded:

"I want *you*, Charley."

Charley laughed heartily now. "Me? What a missionary *I* would make! Kid-glove gospeller I'd be called in the first three days. What a superb Sunday-school teacher I'd make! Why, Henry Vail, you know better. There's just one thing in this world I have a talent for, and that's society. I'm a man of the world in my very fiber. But as for following in your illustrious footsteps—I wish I could be so good a man, but you see I'm not built in that way. I'm a man of the world."

"That's just what I want," said Henry Vail, looking with the same tender wistfulness into his friend's eyes. "If I'd wanted a missionary I shouldn't have come to you. If I'd wanted a Sunday-school teacher I could have found twenty better; and as for tract distributing and Bible reading, you couldn't do either if you'd try. What I want for Huckleberry Street more than I want anything else is a man of the world. You are a man of the world—of the whole world. I have seen a restaurant waiter stop and gape and listen to your talk. I have seen a coal-heaver delighted with your manners when you paid him. Charley, you're the most magnificent man of the world I ever saw. Must a man of the world be useless? I tell you I want you for God and Huckleberry Street, and I mean to have you some day, old fellow." And the perfect assurance with which he said this, and the settled conviction of final success that was visible in his quiet gray eyes, fascinated Charley Vanderhuyn, and he felt spellbound, like the wedding guest held by the "Ancient Mariner."

"I tell you what, Henry," he said presently, "I've got no call. I'm an Epicurean. I say to you, in the words of an American poet:

'Take the current of your nature, make it stagnant if you will:
Dam it up to drudge forever at the service of your will.
Mine the rapture and the freedom of the torrent on the hill!
I shall wander o'er the meadows where the fairest blossoms call:
Though the ledges seize and fling me headlong from the rocky wall,
I shall leave a rainbow hanging o'er the ruins of my fall.'"

"Charley, I don't want to preach," said Vail; "but you know that this doctrine of mere selfish floating on the current of impulse which your traveler poet teaches is devilish laziness, and devilish laziness always tends to something worse. You may live such a life, and quote such poetry, but you don't believe that a man should flow on like a purposeless river. The lines you quoted bear the mark of a restless desire to apologize to conscience for a fearful waste of power and possibility. No," he said, rising, "I don't want that check. This one will do; but you won't forget that God and Huckleberry Street want you, and they will have you, too, noble-hearted fellow! Good night! God bless you!" and he shook Charley's hand and went out into the night to seek his home in Huckleberry Street. And the genial Charley never saw his brave friend again. Yes, he did, too. Or did he?

II.

The month of December, four years ago, was a month of much festivity in the metropolis. Charley was wanted nearly every night to grace some gathering or other, and Charley was too obliging to refuse to go where he was wanted—that is, when he was wanted in Fifth Avenue or Thirty-fourth Street. As for Huckleberry Street and Greenfield Court, they were fast fading out of Charley's mind. He knew that Henry Vail would introduce the subject when he came for his January check, and he expected some annoyance from the discussion of the question—annoyance, because there was something in his own breast that answered to Vail's appeal. Charley was more than an Epicurean. To eat and drink, to laugh and talk, and die, was not enough for such a soul. He mentally compared himself to Felix, and said that Vail wouldn't let him forget his duty, anyhow. But for the present it was too delightful to him to honor the entertainment given by the Honorable Mr. So-and-so and Mrs. So-and-so; it was pleasant to be assured by Mrs. Forty-Millions that her party would fail but for his presence. And then he had just achieved the end of his ambition. He was president of the Hasheesh Club. He took his seat at the head of the table on Christmas Eve.

Now, patient reader, we draw near to the time when Charley uttered the exclamation set down at the head of this story. Bear a little longer with my roundabout way of telling. It is Christmastide anyway; why should we hurry ourselves through this happy season?

Just as Charley went into the door of the clubhouse—you remember the Hasheesh clubhouse was in Madison Avenue then—just as Charley entered he met the burly form and genial face of the eminent Dr. Van Doser, who said, "Well, Vanderhuyn, how's your cousin Vail?"—"Is he sick?" asked Charley, struck with a foreboding that made him tremble.

"Sick? Didn't you know? Well, that's just like Vail. He was taken with small-pox two weeks ago, and I wanted to take the risk of penalties and not report his case, but he said if I didn't he would do it himself; that sanitary regulations requiring small-pox patients to go to a hospital were necessary, and that it became one in his position to set a good example to Huckleberry Street. So I was compelled to report him and let him go to the island. And he hasn't let you know? For fear you would try to communicate with him probably, and thus expose yourself to infection. Extraordinary man, that Vail. I never saw his like," and with that the doctor turned to speak to some gentlemen who had just come in.

And so Charley's Christmas Eve dinner at the Hasheesh Club was spoiled. There are two inconvenient things in this world, a conscience and a tender heart—and Charley Vanderhuyn was plagued with both. While going through with the toasts, his mind was busy with poor Henry Vail suffering in a small-pox hospital. In his graceful response to the sentiment, "The President of the Hasheesh Club," he alluded to the retiring president, and made some witty remark—I forget what—about his being a denizen of Lexington Avenue; but in saying Lexington Avenue he came near slipping into Huckleberry Street, and in fact he did get the first syllable out before he checked himself. He was horrified afterward to think how near he had come, later in the evening, to addressing the company as "Gentlemen of the Small-pox Hospital."

Charley drank more wine and punch than usual. Those who sat near him looked at one another significantly, in a way that implied their belief that Vanderhuyn was too much elated over his election. Little did they know that at that moment the presidency of the famous Hasheesh Club appeared to Charley the veriest bawble in the world. If he had not known how futile would be any attempt to gain an entrance to the small-pox hospital, he would have excused himself and started for the island on the instant.

But it was one o'clock before Charley got away. Out of the brilliantly lighted rooms he walked, stunned with grief, and a little heavy with the wine and punch he had drunk, for in his preoccupation of mind he had forgotten to be as cautious as usual. Following an impulse, he took a car and went directly downtown, and then made his way to Huckleberry Street. He stopped at a saloon door and asked if they could tell him where Mr. Vail's rooms were.

"The blissed man as wint about like a saint? Shure and I can," said the boozy Irishman. "It's right ferninst where yer afther stanin, up the stairs on the corner of Granefield Coort—over there, bedad."

Seeing a light in the rooms indicated by the man, Charley crossed over, passed through a sorrowful-looking crowd at the door, and went up the stairs. He found the negro woman who kept the rooms for Vail standing talking to an Irish woman. Both the women were deeply pitted with small-pox.

He inquired if they could tell him how Mr. Vail was.

"O honey, he's done dead sence three o'clock," said the black woman, sitting down in a chair and beginning to wipe her eyes on her apron. "This Misses Mcgroarty's jist done tole me this minute."

The Irish woman came round in front of Mr. Vanderhuyn and looked inquisitively at him a moment, and then said, "Faix, mister, and is yer name Charley?"

"Why do you ask?" said Vanderhuyn.

"Because I thought, mebbe, you might be after him, the gentleman. It's me husband, Pat Mcgroarty, as is a nurruss in the horsepital, and a good one as iver ye seed, and it's Pat as has been a-tellin me about that blissed saint of a man, as how in his delairyum he kept a-talkin to Charley all the time, and Pat said as he seemed to have something on his mind he wanted to say to Charley. An' whin I see yer face, sich a gintleman's face as ye've got, too, I says shure that must be Charley."

"What did he say?" asked Vanderhuyn.

"Shure, and Pat said it wasn't much he could gether, for he was in a awful delairyum, ye know, but he would keep a-sayin', 'Charley, Charley, God and Huckleberry Street want you.' Pat says he'd say it so awful as would make him shiver, that God and Huckleberry Street wanted Charley. Shure it must a bin the delairyum, you know, that made him mix up things loike, and put God and Huckleberry Street together, when its more loike the divil would seem more proper to go with Huckleberry Street, ye know. But if yer name's Charley, and yer loike the loikes of him as is dead, shure Huckleberry Street is after wantin' of you, bad enough."

"My name's Charley, but I'm not a bit like him, though, I'm sorry to say, my good woman. Tell your husband to come and see me—there's my number."

Charley went out, and the men at the door whispered, "That must be the rich man as give him all the money." He took the last car uptown, and he who had been two hours before in that brilliant company at the Hasheesh was now one of ten people riding in a street car. Of his fellow-passengers six were drunken men and two were low women of the town; one of them had no bonnet, and lacked a penny of enough to pay her fare, but the conductor mercifully let her ride, remarking to Vanderhuyn, who stood on the platform, that "the poor devil has a hard life any how." Said I not a minute ago, that the antipodes live not around the world, but around the street corner? Antipodes ride in the same street car.

As the car was passing Mott Street, a passenger, half drunk, came out, turned his haggard face a moment toward the face of Charley Vanderhuyn, and then, with an exclamation of startled recognition, leaped from the car and hurried away in the darkness. It was not till the car had gone three blocks farther that Vanderhuyn guessed, from the golden hair, that this was Perdue, the brilliant "Baron Bertram" of the early days of the Hasheesh Club.

When Charley got back to his luxurious apartment he was possessed with a superstitious feeling. He took up the paper weight that Henry Vail had held in his hand the very last night he was in this parlor, and he thought the whole conversation over as he smoked his cigar, fearing to put out his light.

"Confound the man that invented ghost stories for a Christmas amusement!" he said, as he remembered Old Scrooge and Tiny Tim. "Well, I'm not Old Scrooge, anyhow, if I'm not as good as poor Henry Vail."

I do not know whether it was the reaction from the punch he had drunk, or the sudden shock of Vail's death, or the troubled conscience, or from all three, but when he got into bed he found himself shaking with nervousness.

He had been asleep an hour, perhaps, when he heard a genuine Irish voice say, "Faix, mister, and is yer name Charley?"

He started up—looked around the room. He had made so much concession to his nervous feeling that he had not turned the gas quite out, as was his custom. The dim duskiness made him shudder; he expected to see the Huckleberry Street Irish woman looking at him. But he shook off his terror a little, uttered another malediction on the man that invented Christmas ghost stories, concluded that his illusion must have come from his lying on his left side, turned over, and reflected that by so doing he would relieve his heart and stomach from the weight of his liver, repeated this physiological reflection in a soothing way two or three times, dropped off into a quiet snooze, and almost immediately found himself sitting bolt upright in bed, shaking with a chill terror, sure that the Irish voice had again asked the question, "Faix, mister, and is yer name Charley?" He had a feeling, though his back was toward the table, that some one sat at the table. Charley was no coward, but it took him a minute or two to shake off his terror and regain enough self-control to look around.

For a moment he saw, or thought he saw, a form sitting at the table, then it disappeared, and then, after a good while, Charley got himself composed to sleep again, this time with his head well bolstered, to reduce the circulation in the brain, as he reflected.

He did not get to sleep, however, for before he became unconscious the Irish voice from just above the carved headboard spoke out so clear now that there could be no mistake, "Faix, mister, and is yer name Charley?" It was then that he rose in bed and uttered the exclamation which I set down in the first line of this story. Charley Vanderhuyn could not tell whether he meant Charles Dickens or Nick. Perhaps you can. Indeed, it doesn't seem to matter much, after all.

III.

A narrative of this sort, like a French sermon, divides itself into three parts. I have now got through the preliminary tanglements of the history of the founding of the Christmas Club, and I hope to be able to tell the remainder of the story with as few digressions as possible, for at Christmastide a body doesn't want his stories to stretch out to eternity, even if they are ghostly.

Charley Vanderhuyn said "The Dickens!" and though his meaning was indefinite, he really meant it, whatever it might be. He looked up at the ornamental figure carved on the rich headboard of his bed as if he suspected that the headboard of English walnut had spoken in Irish. He looked at the headboard intently a long time, partly because the Irish voice had come from that direction, and partly because he was afraid to look round toward the table. He *knew*, just as well before he looked around as he did afterward, what he should see. He saw it before he looked round by some other vision than that of his eyes, and that was what made him shiver so. He knew that the persistent gray eyes were upon him, that they would never move until he looked round. *He could feel the look before he saw it.*

At last he turned slowly. Sure enough, in that very chair by the table sat the Presence, the Ghost—the—it was Henry Vail; or was it? There, in the dim light, was the aquiline nose like an eagle's beak, there were the steady, unwavering gray eyes, with that same earnest, wistful look fastened on Vanderhuyn; the features were Vail's, but the face was plowed and pitted fearfully as with the small-pox. All this Charley saw, while seeing through the ghost and beyond—the carving on the rosewood dressing case was quite as visible through the unsubstantial apparition as before. Charley was not ordinarily superstitious, and he quickly reasoned that his excited imagination had confounded the features of Harry Vail's face with the pock-marked visage of the Huckleberry Street Irish woman. So he shook himself, rubbed his eyes and looked again. The apparition this time was much more distinct, and it lifted the paper weight, as Henry had three weeks before. Charley was so sure that it was Henry Vail himself that he began to get up to shake hands with his friend, but the perfect transparency of the apparition checked him, and he hid his face in his hands a moment, in a terror that he could no longer conceal from himself.

"What do you want?" he said at last, lifting his eyes.

"I want you, Charley!" said the ghost.

Now I hardly know how to describe to you the manner in which the ghost replied. It was not speech, nor any attempt at speech. You have seen a mesmerist or biologist, or whatever-you-call-him-ist, communicate with a man under his spell without speech. He looks at him, *wills* that a distinct impression shall be made on his victim, and the poor fellow does or says as the master spirit wishes him. By some such subtle influence the ghost, without the intervention of sound or the sense of hearing, conveyed this reply to Charley. There was no doubt about the reply. It was far more distinct than speech, an impression made directly upon the consciousness.

Charley arose and dressed himself under some sort of fascination. His own will had abdicated; the tender, eager, wistful eyes of Vail held him fast, and he did not feel either inclination or power to resist. The eyes directed him to one article of clothing, and then to another, until he found himself muffled to the ears for a night walk.

"Where are we going?" asked Charley huskily.

"To Huckleberry Street," answered the eyes, without a sound, and in a minute more the two were passing down the silent streets. They met several policemen and private watchmen, but Vanderhuyn observed that no one took notice either of him or the ghost. The feet of the watchmen made a grinding noise in the crisp snow, but Charley was horrified to find that his own tread and that of his companion made no sound whatever as their feet fell upon the icy sidewalks. Was he, then, out of the body also? This silence and this loss of the power of choice made him doubtful, indeed, whether he were dead or alive.

In Huckleberry Street they went first to a large saloon, where a set of roysterers were having a Christmas-Eve spree preparatory to a Christmas-morning headache. Charley could not imagine why the ghost had brought him here, to be smothered with the smell of this villainous tobacco, for to nothing was Charley more sensitive than to the smell of a poor cigar or a cheap pipe. He thought if he should have to stay here long he would like to distribute a box of his best brand among these smokers, so as to give the room the odor of the Hasheesh Club. At first it seemed a Babel of voices; there were men of several different nationalities talking in three or four languages. Six men were standing at the long counter drinking—one German, two Irishmen, a Portuguese sailor, a white American, and a black one. The spirit of Vail seemed to be looking for somebody; it peered round from table to table, where men slammed down the cards so as to make as much noise as possible. Nobody paid the least attention to the two strangers, and at last it flashed upon Vanderhuyn that he and Vail were both invisible to the throng around them.

The Presence stopped in front of a table where two young men sat. They were playing euchre, and they were drinking. It is an old adage that truth is told in wine, and with some men sense comes with whiskey.

"I say, Joe," said one, "blamed ef it 'taint too bad; you and me spendin' our time this way! The ole woman's mos' broke 'r heart over me t'day. Sh' said I ought be the s'port 'f her ole dage, 'stid 'f boozin' roun' thish yer way. 'S so! Tell you, Joe, 's so! Blam'd 'f 'taint. Hey? W'at y' say? Hey?"

"Of course 'tis, Ben," growled the other; "we all know that. But what's a feller goin' to do for company? Go on; it's your deal."

"Who kyeers fer th' deal? I d—on't. Now, Joe, I says, t—to th' ole lady, y' see, I says, a young man can't live up a dingy stairs on th' top floor al'ays, and never git no comp'ny. Can't do it. I don't want t' 'rink much, but I c—ome here to git comp'ny. Comp'ny drinks, and I git drunk 'f—fore I know—'fore you——pshaw! deal yerself 'f you want t' play."

After a while he put the cards down again, and began:

"What think I done wunst? He, he! Went to th' Young Men's Chrissen Soshiashen. Ole lady, you know, coaxed. He! he! You bet! Prayer meetin', Bible class, or somethi'n. All slick young fellers 'th side whiskers. Talked pious, an' so genteel, you know. I went there fer comp'ny! Didn go no more. Druther git drunk at the 'free-and-easy' ever' night, by George, 'n to be a slick kind 'f feller 'th side whiskers a lis'nin' t' myself make purty speeches 'n a prayer Bible class meetin' or such, you know. Hey? w'at ye say? Hey? 'S comp'ny a feller wants, and 's comp'ny a feller's got t' have, by cracky! Hey? W'at ye say? Hey, Joe?"

"Blam'd 'f 'tain't," said Joe.

"That's w'at them rich fellers goes to the club fer? Hey? w'at ye say, Joe? Hey?"

"Yes, of course."

"Wish I had a club! Better'n this place to go to. Vail, he used to do a fellow good. If he'd a lived he'd a pulled me out this yer, would, you, know. He got 's eyes onto me, and they say when he got 's eyes onto feller never let go, you know. Done me good.

Made me 'shamed. Does feller good t' be 'shamed, Joe. Don't it? Hey? W'at you say?"

"Yes," said Joe.

"But w'en a feller's lonesome, a young feller, I mean; he's got to have company if he has to go down to Davy Joneses, and play seven up with Ole Nick. Hey, Joe? W'at you say? Hey?"

"I s'pose so," said Joe; "but come, deal, old fellow; don't go to preachin'."

I have heard Charley say that he never heard anything half so distinctly in his life as he felt what the apparition said to him when their eyes met at that moment.

"God and Huckleberry Street want you, Charley."

Charley looked away restively, and then caught the eyes of the ghost again, and this time the ghost said—

"And they're going to have you, too."

I have heard Charley tell of several other visits they made that night; but, as I said before, even a Christmas yarn and a ghost story must not spin itself out, like Banquo's line, to the crack of doom. However true or authentic a story may be—and you can easily verify this by asking any member of the Christmas Club in Huckleberry Street—however true a yarn may be, it must not be so long that it can never be wound up.

The very last of the wretched places they looked in upon was a bare room in a third story. There was a woman sitting on a box in one corner, holding a sick child. A man with golden hair was pacing the floor.

"There's that devil again!" he said, pointing to the blank wall. "Now he's gone. You see, Carrie, I could quit if I had anybody to help me. Oh! I heard to-night that Charley Vanderhuyn had been elected president of the Hasheesh. And I saw him an hour ago on a Second Avenue car. I wish Charley would come and talk to me. He'd give me money, but 'taint money. I could make money if I could let whiskey alone. I used to love to hear Charley talk better than to live. I believe it was the ruin of me. But he don't seem to care for a fellow when his clothes get shabby. See there!" and he picked up a piece of wood and threw it at the wall, startling his wife and making the child cry. "I hit him that time! I wish I could hear Charley Vanderhuyn talk once more. His talk is enough to drive devils away any time. Great God, what an awful Christmas this is!"

Charley wanted to begin to talk on the spot, but when he found that poor "Baron Bertram" could neither see him nor hear a word he spoke, he had a fearful sense of being a disembodied spirit. The ghost looked wistfully at him, and said, "God and Huckleberry Street want *you*, Charley."

Charley was very loath to leave Perdue and his wife in this condition; he would have loved dearly to while away the dreary night for them, but he could not speak to them, and the eyes of the ghost bade him follow, and the two went swiftly back to Charley's rooms again.

Then the apparition sat down by the table and fastened its sad and wistful eyes upon the soul of Charley Vanderhuyn. Not a word did it speak. But the look, the old tender, earnest look of Henry Vail, drew Charley's heart into his eyes and made him weep. There Vail sat, still and wistful, until Charley, roused by all that he had seen, resolved to do what he could for Huckleberry Street. He made no communication of his purpose to the ghost. He meant to keep it close in his own breast. But no sooner had he formed the purpose than a smile—the old familiar smile—came across the face of Vail, the hideous scars of his loathsome disease disappeared, and the face began to shine, while a faint aureole appeared about his head. And Vanderhuyn became conscious that the room was full of other mysterious beings. And to his regret Vail ceased now to regard his friend any more, but looked about him at the Huckleberry Street angels, who seemed to be pulling him away. He and they vanished slowly, and on the wall there shone some faint luminous letters, which Vanderhuyn tried to read, but the light of the Christmas dawn disturbed his vision, and he was able to see only the latter part, and even that was not clear to his eyes, but he partly read and partly remembered the words, "When ye fail on earth they may receive you into everlasting habitations."

He rang for his servant, had the fire replenished, opened his desk and began to write letters. First he resigned the presidency of the Hasheesh Club. Next he begged that Mrs. Rear-Admiral Albatross would excuse him from her Christmas dinner. Unforeseen circumstances, and the death of an intimate friend, were his apologies. Then he sent his regrets, and declined all the invitations to holiday parties. He canceled his engagements to make New-Year's calls in company with Bird, the painter. Then he had breakfast, ordered his carriage, and drove to Huckleberry Street. On the way down he debated what he should do. He couldn't follow in Vail's footsteps. He was not a missionary. He went first and found Perdue, who had been fighting off a threatened attack of tremens all night, relieved the necessities of his family, and took the golden-haired fellow into his carriage. He ordered the coachman to drive the whole length of Huckleberry Street slowly.

"Perdue, what can I do down here? Vail always said that I could do something, if I would try."

"Why, Charley, start a club. That's what these fellows need. How I should like to hear you talk again!"

IV.

How provoking this is! I thought I should get through with three parts. But Christmas is a time when a man cannot avoid a tendency to long stories. One cannot quite control one's self in a time of mirth, and here my history has grown until I shall have to put on a mansard roof to accommodate it. For in all these three parts I have told you about everything but what my title promised. If you have ever gone through Huckleberry Street—of course you never have gone through such a street except by accident, since you are neither poor, vicious, nor benevolent, and only the poor, the vicious, and the benevolent ever go there intentionally—but if you have ever happened to go there of late years, you have seen the Christmas Club building. For on that very morning, with poor "Baron Bertram" in the carriage, Charley resolved to found a club in Huckleberry Street. And what house so good as the one in which Henry Vail had lived?

So he drove up to the house on the corner of Greenfield Court and began to examine it. It was an old-fashioned house; and in its time, when the old families inhabited the downtown streets, it had been an aristocratic mansion. The lower floor was occupied by a butcher's shop, and in the front room, where an old family had once entertained its guests, cheap roasts were being dispensed to the keepers of low boarding houses. The antique fireplace and the ancient mantelpiece were forced to keep company with meat blocks and butchers' cleavers. Above this were Henry Vail's rooms, where the old chambers had been carefully restored; and above these the third story and attic were crowded with tenants. But everywhere the house had traces of its former gentility.

"Good!" said Charley; "Vail preserved his taste for the antique to the last."

"Perdue, what do you think of this for a club-house?"

"Just the thing if you can get it. Ten chances to one it belongs to some saloon-keeper who wouldn't rent it for purposes of civilization."

"O!, I'll get it! Such men are always susceptible to the influence of money, and I'm sure this is the spot, or Vail wouldn't have chosen it."

And with that Charley and the delighted Perdue drove to the house of Charley's business agent, the same who had been his father's manager.

"Mr. Johnston," said Charley, "I don't like to ask you to work on Christmas, but I want you to find out to-day, if you can, who owns No. 164 Huckleberry Street."

"Do you mean the house Mr. Vail lived in?"

"Yes, that's it. Look it up for me, if you can."

"Oh, that's not hard. The house belongs to you."

"To me! I didn't know I had anything there."

"Yes, that house was your grandfather's, and your mother lived there in her childhood, and your father wouldn't sell it. It brought good rent, and I have never bothered you about it."

"And you let Harry pay me rent?"

"Well, sir, he asked me not to mention to you that he was in your house. He liked to pay his own way. Strange man, that Mr. Vail! I heard from another tenant last night that he was dead."

"Perdue," said Charley, "I wish you would go down there to-day and find out what each tenant in that house will sell his lease for and give possession immediately. Give them a note to Johnston stating the amount, and I want Johnston to give them something over the amount agreed on. I must be on good terms with Huckleberry Street."

Johnston wondered what whim Charley had in his head. "Baron Bertram" completed his negotiations for the leases of the tenants, and then went off and drank Charley's health in so many saloons that he went home entirely drunk, and the next morning was ashamed to see Vanderhuyn. But Charley never even looked a disapproval at him. He had learned from Vail how easy it is for reformers to throw their influence on the wrong side in such a life-and-death struggle as that of Perdue's. In the year that followed he had to forgive him many more than seven times. But Perdue grew stronger in the sunlight of Vanderhuyn's steady friendship.

They had a great time opening the club on New Year's Eve. There was a banquet, not quite in Delmonico's style, nor quite so fine as those at the Hasheesh. But still it was a grand affair to the dilapidated wrecks that Charley gathered about him. Charley was president, and Vail's portrait hung over the mantelpiece, with this inscription beneath: "The Founder of the Club." Most of Charley's fine paintings were here, and the rooms were indeed brilliant. And if lemonade and root beer and good strong coffee could have made people drunk, there would not have been one sober man there. But Ben delighted "the old lady" by going home sober, owning it was better than the free-and-easy, and his friends all agreed with him. To Charley, as he looked round on them, this was a far grander moment than when, one week before, he had presided over the gay company at the Hasheesh. Here were good cheer, laughter, funny stories, and a New Year's Eve worth the having. The gray eyes of the portrait over the antique mantel-piece seemed happy and satisfied.

"Gentlemen," said Charley, "I rise to propose the memory of our founder," and he proceeded to set forth the virtues of Henry Vail. If there had been a reporter present he could have inserted in parenthesis, at several places in Charley's speech, the words, "great applause"; and if he had reported its effect exactly, he would, at several other places, have inserted the words "great sensation," which, in reporter's phrase, expresses any great emotion, especially one which makes an audience weep. In conclusion, Charley lifted his glass of lemonade, and said, "To the memory of Henry Vail, the Founder of the Christmas Club."

"Christmas!" said Baron Bertram, "a good name! For this man," pointing to Charley, "receiveth sinners and eateth with them" (applause).

I have done. Dear friends, a Merry Christmas to you all!

THE GHOST OF CHARLOTTE CRAY

CRAY
by
Florence Marryat
1878

Mr. Sigismund Braggett was sitting in the little room he called his study, wrapped in a profound—not to say a mournful—reverie. Now, there was nothing in the present life nor surroundings of Mr. Braggett to account for such a demonstration. He was a publisher and bookseller; a man well to do, with a thriving business in the city, and the prettiest of all pretty villas at Streatham. And he was only just turned forty; had not a grey hair in his head nor a false tooth in his mouth; and had been married but three short months to one of the fairest and most affectionate specimens of English womanhood that ever transformed a bachelor's quarters into Paradise.

What more could Mr. Sigismund Braggett possibly want? Nothing! His trouble lay in the fact that he had got rather more than he wanted. Most of us have our little peccadilloes in this world—awkward reminiscences that we would like to bury five fathoms deep, and never hear mentioned again, but that have an uncomfortable habit of cropping up at the most inconvenient moments; and no mortal is more likely to be troubled with them than a middle-aged bachelor who has taken to matrimony.

Mr. Sigismund Braggett had no idea what he was going in for when he led the blushing Emily Primrose up to the altar, and swore to be hers, and hers only, until death should them part. He had no conception a woman's curiosity could be so keen, her tongue so long, and her inventive faculties so correct. He had spent whole days before the fatal moment of marriage in burning letters, erasing initials, destroying locks of hair, and making offerings of affection look as if he had purchased them with his own money. But it had been of little avail. Mrs. Braggett had swooped down upon him like a beautiful bird of prey, and wheedled, coaxed, or kissed him out of half his secrets before he knew what he was about. But he had never told her about Charlotte Cray. And now he almost wished that he had done so, for Charlotte Cray was the cause of his present dejected mood.

Now, there are ladies *and* ladies in this world. Some are very shy, and will only permit themselves to be wooed by stealth. Others, again, are the pursuers rather than the pursued, and chase the wounded or the dying even to the very doors of their stronghold, or lie in wait for them like an octopus, stretching out their tentacles on every side in search of victims.

And to the latter class Miss Charlotte Cray decidedly belonged. Not a person worth mourning over, you will naturally say. But, then. Mr Sigismund Braggett had not behaved well to her. She was one of the "peccadilloes." She was an authoress—not an author, mind you, which term smacks more of the profession than the sex—but an 'authoress' with lots of the "ladylike" about the plots of her stories and the metre of her rhymes. They had come together in the sweet connection of publisher and writer—had met first in a dingy, dusty little office at the back of his house of business, and laid the foundation of their friendship with the average amount of chaffering and prevarication that usually attend such proceedings.

Mr. Braggett ran a risk in publishing Miss Cray's tales or verses, but he found her useful in so many other ways that he used occasionally to hold forth a sop to Cerberus in the shape of publicity for the sake of keeping her in his employ. For Miss Charlotte Cray—who was as old as himself, and had arrived at the period of life when women are said to pray "Any, good Lord, any!"—was really a clever woman, and could turn her hand to most things required of her, or upon which she had set her mind; and she had most decidedly set her mind upon marrying Mr Braggett, and he—to serve his own purposes—had permitted her to cherish the idea, and this was the Nemesis that was weighing him down in the study at the present moment. He had complimented Miss Cray, and given her presents, and taken her out a-pleasuring, all because she was useful to him, and did odd jobs that no one else would undertake, and for less than any one else would have accepted; and he had known the while that she was in love with him, and that she believed he was in love with her.

He had not thought much of it at the time. He had not then made up his mind to marry Emily Primrose, and considered that what pleased Miss Cray, and harmed no one else, was fair play for all sides. But he had come to see things differently now. He had been married three months, and the first two weeks had been very bitter ones to him. Miss Cray had written him torrents of reproaches during that unhappy period, besides calling day after day at his office to deliver them in person. This and her threats had frightened him out of his life. He had lived in hourly terror lest the clerks should overhear what passed at their interviews, or that his wife should be made acquainted with them.

He had implored Miss Cray, both by word of mouth and letter, to cease her persecution of him; but all the reply he received was that he was a base and perjured man, and that she should continue to call at his office, and write to him through the penny post, until he had introduced her to his wife. For therein lay the height and depth of his offending. He had been afraid to bring Emily and Miss Cray together, and the latter resented the omission as an insult. It was bad enough to find that Sigismund Braggett, whose hair she wore next her heart, and whose photograph stood as in a shrine upon her bedroom mantelpiece, had married another woman, without giving her even the chance of a refusal, but it was worse still to come to the conclusion that he did not intend her to have a glimpse into the garden of Eden he had created for himself.

Miss Cray was a lady of vivid imagination and strong aspirations. All was not lost in her ideas, although Mr Braggett *had* proved false to the hopes he had raised. Wives did not live for ever; and the chances and changes of this life were so numerous, that stranger things had happened than that Mr Braggett might think fit to make better use of the second opportunity afforded him than he had done of the first. But if she were not to continue even his friend, it was too hard. But the perjured publisher had continued resolute, notwithstanding all Miss Cray's persecution, and now he had neither seen nor heard from her for a month; and, man-like, he was beginning to wonder what had become of her, and whether she had found anybody to console her for his untruth. Mr Braggett did not wish to comfort Miss Cray himself; but he did not quite like the notion of her being comforted.

After all—so he soliloquised—he had been very cruel to her; for the poor thing was devoted to him. How her eyes used to sparkle and her cheek to flush when she entered his office, and how eagerly she would undertake any work for him, however disagreeable to perform! He knew well that she had expected to be Mrs. Braggett, and it must have been a terrible disappointment to her when he married Emily Primrose.

Why had he not asked her out to Violet Villa since? What harm could she do as a visitor there? particularly if he cautioned her first as to the peculiarity of Mrs. Braggett's disposition, and the quickness with which her jealousy was excited. It was close upon Christmas-time, the period when all old friends meet together and patch up, if they cannot entirely forget, everything that has annoyed them in the past. Mr. Braggett pictured to himself the poor old maid sitting solitary in her small rooms at Hammersmith, no longer able to live in the expectation of seeing his manly form at the wicket-gate, about to enter and cheer her solitude. The thought smote him as a two-edged sword, and he sat down at once and penned Miss Charlotte a note, in which he inquired after her health, and hoped that they should soon see her at Violet Villa.

He felt much better after this note was written and despatched. He came out of the little study and entered the cheerful drawing-room, and sat with his pretty wife by the light of the fire, telling her of the lonely lady to whom he had just proposed to introduce her.

"An old friend of mine, Emily. A clever, agreeable woman, though rather eccentric. You will be polite to her, I know, for my sake."

"An *old* woman, is she?" said Mrs Braggett, elevating her eyebrows. "And what do you call 'old,' Siggy, I should like to know?"

"Twice as old as yourself, my dear—five-and-forty at the very least, and not personable-looking, even for that age. Yet I think you will find her a pleasant companion, and I am sure she will be enchanted with you."

"I don't know that: clever women don't like me, as a rule, though I don't know why."

"They are jealous of your beauty, my darling; but Miss Cray is above such meanness, and will value you for your own sake."

"She'd better not let me catch her valuing me for *yours*," responded Mrs Braggett, with a flash of the eye that made her husband ready to regret the dangerous experiment he was about to make of bringing together two women who had each, in her own way, a claim upon him, and each the will to maintain it.

So he dropped the subject of Miss Charlotte Cray, and took to admiring his wife's complexion instead, so that the evening passed harmoniously, and both parties were satisfied.

For two days Mr Braggett received no answer from Miss Cray, which rather surprised him. He had quite expected that on the reception of his invitation she would rush down to his office and into his arms, behind the shelter of the ground-glass door that enclosed his chair of authority. For Miss Charlotte had been used on occasions to indulge in rapturous demonstrations of the sort, and the remembrance of Mrs Braggett located in Violet Villa would have been no obstacle whatever to her. She believed she had a prior claim to Mr Braggett. However, nothing of the kind happened, and the perjured publisher was becoming strongly imbued with the idea that he must go out to Hammersmith and see if he could not make his peace with her in person, particularly as he had several odd jobs for Christmas-tide, which no one could undertake so well as herself, when a letter with a black-edged border was put into his hand. He opened it mechanically, not knowing the writing; but its contents shocked him beyond measure.

'HONOURED SIR,—I am sorry to tell you that Miss Cray died at my house a week ago, and was buried yesterday. She spoke of you several times during her last illness, and if you would like to hear any further particulars, and will call on me at the old address, I shall be most happy to furnish you with them.

"Yours respectfully,

"Mary Thompson."

When Mr. Braggett read this news, you might have knocked him over with a feather. It is not always true that a living dog is better than a dead lion. Some people gain considerably in the estimation of their friends by leaving this world, and Miss Charlotte Cray was one of them. Her persecution had ceased for ever, and her amiable weaknesses were alone held in remembrance. Mr. Braggett felt a positive relief in the knowledge that his dead friend and his wife would never now be brought in contact with each other; but at the same time he blamed himself more than was needful, perhaps, for not having seen nor communicated with Miss Cray for so long before her death. He came down to breakfast with a portentously grave face that morning, and imparted the sad intelligence to Mrs Braggett with the air of an undertaker. Emily wondered, pitied, and sympathised, but the dead lady was no more to her than any other stranger; and she was surprised her husband looked so solemn over it all. Mr. Braggett, however, could not dismiss the subject easily from his mind. It haunted him during the business hours of the morning, and as soon as he could conveniently leave his office, he posted away to Hammersmith. The little house in which Miss Cray used to live looked just the same, both inside and outside: how strange it seemed that *she* should have flown away from it for ever! And here was her landlady, Mrs. Thompson, bobbing and curtseying to him in the same old black net cap with artificial flowers in it, and the same stuff gown she had worn since he first saw her, with her apron in her hand, it is true, ready to go to her eyes as soon as a reasonable opportunity occurred, but otherwise the same Mrs. Thompson as before. And yet she would never wait upon *her* again.

"It was all so sudden, sir," she said, in answer to Mr. Braggett's inquiries, "that there was no time to send for nobody."

"But Miss Cray had my address."

"Ah! perhaps so; but she was off her head, poor dear, and couldn't think of nothing. But she remembered you, sir, to the last; for the very morning she died, she sprung up in bed and called out, 'Sigismund! Sigismund!' as loud as ever she could, and she never spoke to anybody afterwards, not one word."

"She left no message for me?"

"None, sir. I asked her the day before she went if I was to say nothing to you for her (knowing you was such friends), and all her answer was, 'I wrote to him. He's got my letter.' So I thought, perhaps, you had heard, sir."

"Not for some time past. It seems terribly sudden to me, not having heard even of her illness. Where is she buried?"

"Close by in the churchyard, sir. My little girl will go with you and show you the place, if you'd like to see it."

Mr. Braggett accepted her offer and left. When he was standing by a heap of clods they called a grave, and had dismissed the child, he drew out Miss Cray's last letter, which he carried in his pocket, and read it over.

"You tell me that I am not to call at your office again, except on business" (so it ran), "nor to send letters to your private address, lest it should come to the knowledge of your wife, and create unpleasantness between you; but I *shall* call, and I *shall* write, until I have seen Mrs. Braggett, and, if you don't take care, I will introduce myself to her and tell her the reason you have been afraid to do so."

This letter had made Mr. Braggett terribly angry at the time of reception. He had puffed and fumed, and cursed Miss Charlotte by all his gods for daring to threaten him. But he read it with different feelings now Miss Charlotte was down there, six feet beneath the ground he stood on, and he could feel only compassion for her frenzy, and resentment against himself for having excited it. As he travelled home from Hammersmith to Streatham, he was a very dejected publisher indeed.

He did not tell Mrs. Braggett the reason of his melancholy, but it affected him to that degree that he could not go to office on the following day, but stayed at home instead, to be petted and waited upon by his pretty wife, which treatment resulted in a complete cure. The next morning, therefore, he started for London as briskly as ever, and arrived at office before his usual time. A clerk, deputed to receive all messages for his master, followed him behind the ground-glass doors, with a packet of letters.

"Mr. Van Ower was here yesterday, sir. He will let you have the copy before the end of the week, and Messrs Hanleys' foreman called on particular business, and will look in today at eleven. And Mr. Ellis came to ask if there was any answer to his letter yet; and Miss Cray called, sir; and that's all."

"*Who* did you say?" cried Braggett.

"Miss Cray, sir. She waited for you above an hour, but I told her I thought you couldn't mean to come into town at all, so she went."

"Do you know what you're talking about, Hewetson? You said *Miss Cray!*"

"And I meant it, sir—Miss Charlotte Cray. Burns spoke to her as well as I."

"Good heavens!" exclaimed Mr. Braggett, turning as white as a sheet. "Go at once and send Burns to me." Burns came.

"Burns, who was the lady that called to see me yesterday?"

"Miss Cray, sir. She had a very thick veil on, and she looked so pale that I asked her if she had been ill, and she said 'Yes.' She sat in the office for over an hour, hoping you'd come in, but as you didn't, she went away again."

"Did she lift her veil?"

"Not whilst I spoke to her, sir."

"How do you know it was Miss Cray, then?"

The clerk stared. "Well, sir, we all know her pretty well by this time."

"Did you ask her name?"

"No, sir; there was no need to do it."

"You're mistaken, that's all, both you and Hewetson. It couldn't have been Miss Cray! I know for certain that she is—is—is—not in London at present. It must have been a stranger."

"It was not, indeed, sir, begging your pardon. I could tell Miss Cray anywhere, by her figure and her voice, without seeing her face. But I did see her face, and remarked how awfully pale she was—just like death, sir!"

"There! there! that will do! It's of no consequence, and you can go back to your work."

But any one who had seen Mr. Braggett, when left alone in his office, would not have said he thought the matter of no consequence. The perspiration broke out upon his forehead, although it was December, and he rocked himself backward and forward in his chair with agitation.

At last he rose hurriedly, upset his throne, and dashed through the outer premises in the face of twenty people waiting to speak to him. As soon as he could find his voice, he hailed a hansom, and drove to Hammersmith. Good Mrs. Thompson opening the door to him, thought he looked as if he had just come out of a fever.

"Lor' bless me, sir! whatever's the matter?"

"Mrs. Thompson, have you told me the truth about Miss Cray? Is she really dead?"

"*Really dead*, sir! Why, I closed her eyes, and put her in the coffin with my own hands! If she ain't dead, I don't know who is! But if you doubt my word, you'd better ask the doctor that gave the certificate for her."

"What is the doctor's name?"

"Dodson; he lives opposite."

"You must forgive my strange questions, Mrs. Thompson, but I have had a terrible dream about my poor friend, and I think I should like to talk to the doctor about her."

"Oh, very good, sir," cried the landlady, much offended. "I'm not afraid of what the doctor will tell you. She had excellent nursing and everything as she could desire, and there's nothing on my conscience on that score, so I'll wish you good morning." And with that Mrs. Thompson slammed the door in Mr. Braggett's face.

He found Dr Dodson at home.

"If I understand you rightly," said the practitioner, looking rather steadfastly in the scared face of his visitor, "you wish, as a friend of the late Miss Cray's, to see a copy of the certificate of her death? Very good, sir; here it is. She died, as you will perceive, on the twenty-fifth of November, of peritonitis. She had, I can assure you, every attention and care, but nothing could have saved her."

"You are quite sure, then, she is dead?" demanded Mr. Braggett, in a vague manner.

The doctor looked at him as if he were not quite sure if he were sane.

"If seeing a patient die, and her corpse coffined and buried, is being sure she is dead, I am in no doubt whatever about Miss Cray."

"It is very strange—most strange and unaccountable," murmured poor Mr. Braggett, in reply, as he shuffled out of the doctor's passage, and took his way back to the office.

Here, however, after an interval of rest and a strong brandy and soda, he managed to pull himself together, and to come to the conclusion that the doctor and Mrs. Thompson *could* not be mistaken, and that, consequently, the clerks *must*. He did not mention the subject again to them, however; and as the days went on, and nothing more was heard of the mysterious stranger's visit, Mr. Braggett put it altogether out of his mind.

At the end of a fortnight, however, when he was thinking of something totally different, young Hewetson remarked to him, carelessly,—

"Miss Cray was here again yesterday, sir. She walked in just as your cab had left the door."

All the horror of his first suspicions returned with double force upon the unhappy man's mind.

"Don't talk nonsense!" he gasped, angrily, as soon as he could speak. "Don't attempt to play any of your tricks on me, young man, or it will be the worse for you, I can tell you."

"Tricks, sir!" stammered the clerk. "I don't know what you are alluding to. I am only telling you the truth. You have always desired me to be most particular in letting you know the names of the people who call in your absence, and I thought I was only doing my duty in making a point of ascertaining them——"

"Yes, yes! Hewetson, of course," replied Mr Braggett, passing his handkerchief over his brow, "and you are quite right in following my directions as closely as possible; only—in this case you are completely mistaken, and it is the second time you have committed the error."

"Mistaken!"

"Yes!—as mistaken as it is possible for a man to be! Miss Cray *could* not have called at this office yesterday."

"But she did, sir."

"Am I labouring under some horrible nightmare?" exclaimed the publisher, "or are we playing at cross purposes? Can you mean the Miss Cray I mean?"

"I am speaking of Miss Charlotte Cray, sir, the author of 'Sweet Gwendoline,'—the lady who has undertaken so much of our compilation the last two years, and who has a long nose, and wears her hair in curls. I never knew there was another Miss Cray; but if there are two, that is the one I mean."

"Still I *cannot* believe it, Hewetson, for the Miss Cray who has been associated with our firm died on the twenty-fifth of last month."

"*Died*, sir! Is Miss Cray dead? Oh, it can't be! It's some humbugging trick that's been played upon you, for I'd swear she was in this room yesterday afternoon, as full of life as she's ever been since I knew her. She didn't talk much, it's true, for she seemed in a hurry to be off again, but she had got on the same dress and bonnet she was in here last, and she made herself as much at home in the office as she ever did. Besides," continued Hewetson, as though suddenly remembering something, "she left a note for you, sir."

"A note! Why did you not say so before?"

"It slipped my memory when you began to doubt my word in that way, sir. But you'll find it in the bronze vase. She told me to tell you she had placed it there."

Mr Braggett made a dash at the vase, and found the three-cornered note as he had been told. Yes! it was Charlotte's handwriting, or the facsimile of it, there was no doubt of that; and his hands shook so he could hardly open the paper. It contained these words:

"You tell me that I am not to call at your office again, except on business, nor to send letters to your private address, lest it should come to the knowledge of your wife, and create unpleasantness between you; but I *shall* call, and I *shall* write until I have seen Mrs. Braggett, and if you don't take care I will introduce myself to her, and tell her the reason you have been afraid to do so."

Precisely the same words, in the same writing of the letter he still carried in his breast-pocket, and which no mortal eyes but his and hers had ever seen. As the unhappy man sat gazing at the opened note, his whole body shook as if he were attacked by ague.

"It is Miss Cray's handwriting, isn't it, sir?"

"It looks like it, Hewetson, but it cannot be. I tell you it is an impossibility! Miss Cray died last month, and I have seen not only her grave, but the doctor and nurse who attended her in her last illness. It is folly, then, to suppose either that she called here or wrote that letter."

"Then *who could it have been*, sir?" said Hewetson, attacked with a sudden terror in his turn.

"That is impossible for me to say; but should the lady call again, you had better ask her boldly for her name and address."

"I'd rather you'd depute the office to anybody but me, sir," replied the clerk, as he hastily backed out of the room.

Mr. Braggett, dying with suspense and conjecture, went through his business as best he could, and hurried home to Violet Villa.

There he found that his wife had been spending the day with a friend, and only entered the house a few minutes before himself.

"Siggy, dear!" she commenced, as soon as he joined her in the drawing-room after dinner; "I really think we should have the fastenings and bolts of this house looked to. Such a funny thing happened whilst I was out this afternoon. Ellen has just been telling me about it."

"What sort of a thing, dear?"

"Well, I left home as early as twelve, you know, and told the servants I shouldn't be back until dinner-time; so they were all enjoying themselves in the kitchen, I suppose, when cook told Ellen she heard a footstep in the drawing-room. Ellen thought at first it must be cook's fancy, because she was sure the front door was fastened; but when they listened, they all heard the noise together, so she ran upstairs, and what on earth do you think she saw?"

"How can I guess, my dear?"

"Why, a lady, seated in this very room, as if she was waiting for somebody. She was oldish, Ellen says, and had a very white face, with long curls hanging down each side of it; and she wore a blue bonnet with white feathers, and a long black cloak, and—"

"Emily, Emily! Stop! You don't know what you're talking about. That girl is a fool: you must send her away. That is, how could the lady have got in if the door was closed? Good heavens! you'll all drive me mad between you with your folly!" exclaimed Mr. Braggett, as he threw himself back in his chair, with an exclamation that sounded very like a groan.

Pretty Mrs. Braggett was offended. What had she said or done that her husband should doubt her word? She tossed her head in indignation, and remained silent. If Mr. Braggett wanted any further information, he would have to apologise.

"Forgive me, darling," he said, after a long pause. "I don't think I'm very well this evening, but your story seemed to upset me."

"I don't see why it should upset you," returned Mrs Braggett. "If strangers are allowed to come prowling about the house in this way, we shall be robbed some day, and then you'll say I should have told you of it."

"Wouldn't she—this person — give her name?"

"Oh! I'd rather say no more about it. You had better ask Ellen."

"No, Emily! I'd rather hear it from you."

"Well, don't interrupt me again, then. When Ellen saw the woman seated here, she asked her her name and business at once, but she gave no answer, and only sat and stared at her. And so Ellen, feeling very uncomfortable, had just turned round to call up cook, when the woman got up, and dashed past her like a flash of lightning, and they saw nothing more of her!"

"Which way did she leave the house?"

"Nobody knows any more than how she came in. The servants declare the hall-door was neither opened nor shut—but, of course, it must have been. She was a tall gaunt woman, Ellen says, about fifty, and she's sure her hair was dyed. She must have come to steal something, and that's why I say we ought to have the house made more secure. Why, Siggy! Siggy! what's the matter? Here, Ellen! Jane! come, quick, some of you! Your master's fainted!"

And, sure enough, the repeated shocks and horrors of the day had had such an effect upon poor Mr. Braggett, that for a moment he did lose all consciousness of what surrounded him. He was thankful to take advantage of the Christmas holidays, to run over to Paris with his wife, and try to forget, in the many marvels of that city, the awful fear that fastened upon him at the mention of anything connected with home. He might be enjoying himself to the top of his bent; but directly the remembrance of Charlotte Cray crossed his mind, all sense of enjoyment vanished, and he trembled at the mere thought of returning to his business, as a child does when sent to bed in the dark.

He tried to hide the state of his feelings from Mrs Braggett, but she was too sharp for him. The simple, blushing Emily Primrose had developed, under the influence of the matrimonial forcing-frame, into a good watch-dog, and nothing escaped her notice.

Left to her own conjecture, she attributed his frequent moods of dejection to the existence of some other woman, and became jealous accordingly. If Siggy did not love her, why had he married her? She felt certain there was some other horrid creature who had engaged his affections and would not leave him alone, even now that he was her own lawful property. And to find out who the 'horrid creature' was became Mrs. Emily's constant idea. When she had found out, she meant to give her a piece of her mind, never fear! Meanwhile Mr. Braggett's evident distaste to returning to business only served to increase his wife's suspicions. A clear conscience, she argued, would know no fear. So they were not a happy couple, as they set their faces once more towards England. Mr. Braggett's dread of re-entering his office amounted almost to terror, and Mrs. Braggett, putting this and that together, resolved that she would fathom the mystery, if it lay in feminine *finesse* to do so. She did not whisper a word of her intentions to dear Siggy, you may be sure of that! She worked after the manner of her amiable sex, like a cat in the dark, or a worm boring through the earth, and appearing on the surface when least expected.

So poor Mr. Braggett brought her home again, heavy at heart indeed, but quite ignorant that any designs were being made against him. I think he would have given a thousand pounds to be spared the duty of attending office the day after his arrival. But it was necessary, and he went, like a publisher and a Briton. But Mrs. Emily had noted his trepidation and his fears, and laid her plans accordingly. She had never been asked to enter those mysterious precincts, the house of business. Mr. Braggett had not thought it necessary that her blooming loveliness should be made acquainted with its dingy, dusty accessories, but she meant to see them for herself today. So she waited till he had left Violet Villa ten minutes, and then she dressed and followed him by the next train to London.

Mr. Sigismund Braggett meanwhile had gone on his way, as people go to a dentist, determined to do what was right, but with an indefinite sort of idea that he might never come out of it alive. He dreaded to hear what might have happened in his absence, and he delayed his arrival at the office for half-an-hour, by walking there instead of taking a cab as usual, in order to put off the evil moment. As he entered the place, however, he saw at a glance that his efforts were vain, and that something had occurred. The customary formality and precision of the office were upset, and the clerks, instead of bending over their ledgers, or attending to the demands of business, were all huddled together at one end whispering and gesticulating to each other. But as soon as the publisher appeared, a dead silence fell upon the group, and they only stared at him with an air of horrid mystery.

"What is the matter now?" he demanded, angrily, for like most men when in a fright which they are ashamed to exhibit, Mr. Sigismund Braggett tried to cover his want of courage by bounce.

The young man called Hewetson advanced towards him, with a face the colour of ashes, and pointed towards the ground-glass doors dumbly.

"What do you mean? Can't you speak? What's come to the lot of you, that you are neglecting my business in this fashion to make fools of yourselves?"

"If you please, sir, she's in there."

Mr Braggett started back as if he'd been shot. But still he tried to have it out.

"*She!* Who's *she?*"

"Miss Cray, sir."

"Haven't I told you already that's a lie."

"Will you judge for yourself, Mr Braggett?" said a grey-haired man, stepping forward. "I was on the stairs myself just now when Miss Cray passed me, and I have no doubt whatever but that you will find her in your private room, however much the reports that have lately reached you may seem against the probability of such a thing."

Mr Braggett's teeth chattered in his head as he advanced to the ground-glass doors, through the panes of one of which there was a little peephole to ascertain if the room were occupied or not. He stooped and looked in. At the table, with her back towards him, was seated the well-known figure of Charlotte Cray. He recognised at once the long black mantle in which she was wont to drape her gaunt figure—the blue bonnet, with its dejected-looking, uncurled feather—the lank curls which rested on her shoulders—and the black leather bag, with a steel clasp, which she always carried in her hand. It was the embodiment of Charlotte Cray, he had no doubt of that; but how could he reconcile the fact of her being there with the damp clods he had seen piled upon her grave, with the certificate of death, and the doctor's and landlady's assertion that they had watched her last moments?

At last he prepared, with desperate energy, to turn the handle of the door. At that moment the attention of the more frivolous of the clerks was directed from his actions by the entrance of an uncommonly pretty woman at the other end of the outer office. Such a lovely creature as this seldom brightened the gloom of their dusty abiding-place. Lilies, roses, and carnations vied with each other in her complexion, whilst the sunniest of locks, and the brightest of blue eyes, lent her face a girlish charm not easily described. What could this fashionably-attired Venus want in their house of business?

"Is Mr. Braggett here? I am Mrs. Braggett. Please show me in to him immediately."

They glanced at the ground-glass doors of the inner office. They had already closed behind the manly form of their employer.

"This way, madam," one said, deferentially, as he escorted her to the presence of Mr. Braggett.

Meanwhile, Sigismund had opened the portals of the Temple of Mystery, and with trembling knees entered it. The figure in the chair did not stir at his approach. He stood at the door irresolute. What should he do or say?

"Charlotte," he whispered.

Still she did not move.

At that moment his wife entered.

"Oh, Sigismund!" cried Mrs Emily, reproachfully, "I knew you were keeping something from me, and now I've caught you in the very act. Who is this lady, and what is her name? I shall refuse to leave the room until I know it."

At the sound of her rival's voice, the woman in the chair rose quickly to her feet and confronted them. Yes! there was Charlotte Cray, precisely similar to what she had appeared in life, only with an uncertainty and vagueness about the lines of the familiar features that made them ghastly.

She stood there, looking Mrs Emily full in the face, but only for a moment, for, even as she gazed, the lineaments grew less and less distinct, with the shape of the figure that supported them, until, with a crash, the apparition seemed to fall in and disappear, and the place that had known her was filled with empty air.

"Where is she gone?" exclaimed Mrs Braggett, in a tone of utter amazement.

"Where is *who* gone?" repeated Mr. Braggett, hardly able to articulate from fear.

"The lady in the chair!"

"There was no one there except in your own imagination. It was my great-coat that you mistook for a figure," returned her husband hastily, as he threw the article in question over the back of the armchair.

"But how could that have been?" said his pretty wife, rubbing her eyes. "How could I think a coat had eyes, and hair, and features? I am sure I saw a woman seated there, and that she rose and stared at me. Siggy! tell me it was true. It seems so incomprehensible that I should have been mistaken."

"You must question your own sense. You see that the room is empty now, except for ourselves, and you know that no one has left it. If you like to search under the table, you can."

"Ah! now, Siggy, you are laughing at me, because you know that would be folly. But there was certainly some one here—only, where can she have disappeared to?"

"Suppose we discuss the matter at a more convenient season," replied Mr. Braggett, as he drew his wife's arm through his arm. "Hewetson! you will be able to tell Mr Hume that he was mistaken. Say, also, that I shall not be back in the office today. I am not so strong as I thought I was, and feel quite unequal to business. Tell him to come out to Streatham this evening with my letters, and I will talk with him there."

What passed at that interview was never disclosed; but pretty Mrs Braggett was much rejoiced, a short time afterwards, by her husband telling her that he had resolved to resign his active share of the business, and devote the rest of his life to her and Violet Villa. He would have no more occasion, therefore, to visit the office, and be exposed to the temptation of spending four or five hours out of every twelve away from her side. For, though Mrs Emily had arrived at the conclusion that the momentary glimpse she caught of a lady in Siggy's office must have been a delusion, she was not quite satisfied by his assertions that she would never have found a more tangible cause for her jealousy.

But Sigismund Braggett knew more than he chose to tell Mrs. Emily. He knew that what she had witnessed was no delusion, but a reality; and that Charlotte Cray had carried out her dying determination, to call at his office and his private residence, *until she had seen his wife!*

THE WRAITH OF BARNJUM
by
F. Ansty
1879

I always detested Barnjum; everything the fellow said and did jarred upon me somehow in an absolutely indescribable manner, and I have since learnt that there was something about me which inspired Barnjum with an utterly unreasonable aversion.

And yet, in spite of all this, with that strangely irresistible attraction which so often embitters a mutual antipathy, we were continually seeking one another's society with an ever unsatiated zest.

So essentially unlike were we in every respect—I, with my innate culture and refinement, my almost fastidious exclusiveness in the choice of associates; he, a great red coarse brute, whose conversation was characterised by nothing more attractive than unflattering bluntness and commonplace profanity, that I often asked him with a genuine wish to be informed—what had I in common with him? It was his proudest boast that he invariably called a spade a spade; this I merely mention to show the kind of man he was, and to convey some idea of the intolerable burden of our ill-assorted companionship.

At last, one ill-starred day, we agreed to go on a walking tour in North Wales together (I hardly know why, but possibly we thought it would annoy one another), and in less than a week had started upon a journey from which but one of us was fated to return!

I pass by the painful details of the first few days of that unhappy tour; I will say nothing of Barnjum's sordid animalism, of his consummate selfishness, his ultra-bucolic indifference to the allurements of nature, or even of the mean way in which he contrived to let me in for railway-tickets and hotel-bills; for I wish to state the facts as impartially as possible, and shrink from being suspected of any attempt to prejudice the reader unduly in my favour.

I pass then to the day, when my disgust, so long pent up, so slightly concealed, culminated in one grand outburst of a not ignoble indignation—to the hour when I summoned moral courage to sever the bonds which linked us so unequally, and which we both so thoroughly loathed.

I remember it so well—that brilliant June morning when we left the Temperance Hotel, Doldwyddlm, and scaled in sulky silence the craggy heights of Cader Idris, which I believe still overhang that picturesque village, while, as we ascended, an ever-changing, ever-widening panorama unrolled itself before my delighted eyes.

The air up there was keen and bracing, and I recollect that I could not repress an æsthetic shudder at the repulsively crude tone which Barnjum's nose was acquiring under its influence.

I mentioned it as a friend, when he retorted with the brutal personality which formed so strong an ingredient of his character.

"Hang it, Buster" (my name is Buster), he said, with his accustomed profanity; "if you could see yourself now in that suit of yours and that hat, you'd let my nose alone."

I replied with a sarcasm that was, I felt afterwards, a little too crushing, that I had every intention of doing so; and he remarked offensively enough that no one could help his nose getting red, but that any man in my position could at least *dress* like a gentleman.

I took no notice of this insult—a Buster can afford to pass them by (indeed I find it actually cheaper to do so), and I flatter myself that my dress is distinguished by a studied looseness and carelessness which are not wholly destitute of the artistically picturesque.

We presently found ourselves skirting the edge of a huge chasm whose steep sides sloped sheer down into the slate-blue waters of the lake below; the view from where we stood was magnificent, to our right were the Peaks of Dolgelly and the plain of Capel Curig, below were sun-lit waters with a dancing fleet of herring-boats, and there over on the left sparkled the falls of Y-Dydd. It was a view which even the most ardent sightseers have hitherto managed to miss, but that only requires to be known to gain a world-wide celebrity. As my eye took it all in, I longed to say something worthy of the occasion, and being possessed of a considerable fund of delicately dried humour, I busied myself in the construction of a remark which, while blending one or more of the quaint names of the vicinity into one sentence, should yet distinctly suggest an entirely different impression, at the same time, even to my dull-witted companion.

Some men have an especial talent for this species of intellectual exercise.

But Barnjum anticipated me: "*You* ought to live up here, Buster," he said, "on the top. You were made for this old mountain."

I was not displeased, for, Londoner as I am, I love the heights with all a poet's enthusiasm.

"Perhaps I was," I said; "but why do you think so?"

"Why," he said, with his odious grin, "this is Cader Idris, ain't it? and you're a *cad awry dressed*, ain't you?—'Cader Idrissed,' don't you see?" (he was dastard enough to explain)—"that's why."

He had been laboriously leading up to this for the last ten minutes. I can conscientiously declare that it was not the personal outrage that roused me; but a paltry verbal quibble like that, uttered amidst such scenery and at that altitude, required a protest in the name of indignant nature, and I protested accordingly, though with an imprudent impetuosity which I cannot bring myself to approve even now.

He happened to be standing on the brink of the abyss, and had just turned his back upon me, when, with a passionate thrust of my right foot, I launched him into space with the chuckle at his unhallowed jest yet hovering upon his lips. I am aware that it was a liberty which, under ordinary circumstances, even the licence of a life-long friendship would hardly have excused, but I felt it due to myself to let him see plainly that I desired our acquaintanceship to cease from that moment, and a more delicate hint would have been thrown away upon him.

I waited till the dull metallic clang of his head, as it repeatedly struck upon the rocks in his descent, had died away on the breeze, and then I slowly and thoughtfully retraced my steps and left a spot which was already becoming associated with memories the reverse of pleasurable.

I took the next up-train, and succeeded in dismissing all thoughts of Barnjum from my mind till I reached town; if I allowed myself to dwell upon the subject at all, it was to experience a certain relief in the reflection that we understood one another at last. But when I had paid my cab, and was ringing the bell before my lodgings, the driver called me back: "Beg pardon, sir," he said hoarsely, "but you've bin and left something white in the cab."

I turned and looked in; there, grinning at me from the interior over the folding doors of the hansom, was the wraith of Barnjum.

I had presence of mind to reward the man for his honesty and go upstairs to my rooms with as little noise as possible; Barnjum's ghost followed me in and sat down coolly before the fire in my armchair, when I took the opportunity to examine the apparition thoroughly.

It was quite the conventional ghost, filmy, transparent and shadowy enough, and a very tolerable likeness of Barnjum; and before I retired, I had thrown both my boots and the contents of my book-case through the thing without appearing to do more than temporarily inconvenience it, which convinced me that it was a being from another world.

Its choice of garments certainly struck me as unusual, however, for, while I cheerfully allow that it is becoming, if not desirable, for apparitions to assume robes of some description, Barnjum's ghost rejoiced in a combination of costume which I have never seen before or since either on the person of spirit or mortal.

It wore that evening, to the best of my recollection, striped pantaloons, a surplice, and a cocked hat, but it subsequently went through such rapid and eccentric changes of costume that I can only explain them on the supposition that there is a vast supernatural theatrical wardrobe somewhere, and that Barnjum's ghost had the run of it.

Before I had been in very long, my landlady came up and saw it, when she objected very strongly, declaring that she wouldn't have no such things about her house, and if I must keep ghosts, I had better go somewhere else; but I pacified her at last by representing that I was only taking care of it for a friend.

When she had gone I sat up till late, thinking calmly over my position and the complications that might ensue from it.

And here I could, of course, if I chose, harrow the reader's feelings and work upon his sympathies by a graphic description of my terror, or an elaborate analysis of my remorse; but I prefer the less effective but more straightforward course of stating nothing but the plain facts, and of describing nothing but my actual feelings. My first impression had not unnaturally been that it was all nerves or indigestion, but I soon saw the improbability of a cabman being plagued by a digestion, or a landlady by a morbid excess of imagination, and admitted to myself that it was a real ghost and would probably continue to haunt me for the rest of my natural life.

I was disgusted with such an exhibition of low malice on Barnjum's part, pardonable perhaps in a Christmas annual with a full-page illustration, but an anachronism in real life and the height of summer; still I brought common sense to bear upon the subject, and told myself philosophically that I had made my ghost and must live with it.

At the worst Barnjum in the spirit was a decided improvement upon Barnjum in the flesh, and I was glad to find that the spirit was not a talking variety and consequently unlikely to tell tales; and luckily for me, as Barnjum was quite unknown about town— his only relative being an aunt at Camberwell—it was improbable that any suspicion would be excited by chance recognition in the circle to which I belonged. It would be folly to shut one's eyes to the fact that it might require considerable nerve to re-enter society in the company of a fancifully attired apparition which nobody would know anything about. Society would sneer perhaps at first, and make remarks, but then I was not without tact and knowledge of the world, and was well aware that men have overcome far more formidable objects to social success.

So that, instead of giving way to unreasonable panic, I took the more manly course of determining to live it down, though, alas! I was doomed to find fate too strong for me in this respect, and to see myself bitterly punished for my indiscretion. When I went out next morning after breakfast, Barnjum's ghost came too and followed me all down St. James's Street, much to my embarrassment, and in fact for weeks after it scarcely ever left me, rendering me the innocent victim of mingled aversion and curiosity.

At first I affected to be unaware of anything unusual, and ascribed it to other people's diseased fancy, but, as the whole town soon began to ring with the story, this dissimulation became too difficult to sustain, so I gave out that it was an artfully contrived piece of spectral mechanism, of which I was the inventor and sole patentee.

This gained me no small reputation in the scientific world, a result which lasted till Maskelyne and Cooke grew envious and declared that they knew the secret of it, and could manufacture a much better spectral machine themselves, which they presently did.

Then I admitted in confidence to two of the aristocracy that it was a bonâ-fide apparition, and that I rather liked such things about me. This frankness afforded me a temporary salvation, for the story went the round of the Pall-Mall clubs and Belgravian boudoirs till I found myself a lion of the largest size.

I was asked out everywhere on the tacit understanding that I was to bring the ghost too, and Barnjum's ghost, as all of gentle birth who read this will well remember, appeared at all the best houses in town for the remainder of the season, while, in the autumn, several wealthy people of the Manchester School asked me down for some shooting, solely, I honestly believe, in the hope that they would persuade the ghost to remain with them permanently and impart the necessary air of ancestral mystery and legend to their bran-new palaces; and I devoutly wish they had. But the novelty soon wore off—too soon in fact—for, fickle as society is, I have no hesitation in asserting that we ought to have lasted it at least another season, if Barnjum's ghost had not persisted in making itself so ridiculously cheap that society was as sick of it as I was myself in a fortnight.

And from that time I saw only the reverse of the medal; I soon noticed that the phantom had a trick of illuminating itself with a bilious green light in the evenings, which rendered it a depressing companion for any one inclined to low spirits; I still saw a good deal of it, though it occasionally absented itself for days together, which only made me more uneasy however than while I had it under my eye. So great was my dread that the people at the Polytechnic, or some one else who understands spectres, should get hold of it, and perhaps compel it to compromise me, that I must have spent pounds in advertisements about it.

I had to leave the rooms where I had been so comfortable; my landlady said the street was blocked up by a mob of the lowest description from seven till twelve every evening, and she really could not put up with it any longer.

I found that this was owing to Barnjum's ghost getting out upon the roof every night after dark and playing the fool among the chimney-pots, which led to my being indicted five times for committing a common nuisance by obstructing the thoroughfare, and once for collecting an unlawful assembly; I spent all my spare cash in fines.

It is true that there were portraits of us both in the illustrated weekly papers, but this was small comfort, and did not blind me to the fact that Barnjum's ghost was slowly but surely ruining me both in fortune and reputation.

Shortly after this it followed me to the Underground Railway, and there behaved in a manner that very justly incensed the authorities, and led to a lawsuit which made a nine days' sensation in the legal world.

I refer to the celebrated case of "The Metropolitan District Railway v. Buster," in which the important principle was once for all decided by the court that no railway company is bound by the terms of its contract to carry ghosts, spectres, or any other supernatural beings, and that the company can exact a heavy penalty from passengers infringing its regulations in this respect.

This was of course a decision against me, and carried heavy costs, which my private fortune was just sufficient to meet.

But Barnjum's ghost was alienating me from society also, for at one of the best balls of the season, at a house where I had just succeeded with infinite pains in establishing a precarious footing, that miserable phantom ruined me for ever by executing a shadowy but unspeakably offensive species of cancan between the dances. I apologised to my hostess, feeling indirectly responsible for its behaviour, but the affair got into the weekly society journals, and she never either forgave or recognised me again.

It was about this time, too, that the committee at my club—the most exclusive in London—requested me to resign, intimating that, in introducing a spirit of disreputable character amongst them (it had followed me into the building arrayed in a highland costume and a tall hat), I had abused the privileges of membership.

I was at the bar, but no respectable firm of solicitors would employ a man who had such an unprofessional thing as a phantom about his chambers, so that I soon found myself obliged to throw up my profession, and I had no sooner changed my last sovereign than I was summoned for keeping a ghost without a licence!

Some men would have given up in despair there and then, but I was made of sterner stuff; besides, an idea had occurred to me by which I might possibly turn the tables upon my shadowy persecutor: it was this—Barnjum's ghost had ruined me, but why should I not endeavour to turn an honest penny by Barnjum's ghost? It was genuine—it was in some respects original—there were valuable moral lessons to be learnt from it, and though it had long failed to attract in town, I saw no reason why it should not make a great hit in the provinces.

So that in a very short time I had made all the necessary preliminary arrangements for running Barnjum's ghost on a short provincial tour, and had decided to open at Tenby in South Wales.

I took every precaution, travelling by night and keeping indoors all day, lest the shade, which was deplorably destitute of all professional pride, should get about and exhibit itself beforehand for nothing; so when it first burst upon a Welsh audience from the platform of the Assembly Rooms, Tenby, no ghost could have been more enthusiastically received, and for the first and last time I felt positively proud of it.

But after the applause had subsided there was an awkward pause. It had not occurred to me that it would be necessary to say anything in particular during the exhibition, beyond the customary assurance that there was no deception and no concealed mechanism, which I could give with a good conscience; but it seems that the audience had expected a comic duologue, with incidental music and dances.

This I was wholly unequal to, even supposing Barnjum's ghost had consented to play up to me, which I could scarcely, under the circumstances, expect it to do. As it was, it did nothing at all except grimace at the audience and make an idiotic fool of itself and me, which soon exhausted and disgusted them. I could have made a far deeper impression upon them with an ordinary magic lantern; and at last, goaded to madness, they rose as one man, hurled chairs through the ghost at me, and wrecked the stage before leaving in a whirlwind of righteous indignation.

It was all over. I was a ruined man, and my weak trust in the humanity of a spectre had put the finishing touch to my misfortune. I paid for the smashed windows and broken chairs, and took a third- lass ticket to London that night, with feelings that can neither be envied nor described.

It was Christmas Eve, and I was sitting gloomily in my shabby Bloomsbury lodgings, watching, with a bitter loathing, Barnjum's ghost, arrayed in a Roman toga and top boots, gliding aimlessly about the horsehair furniture. I was completely and utterly miserable, and bitterly did I now repent my conduct in parting with Barnjum so abruptly by the bleak cliff side, that bright June morning, six short months ago. Nemesis, in the form of a weak-minded but remorseless phantom, had hounded me down to poverty and ruin. I felt so low-spirited just then that I had serious thoughts of seeking out a police-inspector, and sobbing out the truth upon his breast, from which I infer that my liver must have been very much out of order. I cursed my fate, and the day I was born. I cursed Barnjum and his insidious shade, when suddenly there came a tap at the door.

It opened, and the figure of Barnjum, as he had appeared in the flesh, strode solemnly in. "Villain, cowardly villain!" was its first observation.

"So long as your—your proprietor contented himself with one apparition," I said, with a sort of desperate calm, "I bore it—I did not enjoy it, but I endured it. But *two* ghosts is really carrying it too far . . . It is more than any one man's fair allowance. I defy you both . . . I will find means to escape you . . . I will leave the world!" I cried, growing excited. "Other people can be ghosts as well as you. . . . One step more and I blow my brains out."

There was no firearm of any description in the house, but I meant what I said.

"You couldn't do better," said the figure; "but it happens I'm not a ghost. I'm alive; and to come back to the point—scoundrel!"

"If you *are* alive," I said, divided between relief and alarm, "will you have the goodness to tell me what right you have to that apparition? It's been annoying me very much."

"I know nothing about it," he said; "but I hope it will go on annoying you. It serves you right."

I appealed to his better feelings.

"It is sad," I said, "to meet again like this; we parted, I know, not on the best of terms, but it is ridiculous to cherish an old grudge all this time. Don't you see the absurdity of it yourself?"

But he didn't.

"It is Christmas Eve, Barnjum," I continued; "Christmas Eve. At this hour thousands of throbbing human hearts are speeding the cheap but genial Christmas card to those of their relations they consider at all likely to respond with a turkey; the imaginative costermonger is investing soiled evergreens with a purely fictitious value, and the cheery publican is sending the member of his village goose-club away rejoicing with a shot-distended bird and a bottle of poisonous port. Hear my appeal: if I have wronged you, I have suffered. That detestable thing has poisoned my happiest hours, and clouded my prosperity at the zenith of its brightness; it has been, in short, the deuce of a nuisance! I ask you, as a man, as an individual, to call it off. You can do it if you choose, you know you can. I'd do it for *you!*"

Barnjum hesitated a moment; some waits outside struck up 'Silver Threads among the Gold,' and as he listened his face twitched—he burst into tears; I had conquered.

"Be it so!" he said between his sobs; and then turning to the ghost, "Here—you—what's your name? Avaunt!—D'ye hear?—Hook it!"

To my joy it obeyed him immediately; for, as he spoke, it gave way all over, and shrivelling up into a sort of cobweb, was drawn by the draught into the fireplace and carried up the chimney.

THE OPEN DOOR
by
Margaret O. Wilson Oliphant
1882

I took the house of Brentwood on my return from India in 18—, for the temporary accommodation of my family, until I could find a permanent home for them. It had many advantages which made it peculiarly appropriate. It was within reach of Edinburgh; and my boy Roland, whose education had been considerably neglected, could go in and out to school, which was thought to be better for him than either leaving home altogether or staying there always with a tutor. The first of these expedients would have seemed preferable to me; the second commended itself to his mother. The doctor, like a judicious man, took the midway between. "Put him on his pony, and let him ride into the Academy every morning; it will do him all the good in the world," Dr. Simson said; "and when it is bad weather, there is the train." His mother accepted this solution of the difficulty more easily than I could have hoped; and our pale-faced boy, who had never known anything more invigorating than Simla, began to encounter the brisk breezes of the North in the subdued severity of the month of May. Before the time of the vacation in July we had the satisfaction of seeing him begin to acquire something of the brown and ruddy complexion of his schoolfellows. The English system did not commend itself to Scotland in these days. There was no little Eton at Fettes; nor do I think, if there had been, that a genteel exotic of that class would have tempted either my wife or me. The lad was doubly precious to us, being the only one left us of many; and he was fragile in body, we believed, and deeply sensitive in mind. To keep him at home, and yet to send him to school,—to combine the advantages of the two systems,—seemed to be everything that could be desired. The two girls also found at Brentwood everything they wanted. They were near enough to Edinburgh to have masters and lessons as many as they required for completing that never-ending education which the young people seem to require nowadays. Their mother married me when she was younger than Agatha; and I should like to see them improve upon their mother! I myself was then no more than twenty-five,—an age at which I see the young fellows now groping about them, with no notion what they are going to do with their lives. However; I suppose every generation has a conceit of itself which elevates it, in its own opinion, above that which comes after it.

Brentwood stands on that fine and wealthy slope of country— one of the richest in Scotland—which lies between the Pentland Hills and the Firth. In clear weather you could see the blue gleam—like a bent bow, embracing the wealthy fields and scattered houses—of the great estuary on one side of you, and on the other the blue heights, not gigantic like those we had been used to, but just high enough for all the glories of the atmosphere, the play of clouds, and sweet reflections, which give to a hilly country an interest and a charm which nothing else can emulate. Edinburgh, with its two lesser heights—the Castle and the Calton Hill—its spires and towers piercing through the smoke, and Arthur's Seat lying crouched behind, like a guardian no longer very needful, taking his repose beside the well-beloved charge, which is now, so to speak, able to take care of itself without him— lay at our right hand. From the lawn and drawing-room windows we could see all these varieties of landscape. The colour was sometimes a little chilly, but sometimes, also, as animated and full of vicissitude as a drama. I was never tired of it. Its colour and freshness revived the eyes which had grown weary of arid plains and blazing skies. It was always cheery, and fresh, and full of repose.

The village of Brentwood lay almost under the house, on the other side of the deep little ravine, down which a stream—which ought to have been a lovely, wild, and frolicsome little river— flowed between its rocks and trees. The river, like so many in that district, had, however, in its earlier life been sacrificed to trade, and was grimy with paper-making. But this did not affect our pleasure in it so much as I have known it to affect other streams. Perhaps our water was more rapid; perhaps less clogged with dirt and refuse. Our side of the dell was charmingly *accidenté*, and clothed with fine trees, through which various paths wound down to the river-side and to the village bridge which crossed the stream. The village lay in the hollow, and climbed, with very prosaic houses, the other side. Village architecture does not flourish in Scotland. The blue slates and the grey stone are sworn foes to the picturesque; and though I do not, for my own part, dislike the interior of an old-fashioned pewed and galleried church, with its little family settlements on all sides, the square box outside, with its bit of a spire like a handle to lift it by, is not an improvement to the landscape. Still a cluster of houses on differing elevations, with scraps of garden coming in between, a hedgerow with clothes laid out to dry, the opening of a street with its rural sociability, the women at their doors, the slow wagon lumbering along, gives a centre to the landscape. It was cheerful to look at, and convenient in a hundred ways. Within ourselves we had walks in plenty, the glen being always beautiful in all its phases, whether the woods were green in the spring or ruddy in the autumn. In the park which surrounded the house were the ruins of the former mansion of Brentwood, a much smaller and less important house than the solid Georgian edifice which we inhabited. The ruins were picturesque, however, and gave importance to the place. Even we, who were but temporary tenants, felt a vague pride in them, as if they somehow reflected a certain consequence upon ourselves. The old building had the remains of a tower, an indistinguishable mass of mason-work, over-grown with ivy; and the shells of walls attached to this were half filled up with soil. I had never examined it closely, I am ashamed to say. There was a large room, or what had been a large room, with the lower part of the windows still existing, on the principal floor, and underneath other windows, which were perfect, though half filled up with fallen soil, and waving with a wild growth of brambles and chance growths of all kinds. This was the oldest part of all. At a little distance were some very commonplace and disjointed fragments of building, one of them suggesting a certain pathos by its very commonness and the complete wreck which it showed. This was the end of a low gable, a bit of grey wall, all incrusted with lichens, in which was a common doorway. Probably it had been a servants' entrance, a backdoor, or opening into what are called "the offices" in Scotland. No offices remained to be entered,—pantry and kitchen had all been swept out of being; but there stood the doorway open and vacant, free to all the winds, to the rabbits, and every wild creature. It struck my eye, the first time I went to Brentwood, like a melancholy comment upon a life that was over. A door that led to nothing,—closed once, perhaps, with anxious care, bolted and guarded, now void of any meaning. It impressed me, I remember, from the first; so perhaps it may be said that my mind was prepared to attach to it an importance which nothing justified.

The summer was a very happy period of repose for us all. The warmth of Indian suns was still in our veins. It seemed to us that we could never have enough of the greenness, the dewiness, the freshness of the northern landscape. Even its mists were pleasant to us, taking all the fever out of us, and pouring in vigour and refreshment. In autumn we followed the fashion of the time, and went away for change which we did not in the least require. It was when the family had settled down for the winter, when the days were short and dark, and the rigorous reign of frost upon us, that the incidents occurred which alone could justify me in intruding upon the world my private affairs. These incidents were, however, of so curious a character, that I hope my inevitable references to my own family and pressing personal interests will meet with a general pardon.

I was absent in London when these events began. In London an old Indian plunges back into the interests with which all his previous life has been associated, and meets old friends at every step. I had been circulating among some half-dozen of these,—enjoying the return to my former life in shadow, though I had been so thankful in substance to throw it aside,—and had missed some of my home letters, what with going down from Friday to Monday to old Benbow's place in the country, and stopping on the way back to dine and sleep at Sellar's and to take a look into Cross's stables, which occupied another day. It is never safe to miss one's letters. In this transitory life, as the Prayer-book says, how can one ever be certain what is going to happen? All was well at home. I knew exactly (I thought) what they would have to say to me: "The weather has been so fine, that Roland has not once gone by train, and he enjoys the ride beyond anything." "Dear papa, be sure that you don't forget anything, but bring us so-and-so, and so-and-so,"—a list as long as my arm. Dear girls and dearer mother! I would not for the world have forgotten their commissions, or lost their little letters, for all the Benbows and Crosses in the world.

But I was confident in my home-comfort and peacefulness. When I got back to my club, however, three or four letters were lying for one, upon some of which I noticed the "immediate," "urgent," which old-fashioned people and anxious people still believe will influence the post-office and quicken the speed of the mails. I was about to open one of these, when the club porter brought me two telegrams, one of which, he said, had arrived the night before. I opened, as was to be expected, the last first, and this was what I read: "Why don't you come or answer? For God's sake, come. He is much worse." This was a thunderbolt to fall upon a man's head who had one only son, and he the light of his eyes! The other telegram, which I opened with hands trembling so much that I lost time by my haste, was to much the same purport: "No better; doctor afraid of brain-fever. Calls for you day and night. Let nothing detain you." The first thing I did was to look up the time-tables to see if there was any way of getting off sooner than by the night-train, though I knew well enough there was not; and then I read the letters, which furnished, alas! too clearly, all the details. They told me that the boy had been pale for some time, with a scared look. His mother had noticed it before I left home, but would not say anything to alarm me. This look had increased day by day: and soon it was observed that Roland came home at a wild gallop through the park, his pony panting and in foam, himself "as white as a sheet," but with the perspiration streaming from his forehead. For a long time he had resisted all questioning, but at length had developed such strange changes of mood, showing a reluctance to go to school, a desire to be fetched in the carriage at night,—which was a ridiculous piece of luxury,—an unwillingness to go out into the grounds, and nervous start at every sound, that his mother had insisted upon an explanation. When the boy—our boy Roland, who had never known what fear was—began to talk to her of voices he had heard in the park, and shadows that had appeared to him among the ruins, my wife promptly put him to bed and sent for Dr. Simson, which, of course, was the only thing to do.

I hurried off that evening, as may be supposed, with an anxious heart. How I got through the hours before the starting of the train, I cannot tell. We must all be thankful for the quickness of the railway when in anxiety; but to have thrown myself into a post-chaise as soon as horses could be put to, would have been a relief. I got to Edinburgh very early in the blackness of the winter morning, and scarcely dared look the man in the face, at whom I gasped, "What news?" My wife had sent the brougham for me, which I concluded, before the man spoke, was a bad sign. His answer was that stereotyped answer which leaves the imagination so wildly free,—"Just the same." Just the same! What might that mean? The horses seemed to me to creep along the long dark country road. As we dashed through the park, I thought I heard some one moaning among the trees, and clenched my fist at him (whoever he might be) with fury. Why had the fool of a woman at the gate allowed any one to come in to disturb the quiet of the place? If I had not been in such hot haste to get home, I think I should have stopped the carriage and got out to see what tramp it was that had made an entrance, and chosen my grounds, of all places in the world,—when my boy was ill!—to grumble and groan in. But I had no reason to complain of our slow pace here. The horses flew like lightning along the intervening path, and drew up at the door all panting, as if they had run a race. My wife stood waiting to receive me, with a pale face, and a candle in her hand, which made her look paler still as the wind blew the flame about. "He is sleeping," she said in a whisper, as if her voice might wake him. And I replied, when I could find my voice, also in a whisper, as though the jingling of the horses' furniture and the sound of their hoofs must not have been more dangerous. I stood on the steps with her a moment, almost afraid to go in, now that I was here; and it seemed to me that I saw without observing, if I may say so, that the horses were unwilling to turn round, though their stables lay that way, or that the men were unwilling. These things occurred to me afterwards, though at the moment I was not capable of anything but to ask questions and to hear of the condition of the boy.

I looked at him from the door of his room, for we were afraid to go near, lest we should disturb that blessed sleep. It looked like actual sleep—not the lethargy into which my wife told me he would sometimes fall. She told me everything in the next room, which communicated with his, rising now and then and going to the door of communication; and in this there was much that was very startling and confusing to the mind. It appeared that ever since the winter began, since it was early dark, and night had fallen before his return from school, he had been hearing voices among the ruins—at first only a groaning, he said, at which his pony was as much alarmed as he was, but by degrees a voice. The tears ran down my wife's cheeks as she described to me how he would start up in the night and cry out, "Oh, mother, let me in! oh, mother, let me in!" with a pathos which rent her heart. And she sitting there all the time, only longing to do everything his heart could desire! But though she would try to soothe him, crying, "You are at home, my darling. I am here. Don't you know me? Your mother is here!" he would only stare at her, and after a while spring up again with the same cry. At other times he would be quite reasonable, she said, asking eagerly when I was coming, but declaring that he must go with me as soon as I did so, "to let them in." "The doctor thinks his nervous system must have received a shock," my wife said. "Oh, Henry, can it be that we have pushed him on too much with his work—a delicate boy like Roland?—and what is his work in comparison with his health? Even you would think little of honours or prizes if it hurt the boy's health." Even I! +as if I were an inhuman father sacrificing my child to my ambition. But I would not increase her trouble by taking any notice. After awhile they persuaded me to lie down, to rest, and to eat, none of which things had been possible since I received their letters. The mere fact of being on the spot, of course, in itself was a great thing; and when I knew that I could be called in a moment, as soon as he was awake and wanted me, I felt capable, even in the dark, chill morning twilight, to snatch an hour or two's sleep. As it happened, I was so worn out with the strain of anxiety, and he so quieted and consoled by knowing I had come, that I was not disturbed till the afternoon, when the twilight had again settled down. There was just daylight enough to see his face when I went to him; and what a change in a fortnight! He was paler and more worn, I thought, than even in those dreadful days in the plains before we left India. His hair seemed to me to have grown long and lank; his eyes were like blazing lights projecting out of his white face. He got hold of my hand in a cold and tremulous clutch, and waved to everybody to go away. "Go away—even mother," he said,—"go away." This went to her heart; for she did not like that even I should have more of the boy's confidence than herself; but my wife has never been a woman to think of herself, and she left us alone. "Are they all gone?" he said eagerly. "They would not let me speak. The doctor treated me as if I were a fool. You know I am not a fool, papa."

"Yes, yes, my boy, I know. But you are ill, and quiet is so necessary. You are not only not a fool, Roland, but you are reasonable and understand. When you are ill you must deny yourself; you must not do everything that you might do being well."

He waved his thin hand with a sort of indignation. "Then, father, I am not ill," he cried. "Oh, I thought when you came you would not stop me,—you would see the sense of it! What do you think is the matter with me, all of you? Simson is well enough; but he is only a doctor. What do you think is the matter with me? I am no more ill than you are. A doctor, of course, he thinks you are ill the moment he looks at you—that's what he's there for—and claps you into bed."

"Which is the best place for you at present, my dear boy."

"I made up my mind," cried the little fellow, "that I would stand it till you came home. I said to myself, I won't frighten mother and the girls. But now, father," he cried, half jumping out of bed, "it's not illness,—it's a secret."

His eyes shone so wildly, his face was so swept with strong feeling, that my heart sank within me. It could be nothing but fever that did it, and fever had been so fatal. I got him into my arms to put him back into bed. "Roland," I said, humouring the poor child, which I knew was the only way, "if you are going to tell me this secret to do any good, you know you must be quite quiet, and not excite yourself. If you excite yourself, I must not let you speak."

"Yes, father," said the boy. He was quiet directly, like a man, as if he quite understood. When I had laid him back on his pillow, he looked up at me with that grateful, sweet look with which children, when they are ill, break one's heart, the water coming into his eyes in his weakness. "I was sure as soon as you were here you would know what to do," he said.

"To be sure, my boy. Now keep quiet, and tell it all out like a man." To think I was telling lies to my own child! for I did it only to humour him, thinking, poor little fellow, his brain was wrong.

"Yes, father. Father, there is some one in the park,—some one that has been badly used."

"Hush, my dear; you remember there is to be no excitement. Well, who is this somebody, and who has been ill-using him? We will soon put a stop to that."

"Ah," cried Roland, "but it is not so easy as you think. I don't know who it is. It is just a cry. Oh, if you could hear it! It gets into my head in my sleep. I heard it as clear—as clear;—and they think that I am dreaming—or raving perhaps," the boy said, with a sort of disdainful smile.

This look of his perplexed me; it was less like fever than I thought. "Are you quite sure you have not dreamt it, Roland?" I said.

"Dreamt?—that!" He was springing up again when he suddenly bethought himself, and lay down flat, with the same sort of smile on his face. "The pony heard it, too," he said. "She jumped as if she had been shot. If I had not grasped at the reins,—for I was frightened, father——"

"No shame to you, my boy," said I, though I scarcely knew why.

"If I hadn't held to her like a leech, she'd have pitched me over her head, and never drew breath till we were at the door. Did the pony dream it?" he said, with a soft disdain, yet indulgence for my foolishness. Then he added slowly, "It was only a cry the first time, and all the time before you went away. I wouldn't tell you, for it was so wretched to be frightened. I thought it might be a hare or a rabbit snared, and I went in the morning and looked; but there was nothing. It was after you went I heard it really first; and this is what he says." He raised himself on his elbow close to me, and looked me in the face. "'Oh, mother, let me in! oh, mother, let me in!'" As he said the words a mist came over his face, the mouth quivered, the soft features all melted and changed, and when he had ended these pitiful words, dissolved in a shower of heavy tears.

Was it a hallucination? Was it the fever of the brain? Was it the disordered fancy caused by great bodily weakness? How could I tell? I thought it wisest to accept it as if it were all true.

"This is very touching, Roland," I said.

"Oh, if you had just heard it, father! I said to myself, if father heard it he would do something; but mamma, you know, she's given over to Simson, and that fellow's a doctor, and never thinks of anything but clapping you into bed."

"We must not blame Simson for being a doctor, Roland."

"No, no," said my boy, with delightful toleration and indulgence; "oh, no; that's the good of him—that's what he's for; I know that. But you—you are different; you are just father; and you'll do something,—directly, papa, directly,—this very night."

"Surely," I said. "No doubt it is some little lost child."

He gave me a sudden, swift look, investigating my face as though to see whether, after all, this was everything my eminence as "father" came to,—no more than that. Then he got hold of my shoulder, clutching it with his thin hand. "Look here," he said, with a quiver in his voice; "suppose it wasn't living at all!"

"My dear boy, how then could you have heard it?" I said.

He turned away from me with a pettish exclamation,—"As if you didn't know better than that!"

"Do you want to tell me it is a ghost?" I said.

Roland withdrew his hand; his countenance assumed an aspect of great dignity and gravity; a slight quiver remained about his lips. "Whatever it was—you always said we were not to call names. It was something—in trouble. Oh, father, in terrible trouble!"

"But, my boy," I said—I was at my wits' end—"if it was a child that was lost, or any poor human creature——but, Roland, what do you want me to do?"

"I should know if I was you," said the child eagerly. "That is what I always said to myself,—Father will know. Oh, papa, papa, to have to face it night after night, in such terrible, terrible trouble! and never to be able to do it any good! I don't want to cry; it's like a baby, I know; but I can't help it;—out there all by itself in the ruin, and nobody to help it! I can't bear it! I can't bear it!" cried my generous boy. And in his weakness he burst out, after many attempts to restrain it, into a great childish fit of sobbing and tears.

I do not know that I ever was in a greater perplexity in my life; and afterwards, when I thought of it, there was something comic in it too. It is bad enough to find your child's mind possessed with the conviction that he has seen—or heard—a ghost. But that he should require you to go instantly and help that ghost was the most bewildering experience that had ever come my way. I am a sober man myself, and not superstitious—at least any more than everybody is superstitious. Of course I do not believe in ghosts; but I don't deny, any more than other people, that there are stories which I cannot pretend to understand. My blood got a sort of chill in my veins at the idea that Roland should be a ghost-seer; for that generally means a hysterical temperament and weak health, and all that men most hate and fear for their children. But that I should take up his ghost and right its wrongs, and save it from its trouble, was such a mission as was enough to confuse any man. I did my best to console my boy without giving any promise of this astonishing kind; but he was too sharp for me: he would have none of my caresses. With sobs breaking in at intervals upon his voice, and the rain-drops hanging on his eyelids, he yet returned to the charge.

"It will be there now!—it will be there all the night! Oh, think, papa, think if it was me! I can't rest for thinking of it. Don't!" he cried, putting away my hand,—"don't! You go and help it, and mother can take care of me."

"But, Roland, what can I do?"

My boy opened his eyes, which were large with weakness and fever, and gave me a smile such, I think, as sick children only know the secret of. "I was sure you would know as soon as you came. I always said, Father will know. And mother," he cried, with a softening of repose upon his face, his limbs relaxing, his form sinking with a luxurious ease in his bed—"mother can come and take care of me."

I called her, and saw him turn to her with the complete dependence of a child; and then I went away and left them, as perplexed a man as any in Scotland. I must say, however, I had this consolation, that my mind was greatly eased about Roland. He might be under a hallucination; but his head was clear enough, and I did not think him so ill as everybody else did. The girls were astonished even at the ease with which I took it. "How do you think he is?" they said in a breath, coming round me, laying hold of me. "Not half so ill as I expected," I said; "not very bad at all." "Oh, papa, you are a darling!" cried Agatha, kissing me, and crying upon my shoulder; while little Jeanie, who was as pale as

Roland, clasped both her arms round mine, and could not speak at all. I knew nothing about it, not half so much as Simson; but they believed in me: they had a feeling that all would go right now. God is very good to you when your children look to you like that. It makes one humble, not proud. I was not worthy of it; and then I recollected that I had to act the part of a father to Roland's ghost, which made me almost laugh, though I might just as well have cried. It was the strangest mission that ever was entrusted to mortal man.

It was then I remembered suddenly the looks of the men when they turned to take the brougham to the stables in the dark that morning. They had not liked it, and the horses had not liked it. I remembered that even in my anxiety about Roland I had heard them tearing along the avenue back to the stables, and had made a memorandum mentally that I must speak of it. It seemed to me that the best thing I could do was to go to the stables now and make a few inquiries. It is impossible to fathom the minds of rustics; there might be some devilry of practical joking, for anything I knew; or they might have some interest in getting up a bad reputation for the Brentwood avenue. It was getting dark by the time I went out, and nobody who knows the country will need to be told how black is the darkness of a November night under high laurel-bushes and yew-trees. I walked into the heart of the shrubberies two or three times, not seeing a step before me, till I came out upon the broader carriage-road, where the trees opened a little, and there was a faint grey glimmer of sky visible, under which the great limes and elms stood darkling like ghosts; but it grew black again as I approached the corner where the ruins lay. Both eyes and ears were on the alert, as may be supposed; but I could see nothing in the absolute gloom, and, so far as I can recollect, I heard nothing. Nevertheless there came a strong impression upon me that somebody was there. It is a sensation which most people have felt. I have seen when it has been strong enough to awake me out of sleep, the sense of some one looking at me. I suppose my imagination had been affected by Roland's story; and the mystery of the darkness is always full of suggestions. I stamped my feet violently on the gravel to rouse myself, and called out sharply, "Who's there?" Nobody answered, nor did I expect any one to answer, but the impression had been made. I was so foolish that I did not like to look back, but went sideways, keeping an eye on the gloom behind. It was with great relief that I spied the light in the stables, making a sort of oasis in the darkness. I walked very quickly into the midst of that lighted and cheerful place, and thought the clank of the groom's pail one of the pleasantest sounds I had ever heard. The coachman was the head of this little colony, and it was to his house I went to pursue my investigations. He was a native of the district, and had taken care of the place in the absence of the family for years; it was impossible but that he must know everything that was going on, and all the traditions of the place. The men, I could see, eyed me anxiously when I thus appeared at such an hour among them, and followed me with their eyes to Jarvis's house, where he lived alone with his old wife, their children being all married and out in the world. Mrs. Jarvis met me with anxious questions. How was the poor young gentleman? But the others knew, I could see by their faces, that not even this was the foremost thing in my mind.

*   *   *

"Noises?—ou ay, there'll be noises—the wind in the trees, and the water soughing down the glen. As for tramps, Cornel, no, there's little o' that kind o' cattle about here; and Merran at the gate's a careful body." Jarvis moved about with some embarrassment from one leg to another as he spoke. He kept in the shade, and did not look at me more than he could help. Evidently his mind was perturbed, and he had reasons for keeping his own counsel. His wife sat by, giving him a quick look now and then, but saying nothing. The kitchen was very snug and warm and bright,—as different as could be from the chill and mystery of the night outside.

"I think you are trifling with me, Jarvis," I said.

"Triflin', Cornel? no me. What would I trifle for? If the deevil himsel was in the auld hoose, I have no interest in't one way or another——"

"Sandy, hold your peace!" cried his wife imperatively.

"And what am I to hold my peace for, wi' the Cornel standing there asking a' thae questions? I'm saying, if the deevil himsel——"

"And I'm telling ye hold your peace!" cried the woman, in great excitement. "Dark November weather and lang nichts, and us that ken a' we ken. How daur ye name—a name that shouldna be spoken?" She threw down her stocking and got up, also in great agitation. "I tell't ye you never could keep it. It's no a thing that will hide; and the haill toun kens as weel as you or me. Tell the Cornel straight out, or see, I'll do it. I dinna hold wi' your secrets: and a secret that the haill toun kens!" She snapped her fingers with an air of large disdain. As for Jarvis, ruddy and big as he was, he shrank to nothing before this decided woman. He repeated to her two or three times her own adjuration, "Hold your peace!" then, suddenly changing his tone, cried out, "Tell him then, confound ye! I'll wash my hands o't. If a' the ghosts in Scotland were in the auld hoose, is that ony concern o' mine?"

After this I elicited without much difficulty the whole story. In the opinion of the Jarvises, and of everybody about, the certainty that the place was haunted was beyond all doubt. As Sandy and his wife warmed to the tale, one tripping up another in their eagerness to tell everything, it gradually developed as distinct a superstition as I ever heard, and not without poetry and pathos. How long it was since the voice had been heard first, nobody could tell with certainty. Jarvis's opinion was that his father, who had been coachman at Brentwood before him, had never heard anything about it, and that the whole thing had arisen within the last ten years, since the complete dismantling of the old house; which was a wonderfully modern date for a tale so well authenticated. According to these witnesses, and to several whom I questioned afterwards, and who were all in perfect agreement, it was only in the months of November and December that "the visitation" occurred. During these months, the darkest of the year, scarcely a night passed without the recurrence of these inexplicable cries. Nothing, it was said, had ever been seen—at least, nothing that could be identified. Some people, bolder or more imaginative than the others, had seen the darkness moving, Mrs. Jarvis said, with unconscious poetry. It began when night fell, and continued, at intervals, till day broke. Very often it was only all inarticulate cry and moaning, but sometimes the words which had taken possession of my poor boy's fancy had been distinctly audible,— "Oh, mother, let me in!" The Jarvises were not aware that there had ever been any investigation into it. The estate of Brentwood had lapsed into the hands of a distant branch of the family, who had lived but little there; and of the many people who had taken it, as I had done, few had remained through two Decembers. And nobody had taken the trouble to make a very close examination into the facts. "No, no," Jarvis said, shaking his head, "No, no, Cornel. Wha wad set themsels up for a laughin'-stock to a' the country-side, making a wark about a ghost? Naebody believes in ghosts. It bid to be the wind in the trees, the last gentleman said, or some effec' o' the water wrastlin' among the rocks. He said it was a' quite easy explained: but he gave up the hoose. And when you cam, Cornel, we were awfu' anxious you should never hear. What for should I have spoiled the bargain and hairmed the property for no-thing?"

"Do you call my child's life nothing?" I said in the trouble of the moment, unable to restrain myself. "And instead of telling this all to me, you have told it to him—to a delicate boy, a child unable to sift evidence or judge for himself, a tender-hearted young creature——"

I was walking about the room with an anger all the hotter that I felt it to be most likely quite unjust. My heart was full of bitterness against the stolid retainers of a family who were content to risk other people's children and comfort rather than let a house be empty. If I had been warned I might have taken precautions, or left the place, or sent Roland away, a hundred things which now I could not do; and here I was with my boy in a brain-fever, and his life, the most precious life on earth, hanging in the balance, dependent on whether or not I could get to the reason of a *banal* commonplace ghost-story! I paced about in high wrath, not seeing what I was to do; for to take Roland away, even if he were able to travel, would not settle his agitated mind; and I feared even that a scientific explanation of refracted sound or reverberation, or any other of the easy certainties with which we elder men are silenced, would have very little effect upon the boy.

"Cornel," said Jarvis solemnly, "and *she'll* bear me witness— the young gentleman never heard a word from me—no, nor from either groom or gardener; I'll gie ye my word for that. In the first place, he's no a lad that invites ye to talk. There are some that are, and some that arena. Some will draw ye on, till ye've tellt them a' the clatter of the toun, and a' ye ken, and whiles mair. But Maister Roland, his mind's fu' of his books. He's aye civil and kind, and a fine lad; but no that sort. And ye see it's for a' our interest, Cornel, that you should stay at Brentwood. I took it upon me mysel to pass the word,—'No a syllable to Maister Roland, nor to the young leddies—no a syllable.' The women-servants, that have little reason to be out at night, ken little or nothing about it. And some think it grand to have a ghost so long as they're no in the way of coming across it. If you had been tellt the story to begin with, maybe ye would have thought so yourself."

This was true enough, though it did not throw any light upon my perplexity. If we had heard of it to start with, it is possible that all the family would have considered the possession of a ghost a distinct advantage. It is the fashion of the times. We never think what a risk it is to play with young imaginations, but cry out, in the fashionable jargon, "A ghost!—nothing else was wanted to make it perfect." I should not have been above this myself. I should have smiled, of course, at the idea of the ghost at all, but then to feel that it was mine would have pleased my vanity. Oh, yes, I claim no exemption. The girls would have been delighted. I could fancy their eagerness, their interest, and excitement. No; if we had been told, it would have done no good—we should have made the bargain all the more eagerly, the fools that we are. "And there has been no attempt to investigate it," I said, "to see what it really is?"

"Eh, Cornel," said the coachman's wife, "wha would investigate, as ye call it, a thing that nobody believes in? Ye would be the laughin'-stock of a' the country-side, as my man says."

"But you believe in it," I said, turning upon her hastily. The woman was taken by surprise. She made a step backward out of my way.

"Lord, Cornel, how ye frichten a body! Me!—there's awfu' strange things in this world. An unlearned person doesna ken what to think. But the minister and the gentry they just laugh in your face. Inquire into the thing that is not! Na, na, we just let it be——"

"Come with me, Jarvis," I said hastily, "and we'll make an attempt at least. Say nothing to the men or to anybody. I'll come back after dinner, and we'll make a serious attempt to see what it is, if it is anything. If I hear it,—which I doubt,—you may be sure

I shall never rest till I make it out. Be ready for me about ten o'clock."

"Me, Cornel!" Jarvis said, in a faint voice. I had not been looking at him in my own preoccupation, but when I did so, I found that the greatest change had come over the fat and ruddy coachman. "Me, Cornel!" he repeated, wiping the perspiration from his brow. His ruddy face hung in flabby folds, his knees knocked together, his voice seemed half extinguished in his throat. Then he began to rub his hands and smile upon me in a deprecating, imbecile way. "There's nothing I wouldna do to pleasure ye, Cornel," taking a step further back. "I'm sure *she* kens I've aye said I never had to do with a mair fair, weel-spoken gentleman——" Here Jarvis came to a pause, again looking at me, rubbing his hands.

"Well?" I said.

"But eh, sir!" he went on, with the same imbecile yet insinuating smile, "if ye'll reflect that I am no used to my feet. With a horse atween my legs, or the reins in my hand, I'm maybe nae worse than other men; but on fit, Cornel—It's no the— bogles—but I've been cavalry, ye see," with a little hoarse laugh, "a' my life. To face a thing ye dinna understan'—on your feet, Cornel."

"Well, sir, if *I* do it," said I tartly, "why shouldn't you?"

"Eh, Cornel, there's an awfu' difference. In the first place, ye tramp about the haill countryside, and think naething of it; but a walk tires me mair than a hunard miles' drive; and then ye're a gentleman, and do your ain pleasure; and you're no so auld as me; and it's for your ain bairn, ye see, Cornel; and then——"

"He believes in it, Cornel, and you dinna believe in it," the woman said.

"Will you come with me?" I said, turning to her.

She jumped back, upsetting her chair in her bewilderment. "Me!" with a scream, and then fell into a sort of hysterical laugh. "I wouldna say but what I would go; but what would the folk say to hear of Cornel Mortimer with an auld silly woman at his heels?"

The suggestion made me laugh too, though I had little inclination for it. "I'm sorry you have so little spirit, Jarvis," I said. "I must find some one else, I suppose."

Jarvis, touched by this, began to remonstrate, but I cut him short. My butler was a soldier who had been with me in India, and was not supposed to fear anything,—man or devil,—certainly not the former; and I felt that I was losing time. The Jarvises were too thankful to get rid of me. They attended me to the door with the most anxious courtesies. Outside, the two grooms stood close by, a little confused by my sudden exit. I don't know if perhaps they had been listening,—at least standing as near as possible, to catch any scrap of the conversation. I waved my hand to them as I went past, in answer to their salutations, and it was very apparent to me that they also were glad to see me go.

And it will be thought very strange, but it would be weak not to add, that I myself, though bent on the investigation I have spoken of, pledged to Roland to carry it out, and feeling that my boy's health, perhaps his life, depended on the result of my inquiry,—I felt the most unaccountable reluctance to pass these ruins on my way home. My curiosity was intense; and yet it was all my mind could do to pull my body along. I daresay the scientific people would describe it the other way, and attribute my cowardice to the state of my stomach. I went on; but if I had followed my impulse, I should have turned and bolted. Everything in me seemed to cry out against it: my heart thumped, my pulses all began, like sledge-hammers, beating against my ears and every sensitive part. It was very dark, as I have said; the old house, with its shapeless tower, loomed a heavy mass through the darkness, which was only not entirely so solid as itself. On the other hand, the great dark cedars of which we were so proud seemed to fill up the night. My foot strayed out of the path in my confusion and the gloom together, and I brought myself up with a cry as I felt myself knock against something solid. What was it? The contact with hard stone and lime and prickly bramble-bushes restored me a little to myself. "Oh, it's only the old gable," I said aloud, with a little laugh to reassure myself. The rough feeling of the stones reconciled me. As I groped about thus, I shook off my visionary folly. What so easily explained as that I should have strayed from the path in the darkness? This brought me back to common existence, as if I had been shaken by a wise hand out of all the silliness of superstition. How silly it was, after all! What did it matter which path I took? I laughed again, this time with better heart, when suddenly, in a moment, the blood was chilled in my veins, a shiver stole along my spine, my faculties seemed to forsake me. Close by me, at my side, at my feet, there was a sigh. No, not a groan, not a moaning, not anything so tangible,—a perfectly soft, faint, inarticulate sigh. I sprang back, and my heart stopped beating. Mistaken! no, mistake was impossible. I heard it as clearly as I hear myself speak; a long, soft, weary sigh, as if drawn to the utmost, and emptying out a load of sadness that filled the breast. To hear this in the solitude, in the dark, in the night (though it was still early), had an effect which I cannot describe. I feel it now,—something cold creeping over me, up into my hair, and down to my feet, which refused to move. I cried out, with a trembling voice, "Who is there?" as I had done before—but there was no reply.

I got home I don't quite know how; but in my mind there was no longer any indifference as to the thing, whatever it was, that haunted these ruins. My scepticism disappeared like a mist. I was as firmly determined that there was something as Roland was. I did not for a moment pretend to myself that it was possible I could be deceived; there were movements and noises which I understood all about, cracklings of small branches in the frost, and little rolls of gravel on the path, such as have a very eerie sound sometimes, and perplex you with wonder as to who has done it, *when there is no real mystery;* but I assure you all these little movements of nature don't affect you one bit when *there is something.* I understood *them.* I did not understand the sigh. That was not simple nature; there was meaning in it—feeling, the soul of a creature invisible. This is the thing that human nature trembles at—a creature invisible, yet with sensations, feelings, a power somehow of expressing itself. I had not the same sense of unwillingness to turn my back upon the scene of the mystery which I had experienced in going to the stables; but I almost ran home, impelled by eagerness to get everything done that had to be done, in order to apply myself to finding it out. Bagley was in the hall as usual when I went in. He was always there in the afternoon, always with the appearance of perfect occupation, yet, so far as I know, never doing anything. The door was open, so that I hurried in without any pause, breathless; but the sight of his calm regard, as he came to help me off with my overcoat, subdued me in a moment. Anything out of the way, anything incomprehensible, faded to nothing in the presence of Bagley. You saw and wondered how *he* was made: the parting of his hair, the tie of his white neck-cloth, the fit of his trousers, all perfect as works of art; but you could see how they were done, which makes all the difference. I flung myself upon him, so to speak, without waiting to note the extreme unlikeness of the man to anything of the kind I meant. "Bagley," I said, "I want you to come out with me to-night to watch for—"

"Poachers, Colonel?" he said, a gleam of pleasure running all over him.

"No, Bagley; a great deal worse," I cried.

"Yes, Colonel; at what hour, sir?" the man said; but then I had not told him what it was.

It was ten o'clock when we set out. All was perfectly quiet indoors. My wife was with Roland, who had been quite calm, she said, and who (though, no doubt, the fever must run its course) had been better ever since I came. I told Bagley to put on a thick greatcoat over his evening coat, and did the same myself—with strong boots; for the soil was like a sponge, or worse. Talking to him, I almost forgot what we were going to do. It was darker even than it had been before, and Bagley kept very close to me as we went along. I had a small lantern in my hand, which gave us a partial guidance. We had come to the corner where the path turns. On one side was the bowling-green, which the girls had taken possession of for their croquet-ground—a wonderful enclosure surrounded by high hedges of holly, three hundred years old and more; on the other, the ruins. Both were black as night; but before we got so far, there was a little opening in which we could just discern the trees and the lighter line of the road. I thought it best to pause there and take breath. "Bagley," I said, "there is something about these ruins I don't understand. It is there I am going. Keep your eyes open and your wits about you. Be ready to pounce upon any stranger you see,—anything, man or woman. Don't hurt, but seize anything you see." "Colonel," said Bagley, with a little tremor in his breath, "they do say there's things there—as is neither man nor woman." There was no time for words. "Are you game to follow me, my man? that's the question," I said. Bagley fell in without a word, and saluted. I knew then I had nothing to fear.

We went, so far as I could guess, exactly as I had come; when I heard that sigh. The darkness, however, was so complete that all marks, as of trees or paths, disappeared. One moment we felt our feet on the gravel, another sinking noiselessly into the slippery grass, that was all. I had shut up my lantern, not wishing to scare any one, whoever it might be. Bagley followed, it seemed to me, exactly in my footsteps as I made my way, as I supposed, towards the mass of the ruined house. We seemed to take a long time groping along seeking this; the squash of the wet soil under our feet was the only thing that marked our progress. After a while I stood still to see, or rather feel, where we were. The darkness was very still, but no stiller than is usual in a winter's night. The sounds I have mentioned—the crackling of twigs, the roll of a pebble, the sound of some rustle in the dead leaves, or creeping creature on the grass—were audible when you listened, all mysterious enough when your mind is disengaged, but to me cheering now as signs of the livingness of nature, even in the death of the frost. As we stood still there came up from the trees in the glen the prolonged hoot of an owl. Bagley started with alarm, being in a state of general nervousness, and not knowing what he was afraid of. But to me the sound was encouraging and pleasant, being so comprehensible. "An owl," I said, under my breath. "Y—es, Colonel," said Bagley, his teeth chattering. We stood still about five minutes, while it broke into the still brooding of the air, the sound widening out in circles, dying upon the darkness. This sound, which is not a cheerful one, made me almost gay. It was natural, and relieved the tension of the mind. I moved on with new courage, my nervous excitement calming down.

When all at once, quite suddenly, close to us, at our feet, there broke out a cry. I made a spring backwards in the first moment of surprise and horror, and in doing so came sharply against the same rough masonry and brambles that had struck me before. This new sound came upwards from the ground—a low, moaning, wailing voice, full of suffering and pain. The contrast between it and the hoot of the owl was indescribable; the one with a wholesome wildness and naturalness that hurt nobody—the other, a sound that made one's blood curdle, full of human misery. With a great deal of fumbling—for in spite of everything I could do to keep up my courage my hands shook,—I managed to remove the slide of my lantern. The light leaped out like something living, and made the place visible in a moment. We were what would have been inside the ruined building had anything remained but the gable-wall which I have described. It was close to us, the vacant door-way in it going out straight into the blackness outside. The light showed the bit of wall, the ivy glistening upon it in clouds of dark green, the bramble-branches waving, and below, the open door—a door that led to nothing. It was from this the voice came which died out just as the light flashed upon this strange scene. There was a moment's silence, and then it broke forth again. The sound was so near, so penetrating, so pitiful, that, in the nervous start I gave, the light fell out of my hand. As I groped for it in the dark my hand was clutched by Bagley, who, I think, must have dropped upon his knees; but I was too much perturbed myself to think much of this. He clutched at me in the confusion of his terror, forgetting all his usual decorum. "For God's sake, what is it, sir?" he gasped. If I yielded, there was evidently an end of both of us. "I can't tell," I said, "any more than you; that's what we've got to find out: up, man, up!" I pulled him to his feet. "Will you go round and examine the other side, or will you stay here with the lantern?" Bagley gasped at me with a face of horror. "Can't we stay together, Colonel?" he said; his knees were trembling under him. I pushed him against the corner of the wall, and put the light into his hands. "Stand fast till I come back; shake yourself together, man; let nothing pass you," I said. The voice was within two or three feet of us; of that there could be no doubt.

I went myself to the other side of the wall, keeping close to it. The light shook in Bagley's hand, but, tremulous though it was, shone out through the vacant door, one oblong block of light marking all the crumbling corners and hanging masses of foliage. Was that something dark huddled in a heap by the side of it? I pushed forward across the light in the door-way, and fell upon it with my hands; but it was only a juniper-bush growing close against the wall. Meanwhile, the sight of my figure crossing the door-way had brought Bagley's nervous excitement to a height: he flew at me, gripping my shoulder. "I've got him, Colonel! I've got him!" he cried, with a voice of sudden exultation. He thought it was a man, and was at once relieved. But at that moment the voice burst forth again between us, at our feet—more close to us than any separate being could be. He dropped off from me, and fell against the wall, his jaw dropping as if he were dying. I suppose, at the same moment, he saw that it was me whom he had clutched. I, for my part, had scarcely more command of myself. I snatched the light out of his hand, and flashed it all about me wildly. Nothing,—the juniper-bush which I thought I had never seen before, the heavy growth of the glistening ivy, the brambles waving. It was close to my ears now, crying, crying, pleading as if for life. Either I heard the same words Roland had heard, or else, in my excitement, his imagination got possession of mine. The voice went on, growing into distinct articulation, but wavering about, now from one point, now from another, as if the owner of it were moving slowly back and forward. "Mother! mother!" and then an outburst of wailing. As my mind steadied, getting accustomed (as one's mind gets accustomed to anything), it seemed to me as if some uneasy, miserable creature was pacing up and down before a closed door. Sometimes—but that must have been excitement—I thought I heard a sound like knocking, and then another burst, "Oh, mother! mother!" All this close, close to the space where I was standing with my lantern, now before me, now behind me: a creature restless, unhappy, moaning, crying, before the vacant door-way, which no one could either shut or open more.

"Do you hear it, Bagley? do you hear what it is saying?" I cried, stepping in through the door-way. He was lying against the wall—his eyes glazed, half dead with terror. He made a motion of his lips as if to answer me, but no sounds came; then lifted his hand with a curious imperative movement as if ordering me to be silent and listen. And how long I did so I cannot tell. It began to have an interest, an exciting hold upon me, which I could not describe. It seemed to call up visibly a scene any one could understand—a something shut out, restlessly wandering to and fro; sometimes the voice dropped, as if throwing itself down—sometimes wandered off a few paces, growing sharp and clear. "Oh, mother, let me in! oh, mother, mother, let me in! oh, let me in!" Every word was clear to me. No wonder the boy had gone wild with pity. I tried to steady my mind upon Roland, upon his conviction that I could do something, but my head swam with the excitement, even when I partially overcame the terror. At last the words died away, and there was a sound of sobs and moaning. I cried out, "In the name of God, who are you?" with a kind of feeling in my mind that to use the name of God was profane, seeing that I did not believe in ghosts or anything supernatural; but I did it all the same, and waited, my heart giving a leap of terror lest there should be a reply. Why this should have been I cannot tell, but I had a feeling that if there was an answer it would be more than I could bear. But there was no answer; the moaning went on, and then, as if it had been real, the voice rose a little higher again, the words recommenced, "Oh, mother, let me in! oh, mother, let me in!" with an expression that was heart-breaking to hear.

As if it had been real! What do I mean by that? I suppose I got less alarmed as the thing went on. I began to recover the use of my senses,—I seemed to explain it all to myself by saying that this had once happened, that it was a recollection of a real scene. Why there should have seemed something quite satisfactory and composing in this explanation I cannot tell, but so it was. I began to listen almost as if it had been a play, forgetting Bagley, who, I almost think, had fainted, leaning against the wall. I was startled out of this strange spectatorship that had fallen upon me by the sudden rush of something which made my heart jump once more, a large black figure in the door-way waving its arms. "Come in! come in! come in!" it shouted out hoarsely at the top of a deep bass voice, and then poor Bagley fell down senseless across the threshold. He was less sophisticated than I,—he had not been able to bear it any longer. I took him for something supernatural, as he took me, and it was some time before I awoke to the necessities of the moment. I remembered only after, that from the time I began to give my attention to the man, I heard the other voice no more. It was some time before I brought him to. It must have been a strange scene: the lantern making a luminous spot in the darkness, the man's white face lying on the black earth, I over him, doing what I could for him, probably I should have been thought to be murdering him had any one seen us. When at last I succeeded in pouring a little brandy down his throat, he sat up and looked about him wildly. "What's up?" he said; then recognizing me, tried to struggle to his feet with a faint "Beg your pardon, Colonel." I got him home as best I could, making him lean upon my arm. The great fellow was as weak as a child. Fortunately he did not for some time remember what had happened. From the time Bagley fell the voice had stopped, and all was still.

"You've got an epidemic in your house, Colonel," Simson said to me next morning. "What's the meaning of it all? Here's your butler raving about a voice. This will never do, you know; and so far as I can make out, you are in it too."

"Yes, I am in it, Doctor. I thought I had better speak to you. Of course you are treating Roland all right, but the boy is not raving, he is as sane as you or me. It's all true."

"As sane as—I—or you. I never thought the boy insane. He's got cerebral excitement, fever. I don't know what you've got. There's something very queer about the look of your eyes."

"Come," said I, "you can't put us all to bed, you know. You had better listen and hear the symptoms in full."

The Doctor shrugged his shoulders, but he listened to me patiently. He did not believe a word of the story, that was clear; but he heard it all from beginning to end. "My dear fellow," he said, "the boy told me just the same. It's an epidemic. When one person falls a victim to this sort of thing, it's as safe as can be—there's always two or three."

"Then how do you account for it?" I said.

"Oh, account for it!—that's a different matter; there's no accounting for the freaks our brains are subject to. If it's delusion, if it's some trick of the echoes or the winds—some phonetic disturbance or other——"

"Come with me to-night, and judge for yourself," I said.

Upon this he laughed aloud, then said, "That's not such a bad idea; but it would ruin me forever if it were known that John Simson was ghost-hunting."

"There it is," said I; "you dart down on us who are unlearned with your phonetic disturbances, but you daren't examine what the thing really is for fear of being laughed at. That's science!"

"It's not science—it's common-sense," said the Doctor. "The thing has delusion on the front of it. It is encouraging an unwholesome tendency even to examine. What good could come of it? Even if I am convinced, I shouldn't believe."

"I should have said so yesterday; and I don't want you to be convinced or to believe," said I. "If you prove it to be a delusion, I shall be very much obliged to you for one. Come; somebody must go with me."

"You are cool," said the Doctor. "You've disabled this poor fellow of yours, and made him—on that point—a lunatic for life; and now you want to disable me. But, for once, I'll do it. To save appearance, if you'll give me a bed, I'll come over after my last rounds."

It was agreed that I should meet him at the gate, and that we should visit the scene of last night's occurrences before we came to the house, so that nobody might be the wiser. It was scarcely possible to hope that the cause of Bagley's sudden illness should not somehow steal into the knowledge of the servants at least, and it was better that all should be done as quietly as possible. The day seemed to me a very long one. I had to spend a certain part of it with Roland, which was a terrible ordeal for me—for what could I say to the boy? The improvement continued, but he was still in a very precarious state, and the trembling vehemence with which he turned to me when his mother left the room filled me with alarm. "Father?" he said quietly. "Yes, my boy, I am giving my best attention to it—all is being done that I can do. I have not come to any conclusion—yet. I am neglecting nothing you said," I cried. What I could not do was to give his active mind any encouragement to dwell upon the mystery. It was a hard predicament, for some satisfaction had to be given him. He looked at me very wistfully, with the great blue eyes which shone so large and brilliant out of his white and worn face. "You must trust me," I said. "Yes, father. Father knows—father knows," he said to himself, as if to soothe some inward doubt. I left him as soon as I could. He was about the most precious thing I had on earth, and his health my first thought; but yet somehow, in the excitement of this other subject, I put that aside, and preferred not to dwell upon Roland, which was the most curious part of it all.

That night at eleven I met Simson at the gate. He had come by train, and I let him in gently myself. I had been so much absorbed in the coming experiment that I passed the ruins in going to meet him, almost without thought, if you can understand that. I had my lantern; and he showed me a coil of taper which he had ready for use. "There is nothing like light," he said, in his scoffing tone. It was a very still night, scarcely a sound, but not so dark. We could keep the path without difficulty as we went along. As we approached the spot we could hear a low moaning, broken occasionally by a bitter cry. "Perhaps that is your voice," said the Doctor; "I thought it must be something of the kind. That's a poor brute caught in some of these infernal traps of yours; you'll find it among the bushes somewhere." I said nothing. I felt no particular fear, but a triumphant satisfaction in what was to follow. I led him to the spot where Bagley and I had stood on the previous night. All was silent as a winter night could be—so silent that we heard far off the sound of the horses in the stables, the shutting of a window at the house. Simson lighted his taper and went peering about, poking into all the corners. We looked like two conspirators lying in wait for some unfortunate traveller; but not a sound broke the quiet. The moaning had stopped before we came up; a star or two shone over us in the sky, looking down as if surprised at our strange proceedings. Dr. Simson did nothing but utter subdued laughs under his breath. "I thought as much," he said. "It is just the same with tables and all other kinds of ghostly apparatus; a sceptic's presence stops everything. When I am present nothing ever comes off. How long do you think it will be necessary to stay here? Oh, I don't complain; only when *you* are satisfied, *I* am—quite."

I will not deny that I was disappointed beyond measure by this result. It made me look like a credulous fool. It gave the Doctor such a pull over me as nothing else could. I should point all his morals for years to come; and his materialism, his scepticism, would be increased beyond endurance. "It seems, indeed," I said, "that there is to be no—" "Manifestation," he said, laughing; "that is what all the mediums say. No manifestations, in consequence of the presence of an unbeliever." His laugh sounded very uncomfortable to me in the silence; and it was now near midnight. But that laugh seemed the signal; before it died away the moaning we had heard before was resumed. It started from some distance off, and came towards us, nearer and nearer, like some one walking along and moaning to himself. There could be no idea now that it was a hare caught in a trap. The approach was slow, like that of a weak person, with little halts and pauses. We heard it coming along the grass straight towards the vacant door-way. Simson had been a little startled by the first sound. He said hastily,

"That child has no business to be out so late." But he felt, as well as I, that this was no child's voice. As it came nearer, he grew silent, and, going to the door-way with his taper, stood looking out towards the sound. The taper being unprotected blew about in the night air, though there was scarcely any wind. I threw the light of my lantern steady and white across the same space. It was in a blaze of light in the midst of the blackness. A little icy thrill had gone over me at the first sound, but as it came close, I confess that my only feeling was satisfaction. The scoffer could scoff no more. The light touched his own face, and showed a very perplexed countenance. If he was afraid, he concealed it with great success, but he was perplexed. And then all that had happened on the previous night was enacted once more. It fell strangely upon me with a sense of repetition. Every cry, every sob seemed the same as before. I listened almost without any emotion at all in my own person, thinking of its effect upon Simson. He maintained a very bold front, on the whole. All that coming and going of the voice was, if our ears could be trusted, exactly in front of the vacant, blank door-way, blazing full of light, which caught and shone in the glistening leaves of the great hollies at a little distance. Not a rabbit could have crossed the turf without being seen—but there was nothing. After a time, Simson, with a certain caution and bodily reluctance, as it seemed to me, went out with his roll of taper into this space. His figure showed against the holly in full outline. Just at this moment the voice sank, as was its custom, and seemed to fling itself down at the door. Simson recoiled violently, as if some one had come up against him, then turned, and held his taper low, as if examining something. "Do you see anybody?" I cried in a whisper, feeling the chill of nervous panic steal over me at this action. "It's nothing but a—confounded juniper-bush," he said. This I knew very well to be nonsense, for the juniper-bush was on the other side. He went about after this round and round, poking his taper everywhere, then returned to me on the inner side of the wall. He scoffed no longer; his face was contracted and pale. "How long does this go on?" he whispered to me, like a man who does not wish to interrupt some one who is speaking. I had become too much perturbed myself to remark whether the successions and changes of the voice were the same as last night. It suddenly went out in the air almost as he was speaking, with a soft reiterated sob dying away. If there had been anything to be seen, I should have said that the person was at that moment crouching on the ground close to the door.

We walked home very silent afterwards. It was only when we were in sight of the house that I said, "What do you think of it?" "I can't tell what to think of it," he said quickly. He took—though he was a very temperate man—not the claret I was going to offer him, but some brandy from the tray, and swallowed it almost undiluted. "Mind you, I don't believe a word of it," he said, when he had lighted his candle; "but I can't tell what to think," he turned round to add, when he was half-way upstairs.

All of this, however, did me no good with the solution of my problem. I was to help this weeping, sobbing thing, which was already to me as distinct a personality as anything I knew—or what should I say to Roland? It was on my heart that my boy would die if I could not find some way of helping this creature. You may be surprised that I should speak of it in this way. I did not know if it was man or woman; but I no more doubted that it was a soul in pain than I doubted my own being; and it was my business to soothe this pain—to deliver it, if that was possible. Was ever such a task given to an anxious father trembling for his only boy? I felt in my heart, fantastic as it may appear, that I must fulfil this somehow, or part with my child; and you may conceive that rather than do that I was ready to die. But even my dying would not have advanced me—unless by bringing me into the same world with that seeker at the door.

Next morning Simson was out before breakfast, and came in with evident signs of the damp grass on his boots, and a look of worry and weariness, which did not say much for the night he had passed. He improved a little after breakfast, and visited his two patients, for Bagley was still an invalid. I went out with him on his way to the train, to hear what he had to say about the boy. "He is going on very well," he said; "there are no complications as yet. But mind you, that's not a boy to be trifled with, Mortimer. Not a word to him about last night." I had to tell him then of my last interview with Roland, and of the impossible demand he had made upon me, by which, though he tried to laugh, he was much discomposed, as I could see. "We must just perjure ourselves all round," he said, "and swear you exorcised it;" but the man was too kind-hearted to be satisfied with that. "It's frightfully serious for you, Mortimer. I can't laugh as I should like to. I wish I saw a way out of it, for your sake. By the way," he added shortly, "didn't you notice that juniper-bush on the left-hand side?" "There was one on the right hand of the door. I noticed you made that mistake last night." "Mistake!" he cried, with a curious low laugh, pulling up the collar of his coat as though he felt the cold,—"there's no juniper there this morning, left or right. Just go and see." As he stepped into the train a few minutes after, he looked back upon me and beckoned me for a parting word. "I'm coming back to-night," he said.

I don't think I had any feeling about this as I turned away from that common bustle of the railway which made my private preoccupations feel so strangely out of date. There had been a distinct satisfaction in my mind before, that his scepticism had been so entirely defeated. But the more serious part of the matter pressed upon me now. I went straight from the railway to the manse, which stood on a little plateau on the side of the river opposite to the woods of Brentwood. The minister was one of a class which is not so common in Scotland as it used to be. He was a man of good family, well educated in the Scotch way, strong in philosophy, not so strong in Greek, strongest of all in experience,—a man who had "come across," in the course of his life, most people of note that had ever been in Scotland—and who was said to be very sound in doctrine, without infringing the toleration with which old men, who are good men, are generally endowed. He was old-fashioned; perhaps he did not think so much about the troublous problems of theology as many of the young men, nor ask himself any hard questions about the Confession of Faith—but he understood human nature, which is perhaps better. He received me with a cordial welcome. "Come away, Colonel Mortimer," he said; "I'm all the more glad to see you, that I feel it's a good sign for the boy. He's doing well?—God be praised—and the Lord bless him and keep him. He has many a poor body's prayers, and that can do nobody harm."

"He will need them all, Dr. Moncrieff," I said, "and your counsel too." And I told him the story—more than I had told

Simson. The old clergyman listened to me with many suppressed exclamations, and at the end the water stood in his eyes.

"That's just beautiful," he said. "I do not mind to have heard anything like it; it's as fine as Burns when he wished deliverance to one—that is prayed for in no kirk. Ay, ay! so he would have you console the poor lost spirit? God bless the boy! There's something more than common in that, Colonel Mortimer. And also the faith of him in his father!—I would like to put that into a sermon." Then the old gentleman gave me an alarmed look, and said, "No, no; I was not meaning a sermon; but I must write it down for the 'Children's Record.'" I saw the thought that passed through his mind. Either he thought, or he feared I would think, of a funeral sermon. You may believe this did not make me more cheerful.

I can scarcely say that Dr. Moncrieff gave me any advice. How could any one advise on such a subject? But he said, "I think I'll come too. I'm an old man; I'm less liable to be frightened than those that are further off the world unseen. It behoves me to think of my own journey there. I've no cut-and-dry beliefs on the subject. I'll come too; and maybe at the moment the Lord will put into our heads what to do."

This gave me a little comfort—more than Simson had given me. To be clear about the cause of it was not my grand desire. It was another thing that was in my mind—my boy. As for the poor soul at the open door, I had no more doubt, as I have said, of its existence than I had of my own. It was no ghost to me. I knew the creature, and it was in trouble. That was my feeling about it, as it was Roland's. To hear it first was a great shock to my nerves, but not now; a man will get accustomed to anything. But to do something for it was the great problem; how was I to be serviceable to a being that was invisible, that was mortal no longer? "Maybe at the moment the Lord will put it into our heads." This is very old-fashioned phraseology, and a week before, most likely, I should have smiled (though always with kindness) at Dr. Moncrieff's credulity; but there was a great comfort, whether rational or otherwise I cannot say, in the mere sound of the words.

The road to the station and the village lay through the glen—not by the ruins; but though the sunshine and the fresh air, and the beauty of the trees, and the sound of the water were all very soothing to the spirits, my mind was so full of my own subject that

I could not refrain from turning to the right hand as I got to the top of the glen, and going straight to the place which I may call the scene of all my thoughts. It was lying full in the sunshine, like all the rest of the world. The ruined gable looked due east, and in the present aspect of the sun the light streamed down through the doorway as our lantern had done, throwing a flood of light upon the damp grass beyond. There was a strange suggestion in the open door—so futile, a kind of emblem of vanity—all free around, so that you could go where you pleased, and yet that semblance of an enclosure—that way of entrance, unnecessary, leading to nothing. And why any creature should pray and weep to get in—to nothing: or be kept out—by nothing! You could not dwell upon it, or it made your brain go round. I remembered, however, what Simson said about the juniper, with a little smile on my own mind as to the inaccuracy of recollection which even a scientific man will be guilty of. I could see now the light of my lantern gleaming upon the wet glistening surface of the spiky leaves at the right hand—and he ready to go to the stake for it that it was the left! I went round to make sure. And then I saw what he had said. Right or left there was no juniper at all. I was confounded by this, though it was entirely a matter of detail: nothing at all: a bush of brambles waving, the grass growing up to the very walls. But after all, though it gave me a shock for a moment, what did that matter? There were marks as if a number of footsteps had been up and down in front of the door, but these might have been our steps; and all was bright and peaceful and still. I poked about the other ruin— the larger ruins of the old house—for some time, as I had done before. There were marks upon the grass here and there, I could not call them footsteps, all about; but that told for nothing one way or another. I had examined the ruined rooms closely the first day. They were half filled up with soil and *débris*, withered brackens and bramble—no refuge for any one there. It vexed me that Jarvis should see me coming from that spot when he came up to me for his orders. I don't know whether my nocturnal expeditions had got wind among the servants, but there was a significant look in his face. Something in it I felt was like my own sensation when Simson in the midst of his scepticism was struck dumb. Jarvis felt satisfied that his veracity had been put beyond question. I never spoke to a servant of mine in such a peremptory tone before. I sent him away "with a flea in his lug," as the man described it afterwards. Interference of any kind was intolerable to me at such a moment.

But what was strangest of all was, that I could not face Roland. I did not go up to his room, as I would have naturally done, at once. This the girls could not understand. They saw there was some mystery in it. "Mother has gone to lie down," Agatha said; "he has had such a good night." "But he wants you so, papa!" cried little Jeanie, always with her two arms embracing mine in a pretty way she had. I was obliged to go at last—but what could I say? I could only kiss him, and tell him to keep still—that I was doing all I could. There is something mystical about the patience of a child. "It will come all right, won't it, father?" he said. "God grant it may! I hope so, Roland." "Oh, yes, it will come all right." Perhaps he understood that in the midst of my anxiety I could not stay with him as I should have done otherwise. But the girls were more surprised than it is possible to describe. They looked at me with wondering eyes. "If I were ill, papa, and you only stayed with me a moment, I should break my heart," said Agatha. But the boy had a sympathetic feeling. He knew that of my own will I would not have done it. I shut myself up in the library, where I could not rest, but kept pacing up and down like a caged beast. What could I do? and if I could do nothing, what would become of my boy? These were the questions that, without ceasing, pursued each other through my mind.

Simson came out to dinner, and when the house was all still, and most of the servants in bed, we went out and met Dr. Moncrieff, as we had appointed, at the head of the glen. Simson, for his part, was disposed to scoff at the Doctor. "If there are to be any spells, you know, I'll cut the whole concern," he said. I did not make him any reply. I had not invited him; he could go or come as he pleased. He was very talkative, far more so than suited my humour, as we went on. "One thing is certain, you know; there must be some human agency," he said. "It is all bosh about apparitions. I never have investigated the laws of sound to any great extent, and there's a great deal in ventriloquism that we don't know much about." "If it's the same to you," I said, "I wish you'd keep all that to yourself, Simson. It doesn't suit my state of mind." "Oh, I hope I know how to respect idiosyncrasy," he said. The very tone of his voice irritated me beyond measure. These scientific fellows, I wonder people put up with them as they do, when you have no mind for their cold-blooded confidence. Dr. Moncrieff met us about eleven o'clock, the same time as on the previous night. He was a large man, with a venerable countenance and white hair—old, but in full vigour, and thinking less of a cold night walk than many a younger man. He had his lantern, as I had. We were fully provided with means of lighting the place, and we were all of us resolute men. We had a rapid consultation as we went up, and the result was that we divided to different posts. Dr. Moncrieff remained inside the wall—if you can call that inside where there was no wall but one. Simson placed himself on the side next the ruins, so as to intercept any communication with the old house, which was what his mind was fixed upon. I was posted on the other side. To say that nothing could come near without being seen was self-evident. It had been so also on the previous night. Now, with our three lights in the midst of the darkness, the whole place seemed illuminated. Dr. Moncrieff's lantern, which was a large one, without any means of shutting up—an old-fashioned lantern with a pierced and ornamental top—shone steadily, the rays shooting out of it upward into the gloom. He placed it on the grass, where the middle of the room, if this had been a room, would have been. The usual effect of the light streaming out of the door-way was prevented by the illumination which Simson and I on either side supplied. With these differences, everything seemed as on the previous night.

And what occurred was exactly the same, with the same air of repetition, point for point, as I had formerly remarked. I declare that it seemed to me as if I were pushed against, put aside, by the owner of the voice as he paced up and down in his trouble,— though these are perfectly futile words, seeing that the stream of light from my lantern, and that from Simson's taper, lay broad and clear, without a shadow, without the smallest break, across the entire breadth of the grass. I had ceased even to be alarmed, for my part. My heart was rent with pity and trouble—pity for the poor suffering human creature that moaned and pleaded so, and trouble for myself and my boy. God! if I could not find any help—and what help could I find?—Roland would die.

We were all perfectly still till the first outburst was exhausted, as I knew (by experience) it would be. Dr. Moncrieff, to whom it was new, was quite motionless on the other side of the wall, as we were in our places. My heart had remained almost at its usual beating during the voice. I was used to it; it did not rouse all my pulses as it did at first. But just as it threw itself sobbing at the door (I cannot use other words), there suddenly came something which sent the blood coursing through my veins, and my heart into my mouth. It was a voice inside the wall—the minister's well-known voice. I would have been prepared for it in any kind of adjuration, but I was not prepared for what I heard. It came out with a sort of stammering, as if too much moved for utterance. "Willie, Willie! Oh, God preserve us! is it you?"

These simple words had an effect upon me that the voice of the invisible creature had ceased to have. I thought the old man, whom I had brought into this danger, had gone mad with terror. I made a dash round to the other side of the wall, half crazed myself with the thought. He was standing where I had left him, his shadow thrown vague and large upon the grass by the lantern which stood at his feet. I lifted my own light to see his face as I rushed forward. He was very pale, his eyes wet and glistening, his mouth quivering with parted lips. He neither saw nor heard me. We that had gone through this experience before, had crouched towards each other to get a little strength to bear it. But he was not even aware that I was there. His whole being seemed absorbed in anxiety and tenderness. He held out his hands, which trembled, but it seemed to me with eagerness, not fear. He went on speaking all the time. "Willie, if it is you—and it's you, if it is not a delusion of Satan,—Willie, lad! why come ye here frighting them that know you not? Why came ye not to me?"

He seemed to wait for an answer. When his voice ceased, his countenance, every line moving, continued to speak. Simson gave me another terrible shock, stealing into the open door-way with his light, as much awe-stricken, as wildly curious, as I. But the minister resumed, without seeing Simson, speaking to some one else. His voice took a tone of expostulation—

"Is this right to come here? Your mother's gone with your name on her lips. Do you think she would ever close her door on her own lad? Do ye think the Lord will close the door, ye faint-hearted creature? No!—I forbid ye! I forbid ye!" cried the old man. The sobbing voice had begun to resume its cries. He made a step forward, calling out the last words in a voice of command. "I forbid ye! Cry out no more to man. Go home, ye wandering spirit! go home! Do you hear me?—me that christened ye, that have struggled with ye, that have wrestled for ye with the Lord!" Here the loud tones of his voice sank into tenderness. "And her too, poor woman! poor woman! her you are calling upon. She's not here. You'll find her with the Lord. Go there and seek her, not here. Do you hear me, lad? go after her there. He'll let you in, though it's late. Man, take heart! if you will lie and sob and greet, let it be at heaven's gate, and not your poor mother's ruined door."

He stopped to get his breath; and the voice had stopped, not as it had done before, when its time was exhausted and all its repetitions said, but with a sobbing catch in the breath as if overruled. Then the minister spoke again, "Are you hearing me, Will? Oh, laddie, you've liked the beggarly elements all your days. Be done with them now. Go home to the Father—the Father! Are you hearing me?" Here the old man sank down upon his knees, his face raised upwards, his hands held up with a tremble in them, all white in the light in the midst of the darkness. I resisted as long as I could, though I cannot tell why,—then I, too, dropped upon my knees. Simson all the time stood in the door-way, with an expression in his face such as words could not tell, his under lip dropped, his eyes wild, staring. It seemed to be to him, that image of blank ignorance and wonder, that we were praying. All the time the voice, with a low arrested sobbing, lay just where he was standing, as I thought.

"Lord," the minister said—"Lord, take him into Thy everlasting habitations. The mother he cries to is with Thee. Who can open to him but Thee? Lord, when is it too late for Thee, or what is too hard for Thee? Lord, let that woman there draw him inower! Let her draw him inower!"

I sprang forward to catch something in my arms that flung itself wildly within the door. The illusion was so strong, that I never paused till I felt my forehead graze against the wall and my hands clutch the ground—for there was nobody there to save from falling, as in my foolishness I thought. Simson held out his hand to me to help me up. He was trembling and cold, his lower lip hanging, his speech almost inarticulate. "It's gone," he said, stammering,—"it's gone!" We leaned upon each other for a moment, trembling so much, both of us, that the whole scene trembled as if it were going to dissolve and disappear; and yet as long as I live I will never forget it—the shining of the strange lights, the blackness all round, the kneeling figure with all the whiteness of the light concentrated on its white venerable head and uplifted hands. A strange solemn stillness seemed to close all round us. By intervals a single syllable, "Lord! Lord!" came from the old minister's lips. He saw none of us, nor thought of us. I never knew how long we stood, like sentinels guarding him at his prayers, holding our lights in a confused dazed way, not knowing what we did. But at last he rose from his knees, and standing up at his full height, raised his arms, as the Scotch manner is at the end of a religious service, and solemnly gave the apostolical benediction—to what? to the silent earth, the dark woods, the wide breathing atmosphere; for we were but spectators gasping an Amen!

It seemed to me that it must be the middle of the night, as we all walked back. It was in reality very late. Dr. Moncrieff put his arm into mine. He walked slowly, with an air of exhaustion. It was as if we were coming from a death-bed. Something hushed and solemnized the very air. There was that sense of relief in it which there always is at the end of a death-struggle. And nature, persistent, never daunted, came back in all of us, as we returned into the ways of life. We said nothing to each other, indeed, for a time; but when we got clear of the trees and reached the opening near the house, where we could see the sky, Dr. Moncrieff himself was the first to speak. "I must be going," he said; "it's very late, I'm afraid. I will go down the glen, as I came."

"But not alone. I am going with you, Doctor."

"Well, I will not oppose it. I am an old man, and agitation wearies more than work. Yes; I'll be thankful of your arm. To-night, Colonel, you've done me more good turns than one."

I pressed his hand on my arm, not feeling able to speak. But Simson, who turned with us, and who had gone along all this time with his taper flaring, in entire unconsciousness, came to himself, apparently at the sound of our voices, and put out that wild little torch with a quick movement, as if of shame. "Let me carry your lantern," he said; "it is heavy." He recovered with a spring; and in a moment, from the awe-stricken spectator he had been, became himself, sceptical and cynical. "I should like to ask you a question," he said. "Do you believe in Purgatory, Doctor? It's not in the tenets of the Church, so far as I know."

"Sir," said Dr. Moncrief, "an old man like me is sometimes not very sure what he believes. There is just one thing I am certain of—and that is the loving-kindness of God."

"But I thought that was in this life. I am no theologian——"

"Sir," said the old man again, with a tremor in him which I could feel going over all his frame, "if I saw a friend of mine within the gates of hell, I would not despair but his Father would take him by the hand still, if he cried like *yon*."

"I allow it is very strange—very strange. I cannot see through it. That there must be human agency, I feel sure. Doctor, what made you decide upon the person and the name?"

The minister put out his hand with the impatience which a man might show if he were asked how he recognized his brother. "Tuts!" he said, in familiar speech; then more solemnly, "How should I not recognize a person that I know better—far better—than I know you?"

"Then you saw the man?"

Dr. Moncrief made no reply. He moved his hand again with a little impatient movement, and walked on, leaning heavily on my arm. And we went on for a long time without another word, threading the dark paths, which were steep and slippery with the damp of the winter. The air was very still—not more than enough to make a faint sighing in the branches, which mingled with the sound of the water to which we were descending. When we spoke again, it was about indifferent matters—about the height of the river, and the recent rains. We parted with the minister at his own door, where his old housekeeper appeared in great perturbation, waiting for him. "Eh, me, minister! the young gentleman will be worse?" she cried.

"Far from that—better. God bless him!" Dr. Moncrief said.

I think if Simson had begun again to me with his questions, I should have pitched him over the rocks as we returned up the glen; but he was silent, by a good inspiration. And the sky was clearer than it had been for many nights, shining high over the trees, with here and there a star faintly gleaming through the wilderness of dark and bare branches. The air, as I have said, was very soft in them, with a subdued and peaceful cadence. It was real, like every natural sound, and came to us like a hush of peace and relief. I thought there was a sound in it as of the breath of a sleeper, and it seemed clear to me that Roland must be sleeping, satisfied and calm. We went up to his room when we went in. There we found the complete hush of rest. My wife looked up out of a doze, and gave me a smile: "I think he is a great deal better; but you are very late," she said in a whisper, shading the light with her hand that the Doctor might see his patient. The boy had got back something like his own colour. He woke as we stood all round his bed. His eyes had the happy, half-awakened look of childhood, glad to shut again, yet pleased with the interruption and glimmer of the light. I stooped over him and kissed his forehead, which was moist and cool. "It is all well, Roland," I said. He looked up at me with a glance of pleasure, and took my hand and laid his cheek upon it, and so went to sleep.

For some nights after, I watched among the ruins, spending all the dark hours up to midnight patrolling about the bit of wall which was associated with so many emotions; but I heard nothing, and saw nothing beyond the quiet course of nature; nor, so far as I am aware, has anything been heard again. Dr. Moncrieff gave me the history of the youth, whom he never hesitated to name. I did not ask, as Simson did, how he recognized him. He had been a prodigal—weak, foolish, easily imposed upon, and "led away," as people say. All that we had heard had passed actually in life, the Doctor said. The young man had come home thus a day or two after his mother died—who was no more than the housekeeper in the old house—and distracted with the news, had thrown himself down at the door and called upon her to let him in. The old man could scarcely speak of it for tears. To me it seemed as if—heaven help us, how little do we know about anything!—a scene like that might impress itself somehow upon the hidden heart of nature. I do not pretend to know how, but the repetition had struck me at the time as, in its terrible strangeness and incomprehensibility, almost mechanical—as if the unseen actor could not exceed or vary, but was bound to re-enact the whole. One thing that struck me, however, greatly, was the likeness between the old minister and my boy in the manner of regarding these strange phenomena. Dr. Moncrieff was not terrified, as I had been myself, and all the rest of us. It was no "ghost," as I fear we all vulgarly considered it, to him—but a poor creature whom he knew under these conditions, just as he had known him in the flesh, having no doubt of his identity. And to Roland it was the same. This spirit in pain—if it was a spirit—this voice out of the unseen—was a poor fellow-creature in misery, to be succoured and helped out of his trouble, to my boy. He spoke to me quite frankly about it when he got better. "I knew father would find out some way," he said. And this was when he was strong and well, and all idea that he would turn hysterical or become a seer of visions had happily passed away.

I must add one curious fact, which does not seem to me to have any relation to the above, but which Simson made great use of, as the human agency which he was determined to find somehow. We had examined the ruins very closely at the time of these occurrences; but afterwards, when all was over, as we went casually about them one Sunday afternoon in the idleness of that unemployed day, Simson with his stick penetrated an old window which had been entirely blocked up with fallen soil. He jumped down into it in great excitement, and called me to follow. There we found a little hole—for it was more a hole than a room—entirely hidden under the ivy and ruins, in which there was a quantity of straw laid in a corner, as if some one had made a bed there, and some remains of crusts about the floor. Some one had lodged there, and not very long before, he made out; and that this unknown being was the author of all the mysterious sounds we heard he is convinced. "I told you it was human agency," he said triumphantly. He forgets, I suppose, how he and I stood with our lights, seeing nothing, while the space between us was audibly traversed by something that could speak, and sob, and suffer. There is no argument with men of this kind. He is ready to get up a laugh against me on this slender ground. "I was puzzled myself—I could not make it out—but I always felt convinced human agency was at the bottom of it. And here it is—and a clever fellow he must have been," the Doctor says.

Bagley left my service as soon as he got well. He assured me it was no want of respect, but he could not stand "them kind of things." And the man was so shaken and ghastly that I was glad to give him a present and let him go. For my own part, I made a point of staying out the time, two years, for which I had taken Brentwood; but I did not renew my tenancy. By that time we had settled, and found for ourselves a pleasant home of our own.

I must add, that when the Doctor defies me, I can always bring back gravity to his countenance, and a pause in his railing, when I remind him of the juniper-bush. To me that was a matter of little importance. I could believe I was mistaken. I did not care about it one way or other; but on his mind the effect was different. The miserable voice, the spirit in pain, he could think of as the result of ventriloquism, or reverberation, or—anything you please: an elaborate prolonged hoax, executed somehow by the tramp that had found a lodging in the old tower; but the juniper-bush staggered him. Things have effects so different on the minds of different men.

A CHRISTMAS GHOST
A STORY OF CHRISTMAS-TIDE—
A LIVELY EXPERIENCE AND A VERY
HAPPY RESULT
by
Anon
1882

Chapter I.

It was optional with me, of course, to refuse or accept: but somehow I adopted the latter course. I spouse it was easier to write a letter of acquiescence than of apology; or possibly the latent curiosity which I had kept in check for so long had asserted itself at last, to the defeat of reason and resolution.

Three years before I had spent a week at Forrest Hall; and when I brought my stay to an abrupt conclusion, I had almost registered a mental vow that I would never repeat the experiment of a visit again. Yet Mr. Forrester, my host, had been courteous, even cordial; his wife showed herself as agreeable as a foreigner, who spoke English but imperfectly could be; and there was no other visible inmate of the house to give umbrage or disturbance. The adjective may seem expressive; but as it is taken to imply that I suffered annoyance from nocturnal visitations of a spiritual cast, it says too much. It was not thus that my seven days' sojourn at the hall was rendered irritable and almost unendurable. But I need not pause upon a matter which will naturally unfold itself later.

It was on the eve of Christmas day that I drove beneath the ivied portal which gave entrance to the romantic old place that I had once looked upon as my own. It had belonged a few years before to my uncle, Mr. Godfrey Forrester. He had never married; I was his favourite nephew; and though the son of his youngest brother, it had been an assumed, almost settled thing that I, George Forrester, was to be his heir. The disappointment in these expectations came to me before that ominous and momentous day when the will was opened.

Some months before my uncle's decease I divined his intentions regarding the disposal of his property had varied, and that for no fault of mine, but, through a sudden favor shown to another, changes were made which were to work strangely on my after-life.

The son of his eldest brother came back from a long residence in Italy with an only and very lovely young daughter. They were naturally invited to Forrest Hall; and before the visit had ended I knew that a former estrangement between the uncle and nephew was dissipated by the friendly intercourse of the present, and more especially and entirely by the fascination exercised over the old gentleman by the winning brightness and beauty of Lucia Forrester. Her mother was an Italian and was still in her own country while the father and daughter paid this visit of policy to the fast failing owner of Forrest Hall.

They remained with him to the last, and it was found then that, with the exception of a small bequest to myself, the whole of my uncle's property was willed to his elder nephew, in version to his only child Lucia. I had met the latter, had spent a fortnight in the house with her, and had admitted that power of attraction was deep and incontestable. I thought of her now as I was borne swiftly along the drive, and came presently in view of the old Elizabethan mansion, which was her home. Though the weather was bleak, with a piercing wind blowing on the open road without the demense, here there was comparative shelter.

My Uncle Geoffrey had carried out one of his fancies to a successful issue, and had surrounded himself with the green and shade of summer when there was winter elsewhere. The whole grounds were planted thickly with evergreens which flourished almost like trees, so carefully had their luxuriance and growth been promoted; and now, at this Christmas season, outer decorations, as well as inner, might have been specially got up, judging from the glossy holly branches, ivy wreaths and laurel-boughs which filled the view on all sides.

It was evening; the house was very brilliantly lighted up; and as the hall door was thrown open; the warm glow within was all the pleasanter in contrast to the frosty air and flitting moonshine which held the world in a cold spell without. Something else was more inspiriting than all. It was a sight which met my eyes in the first moment of entering. A young lady was crossing the hall, and turning just in the doorway leading to the room opposite she gave me a smile of welcome. She was beautifully dressed in silk of a creamy shade, with some draperies of rich violet velvet, relieving the otherwise colorless picture: for the tint of her skin and hair harmonized with that of her dress, and was scarcely deeper in tone. But there was nothing insipid in a face which beamed with an expression, which had bewitchingly lovely features and a pair of dark blue eyes, set like stars beneath the delicate pencilling of her brows.

"Lucia!" I exclaimed, and sprang forward eagerly. "Have we then met last?"

"Have you come last?" she retorted quickly. "Three invitations and three refusals speak fairly for our friendship, but not for yours."

"An invitation to a place is nothing—the people are everything," I said. "When I was here you absented yourself strangely. Can you wonder I did not come again?"

This was the mere fact of the case. On the occasion of that former Christmas visit my cousin Lucia had not once shown herself. I was told that she was ill, and had felt bound to believe the statement, till it was strangely negatived by a sight which rendered me at once perplexed and indignant. I had started one day for a ride when something went wrong with the equipment of my steed, and I was obliged to return unexpectedly to the house. I was walking along the avenue of the hall, leading the horse by the bridle, when, in a pathway amongst the evergreens, I caught a glimpse of a well-remembered figure. the tall slight proportions, the girlish step, and the pale amber of the hair, which was rolled low upon the neck and rested on the glossy darkness of a seal-skin jacket, were sufficient in themselves to identify the lady; but any doubt or bewilderment on the subject was at once dissipated by. A full view of the face.

Miss Forrester had evidently heard the sound of advancing steps on the drive, for she turned suddenly. A rosy flush mounted to her brow at the moment; but before word or gesture could express questioning surprise on my part she was gone. Hurrying onwards I left the horse in the care of the groom, and went at once to the house. My enquiry for Miss Forrester was met by the reply that the young lady was still unwell, was confined to her room, and could see no one. Half an hour later I had left Forrest Hall, anger having predominated over the feeling of mystification which might have led me to prolong my stay in the hope of dissipating it by penetrations or investigation. I felt my cousin, who was the heiress now, was determined to arrest any incipient attentions of the former heir by showing him, in the most pointed manner, her disinclination even to tolerate his presence. It was galling enough to have to return as an impoverished guest to a place where I had once hoped to dispense hospitality, on my part, without incurring the additional humiliation of being subject to an unjust suspicion.

I could see nothing else in the strange withdrawal of my cousin Lucia from my society. She plainly thought that I might become too audacious as a suitor as I was determined that the inheritance, I had lost should not be regained through her. This was the view of her conduct which I took at the time, and which nettled me so that when an invitation came each succeeding Christmas to spend it at Forrest Hall I refused until the present occasion.

A little silvery laugh and a sweet bewildering glance dissipated everything but a sense of entrancement now. They had been the only reply to my enquiry but they were sufficient to arrest the questionings of the past in the view of a less perplexing future.

I was soon in the drawing room, to which Lucia led the way, and amid the excitement of the Christmas festivities. I was greeted cordially by Mrs. Forrester and my cousin Geoffrey. My hostess was a tall thin lady, scarcely foreign looking in appearance, as her complexion retained in a faded form the traces of fairness almost as dazzling as her daughter's. She was still in the prime of life, but a peculiar air of feebleness was given to her aspect by the way in which she carried her head. It was always slightly on one side, was enveloped with muslin or lace ties high up about the throat, and might have been bandaged on, so nervous was its balance and so little action was allowed its movements. She spoke generally in italics and emphasized her reception of me now in a way which was very gratifying.

"So glad to see you, Mr. Forrester. But you should have come before. Your absence was too bad. Did we offend you?"

I got out of the difficulty with a smile it was easy to summon up with Lucia close by, and ready, as I found, to give me her hand for the next dance.

The evening passed delightfully, though I was rendered a shade uneasy towards its close by the assiduity of a young gentleman who seemed determined to give Miss Forrester the benefit of his entire stock of information. London and literature, the country and sports, all were brought eloquently forward to gain a hold on his companion's attention. He had only been introduced to the young lady that night, I learned, but I could see at once that he was drawing the first parallel, and that, whether effectively or not, the tactics of a siege were beginning.

The next day we had skating. Lucia was an adept in the art, and went skimming over the glassy surface as graceful as a swan on unruffled water. I was out of practice, and was ploughing along in a rather labored fashion when she flew up to me.

"Do be a little more adventurous!" she exclaimed. "The outside edge is the easiest thing in the world. Can you not cut some figures?"

"One, as you see," I rejoined, laughing. "My awkwardness speaks for itself, but this singular state of things supposes anything but an advance in the plural direction."

"You are not so very bad," she said with a critical look. "Mr. Lerrington has come to grief twice already. He offered me his hand at starting, or rather made a clutch at mine, but unfortunately I managed a release."

Mr. Lerrington was the aspiring engineer who had laid himself out to be agreeable on the preceding evening, and whose sanguine nature still kept him up. He was beside us even as Miss Forrester spoke.

"Acmes are not perfection after all," he said gaily. "Something went wrong with mine, but they're all right now;" and he made a successful spin. That Lucia should follow him was not a matter for surprise, but that I should be left behind was certainly one for vexation.

Lucia mystified me, and therefore, attracted me. I wanted to understand her, but that could scarcely be done at a distance. In the present instance I could keep my footing, though speed was beyond me; yet this plainly was the thing desirable. Recklessness may be decried in other paths of life, but on the most slippery one of all it seems a most rightful exchange for prudence, an indispensable impetus to advance.

After a while the young lady grew tire either of the exercise or the escort, and was back again with me. I am afraid I had been contemplating rashness with too favorable an eye, for I was led away by it unwarrantably now. I began to question Lucia respecting her strange disappearance from the scene on the occasion of my last visit. Breaking the ice is hazardous work, and I certainly ought not to have attempted it here. I endangered myself, if not another. Lucia rarely flushed. Shade rather than color passed into her face from the effect of annoyance or emotion. A change of the kind was noticeable as I spoke, and I tried hastily to recover my former footing. But my companion would not let me quite escape any consequences of my temerity.

"You seem to have a good memory," she remarked. "But I am afraid it is only for trifles. Those you should forget, and not even remember that you are forgetting."

"We are apt to estimate matters very differently. "I said. "It might be little to you to keep in a seclusion you had cause to prefer, but your absence was not exactly a trifle to another."

"I know it was not so; but what it could have been is my point of view. Try to look at things in a pleasant light—it makes life easier."

"An effort in that line need not be recommended now," was my response. "There are moments when we have to set realities before us to subdue a too seductive illusion."

"You had better turn to the mainland then, and away from this slippery surface, if this should be one of those instants;" and with the words she was skimming off from me anew.

I saw her rejoin Lerrington, but could scarcely feel jealousy, it was so evident that his society was as indifferent to her as my own. But the fact that she was unimpressionable was not reassuring, taken in conjunction with her own too strong power of fascination I would rather she had shown susceptibility to almost any emotion than have perplexed me by her unruled loveliness.

CHAPTER II.

Was I dreaming or waking? My senses no doubt were enwrapt by the stillness of a frost bound midnight; but surely they were too watchful and observant to be enchanted likewise by the more potent spell of sleep! With my eyes wide open I started upright on my couch. The room I had been allotted on my arrival at Forrest Hall was one hitherto unoccupied buy me. But I could scarcely take exception to its comfort or position in the establishment, considering that it was one chosen by the late master of the house, and which was chosen as "Uncle Geoffrey's room." The bed, an old-fashioned one, faced a large mirror reaching from floor to ceiling and set into the wall. On the right hand side of the four-poster there was a door opening into a dressing closet. This was left unclosed at night; in the summer to give fuller ventilation to the sleeping apartment, which was low and gloomy, and in the winter to admit the subdued warmth and light from a fire that was kindled in a wide grate in the dressing-room.

Such had been the habit in my uncle's life, and I had made no change in the arrangements.

Looking now into the mirror I saw a form reflected at full length. It was moving slowly across the floor in the inner closet and advancing towards the mantelpiece. There was a bright blaze from a wood fire, and the glass being opposite my door and bed, gave back the clear particulars of the scene. It was a strange one; and some ghostly stories, which had been recounted for the benefit of the company by my cousin Lucia that night, came vividly to my mind. The figure I was gazing at was that of my Uncle Geoffrey, clothed in a well-remembered dressing gown of Indian pattern and gorgeous colouring. I saw his spare frame and his bent head just as I had seen them in life. When he had gained the chimney he stretched out his hand towards a large snuff box of tortoise shell, which lay on the marble ledge above.

At this moment I bounded from my couch. My own wakefulness at least was proved by the action; but it led to no further discovery. I lost sight for an instant of the mirror scene; and when I sprang through the open door of communication into the dressing-room, there was no reality here to justify the spectral appearance. The cabinet had its fire light glow and its usual air of comfort, but no occupant. The second door, which gave access to the outer corridor, was closed, and not a sound or footfall disturbed the quietude of the house.

I looked round me. There was no hiding place in the small chamber. Wherever the apparition had come from it had sought the same shrouded precincts again. I paused in a perplexity that was not exactly. I saw little reason for apprehension in a well lit, warm room, which showed no token of habitation, no outer possessions than my own. My coat was on a chair as I had last thrown it; my dressing case open on the table. There was nothing to remind me of a nocturnal intruder, and I could no longer conjure up even the vision of such. I returned to rest, and sleep came later, though it was sometime ere I removed a fixed gaze from the long glass opposite the couch.

I was down early the next morning and the first person I saw in the breakfast room was my cousin Lucia. She had on a beautifully made dress of some warm ruby shade with a bewitching little bow at the throat slumbering in lace.

"Good morning," she said softly. "You are more active than usual. Were your slumbers lighter or more profound? There was some change, I suppose?"

"For the better, of course, since the effect is good," I returned. "But I fear I indulge too much in waking dreams. They are cruelly delusive."

"Then give them up. That cannot be difficult if you dislike them."

"Did I say that? Some of them are only too dear, that is my main objection."

"O, the fault is in yourself, I see, not in the visions. I thought there was a reproach somewhere, but I am glad to find it is your own person."

"Yes, Lucia; I am guilty of a folly no doubt. There might be a cure for it, but I don't look for it."

"Why not? Hopefulness is a pleasant element in life. You ought to cultivate it. I might repay exertion."

What did she mean? Had she understood me; and, speaking to a scarcely breathed longing, was I to know that she fathomed it and was pitiful?

I might have been too daring, but the fortunate entrance of Mrs. Forrester arrested me. Her head was limply adjusted as usual, but there was no dubiousness in her manner; it was decidedly friendly.

I was apt to put in a more tardy appearance in the breakfast room, and her first question ran therefore in the same vein as her daughter's.

Had I slept well? The night had been so cold. She hoped that my fire had been properly attended to? Etc.

"Yes, there was a famous blaze," I responded. "It showed me a good deal more than the daylight brings out;" and then I mentioned the strange apparition in the dressing-room.

Mrs Forrester gazed at me with a sort of terror in her blue eyes and turned white as death. Lucia was perfectly composed, even rallied me playfully on my weak surrender to the sway of Morpheus.

"I make a better fight," she pursued, "but acknowledge myself beaten in the end. You seem to give way at once, and revenge yourself on your opponent by a mere denial of the victory."

"No, no; sleep is no enemy," I interposed. "I never struggle against it; and for that very reason, I suppose, it has less interest in visiting me. Last night, I know, it was very tardy in its advance. But I suppose you won't admit this?"

"Scarcely, with such clear evidence to the contrary. Dreams do not generally come before slumber."

"Walking dreams may, and mine seem to be all of this order."

The conversation dropped here. I did not press it, as I saw the same disturbed, even terrified, look in my hostess' face. She evidently believed in the possibility of an apparition, and especially in the credibility of what I had portrayed. The facts did not lessen my perplexity, but they made me resolve on attempting a solution of it myself.

There was a change in the weather this morning. Low-lying mists wrapped the frozen waters in a warning veil, white and mournful as a shroud. Skating was pronounced unsafe, and Lerrington, with some other gentlemen of the party, started on a shooting excursion. I remained at home, having still hopes that the approach of rain was more distant than appeared, and that the fog might pass off, giving us another day's enjoyment on the ice. Lucia was too fond of the exhilarating pastime to miss it, if it could with any sense of security be managed, and I determined if she were led into rashness it should not be alone.

Doubts or expectations, however, were at once ended when at twelve o'clock a light rain began to fall, and the wind veered full to the south. If my fair cousin could have been seen or spoken to the long hours which succeeded would not have been overclouded. But she absented herself from the drawing room and library during the entire morning and afternoon. I first saw her at dinner time, surrounded by the usual circle of guests, and scarcely inclined to afford me a fair share of her attention or amiability. Lerrington was on the scene and assiduous as ever. He attempted to shine now, but if Lucia listened to him it was scarcely with entrancement. She was evidently bored, or preoccupied at all events, and when the party broke up at an early hour she retired with an abruptness which betrayed a secret relief at her escape from society.

I found my room warm and bright as ever, and sat reading for some time by the fire in the dressing-room. Then I left a lamp burning on a table opposite the door leading to the inner chamber, and betook my self to rest.

In assuming this attitude I was far from feeling a disposition to slumber. On the contrary, I was never more wakeful in my life; but I was resolved that the apparent routine of matters should go on as other nights, and that no marked watchfulness on my part should ever affright a too nervous visitant.

Time passed, midnight approached, and I remembered with a quickening of the pulse, which rose at least to expectation, that it was just at this hour that the mirror before me had reflected such a strange scene on the preceding evening. The moment was exciting. I was not superstitious. It was suspicious rather which entered my thoughts, but this kept every sense strained and acute. The night was a gloomy one, and rain had begun to fall with such weight and persistency that the thick evergreens outside no longer formed a resting canopy, but promoted, as it were, a second shower, which maintained a ceaseless echo of that which came direct from the skies. The sobbing sounds without, the stillness of my low, darkly wainscoted chamber, each had a significance of its own which was somewhat sad and portentous. I could scarcely say what I apprehended, but my memory had gone back to circumstances of a faraway past. I heard when a by that my cousin Geoffrey had lost himself in our uncle's good graces through his habits of wild and reckless extravagance. Having had a final quarrel with him the nephew had gone abroad, where he managed for a time to subsist in some speculative fashion of his own. He married early an Italian lady with a fortune rather more considerable than usually falls to the lot of foreigners, and from this point in his career very little more was heard of him till he returned to Forrest Hall with his daughter, a lovely girl of sixteen, and paid a visit of policy to its fast failing owner. A strange notion crossed my mind as I recalled these details. I felt that it was quite possible, indeed most probable, that my cousin had become involved in fresh embarrassments when he made the successful move which had gained him the Forrest Hall property. Could it be that he had tried to step more quickly into this by any false play with its late master? Had a fictitious death been managed, and was Uncle Geoffrey still alive and a prisoner in some dark and mysterious way in the house? The vision I had seen gave some color to the thought, but it was dismissed again as a mere freak of imagination. Such a scheme, and its accomplishment, I well knew, could scarcely be a reality of days like the present.

Meditation evokes dreaminess, and in order to conquer it I took up a book which I had at hand. Just as I did so I became aware of some change in the light in my room. I raised my eyes to the mirror opposite to me, and saw that a shadowy form was crossing by the table with the lamp on it, towards the chimney-piece in the closet. It was that of my Uncle Geoffrey. Arrayed in the same flowered dressing-gown, with his head bent, and a stick in his hand, he went slowly along, and a faint groan could be heard. The groan chilled my blood; it caused a sort of horror mingled with alarm which was all the more unnerving because it was in a measure indefinite. What could the scene mean? This life-like, yet ghostly, apparition. Whence came it, and for what purpose?

Was it reality or illusion? Action was more to the purpose now than questioning, and the next moment I, too, was in Persian garb, and stealing across the floor of my chamber towards the outer door of this apartment. I had left it ajar, and as I gained the corridor I saw that the dressing-room door, which was close beside, was partly open as well. In a second I closed it noiselessly, turned the key in the lock, and was back again in my former quarters. As I re-entered I paused, and a creeping sensation of unknown dread paralysed further movement. The mirror was full before me, and in it the same reflection, the bowed, mournful figure of my Uncle Geoffrey. He was at the mantle-piece now, was stooping over it wit his back turned towards me, and one hand stretched out in the act of grasping his ancient snuff box. The lid had been raised, though it could scarcely have been with the view of putting the box to its ordinary purpose of use, for the thin fingers of the old man was placing something within the receptacle, not abstracting anything therefrom. To turn away from the glass to gain the inner door of communication with the dressing-room I must necessarily lose the mirrored picture for a second and fail to come directly upon the reality, having first to pass by the foot of the bed. This knowledge held me enchained a moment longer. Then the form, whether spirit or matter, began to glide off, and I felt that the crisis had come. I must follow it at all hazards. With a quick bound I was on the threshold of the cabinet; but an actual cry parted my lips at the instant. The room was empty! All remained as I had left it ere I retired to rest. The lamp was burning brightly, the wood-fire was cheerful, ruddy in its gleam as ever. Nothing ghostly or ghastly threw a lurid coloring on the quiet aspect of the scene. More bewildered, more awe-stricken than if I had beheld the phantom which had been such a vivid revelation, I could only stand and gaze. Then I approached the chimney corner. The tortoise shell box was on the high marble ledge but it was shut. It seemed hard to believe that a pallid hand had but recently been laid on it, had opened it, reclosed it. Yet all this I had seen. It was no trick of the imagination. I had been wakeful, expectant. Involuntarily, half mechanically, I lifted the box, and touched the silver spring at the side. The lid flew back at the action and revealed something novel and unexpected. The interstice within was not filled with the usual contents. A small folded paper had taken their place. To withdraw it was the work of a second. I was not dreaming before; But surely, I said to myself, there must be something of illusion now. The writing I had perused was that of my Uncle Geoffrey. It was clear and unmistakable. The well-remembered characters had a forcible peculiarity of their own, which I for one, was not likely to forget. As I gazed upon them I had present to me a new vision, his aged form, his withered hand. But the substance of the paper was dream like in the extreme and made me pass my hands more than once across my eyes to clear off any filmy veil of drowsiness. Here in a few words, a bequest was made to me. Half the Forrest Hall property was mine without reserve or condition; but an express wish followed on the bequest—that I should become the husband of my cousin Lucia Forrester. The document seemed to be a codicil to my uncle's will and I noticed at once that the date was a later one than that of the testament which had been produced and proved at his death.

When sleep came to me that night I had still the paper in my hand. I knew through disturbed slumbers that I had never let it go, yet if, awakening, I had failed to grasp it or perceive it, I could have felt little surprise. The mode of its discovery, the nature of its contents, scarcely pointed to the scenes of real life. They were more in harmony with the visions which were fleeting. But here was substance and no shadow here. The precious paper was close in my clasp, and at its touch a thrill of delightful hope ran through me. I was no longer an impoverished man, a fortune seeking suitor. However clear I might stand in my own sight of the latter reproach, I had needed hitherto the boldness which could defy the criticism of others. I had it now, and no further delay should interpose between suspense and possible happiness.

When I saw Lucia in the breakfast room that morning she was more bewitching, more beautiful than ever. I was naturally followed still by a sense of mystery, and felt for the first time drawn to a belief in spiritual manifestations. In no other way could I account for the extraordinary scene of the night. I said to myself that my uncle must have appeared to me to make known his will as well as his wishes; and if this were so, I was clearly called upon to carry out the latter. For reasons of my own, I mentioned this second vision in the presence of my cousin Geoffrey and his wife, as well as that of the other members of the party. I gave no details, but spoke of the vividness of the apparition. Again Mrs. Forrester showed a tremor of apprehension, and a deadly pallor in her face. Geoffrey started, too, and then I glanced anxiously towards Lucia. She was smiling and maintained through all my assertions and remarks a gay incredulity. My resolves were taken forthwith. I felt her to be guiltless of any participation in a possible conspiracy to suppress the proofs of my claim to a portion of the property; and an hour or two later I asked her to be my wife. She had been pleasant, if coquettish, with me all the morning, and on the other hand had treated Lerrington with a provoking nonchalance which quickened his perceptions to recall some important engagement in town. He said good bye, and was off from the Hall by an early train.

CHAPTER III.

"You may make what changes in it you please, but it won't change it for me, Lucia. I will never occupy the apartment."

We were standing in the long corridor at Forrest Hall. We implies enough. She was my wife now and thought she had a right to do anything with me. Her designs in the present instance turned fortunately towards a transformation of the house—not in its master. Yet even here I rebelled. When she proposed that Uncle Geoffrey's room and dressing closet should no longer be shut up, but put to some practical use, I uttered the above protest. Though the vision seen in the apartment had pointed only to a path of brightness still there was a mystery associated with it which left a sense of awe on my mind that might be always overshadowing.

The Forrest Hall mansion fell to my share in the new division of the property which had been made on the production of the codicil to the will, and my cousin Geoffrey had gone abroad then with his wife, leaving the bride and bridegroom to settle down in their home.

"There are rooms enough in the house," I added now, "to exercise your taste upon, Lucia. Those in the west wings are newer and brighter. Leave these in the peace which is a rightful enjoyment of the antiquated."

"George, you are superstitious," said the young bride, decisively. "It is not right to humor you in your weakness. I could never have fancied you are so silly—a believer in dreams."

"Life is a dream, if you like," I interposed. "But for me there is as much reality in one episode of it which concerns the night as in any lit up by the clearest sunshine. We may agree on this subject, but that won't alter what is conviction more than impression."

Lucia looked pained. She did not meet me with her usual raillery, nor turn, on the other hand, to reasoning. There was something of a distinct truthfulness in her nature which shrank from letting a misapprehension lie in the mind of another which it was in her power to dispel.

A minute later and I felt her hand stealing within my arm and she was drawing me towards the closed door of Uncle Geoffrey's chamber. Within its precincts, while her sweet eyes both asked pardon for a deception and again sank in bashful confession from my glance, I learnt a full explanation of the strange experience of the past—of all that I had seen in the mirror. The narrative took my fair confessor back to the date of my first visit to Forrest Hall, after her father had become master of it. On the eve of my arrival, in making some arrangements in her room, she chanced to come across an ornamented album which her uncle had placed in her hand on the very day of his death. He had murmured something about a special gift to her, and that he had remembered her wishes. She thought he was wandering at the time, and, being only occupied with watchful attendance on him, she had put it away and not thought of it since. She opened the book now casually and in doing so a paper fell from between the leaves—the very one which came finally into my possession. What followed was told with some rapidity, indeed confusion; but I pressed for no particulars, believing without a word that, however others might have acted, Lucia herself was free from reproach. It appears that her father had made objections to the document on the score of illegality, and had represented that it was better to put aside and not raise up family questionings and contentions. She had held firmly to the view that I should see it in any case, and for that purpose she kept it resolutely in her own hands. Her mother especially urged her to give it up; and, owing to the last clause in it, declared there would be something unmaidenly on her part to bring it forward. Lucia admitted that this plea embarrassed her in a measure. Still she would give no definite assurance as to her suppression of the paper; and she found then that her course of opposition to both parents was resented in an unexpected manner. She was kept a prisoner in her room during my stay; and it was only on one occasion, when I was supposed to be absent for the day, that she was allowed exercise on the grounds. She was on the point of returning to the house when I caught a glimpse of her there, and feeling that she could not well enter into explanations with me in a hurried moment, fled in confusion.

"And later?" I said, "How was it you were able to welcome me at my next visit?"

"I promised," she returned, "that I would not give you the paper—and I did not do so."

"Who did then?"

"No one. You found it yourself."

"Then I am still to live in ghostly intervention? I may not assume you a spirit, yet a woman too?"

"As you please," she murmured, and then, quick and light as the words fell from her, she glided off from the mirror room in which we were standing, and disappeared within the dressing-room. I followed her to find her gone; and while I gazed around me, in something of the old bewilderment, she was back with me again, having entered by the outer door from the corridor.

"What's the secret?" I said. "If you want the rooms to be opened up, you must throw light on them to begin with."

"I am afraid there is not much penetration in your nature," was the reply.

"You would make neither an investor, nor an explorer. I find out things for myself. You should be as clever."

"I am not as inquisitive, I know."

"I know it at all events," she broke in gaily. "If you had only examined the quaint old snuff box in the first instance instead of admiring yourself in the mirror there would have been no need of a vision. But you were too stupid."

"Too vain, I thought."

"I should prefer neither, and as the imputations are so unfounded we needn't quarrel over them. You are quicker than I am, I allow. Will the concession make you complaisant?"

The touch of flattery did its work, and I was enabled to gain a confirmation of my recent surmise that it was she who had personated Uncle Geoffrey. Only one point after this remained to be cleared up; and although she amused herself for some time in leaving the discovery of the matter to my own ingenuity, she grew reasonable presently. Touching some hidden spring in the oak panelling beside the chimney corner a door flew back and she gained access to an inner chamber, which opened in its turn on the corridor. In this way she had made her escape from the dressing closet whenever she found that my watchfulness of her movements extended beyond the scene disclosed in the mirror.

"What did my uncle mean by saying that he remembered your wishes, Lucia?" I asked finally.

"Inquisitorial still?" she exclaimed.

"An enquiring mind that sees for itself but does not question is better. However, if you are dull, I suppose I must only be indulgent. I did not like injustice, sir, that was all."

And with this admission I had to be satisfied. There was no need, indeed, to press for more. My uncle's will had been found; his wishes had been followed. What further could I ask?

WHAT WAS HE?
by
Theo Gift
1883

CHAPTER I.
THE FIRST TIME.

I think it was in the second week of August, 1868, that it happened. I may not be quite right about the time of the month or the month itself; but I am almost sure it was in August; and I know it was that summer, the summer of 1868, that I spent in Switzerland. If I make any mistakes, or there are found any discrepancies in this narrative, I hope the critics will excuse them, and not say sharp things about me, as they do of regular story-writers. I say at once, I do not know how to write a story at all, and have never done such a thing before in my life; but those who have heard the account of these three painful episodes in it have urged me (sorely against my will) to let them be printed here; and, perhaps, if they serve as a warning to anyone—if *he* be still in this world——But I had better tell what I have to tell, and leave you to judge whether I have been wise or not in doing so.

We were staying at a pension kept by a Madame Vambèry, just outside the little town of Abondance, among the Swiss Alps. It was a charming place, a sort of big, rambling chalet, built on the wooded slope of a steep hill, commanding a glorious view of the snowy mountains which framed us in on all sides but one; and looking straight down on the little town, with its picturesque jumble of red roofs and twisted chimneys, and the narrow rock-bound river which girdled its foundations like a dark-blue ribbon spangled with silver, or rushed deep and black under grim old arches which threw back its waters in wreaths of turbid foam.

We were a lively enough party at the chalet, Madame Vambèry being a pleasant woman, and having a knack of getting together young and pleasant inmates. I don't remember all of them, for they went and came; but I can recall a nice little Irish doctor, a handsome High Church clergyman and his sister, who went down regularly every morning to early mass in the town below; a French marquise, middle-aged, but fascinating; a newly-married couple, also French; and Helen Joyce, with whom I was travelling. I was then six-and-twenty, in high health and spirits, and unmarried; while she was still wearing her first widow's weeds. Indeed, it was as a help to recovering her spirits, sorely tried by her husband's death, that I had agreed to spend the year which had still to pass before my John would be ready for me in travelling with her.

I only mention this to show how I came to be there. Otherwise, neither my affairs nor Helen's have anything to do with this narrative, or contain the smallest interest for anyone else.

Unquestionably, the most interesting members of our party were the newly-married couple. They were both very young (she could scarcely have been eighteen) deliciously good-looking, over head and ears in love with one another, and had only been married a week! This last fact, from which the previous one naturally resulted, leaked out from the guileless chatter of the little bride herself, and naturally made them even more the central objects of observation and curiosity than they might otherwise have been; but, indeed, the young wife was pretty and innocent enough to attract notice anywhere—fresh from the convent-school where she had passed all her young life, naive as a babe and playful as a kitten, with big black eyes, most childishly round and liquid, a little head covered with short soft curls, and a complexion of milk and roses.

The husband, however, was even more remarkable for beauty: tall and slenderly made, with a perfectly oval face, long waving hair of a rich auburn colour, with pointed beard and moustachios slightly deeper in tint, and eyes the like of which I had never seen before; which were indeed the chief feature in his face, and which, though I could not call them beautiful, as some did, would have marked the man among a hundred others after years of forgetfulness.

If some of you think that this is an after fancy of mine, not existent at the time, but created by later impressions, you are wrong. What I say of them now I thought then, and even described in a letter which is still extant. 'Eyes not large, but looking so from a singular power of dilation in the pupil produced by any intensity of feeling, pleasant or the reverse; whites very convex, and with the dazzlingly opaque brilliancy of porcelain; iris of a bright golden colour, surrounded by an outer ring of deep greenish gray; the whole shaded, and made additionally noticeable by the straight, sharply-pencilled brows, inky-black, and slightly depressed towards the nose—a peculiarity which became intensified whenever their owner was excited to either irony or vexation, and which lent a curious and, to me, somewhat unpleasant expression to his face.'

The other ladies voted him as handsome as an archangel. Mr. Hume, our clergyman, suggested, half-laughingly, 'A fallen one!' But, whatever our opinions might be, they mattered very little to the subject of them. Those weirdly-brilliant eyes of his, with their orange-tawny light—a light which seemed to come from within, as in those of the leopard and night-hawk—had vision for nothing but the charming face of his young wife, while her innocent gaze seemed to lose itself in wondering admiration as it rested on him.

They were ridiculously in love with one another. We had been talking about the glaciers one day at table d'hote. He had often been in Switzerland, and was describing some of his feats in Alpine climbing, the while his girl-wife listened delightedly, and now and then put in a whisper to one of us:

'*N'est ce pas qu'il est tout à fait montagnard, mon mari?*'

Later in the evening, I happened to be out in the garden. It was not a large one, but had the effect of being so from being laid out in a succession of terraces cut out of the steep hillside, and planted thickly with all manner of flowering shrubs and fragrant, bright-hued blossoms. Strolling along the upper of these terraces, I was gazing out to where the great white mountains showed forth against a sapphire sky set thick with golden star-gleams, and inhaling the delicious fragrance of the pine-woods on the other side of the little river, when I became aware of the presence of our young lovers on the path below me. They were chatting in a little nook formed by the bench and the angle of the wall; he half kneeling on the former, and supporting her as she sat on the wall, her little feet crossed and hanging down in front of her, her slender childish figure pressed against his shoulder. She had on a black lace frock, cut so as to leave the neck and arms bare; and her pretty shoulders, charmingly white and dimpled, glittered like soft mounds of snow in the moonlight, which poured down on her in a silver rain, touching the little curls on her smooth brow, and turning to frosted bronze the crisp waves of her husband's hair, and the glossy leaves of an oleander, which drooped its rosy-flowered branches above them, and swayed softly in the summer breeze.

'*Eh bien, mon chéri,*' I could hear her saying in her clear little child-voice; 'tomorrow, then, thou wilt take me up to the mountains, and show me where to pick the "edelweiss," to take to my mother when we return?'

'If we can find a guide,' the husband answered; 'but they say one ought to engage them the day before, there are so many excursionists here at present.'

The little bride pouted, and struck him a playful blow on the mouth with a bunch of heliotrope which she held in one small white hand. The perfume, crushed against his lips, rose up to me in a sweet, sharp puff.

'Guides! What do we want with guides? Have you not told me how well you know these mountains, and how often you have been over them alone? You shall be my guide, Henri. I want no others, *point d'etrangers.*'

'But suppose any accident should happen to you, *petite ange?*'

'Accident! What accident? We are not going up Mont Blanc, and the *pastear Anglais* takes his sister always with him. *Est-ce que tu me crois poltronne, moi?*'

'*Je te crois tout à fait adorable*, he answered, and, stooping down, lifted her little sandalled shoe and kissed it. I thought it time to retire, and did so; but there had been no vulgar curiosity in my staying so long. They did their love-making perfectly openly, and there were several others besides me enjoying the perfumed air on those terraced walks.

Next evening, when we came home from our drive, we found the whole pension in a state of the greatest excitement and confusion. The marquise was in hysterics, Miss Hume's maid crying bitterly in the hall, while madame, pale as death, and with her hair all limp and unfrizzled, was giving distracted orders to half-a-dozen servants at once. She could only answer our questions in incoherent ejaculations.

'The most frightful accident—our dear young *nouveaux mariés*. Alas! that poor man! No, no, it was not lie; it was his wife; that charming, fresh, all-adorable child. She had ventured too near a crevasse to pluck a flower. The piece of snow on which she stood, loosened by the late rains, had slipped and she had fallen. *Dieu nous garde!* it was too horrible to think of. Some one had heard the cries of the poor husband, and had come to the rescue, but it was too late. She was dead—dead! They were bringing her body home now. *Pour son marie? Hélas!* why ask? They said he had tried to kill himself, too. The guides who lifted her from the crevasse had to restrain him by force from flinging himself in.'

It was too true. We heard it all over again from the Irish doctor, who had started off at once to the scene of the disaster; and I dare say you read it in the *Times* of that week under the head of 'Alpine Accidents,' and with some observations appended to it on the folly of people attempting mountain-climbing without guides. Indeed, there was nothing else to say. As the paper remarked, such fatalities are only too common, and the sole thing which marked this one as specially sad was the extreme youth and recent marriage of the innocent victim.

That same night Miss Hume and I went in to see the body. It had been laid out in a lower room, and hearing that the poor child's mother had been telegraphed for, we had gathered all the white flowers we could find to strew round the corpse, and so soften the sorrowful sight to those to whom it must be agony to gaze upon it.

It was a far more terrible one to us than we had expected. Not that there were any horrible facial wounds or disfigurement.

Curiously enough, as the servants had already told us, there was not a broken bone or a bruise on the whole body. Indeed, it must have been the mere shock of falling from such a giddy height that killed her, for she was found quite uninjured outwardly, lying on a bed of soft snow at the bottom of the crevasse; but to look on the expression of her young face one would have thought she had died in the most awful agony, so ghastly was the look frozen there in death—a look, not of pain, but of unutterable, indescribable fear, of frenzied horror and repulsion; while the tiny waxen hands, which some pious soul had tried to bind together cross-wise on the breast, were bent backwards, with the stiffened fingers curving towards the palm, as though warding off some sudden, unimaginable horror.

Miss Hume could hardly bear the sight. She put her hand over the contorted baby-features, and said faintly:

'Oh, would not one think there was no loving God behind death when a little girl can meet it so! Fancy a mother having only that look to remember her child's face by! Has no one a veil to cover it?'

I said I had, and sending her away, for she was quite unnerved, went to get it.

When I returned I forgot to bring a candle with me, and found the room in darkness, save for a broad stripe of moonlight falling through a window at one end of it upon the bier, which, with its slender white-robed occupant, stood in the centre of the floor. As a clergyman's daughter, and going to be a clergyman's wife, I had no fear of death, and not thinking that there was anyone else in the room, I was going in softly, when I stepped back, shocked and startled at finding myself in the presence of the widower. He had not seen me. He was standing on the further side of the bier his tall figure slightly bent over it, his arms raised high above his head, with the hands wreathed together and waving to and fro, as if in utterance of some prayer or malediction against the woe which had fallen on him; while, though the spot where he stood was all the darker for being just outside that one ray of light, I could see his eyes dilated to double their usual size, and blazing like two un-earthly lamps with a ghastly yellow glare, which seemed to positively irradiate the dark and tortured face beneath them.

Fully believing that the man had gone out of his mind with grief, I fled, pale and terrified, to my room, where I found Helen's maid was already packing our things for going. She said that, considering the state of her mistress's health and spirits, she had persuaded her not to remain in a house with death in it so soon after her own sad loss, and that, after some discussion, Helen had agreed to leave on the morrow. I was not sorry to hear it.

CHAPTER II.
THE SECOND TIME.

'Well, be sure and call me if I can be of any use, Mrs. Critchett.'

'I will, ma'am, thank you; and glad I should be to do so if it were in the night, and the nurse not here. They have engaged one. I made a point of it when I let 'em the rooms; seeing as how that was a thing I could not feel called on for, with my other lodgers to see to and all. But from what she says now, I shouldn't be a bit surprised if it was before the time. These young things never do calculate right with their first.'

'Has she no mother, Mrs. Critchett?'

'She has not, ma'am, which is maybe the reason I feel for her, being young too, as I said, and more ignorant of the world and its wickedness than nine out o' ten gurls nowadays. A most pious and godly young creetur' as ever I see; an' not over-strong. Sits there doing her bits of sewing for the baby as is coming with her Bible on her knee all day long, and sleeps with it under her piller at night. Even my 'usband, he says it's as good as reading a chapter to hear her talk; which no offence to you, ma'am, all the same, as of course she is nothing but a Quaker, which nat'rally you, being a clergyman's wife, might objec' to have anythink to do with.'

'I should object to myself very much, Mrs. Critchett, if I had any such feeling, or my husband either! so don't forget to mention to your young lodger that if she feels nervous or ailing, there is a lady upstairs who will be very glad to come and see her, or to help her in any way.'

It was the winter of 1875. I had been married nearly six years, and John and I were living in lodgings in Guildford Street, Bloomsbury, not far from St. Thomas's Church, where my husband was senior curate. I should have preferred a house of my own; but circumstances made lodgings more practicable to us just then; and these were very clean, comfortable ones, and kept by an exceedingly worthy woman. We had the drawing-rooms and the best bed-rooms above; and besides us there were in the house three other lodgers; a clerk in some City house and his wife, who occupied the dining-rooms, and a queer old bachelor, who lived in one room at the top of the house, and whom we had never yet seen, though he was an older resident than ourselves, and we had lived with Mrs. Critchett for over three years. As for the couple downstairs, they had only been there for three months; and all I knew of them was that I used to get a glimpse, now and then, of a stoutish, thick-set young man, with light hair and a florid complexion, going in to the City of a morning, also that he and his wife had not been married long, and that she was understood to be in a delicate state of health.

Probably for that reason, she went out very seldom, except after dusk, and leaning on her husband's arm; and though I had passed her two or three times on the staircase, or at the door of her room, I had no very distinct impression of her, save of a fair, slenderly-made young woman, with a very good, pure-looking face, to which her simple dove-coloured gowns and muslin caps lent a certain soft attractiveness.

My offer to be of any service to her in her trouble, however, had not come a day too soon, for that very night the summons arrived. About nine o'clock Mrs. Critchett came running to tell me that 'poor Mrs. Jones was took bad. Her husband had gone for the nurse and doctor, and would I mind stepping down and comforting her a bit.' Of course I went. There was not very much for me to do, however, though my inclination to do it was enhanced now that I had time to appreciate more thoroughly the absolute beauty of holiness shining from the pale young face which I found lying so patiently on its pillows below. She was very weak, and suffering a great deal; but she made no complaint or fuss, and indeed hardly spoke, except to utter a gentle ' Thank you,' now and then; or a more pathetic, 'Thou art very good to me, friend. It grieves me to trouble thee.' When the doctor arrived, he said all was going on as well as possible; and, indeed, a very few minutes after Mr. Jones returned with the nurse (who lived at the other side of London, and had not expected to be wanted so soon) everything was over, and there was another tiny citizen the more in the world.

I had gone back to my own rooms by then, not wishing to be in the way, and thinking that between husband, nurse, doctor, and landlady, those very small apartments down-stairs would be sufficiently tenanted. Indeed, I was in the act of telling John, who had just come in, all about it, and what a nice gentle creature the young Quaker wife seemed to be, when the stillness which had followed pleasantly on the late bustle and upset in the house was broken by a sudden hoarse shriek; then an opening and shutting of doors, and the sound of footsteps hurrying to and fro.

'Something is wrong. What can it be, John?' I said, getting up, and looking apprehensively at my husband, and almost in the same moment Mrs. Critchett's maid came to the door with a breathless message:

'Oh, if yon please, ma'am, missus says could you come at once. She thinks Mrs. Jones is going.'

'Going!' By the time I had got from my room to hers, it was plain that she was so far gone that the eyes into which mine looked would never know me or any earthly thing again on this side of the grave. In sober truth, I hardly knew her! The apartment had been tidied and put straight. There was a pleasant glow of fire and lamplight in it, the latter carefully shaded from the face which lay back upon its pillows just as I had left it barely an hour ago. But during that short time such a change had come over the features as no mere womanish pain or distress had had power to bring into them previously; and before which all that exquisite, calm trustfulness, which had been their principal characteristic before, was blotted out as completely as though a livid and alien mask had been pressed down upon them. And such a mask! Such a ghastly presentment of unutterable woe, horror, and repulsion—agonized, terror-stricken repulsion, as I had never, in all my life, seen on any human face before, *save one!*

The face of that girl-bride who perished in the Swiss Alps.

I had forgotten her. The whole incident had slipped from my mind until recalled to it now, seven years afterwards, by that never-to-be-forgotten look of mortal, unendurable terror, repeated even in the very pose of the poor hands which, damp and clammy in death's closing grasp, were yet lifted up with the palm turned outwards and the fingers slightly curved, as though in a last effort to thrust from her something, or some vision, too horrible to see and live.

She was not quite dead, however, though the only sign of life was a faint convulsive shivering of the limbs and lips; and both the nurse and landlady vied with me in striving, by applications of ice, brandy, etc., to recall the fast-ebbing sands of existence, the while the last-named woman answered as well as she could my horror-stricken inquiries as to the cause of the terrible change before me.

'Ma'am, she was going on as well as possible. Very weak, but nothing in the world wrong; though the baby, poor thing, is but a measly bit of a creature, and not like to live, the doctor says. He had done all as was needed, and was in a hurry to get off to another case, so after he'd spoke to Mr. Jones, and told him he might go in and see his wife (as was asking for him), off he went. I let him out myself, and then went into the little back room there to nurse, who was 'tending the baby. She told me she'd just shown the gentleman in here, and bid him be careful not to excite his good lady; but, indeed, there seemed no fear of that, for he went in as soft and quiet as a mouse, while she was lying smiling on her bed like any angel, as calm and still.

"'And an angel she's been all through," I said, when the words were hardly out of my mouth but there came a shriek from this room as you might have heard upstairs, and as hardly sounded like her voice, though we knew it couldn't be no other. Nurse and me we rushed in, and there she was, sitting bolt upright in bed with her arms lifted up and her face like it is now, and him—Mr. Jones, I mean—trying to lie her down and soothe her.

'We put her back almost by force like, for she seemed quite unconscious and stiff, as if she was in a fit; and he began telling us as he'd hardly said a word before a donkey, as was kept in a yard near by, suddenly brayed out loud, and so startled her she sprang up in bed with the scream we heard, when nurse here she stopped him, and bid him run for dear life after the doctor and fetch him back.

"'Never mind what frightened her," said she, "but go this minnit. She's dying now, an' if yon don't catch up with him she'll be gone before you get back."'

There was a knock at the door at that instant, and with the exclamation, 'There he is!' Mrs. Critchett broke off in her narrative and hurried out. A second later and we heard her opening the front door, and speaking volubly to someone there; then steps coming along the corridor, and another voice—a voice that somehow sent a cold, strange thrill through me, though I had no recollection of ever having heard it before—asking in tones which, low as they were, penetrated clearly to where I stood, 'Is she still alive?'

Someone else heard the question besides me—the dying woman! I was holding her, supported on my arm; and at the first sound of that voice I felt a sharp, swift shiver run through her entire frame, while for one instant the secret horror hidden behind those glazed and staring eyeballs flashed into sudden life. The white lips met with a sharp, hissing gasp, and then dropped apart; the hands fell heavily at her side; the eyelids closed.

She had died—died while her husband was still asking if she lived.

Involuntarily I sank down upon my knees and bowed my head upon the bedclothes. At such a moment—the moment when a soul is suddenly torn away from earth and set before the judgment-seat of God—prayer seems the fittest and only attitude for those called on to witness the solemn change. Another step had, however, already entered the room, and as it slowly advanced to the foot of the bed I looked up, meaning to say such poor words of sympathy or comfort as might come to my lips to aid the man so terribly stricken in the first recognition of his bereavement.

They were never uttered! Instead, I found myself staggering dumbly to my feet, with eyes fixed and staring, and a sudden icy coldness at my heart, as though every drop of blood there had been jerked violently upwards to my confused and startled brain. Where— where and when had I seen before—not *this* man now facing me, this plain, dull-browed, sandy-haired English clerk, with whose back-view only I had hitherto been familiar—not him; but *his eyes!* eyes unlike in shape and colour every other feature in his face, dark and sinister, with abnormally dilated pupils, black, sharply-lined brows, with a deep depression towards the centre of the nose, and irides of a lurid orange hue which seemed to glow and scintillate as with some inward flame?

I have no remembrance of how I left the room.

Next morning, before I was up, John spoke very seriously to me, warning me never to say to anyone else what I had told him the previous night, and blaming me for letting my imagination (as he called it) affect my nerves and moral judgment in the way it had done. He pointed out to me that sudden death might not unnaturally leave a more painful expression on the face than a gentle or lingering one, and that it was the recollections suddenly recalled to me by this one when I was tired and over-excited, and not any real resemblance, which had induced me to fancy a similarity between the personality of our fellow-lodger and the handsome young Frenchman of seven years back.

He told me also that he had seen the former several times, and could not detect anything weird or unusual in his eyes save that they, as well as the brows, were rather darker than the general tone of his colouring warranted; and that from what he heard from the nurse and doctor, he was of opinion that the poor young woman's death resulted from perfectly natural causes, and such as would most probably be induced in a nervous woman in her condition by any sudden fright or strain to the system. He said this and a good deal more, and I listened and was silent. I even tried to believe that he was right, and did not ask,

'But *was* she a nervous woman, or one peculiarly the reverse; and why should I, on whose strength and common-sense you have relied for six years, and who have stood with you beside many and many a death-bed, and helped you to comfort all sorts and conditions of mourners, turn suddenly, and without any cause, nervous and fanciful also?'

That evening Mrs. Critchett came to tell me that the baby was dead also, and that the widower had given her notice, saying that he could not bear to stay in the house once the double funeral was over. She added:

'Not that a day-old child can make much difference to him, poor man; and, for my part, I think it's better out of the way. It was miserably delicate from the first, and had the queerest eyes, black and uncanny as a little imp. For that matter there's something about the father's—God forgive me for saying it of him, poor soul!—which always make me feel a bit creepy. Did you ever notice them, ma'am?'

CHAPTER III.
THE THIRD TIME.

What follows is taken from my last year's note-book, the Christmas week of 1882. I copy it just as it stands, without any alteration whatever, save as regards the actual names of the town and people concerned in it. As I am still living in the former, and my husband is rector of the parish, it might possibly be injurious to him or others were I to omit this one caution.

Nov. 25th.—Just a month to Christmas, our first Christmas at the rectory! What a stately, comfortable sound it has, and how well it suits John! He seems actually growing stouter to fit it. Martha tells me that the house adjoining ours is let at last. I am glad of it, for it is a serious drawback to our pretty, cheerful home to be obliged to look out on those desolate, weed-grown gardens, those rows of gaunt and shuttered windows. It is a large house too, and one of the oldest in the place. They say one wing dates back nearly two hundred years; but it belongs to a family who do not live there, and it has been unlet for a long time. I believe there is some talk of its being haunted, and that tenants will not stay in it. I hope the new ones will prove exceptions to the rule. It is quite cheering even to see the huge iron gates standing open, and painters and glaziers already hard at work all over the premises.

Nov. 30th.—I have been listening to a terrible story to-day—a ghost story, too, of all things in the world for a sober rector's wife to give ear to; but as it relates to The Priory (the name by which the house adjoining ours is known), and explains the holy horror with which even the school-children regard that mansion, I thought I might be excused for letting the old woman who comes to mend my carpets give me her version of the legend in question. I need hardly say that she believes in it most implicitly herself.

It seems that about a hundred years ago it belonged to a member of the Thorpe family who had made a very unfortunate marriage. That is to say, he had married a very young and lovely girl who had all the outward semblances of purity and innocence, and who, nevertheless, turned out to be as shamelessly wicked as what old Mrs. Luton calls 'the baddest lot in the town.' Not content with being false to her husband, she used his absence in America, on diplomatic business connected with our ratification of the lately-fought-out independence of the colonies there, to turn the dignified old Priory into a pandemonium of such reckless license and dissipation as filled the whole county with the scandal of the doings there, and caused her dissolute companions to be publicly hooted in the streets of the little township.

It is surmised that she and one of them had planned an elopement to take place before the return of the injured husband from abroad, and so place her in safety from his wrath; but, if so, her scheme was frustrated. Major Thorpe returned three weeks sooner than had been expected, and was met on landing by an old servant who had left The Priory in disgust at the scenes enacted there, and who lost no time in acquainting his master with them.

The scene which followed must have been a terrible one; for even at this distance of time the old woman's voice sank, and she looked furtively about her before telling of it. At first, indeed, Major Thorpe said nought, but struck down and went nigh to murder the man who had dared to blacken his wife's fame to him; but when convinced of the truth of his story, he lifted his two arms to heaven and swore so terrible an oath of vengeance as curdled the very blood of the listener to hear—offering himself to perish everlastingly in the nethermost flames of hell if for those dishonoured seven months of his absence he might be allowed, not only to punish her who had polluted them, but once in seven years to wreak such residue of his wrongs as her mere death could not atone for on some other woman, young and pure and innocent as she had seemed to be, and so satisfy his tortured soul for the worse torture that first woman had inflicted on him.

Next day it was rumoured among some in the town that Major Thorpe had been seen in the neighbourhood; and one old gardener even swore to having seen a figure which he recognised as his master's lurking among the shrubs in The Priory garden; but no hint of this reached the guilty revellers within, or perhaps they might even then have escaped the doom hanging over them.

That same night a sudden cry of 'Fire!' was raised in the quiet old town; and folks, roused from their sleep and rushing to the spot, saw flames pouring from the lower windows of that part of The Priory which the frail Mrs. Thorpe inhabited. The servants, who slept in another wing, were already awaked, and had made good their escape; but all their attempts at rescuing their mistress proved futile, the door opening from the great hall to her suite of apartments being found to be locked and barred; while through crack and keyhole poured a crimson glow which showed that all within was already a sea of roaring flame.

And then, while the shrieks of the victims within and the crowd without rent the air, and while some ran for water and some for ladders, and some fled hiding their eyes for very fear and horror, there was seen at one of the upper windows an awful sight; for there, during the space of one minute, there appeared, as if painted against a curtain of lurid red and framed in wreaths of smoke, three figures—a man and woman, and between them Major Thorpe, holding a hand of each clasped together in the iron clutch of one of his, and with the other levelling a pistol menacingly at the head of the man, whose left arm hung, evidently broken, at his side; the while the woman writhed and shrieked and clung to him with vain cries for mercy.

One second, I say, this was visible. The next there came an awful crash, as though a magazine had exploded at their feet, and in a breath the whole front of the house, roof, windows, walls and all, disappeared and crumbled away in a vast sheet of white flame which shot high into the air and sank down, carrying those three figures with it.

No smallest portion of their bodies was found when the ruins came to be searched afterwards; and in course of time the Thorpe family rebuilt the house as it now stands, and announced it as to let; but already an evil name had accrued to it. People spoke of cries issuing from the empty rooms, and of a shadowy male form seen prowling along the galleries of the one wing of the ancient building still remaining, or in the deserted garden; and though tenants came, it was only to go again the more quickly.

It remains to be seen if the new people (an Indian colonel and his wife) will be braver.

But I am half ashamed to have listened to such a farrago of romance and superstition, after all. I hope no one will whisper a word of it to my little Jo. He is fond of making his way into that garden and playing there.

Dec. 15th.—They are come, and I have seen them; that is, I have had a distant view of them from my bedroom window, as they stood on their lawn together: he, a tall, white-haired, soldierly-looking man, with a long moustache; she, a singularly slender, graceful woman, in black, with a large silver cross round her neck, and seemingly much the younger of the two. People who have met them tell me they are both delightful, and the greatest acquisition to the place that it has had for years; but I fear we are not fated to know much of them. Colonel Thorpe (he is a distant cousin of the owners of the house) is an avowed freethinker, and his beautiful wife—what sounds far worse in the ears of our good townsfolk—a papist! ' A most devout one, too' Lady Fanshawe, our patron's wife, told me. 'Had set her heart on going into a convent when Colonel Thorpe met her, and fell so in love with her he persuaded her to marry him instead. A sweet creature, with a delicious, nun-like unworldliness added to her new matronhood, which makes me quite in love with her myself. You mustn't call there, however. That bad colonel hates parsons, and swears he won't have anyone from a parson's house inside his. Isn't it dreadful of him?'

'And his wife?' I said.

'Oh, my dear, didn't I tell you she was a Romanist, and you know the ill-feeling here against the late rector for his ritualistic tendencies. It would never do for you or your husband to seem to run after her. Your parishioners would be in arms against you at once.'

What narrow, narrow places provincial towns are!

Dec. 23rd.—Something has happened which has upset me terribly; I do not know what to think of it, whether I am under a delusion, or am not so strong as I was; or what it portends, if indeed it portends anything. If John were only here! But he left yesterday for Dullminster on a visit to the bishop, and will not be back till this afternoon. Perhaps, too, he would only laugh at me. Once before, that time in Bloomsbury, he said it was imagination; and now—— But I had better write it all down. Perhaps, if it looks ridiculous on paper, I may be able to feel the foolishness of it myself.

I was going down to the church yesterday afternoon to see about the decorations. There is a narrow lane dividing the Priory grounds from the churchyard, which makes a short cut from our house to the latter; and along this I was hurrying, when, midway in it, I encountered Colonel Thorpe. He was carrying a leather hand-bag, as if bound on a journey, and as it was the first time I had had an opportunity of seeing him close, I naturally slackened my pace a little, so as to get a better view of him. Believe me when I say it, I had no other thought in my mind, no other motive than the natural womanly curiosity to look at one who was not only our nearest neighbour, but a man of good position in the county; and my first glance at the tall, erect figure, the white locks, and long gray moustache, with pointed military tips, gave me a distinct feeling of admiration. In the same moment, however, I was conscious of a change coming over me; a kind of coldness, mingled with a nervous thrill, which quickened as he grew nearer. Instinctively I hung back, a sort of chilled expectancy, though of what I knew not, clogging my steps; while, by contrary impulse, dread, blended with desire, drew my eyes more and more eagerly to his. A double wave of memory seemed to sweep over me—sharp peaks of dazzling snow rising against a sapphire sky, the scent of heaped white flowers on a silent form; and anon a close sick-room, cold, clutching hands, and the wail of a babe near by. A mist was gathering over my gaze, my hands felt cold, my head giddy; and, instead of the man before me, I seemed to see the outline of a window filled with lurid flame, and gleaming out of it a pair of eyes—fierce, dark, with hugely dilated pupils, and irises of a tawny yellow, glowing like two hellish coals with inward fire; the very eyes—God help me now, as I speak the truth!—which seven years before had met mine over the lifeless body of the City clerk's young wife; which once again, seven years before that, had lit with such a wild and ghastly glare the dark face of the young Frenchman in the Swiss chalet! And then, in the same moment, the mist cleared, and I saw the eyes only, and knew that they were in Colonel Thorpe's face, and that *they recognised me!*

Aye, believe it or not, they did; and I knew it; not by any process which I could describe to you—for, indeed, I am not clever at analyses of any sort—hut by that nameless sympathetic flash and thrill, that upleaping something in the gaze, which says to you, and everyone meeting it, whether they can answer it or not, 'I know you!'

There was no syllable spoken, no pause on either side. We met, and passed, and I went on to the church; but in such a tumult of feeling as I pray God I may never experience again: so shaken, and filled by an overpowering sense of some terrible impending calamity, which, nevertheless, I did not think of as affecting me, as shook me to my very centre with impotent terror and anxiety.

For what could I do, or say, that would not proclaim me a hopeless maniac were I to strive to avert an evil, which even in my madness (if madness it was) I could not dare to put into words, if I could find words to put it in, and which all the time I felt myself hopelessly powerless to avert? How could I call at the Priory, intrude on its stately young mistress, and implore her to fly from her home and seek shelter with a stranger like me, or anyone else, from her own natural protector, the husband for whose love she had given up her own holiest hopes and ambitions? And yet it was over her head I knew the doom to be impending; and, hour by hour, as I sat trying to work or read in my own peaceful house, I felt it coming nearer and nearer to the ill-fated one adjoining us, and saw again the mocking, pitiless gleam of those eyes defying me to war against the lost soul behind them.

And it only wanted two days to Christmas! Everything else looked so gay, so tranquil. I even caught a glimpse of her during the day speaking to a couple of poor tramps at the gate, and bringing them bread and meat in her own hands.

I must hurry on.

When night came I could not sleep. I had felt better and more cheerful during the evening. In fact, I had taken the trouble to ascertain that Colonel Thorpe had really been starting for London when I saw him that afternoon, and would not return till next day. The doom, then, whatever it might be, was not to fall immediately on its innocent victim. Providence might even yet show me some means for warding it off, and directly I felt this my spirits rose, and I even felt able to laugh at myself for my forebodings, and to feel glad John was not at home to scold me for them.

But after I was in bed sleep would not come to me. I was not ill or feverish, my head did not ache. There was nothing the matter with me except that, try as I might, my eyes would not close in slumber. I remained wide awake for a couple of hours or more, and at last, wearied of lying thus, got up and went to the window, meaning to look out at the night before lighting a candle and trying to read myself to sleep.

It was then just on the stroke of one. The whole town was asleep and in bed, and over everything reigned that perfect stillness which in London it is impossible to find at any hour. Opposite me was the Priory, shuttered and silent too, and its gardens white with frost and bathed in the full rays of the moon, save where a belt of trees or shrubbery cast darkly-waving shadows on the silvery surface.

I was still gazing, when suddenly one of these shadows seemed to detach itself from the rest, and glide forward with a motion suggestive of some crouching creature unwilling to be seen. Involuntarily the old woman's story of the Priory ghost flashed back upon my mind, and I leant forward to see better; but in the same moment the moon had passed behind a cloud, and the shade disappeared, sucked back into the general obscurity of the shrubs through which it had seemed to be creeping: only for an instant, however! The next, the full silver orb rode out again calm and bright as ever upon the blue expanse, and as it did so the bushes swayed and parted, and out from among them stepped a tall black figure, which stood erect in the moonbeams—no ghost, but a man, and the man I had thought of as at that moment far and safely away—Colonel Thorpe!

There was no mistaking him; no possibility of delusion. For two full seconds he stood there in the white moonlight, dressed as I had seen him earlier in the day, with his blanched hair and long curved moustache glittering in the silver rays, and then plunged again into the shadow, and disappeared in the direction of the house.

January 30th, 1883.—It is many weeks since I have written in my diary. I have been ill for almost the first time in my life—very ill. They would not even let me write letters for some time, but now that I am well and feeling strong again I must add a few words.

I think it was about mid-day on Christmas Eve that the news reached us that young Mrs. Thorpe was dead. The lady's-maid had found her bed unslept in in the morning, and on search being made she was discovered in the library (a room in the older part of the house), on her knees, and stone dead. It seemed that she had told the maid on the previous evening not to wait up for her, as she had promised to do some copying for the Colonel, which might keep her up late; and from her position, combined with the papers on the table and an overturned chair behind her, it was surmised that she had been suddenly startled from her occupation by some sight or sound—though what, none could say—and had actually died of fright.

Colonel Thorpe was away in London at the time; but by a curious chance had left for home before the telegram summoning him arrived, and he appeared among the bewildered and terrified servants within half an hour of their discovery of his wife's body. One of them told me afterwards it was a sight to make the bravest shudder—he standing there gazing at her as if turned into stone, and she, his wife, stretched at his feet with that awful look of terror—the terror that had killed her—still staring dumbly from her dead face, and the silver cross she generally wore held stiffly up in both the poor cold hands, as if in mute appeal to Heaven. The husband has gone abroad again now, and the Priory is once more untenanted. They say it will be pulled down, for that after what has happened this time no one will ever live in it again.

With this fragment from my diary, my story ends. I have nothing more to say, and no arguments to put forward. If, indeed, such a thing be possible as that He who permitted the Evil One to exercise his will on holy Job, and suffered to take place the yet more mysterious temptation of the desert, should, for some unknown dispensation, have allowed the curse of a lost and reckless soul to take actual form and shape, and by the mere revelation for one instant of its infernal personality crush out as instantaneously and irremediably the spark of life in its hapless victims, it is not for me to say; nor is this the place for the discussion of such suggestions. All I wish to repeat, and I do so most earnestly, is that the facts I have narrated did actually take place, and that I, a practical, commonplace, unromantic woman, did actually see and witness them. If to other minds they offer an easy and unalarming explanation, I am glad of it; but I would rather not discuss it with them. I will only mention that both Miss Hume and the landlady in Guildford Street are anxious to confirm my account of the events relative to the latter's lodgings and the Swiss pension.

THE BEESTON GHOST;
OR FORTY YEARS AGO.
A NORFOLK TALE
Edited

by

The Reverend John Swaffield Orton, Rector of Beeston-next-Mileham
1884

CHRISTMAS EVE.

An old-fashioned Christmas Eve; snow on the ground knee deep, on the bare branches of the trees, weighing down the evergreens. The hulver's smooth green leaves and crimson berries peep out brightly from underneath their cold white burden; altogether it is such a night as makes the warm light from the Ploughshare, swimming across the village street, very pleasant to look at.

There are only tallow candles set in last century candlesticks on the landlord's deal tables, for gas has not yet been introduced in towns like Dereham, Swaffham, and Fakenham, and even oil-lamps are a luxury in village life; but the jovial fire, with its great Christmas log, roars up the wide chimney; the landlord has fetched out his best old October-brewed ale in honour of the occasion, and all is merriment and jollity.

The oaken settles all round the room help to keep out the bitter weather. Gradually the room is filled with rustics who mean to make a night of it. The odour of the coarsest tobacco pervades the assembly. Little conversation goes on at first; all seem bent upon thawing their limbs and emptying their mugs. At last conversation begins pretty generally, and a voice that always commands attention is heard above the others.

"I doant moind sich a Christmas as this here sin' my ould mawther died ten yaars ago," remarks Will Spraggs, a corpulent fellow of middle age, shaking off the ashes from his short black pipe on to the clean sanded floor of the "al'us." "The snow war two fut deep, and covered the corfin white at the buryin, and we could scarce carry it to the charchyard for the drifts."

"That war the same yaar as the ould ghoast appared twixt Litcham an Beeston in the drift by the charch pightles," says Jeremiah Shaw. "'T'war a man's skull as moved long the hedge of the tu'npike road, an had eyes blazin' lifelike. Some fules ses it war ye ghoast o' Bonyparty, cos t'war the yaar he knocked off in, spose."

"Never sawr it myssel, but moind mighty well heaarin' of it," Will Spraggs says, warming his hands over the red blaze.

"Turmits makes unkimmon good ghoasteses with a bit of lighted dip in em for eyes," puts in the host with a knowing wink.

"Always thought myssel ould Meg Turner knew more about that there skull than she owned to; t'war jest about the time when her ould chap—he's ded now, poor bohr, war runnin' up sich a score at t' Ploughshare."

"I'd ha put the hakes on her, if she'd ben my missus," remarks a coarse looking, rather surly young man, wearing dufle buskins, at the far end of the porter room, and who had every appearance of a thorough-going poacher.

"Twouldn't do to let the pretty wenches heaar yow say that, if I war yow, Dick," counsels the landlord. "Leastways if yow spect to pick up a deacent looking missus."

"Doant want a missus at all. T'will be a precious long while afore the paarson axes my sibbret. What good be 'em, ses I? 'cept to make the men folks slave and slave for 'em and their young 'uns, and stops all the frolics of a young chap, *surely.* I owes the ould shummaker quite enow for highlows as 'tis."

"But there are ghoasteses, for sartin," observes the landlord's wife, who has come in to snuff the candles. She is a timid woman, not at all "jim," with a doleful "whuling" air, unlike the usual run of cheerful, redcheeked Norfolk landladies. "No one can never make me beleave as 'ow I didn't see a ghoast days afore my poor bohr was killed, sixteen yaars ago come haysel, fighting agin the French. I heaared a rattlin' like in t' keepin' room while I war dustin' these here benches, and a woice callin' 'Mother, mother, mother!' so, tree times, and when I went to find out what it war, I sawr my son, poor bohr, in his sojer's red frock, wi' his sward by his side, an' as white as nip, going out of the back'us door. 'Jem!' ses I, but he taakes no notidge of his silly ould mother, only gie me a kindler whuling look and wanishes away. I shruck out and fell down like a shot bard, and my maaster picked me up—didn't 'ee, Jim bohr? in a deep swound."

"Ben drinkin' some of our maaster's ould ale jest afore, missus," suggests Jerry Shaw.

"For my part I wull never beleave in ghoasteses till I sees 'em with my own oies," says Dick Ryal; "as the proverb ses, 'Seein's beleavin'. Some puir fules as ben frightened 'fore now at a dickey cockin' up 'is heaad behin' a tumb-stun in a charchyard, or gollopin cross the cummin in the dark. Asses therselves, ses I. Ghoasteses is safe to be found out; a pack of rubbish and them as beleaves in 'em, I ses thar know wull craze 'em, and they are born 'uns."

"I sees a sight too much of the charchyard to be afeaard of anything there," remarks the kedge old sexton of Beeston, who is enjoying, much against his conscience, his pipe and glass; for he has just recollected that he left the keys in the big church door in the early part of the evening, but is too comfortable with his "hot pot" to quit his present quarters in order to remedy the mistake. "Twouldn't do for me to be afeaard of dead men."

"My missus ses t' ghoasteses make arful noises up in har ruf o' nights, when I'm hevin' a glass at the Ploughshare," says Jerry Shaw, with a roar. "Doant like bein' by hersel', 'spect; I make rayther short wark of 'em wen I goes hoame."

"Wommen-folks always beleaves in ghoasteses and sperrits and such like," says Dick Ryal, surlily. "A set of 'nation timid fules, that's what I sums 'em to be."

"Well, naarbours, time to shut up shop; t' clock is jest on the stroke," says the landlord. "But drink t' 'ealth of t' King—God bless 'im!—'fore ye all turn out."

"Our missus's tale of t' ghoasteses makes me fare kiney queer all over like; I fare of a malt wash," says Bill Spraggs, with a hearty laugh. "Will yow see me hoame, Dick Ryal? Yow be the sort of chap that doant care if yow do see a ghoast or a sperrit neither. Sartin sure to be found out, eh?" and then he gives him a poke in the ribs.

"That they are," answers Dick, stoutly. "I'd like to see the ghoast or sperrit, if he'd only jest stand still for me to stick-lick 'im like a bohr with my ould oak club. I'll see ye sef' hoame to Woodgate, my old cock; and be sartin sure if I meet the ghoast I'll soll it good tidily."

Twelve o'clock is sounding on the still night air as they go up the wintry road in company. No fog, no damp, as at more modern Christmases; the cold is intense as they wend their way to the churchyard to rectify the sexton's carelessness. Dick Ryal is inclined to be discontented and bad tempered, as he too often is after a third or fourth glass.

"T'will be a mazin' hard winter," snarls he; "an' how us poor folks is to manage to get through I doant 'now. Everythin' is heighen'd 'cept wages t' yaar."

"Yow war alwess a growler, Dick. How du yer think Tom Field manages to keep his missus and five young 'uns, twins, too, t'other day, puir wommen if you can't keep yer'self?"

"Doant 'now; he have got into the mess hisself, and I shan't get him out on't. T' sexton's better off than all we, as gets his livin' out of t' charch an' charchyard; all folks must go to the daisies once, an' then he gets his dues."

"Buryin's ain't what they war in Bees'on parish," replies the sexton, ruefully, "since it war drained an' all these new-fangled schules and insanitary 'provements brought about, quite enow to frighten an old standard like I be. I can 'member as when there war muck'ups afore every housen door, an' a pulk for the ducks, full of black mud jest by the cancers longside of the roads. I don't dispute it when the fever took hould of anybody in them times it used to go slap through the parish, but Providence hev' seen fit to take the best part of my livin' away late yaars. The fees for charchin's an' marryin's ain't worth a sight to me I can assure yer."

"The parish is a good dale healthier than it wes I dow beleave," Bill Spraggs remarks in a meditative tone.

"Those may like the 'provements, as they calls 'em, as doant lose nothing by 'em," says the sexton, doggedly. "Yow duzzy fule! whatever be yer starin' an' gappin' at like a stuck pig?"

For Bill's eyes are riveted upon something; something in the churchyard which is now immediately before them, the narrow strip of land which was used in ancient times for a "butland," (or ground where our village youths used to practise archery,) only intervening between them and the churchyard. Something mysterious, uncanny; some-thing bearing no resemblance to aught of earth.

"Thar! thar! bohr," he gasps, pointing out the spot with his finger, while his hair almost stands on end with terror. "Doant yow see it? Doant yow see sommit goin' along? Thar, up amung t'yew trees! Not a walkin', but kinder sailin' like."

"Are yow tarned duzzy, Bill Spraggs? You luke as if yow had got a stoppage," says the sexton, who is shortsighted and not of an imaginative turn of mind.

"Yow can see it now if yow baint blind as an ould owl; thar 't is, comin' out from the trees an' walkin' 'mong the tumbs," whispers Bill, under his breath. "It's naught of airth, it's a sperrit."

And sure enough, passing out from the shadow of the bushes, and moving swiftly through the churchyard is a figure which can scarcely be mortal. Tall and spectral, it wears a long flowing white garment; on its head a monk's cowl, entirely shading the face if there be a face; under its arm some hideous red object of a distorted round form. It glides along (its garments just sweeping the top of the snow as it goes,) and it is silent, save that once it raises its disengaged arm above its head and gives utterance to a low wail, such as was never heard from mortal lips. Then it disappears; not a footfall, not a sound, save that despairing cry.

Dick Ryal's hair is standing on end; Bill Spraggs is half dead with terror, and even the sexton, in spite of his familiarity with dead men's bones and other ghastly objects, trembles in his shoes. No one is incredulous any longer, for the apparition was distinct enough to be apparent to the dimmest eyes at last.

"It's the ghoast of ould Flupot I have a consait, surely," suggests the sexton, when he has recovered his senses a little; "the ould miser as lived at Dunham, who war paarish pinder thar, an' who sould bergoods an' pinpanches. Folks say as how he fed on nothin' 'cept fyesty goods an' hedge pigs, an' starved his puir old mawther to dead. The naarbours did say how he'd never rest aisy in his grave; an' the sperrit come out jest by his tumb-stun."

"What war it he had under his arm?" whispers Bill Spraggs, in an awe-struck tone; "sumut round an' red, kinder like a body's head kivered wi' bleed, an' its jaw broke tu."

"Doant 'now. I only 'nows as how I shan't fetch them there ould keys out t' charch doors to-night for all the paarsons in Norfolk. They may mob as they like, but better be mobbed by a livin' man than frightened into yer grave by a dead 'un. An' 'sides, I baint 'sackly the man I war, for if I lives I be sixty-two to-yaar."

"P'raps Dick Ryal wool fetch 'em for yer." Bill Spraggs is fond of his joke even in the most terrible moments. "He's not afeared of sperrits, not he!" (Dick's hair is almost white by this time.) "How about lickin' the ghoast with yer oak club, bohr? Durst yow go an' get the keys for t' sexton, an' bate it ace an' douce if yow can find it?"

"That I won't; the sexton hev' all the pay, an' let 'un do the wark, ses I."

"Sartin sure to be found out, eh! Some duzzy fules frightened at a dickey 'mongst the graves, eh! Dick Ryal?" says Bill, with a nudge.

"An' p'raps t'will be found out," replies Dick, shaking; "but I ain't agoing to risk my ould bones in goin' after 'im. So here goes!"

And off down the road he starts at a swinging trot, and the others follow him with the speed of lightning. To see a ghost in company, however shocking even that may be, is *one* thing, and to see one alone is *another*. Fear lends them wings, and they are at home in a brace, of shakes.

Very little sleep did the inhabitants of Beeston-next-Mileham get that night, for the heroes of the adventure straightway awoke their sleeping wives and families and detailed the occurrence with many grievous exagger-ations. Also they called in the neighbours to hear their account of the spectre; and dilated on its awfulness until the very babes and "innocents" shrieked with fear.

Before dawn the ghost had been the object of innumerable strange surmises; he was a monk who had haunted the churchyard from old Papist times; a murderer who had once been buried at Litcham cross-roads, two miles off, but having completed his penance was now supposed to be engaged in looking for a more legitimate resting place; a suicide who had hanged himself near the rectory barn on a lofty elm, the fatal bough of which, made into a walking stick and polished, is still preserved by his fellow servant in the village; the old miser Flupot of Great Dunham; a profligate squire of the last century. Women turned pale as they conversed; children clung to them open-eyed; the very men quaked, for there is something in the supernatural which makes the flesh of the strongest creep on the bones.

So strangely

"Fell (their) Christmas eve."

Only, when the morning was breaking, one stout heart and strong frame left the huddling together assembly, took in his hands a thick stick, and saying not a word to anybody, set out to find

THE GHOST.

CHRISTMAS DAY.

Christmas morning, and the bells ringing merrily at Beeston. The sexton had been early at his post, for the church keys were on his mind, and if they could not be found before service, the congregation would be com-pelled, as he had been, to enter by the small priest's door in the chancel. In the daylight some of his fears on Christmas Eve had melted away. But now the service is about to begin, the parson has already arrived, sermon in hand; hearty and good humoured he enters the vestry.

"What is this?" says he, stopping short and looking round. "Everything seems in strange disorder. Has the church been broken into?"

"Not as I 'now on, sur," replies the sexton, trembling. He is surrounded by his satellites, who have come to support him (in broad daylight) through the trying ordeal, and there is an air of mystery, of could say a great deal more if we would," which strikes the parson strangely.

"Where is my surplice?" he asks the sexton, going to the vestry cupboard. "I am going to have a clean one, perhaps, for Christmas Day—but my hood? And gown?"

"Doant 'now, sur, indeed, 'less—'less the ghoast hev taken 'em off!"

"The ghost, man? What rubbish are you talking? Have you seen a ghost? Has *anybody* seen a ghost?"

"Yes, sur, that they has," answers the sexton, myster-iously. "Will Spraggs, Dick Ryal, an' me, in this here wery charchyard, three witnesses, sur. a sperrit surely; the sperrit I consait of ould Flupot the Dunham miser, as starved hisself an' his ould mawther, an' died worth hundreds of puns, so the chat war, 'sides all this two or three housen an' a three or four acre pightle."

"Was the apparition's face like Flupot's then?" the parson asks, laughing.

"Yow couldn't see its face, sur, t'war kivered up wi' a kinder cowl like, but it riz up over-right his tumb-stun. T'war an awesome sight; in a manner of speakin', not fit for any mort to see."

"A cowl! It was a monk, then, probably," suggests the parson, with a smile. "And you imagine that it wanted some new ecclesiastical vestments, do you, Diggens, and therefore made off with my gown and surplice? You had better send a messenger to Litcham to borrow a surplice for the service."

"I doant suppose the ghoast tooked *them,* sur, 'taint likely. More like they be cut into frocks and shiftnin's 'fore this, fear they should be 'dentified," says honest Diggens, a new idea striking his thick head as he reflects on Flupot's saving propensities during life. "But the keys, sur, wery sorry, sur, but I left 'em by mistake in the charch door yesterday evenin', an' not a soul dare wenture up t' graveyard to fetch 'em arter we'd seen the ghoast. Du yow 'now nothin' about it, Dick Ryal?" turning to that individual somewhat suspiciously.

"No more than yow du yerself; what should I 'now, ye fule?"

"Yow're alwess a grumblin' an' growlin' at summut or t'other, so I thought as how yow had been helpin' yerself."

"Hush, my men," says the parson gently. He had examined the doors and found that they had not been injured by a violent entry; evidently Diggens' carelessness had been the cause of the misfortune. "I am afraid the keys have been in fault, Diggens; let me see if anything else is missing."

He handled reverently the old oak chest or coffer in which the Vessels for Holy Communion were usually kept. Yes, here were signs of damage; the chest had been forcibly opened; and the Sacred Vessels were gone.

"Stolen!" says the clergyman in a grieved tone; "I was afraid so. He breathed a silent prayer, clasping his hands softly, for the poor wretch whom greed, or poverty perchance, (he hoped so) had driven to sacrilege. "This will be a sad Christmas for me, for I fear it is one from among ourselves who has done this," he says. "God pardon me if there be any to whom I have not ministered, any whom I did not succour while I might, and have driven to despair."

"An' will yer forgive me, sur? for I am downright ratified about it," the sexton asks, lingering behind when his companions have quitted the vestry. (He, like the rest of the Beestoners, wishes to stand in the parson's good books.)

"This is the day for forgiveness, is it not?" with a bright smile. "You know *why* I am sorry, *why* I grieve that any one of my parishioners should 'profane the place of His Sanctuary.' But I do not think you will leave the keys in the church door again in a hurry, shall you, Diggens? And now about the ghost, what was it like?"

"Tall an' white, sur, an' shaddery as speckters mostly is. It had a long kinder white robe, as waved about when it glided along like."

"A long white robe!" The parson nodded his head and thought he began to see daylight. "Well, I think we must hunt up this ghost of yours after service, Diggens; and hunt up the thief too, if we can. What is it, Mrs. Field?"

A pale, thin, untidy woman (what the villagers would style a "mawkin") confronts him, curtseying, when he turns round to begin his preparations for the service. Her eyes and manner are wild and despairing.

"Beggin' yer pardon, sur, I'm come to axe yer adwice if yow will give it me," she says. "Tom Field's a missin' sin' yesterday sundown."

"Tom Field! your husband?" laying a kind fatherly hand on her shoulder. "And what do you imagine has become of him, my good woman? What can I do for you?"

"It fares to me that he's agone an' made an end of hisself, sur," the woman answers, suppressing a sob.

She is young still and has a babe at her breast, but had a sad careworn expression of countenance, for she since childhood has worked hard on the land in the gangs in all weathers and seasons.

"If yow would only help me to luk for him, sur, help me to bring him back, I'd bless yer for ever. He war an angain doer when the beer was in, but I've no one else now."

Her emotion is great, and there is moisture in the manly eyes which look into hers so tenderly

"What makes you think he would be likely to do violence to himself?" he asks at length.

"'Cos he war starvin', sur. We're all of us starvin', and pretty nigh famished now. Goods are heighen'd so, an' kindlin' so dear, an' wark is so scarce sin' the ollands are ploughed an' the wheat is dibbled in, an' the swedes an' mangels are all topped. Neither. bite nor sup passed my Tom's lips yesterday, an' my puir mohrs, they ain't tasted a mossel this wery mornin'."

"But why have you not been up to the Rectory and asked for meat or soup or bread? Did you apply for nothing?"

"No, sur, we never axes for doles or charities. 'Taint yer fault, sur; Tom Field is that proud and botty and full of bigoty, he wouldn't axe for nothin' of the paarson wor it ever so. If he knew as how I war atellin' of you this, I doant 'now what he'd say. His ould father as used to live in yonder big town, sur, I means in Norwich; he died starved in his room, rayther than go into the workhousen, where they washes 'em two or three times a week, and makes 'em go about in duffle, a' feeds 'em off a few broth an' no sauce 'cept taters. The Fields is all like that, sur, from the ouldest of 'em down to the youngest boy and child."

The parson paused a moment.

"The service is just about to begin, Mrs. Field, so I can do nothing now; but I will institute a hunt for Tom myself directly it is over. Meanwhile have no fears about a Christmas dinner; for once in a way you must make no scruple about sharing mine at the Rectory; and I think I can almost promise you that Tom shall eat it with you. What is that?"

For there is a shout outside the church,—a shout of wonder and surprise. The noise continues; presently parson, sexton, and churchwardens are on the scene of action. There is quite a crowd in the churchyard, arrested on their way to church, staring, open-mouthed; and Jerry Shaw, pale, hearty, but dirty and breathless, is clutching in his restraining arms

THE GHOST!

"Blest if the ould speckter ain't Tom Field, dressed up in the paarson's surplice!" remarks sexton Diggens.

"He doant luk' so fat in it as the paarson does hisself," a small boy observes, but is promptly suppressed.

And so it was; the apparition which had so appalled the good people of Beeston, and put the sexton at his wits' end, (he had not far to go) was simply a human being in a very emaciated and helpless condition indeed.

Tom Field was lean and cadaverous, but he struggled desperately with his captors. He had been found prostrate in a ditch a few fields off by Jeremiah Shaw, unable to go further owing to his weak and starving condition, with his booty by his side. What had been mistaken for a gory head, were the Sacred Vessels wrapped in an old red handkerchief.

"Hands off! let me go, yer cowards, tree or four of yer on to one," he said, trying to escape from Jerry Shaw's strong hands, and four others who helped to hold him.

"I 'nows I took the Sacrament Wessels. I did; but what would yer do yerself if yer had a wife and young 'uns starvin' at hoame, an' worse fed than the farmer's stock?"

"If I were too proud to tell of my poverty, I would be too proud to steal to relieve it," said the parson solemnly, advancing towards him. "And you have not stolen from man, but from God."

"I 'now as how they war God's Wessels," says the man sullenly. "But men are God's wessels too, and He didn't mane 'em to starve. What are yer blarin' for, mohr?" (looking at his wife shedding tears copiously). "I ses, let me goa, will 'ee? or else take me 'fore the Squire at Litcham at once."

"I do not mean to take you before the Squire," says the parson.

"Well, 'fore the magistrets."

"Nor before the magistrates."

A ray of hope springs up in the haggard miserable face. Mrs. Field clasps her hands, entreating earnestly with her eyes only.

"Nor to send me to Swaffham bridewell?"

"May God pardon me as freely at the last day as I now pardon you in His Name. May God do so unto me and more also, if I do not pardon you as freely as He would Himself (if He were here in Bodily Presence) this day!" said the parson, fervently. "The sin is not against me but against Him, and He alone can forgive. Let us not lose to-day's best blessings by rancour, enmity, and unchari-tableness. My friends, will you not all join with me in thanksgiving for the Christmas joys of Peace and Forgiveness?"

He turned to go into the church followed by a happy grateful crowd, who blessed him with tears in their eyes.

And high from every voice and every place (and especially from a certain seat, newly tenanted, but never afterwards vacant,) rose that glorious thanksgiving which is the most exultant pæan human lips shall know, until they learn before the Great White Throne the new song of Moses and of the Lamb,—"Gloria in excelsis Deo, et in terra pax, hominibus bonæ voluntatis." ("Glory to God in the highest, and on earth peace, good will toward men." *S. Luke* ii. 14.)

FINIS.
"Laus Deo.

THE CHRISTMAS SHADRACH
by
Frank R. Stockton
1891

"I SPOKE OF THE SHADRACH"

Illustrated by Albert Beck Wenzell
Engraved by J. H. E. Whitney

Whenever I make a Christmas present I like it to mean something, not necessarily my sentiments toward the person to whom I give it, but sometimes an expression of what I should like that person to do or to be. In the early part of a certain winter not very long ago, I found myself in a position of perplexity and anxious concern regarding a Christmas present which I wished to make.

The state of the case was this. There was a young lady, the daughter of a neighbour and old friend of my father, who had been gradually assuming relations towards me which were not only unsatisfactory to me, but were becoming more and more so. Her name was Mildred Bronce. She was between twenty and twenty-five years of age, and as fine a woman in every way as one would be likely to meet in a lifetime. She was handsome, of a tender and generous disposition, a fine intelligence, and a thoroughly well-stocked mind. We had known each other for a long time, and when fourteen or fifteen, Mildred had been my favourite companion. She was a little younger than I, and I liked her better than any boy I knew. Our friendship had continued through the years, but of late there had been a change in it; Mildred had become very fond of me, and her fondness seemed to have in it certain elements which annoyed me.

As a girl to make love to no one could be better than Mildred Bronce; but I never made love to her,—at least not earnestly,—and I did not wish that any permanent condition of loving should be established between us. Mildred did not seem to share this opinion, for every day it became plainer to me that she looked upon me as a lover, and that she was perfectly willing to return my affection.

But I had other ideas upon the subject. Into the rural town in which my family passed the greater part of the year there had recently come a young lady, Miss Janet Clinton, to whom my soul went out of my own option. In some respects, perhaps, she was not the equal of Mildred, but she was very pretty, she was small, she had a lovely mouth, was apparently of a clinging nature, and her dark eyes looked into mine with a tingling effect that no other eyes had ever produced. I was in love with her because I wished to be, and the consciousness of this fact caused me a proud satisfaction. This affair was not the result of circumstances, but of my own free will.

I wished to retain Mildred s friendship, I wished to make her happy; and with this latter intent in view I wished very much that she should not disappoint herself in her anticipations of the future.

Each year it had been my habit to make Mildred a Christmas present, and I was now looking for something to give her which would please her and suit my purpose.

When a man wishes to select a present for a lady which, while it assures her of his kind feeling toward her, will at the same time indicate that not only has he no matrimonial inclinations in her direction, but that it would be entirely unwise for her to have any such inclinations in his direction; that no matter with what degree of fondness her heart is disposed to turn toward him, his heart does not turn toward her, and that, in spite of all sentiments induced by long association and the natural fitness of things, she need never expect to be to him anything more than a sister, he has, indeed, a difficult task before him. But such was the task which I set for myself.

Day after day I wandered through the shops. I looked at odd pieces of jewelry and bric-a-brac, and at many a quaint relic or bit of art work which seemed to have a meaning; but nothing had the meaning I wanted. As to books, I found none which satisfied me; not one which was adapted to produce the exact impression that I desired.

One afternoon I was in a little basement shop kept by a fellow in a long overcoat, who, so far as I was able to judge, bought curiosities but never sold any. For some minutes I had been looking at a beautifully decorated saucer of rare workmanship for which there was no cup to match, and for which the proprietor informed me no cup could now be found or manufactured. There were some points in the significance of an article of this sort, given as a present to a lady, which fitted to my purpose, but it would signify too much: I did not wish to suggest to Mildred that she need never expect to find a cup. It would be better, in fact, if I gave her anything of this kind, to send her a cup and saucer entirely unsuited to each other, and which could not, under any conditions, be used together.

I put down the saucer, and continued my search among the dusty shelves and cases.

"How would you like a paper-weight?" the shopkeeper asked. "Here is something a little odd," handing me a piece of dark-coloured mineral nearly as big as my fist, flat on the underside and of a pleasing irregularity above. Around the bottom was a band of arabesque work in some dingy metal, probably German silver. I smiled as I took it.

"This is not good enough for a Christmas present," I said. "I want something odd, but it must have some value."

"Well," said the man, "that has no real value, but there is a peculiarity about it which interested me when I heard of it, and so I bought it. This mineral is a piece of what the iron-workers call shadrach. It is a portion of the iron or iron ore which passes through the smelting-furnaces without being affected by the great heat, and so they have given it the name of one of the Hebrew youths who was cast into the fiery furnace by Nebuchadnezzar, and who came out unhurt. Some people think there is a sort of magical quality about this shadrach, and that it can give out to human beings something of its power to keep their minds cool when they are in danger of being overheated. The old gentleman who had this made was subject to fits of anger, and he thought this piece of shadrach helped to keep him from giving way to them. Occasionally he used to leave it in the house of a hot-tempered neighbour, believing that the testy individual would be cooled down for a time, without knowing how the change had been brought about. I bought a lot of things of the old gentleman's widow, and this among them. I thought I might try it some time, but I never have."

I held the shadrach in my hand, ideas concerning it rapidly flitting through my mind. Why would not this be a capital thing to give to Mildred? If it should, indeed, possess the quality ascribed to it; if it should be able to cool her liking for me, what better present could I give her? I did not hesitate long.

"I will buy this," I said; "but the ornamentation must be of a better sort. It is now too cheap and tawdry-looking."

"I can attend to that for you," said the shopkeeper. "I can have it set in a band of gold or silver filigree-work like this, if you choose."

I agreed to this proposition, but ordered the band to be made of silver, the cool tone of that metal being more appropriate to the characteristics of the gift than the warmer hues of gold.

When I gave my Christmas present to Mildred she was pleased with it; its oddity struck her fancy.

"I don't believe anybody ever had such a paper-weight as that," she said, as she thanked me. "What is it made of?"

I told her, and explained what shadrach was; but I did not speak of its presumed influence over human beings, which, after all, might be nothing but the wildest fancy. I did not feel altogether at my ease, as I added that it was merely a trifle, a thing of no value, except as a reminder of the season.

"The fact that it is a present from you gives it value," she said, as she smilingly raised her eyes to mine.

I left her house—we were all living in the city then—with a troubled conscience. What a deception I was practising upon this noble girl, who, if she did not already love me, was plainly on the point of doing so. She had received my present as if it indicated a warmth of feeling on my part, when, in fact, it was the result of a desire for a cooler feeling on her part.

But I called my reason to my aid, and I showed myself that what I had given Mildred—if it should prove to possess any virtue at all—was, indeed, a most valuable boon. It was something; which would prevent the waste of her affections, the wreck of her hopes. No kindness could be truer, no regard for her happiness more sincere, than the motives which prompted me to give her the shadrach.

I did not soon again see Mildred, but now as often as possible I visited Janet. She always received me with a charming cordiality, and if this should develop into warmer sentiments I was not the man to wish to cool them. In many ways Janet seemed much better suited to me than Mildred. One of the greatest charms of this beautiful girl was a tender trustfulness, as if I were a being on whom she could lean and to whom she could look up. I liked this; it is very different from Mildred's manner; with the latter I had always been well satisfied if I felt myself standing on the same plane.

The weeks and months passed on, and again we were all in the country; and here I saw Mildred often. Our homes were not far apart, and our families were very intimate. With my opportunities for frequent observation, I could not doubt that a change had come over her. She was always friendly when we met, and seemed as glad to see me as she was to see any other member of my family, but she was not the Mildred I used to know. It was plain that my existence did not make the impression on her that it once made. She did not seem to consider it important whether I came or went; whether I was in the room or not; whether I joined a party or stayed away. All this had been very different. I knew well that Mildred had been used to consider my presence as a matter of much importance, and I now felt sure that my Christmas shadrach was doing its work. Mildred was cooling toward me. Her affection, or, to put it more modestly, her tendency to affection, was gently congealing into friendship. This was highly gratifying to my moral nature, for every day I was doing my best to warm the soul of Janet. Whether or not I succeeded in this I could not be sure. Janet was as tender and trustful and charming as ever, but no more so than she had been months before.

Sometimes I thought she was waiting for an indication of an increased warmth of feeling on my part before she allowed the temperature of her own sentiments to rise. But for one reason and another I delayed the solution of this problem. Janet was very fond of company, and although we saw a great deal of each other, we were not often alone. If we two had more frequently walked, driven, or rowed together, as Mildred and I used to do, I think Miss Clinton would soon have had every opportunity of making up her mind about the fervour of my passion.

The summer weeks passed on, and there was no change in the things which now principally concerned me, except that Mildred seemed to be growing more and more indifferent to me. From having seemed to care no more for me than for her other friends, she now seemed to care less for me than for most people. I do not mean that she showed a dislike, but she treated me with a sort of indifference which I did not fancy at all. This sort of thing had gone too far, and there was no knowing how much further it would go. It was plain enough that the shadrach was overdoing the business.

I was now in a state of much mental disquietude. Greatly as I desired to win the love of Janet, it grieved me to think of losing the generous friendship of Mildred—that friendship to which I had been accustomed for the greater part of my life, and on which, as I now discovered, I had grown to depend.

In this state of mind I went to see Mildred. I found her in the library writing. She received me pleasantly, and was sorry her father was not at home, and begged that I would excuse her finishing the note on which she was engaged, because she wished to get it into the post-office before the mail closed. I sat down on the other side of the table, and she finished her note, after which she went out to give it to a servant.

Glancing about me, I saw the shadrach. It was partly under a litter of papers, instead of lying on them. I took it up, and was looking at it when Mildred returned. She sat down and asked me if I had heard of the changes that were to be made in the time-table of the railroad. We talked a little on the subject, and then I spoke of the shadrach, saying carelessly that it might be interesting to analyse the bit of metal; there was a little knob which might be filed off without injuring it in the least,

"You may take it," she said, "and make what experiments you please. I do not use it much; it is unnecessarily heavy for a paper-weight."

From her tone I might have supposed that she had forgotten that I had given it to her. I told her that I would be very glad to borrow the paper weight for a time, and, putting it into my pocket, I went away, leaving her arranging her disordered papers on the table, and giving quite as much regard to this occupation as she had given to my little visit.

I could not feel sure that the absence of the shadrach would cause any diminution in the coolness of her feelings toward me, but there was reason to believe that it would prevent them from growing cooler. If she should keep that shadrach she might in time grow to hate me. I was very glad that I had taken it from her.

My mind easier on this subject, my heart turned more freely toward Janet, and, going to her house the next day I was delighted to find her alone. She was as lovely as ever, and as cordial, but she was flushed and evidently annoyed.

"I am in a bad humour to-day," she said, "and I am glad you came to talk to me and quiet me. Dr. Gilbert promised to take me to drive this afternoon, and we were going over to the hills where they find the wild rhododendron. I am told that it is still in blossom up there, and I want some flowers ever so much—I am going to paint them. And besides, I am crazy to drive with his new horses; and now he sends me a note to say he is engaged."

This communication shocked me, and I began to talk to her about Dr. Gilbert. I soon found that several times she had been driving with this handsome young physician, but never, she said, behind his new horses, nor to the rhododendron hills.

Dr. Hector Gilbert was a fine young fellow, beginning practice in town, and one of my favourite associates. I had never thought of him in connection with Janet, but I could now see that he might make a most dangerous rival. When a young and talented doctor, enthusiastic in his studies, and earnestly desirous of establishing a practice, and who, if his time were not fully occupied, would naturally wish that the neighbours would think that such were the case, deliberately devotes some hours on I know not how many sunny days to driving a young lady into the surrounding country, it may be supposed that he is really in love with her. Moreover, judging from Janet's present mood, this doctor's attentions were not without encouragement.

I went home; I considered the state of affairs; I ran my fingers through my hair; I gazed steadfastly upon the floor. Suddenly I rose. I had an inspiration; I would give the shadrach to Dr. Gilbert.

I went immediately to the doctor's office, and found him there. He was not in a very good humour.

"I have had two old ladies here nearly all the afternoon, and they have bored me to death," he said. "I could not get rid of them, because I found they had made an appointment with each other to visit me to-day and talk over a hospital plan which I proposed some time ago, and which is really very important to me, but I wish they had chosen some other time to come here. What is that thing?"

"That is a bit of shadrach," I said, "made into a paper-weight." And then I proceeded to explain what shadrach is, and what peculiar properties it must possess to resist the power of heat, which melts other metals apparently of the same class; and I added that I thought it might be interesting to analyse a bit of it and discover what fire-proof constituents it possessed.

"I should like to do that," said the doctor, attentively turning over the shadrach in his hand. "Can I take off a piece of it?"

"I will give it to you," said I, "and you can make what use of it you please. If you do analyse it, I shall be very glad indeed to hear the results of your investigations."

The doctor demurred a little at taking the paper-weight with such a pretty silver ring around it, but I assured him that the cost of the whole affair was trifling, and I should be gratified if he would take it. He accepted the gift, and was thanking me, when a patient arrived, and I departed.

I really had no right to give away this paper weight, which, in fact, belonged to Mildred, but there are times when a man must keep his eyes on the chief good, and not think too much about other things. Besides, it was evident that Mildred did not care in the least for the bit of metal, and she had virtually given it to me.

There was another point which I took into consideration. It might be that the shadrach might simply cool Dr. Gilbert's feelings toward me, and that would be neither pleasant nor advantageous. If I could have managed matters so that Janet could have given it to him, it would have been all right. But now all that I could do was to wait and see what would happen. If only the thing would cool the doctor in a general way, that would help. He might then give more thought to his practice and his hospital ladies, and let other people take Janet driving.

About a week after this I met the doctor; he seemed in a hurry, but I stopped him. I had a curiosity to know if he had analysed the shadrach, and asked him about it.

"No," said he; "I haven't done it. I haven't had time. I knocked off a piece of it, and I will attend to it when I get a chance. Good-day."

Of course if the man was busy he could not be expected to give his mind to a trifling matter of that sort, but I thought that he need not have been so curt about it. I stood gazing after him as he walked rapidly down the street. Before I resumed my walk I saw him enter the Clinton house. Things were not going on well. The shadrach had not cooled Dr. Gilbert's feelings toward Janet.

But because the doctor was still warm in his attentions to the girl I loved, I would not in the least relax my attentions to her. I visited her as often as I could find an excuse to do so. There was generally someone else there, but Janet's disposition was of such gracious expansiveness that each one felt obliged to be satisfied with what he got, much as he may have wished for something different.

But one morning Janet surprised me. I met her at Mildred's house, where I had gone to borrow a book of reference. Although I had urged her not to put herself to so much trouble, Mildred was standing on a little ladder looking for the book, because, she said, she knew exactly what I wanted, and she was sure she could find the proper volume better than I could. Janet had been sitting in a window-seat reading, but when I came in she put down her book and devoted herself to conversation with me. I was a little sorry for this, because Mildred was very kindly engaged in doing me a service, and I really wanted to talk to her about the book she was looking for. Mildred showed so much of her old manner this morning that I would have been very sorry to have her think that I did not appreciate her returning interest in me. Therefore, while under other circumstances I would have been delighted to talk to Janet, I did not wish to give her so much of my attention then. But Janet Clinton was a girl who insisted on people attending to her when she wished them to do so, and having stepped through an open door into the garden, she presently called me to her. Of course I had to go.

"I will not keep you a minute from your fellow student," she said, "but I want to ask a favour of you." And into her dark, uplifted eyes there came a look of tender trustfulness clearer than any I had yet seen there. "Don't *you* want to drive me to the rhododendron hills?" she said. "I suppose the flowers are all gone by this time, but I have never been there, and I should like ever so much to go."

I could not help remarking that I thought Dr. Gilbert was going to take her there.

"Dr. Gilbert, indeed!" she said with a little laugh. "He promised once, and didn't come, and the next day he planned for it it rained. I don't think doctors make very good escorts, anyway, for you can't tell who is going to be sick just as you are about to start on a trip. Besides, there is no knowing how much botany I should have to hear, and when I go on a pleasure-drive I don't care very much about studying things. But of course I don't want to trouble you."

"Trouble!" I exclaimed. "It will give me the greatest delight to take you that drive or any other, and at whatever time you please."

"You are always so good and kind," she said, with her dark eyes again upraised. "And now let us go in and see if Mildred has found the book."

I spoke the truth when I said that Janet's proposition delighted me. To take a long drive with that charming girl, and at the same time to feel that she had chosen me as her companion, was a greater joy than I had yet had reason to expect; but it would have been a more satisfying joy if she had asked me in her own house and not in Mildred's; if she had not allowed the love which I hoped was growing up between her and me to interfere with the revival of the old friendship between Mildred and me.

But when we returned to the library Mildred was sitting at a table with a book before her, opened at the passage I wanted.

"I have just found it," she said with a smile. "Draw up a chair, and we will look over these maps together. I want you to show me how he travelled when he left his ship."

"Well, if you two are going to the pole," said Janet, with her prettiest smile, "I will go back to my novel."

She did not seem in the least to object to my geographical researches with Mildred, and if the latter had even noticed my willingness to desert her at the call of Janet, she did not show it. Apparently she was as much a good comrade as she had ever been. This state of things was gratifying in the highest degree. If I could be loved by Janet and still keep Mildred as my friend, what greater earthly joys could I ask?

The drive with Janet was postponed by wet weather. Day after day it rained, or the skies were heavy, and we both agreed that it must be in the bright sunshine that we would make this excursion. When we should make it, and should be alone together on the rhododendron hill, I intended to open my soul to Janet.

It may seem strange to others, and at the time it also seemed strange to me, but there was another reason besides the rainy weather which prevented my declaration of love to Janet. This was a certain nervous anxiety in regard to my friendship for Mildred. I did not in the least waver in my intention to use the best endeavours to make the one my wife, but at the same time I was oppressed by a certain alarm that in carrying out this projcct I might act in such a way as to wound the feelings of the other.

This disposition to consider the feelings of Mildred became so strong that I began to think that my own sentiments were in need of control. It was not right that while making love to one woman I should give so much consideration to my relations with another. The idea struck me that in a measure I had shared the fate of those who had thrown the Hebrew youths into the fiery furnace. My heart had not been consumed by the flames, but in throwing the shadrach into what I supposed were Mildred's affections, it was quite possible that I had been singed by them. At any rate my conscience told me that under the circumstances my sentiments toward Mildred were too warm; in honestly making love to Janet I ought to forget them entirely.

It might have been a good thing, I told myself, if I had not given away the shadrach, but kept it as a gift from Mildred. Very soon after I reached this conclusion it became evident to me that Mildred was again cooling in my direction as rapidly as the mercury falls after sunset on a September day. This discovery did not make my mercury fall; in fact, it brought it for a time nearly to the boiling point. I could not imagine what had happened. I almost neglected Janet, so anxious was I to know what had made this change in Mildred.

Weeks passed on, and I discovered nothing except that Mildred had now become more than indifferent to me. She allowed me to see that my companionship did not give her pleasure. Janet had her drive to the rhododendron hills, but she took it with Dr. Gilbert, and not with me. When I heard of this it pained me, though I could not help admitting that I deserved the punishment; but my surprise was almost as great as my pain, for Janet had recently given me reason to believe that she had a very small opinion of the young doctor. In fact, she had criticised him so severely that I had been obliged to speak in his defence. I now found myself in a most doleful quandary, and there was only one thing of which I could be certain—I needed cooling toward Mildred if I still allowed myself to hope to marry Janet.

One afternoon I was talking to Mr. Bronce in his library, when, glancing towards the table used by his daughter for writing purposes, I was astounded to see, lying on a little pile of letters, the Christmas shadrach. As soon as I could get an opportunity I took it in my hand and eagerly examined it. I had not been mistaken. It was the paper-weight I had given Mildred. There was the silver band around it, and there was the place where a little piece had been knocked off by the doctor. Mildred was not at home, but I determined that I would wait and see her. I would dine with the Bronces; I would spend the evening; I would stay all night; I would not leave the house until I had had this mystery explained. She returned in about half an hour, and greeted me in the somewhat stiff manner she had adopted of late; but when she noticed my perturbed expression and saw that I held the shadrach in my hand, she took a seat by the table, where for some time I had been waiting for her, alone.

"I suppose you want to ask me about that paper-weight?"

"Indeed I do," I replied. "How in the world did you happen to get it again?"

"Again?" she repeated, satirically. "You may well say that. I will explain it to you. Some little time ago I called on Janet Clinton, and on her writing-desk I saw that paper-weight. I remembered it perfectly. It was the one you gave me last Christmas, and afterward borrowed of me, saying that you wanted to analyse it, or something of the sort. I had never used it very much, and of course was willing that you should take it, and make experiments with it if you wanted to; but I must say that the sight of it on Janet Clinton's desk both shocked and angered me. I asked her where she had got it, and she told me a gentleman had given it to her. I did not waste any words in inquiring who this gentleman was, but I determined that she should not rest under a mistake in regard to its proper ownership, and told her plainly that the person who had given it to her had previously given it to me; that it was mine, and he had no right to give it to anyone else. Oh, if that is the case, she exclaimed, take it. I beg of you. I don't care for it, and what is more, I don't care any more for the man who gave it to me than I do for the thing itself. So I took it and brought it home with me. Now you know how I happen to have it again."

For a moment I made no answer. Then I asked her how long it had been since she had received the shadrach from Janet Clinton.

"Oh, I don't remember exactly," she said; "it was several weeks ago."

Now I knew everything; all the mysteries of the past were revealed to me. The young doctor, fervid in his desire to please the woman he loved, had given Janet this novel paper-weight. From that moment she had begun to regard his attentions with apathy, and finally—her nature was one which was apt to go to extremes—to dislike him. Mildred repossessed herself of the shadrach which she took, not as a gift from Janet, but as her rightful property, presented to her by me. And this horrid little object, probably with renewed power, had cooled, almost frozen, indeed, the sentiments of that dear girl toward me. Then, too, had the spell been taken from Janet's inclinations, and she had gone to the rhododendron hills with Doctor Gilbert.

One thing was certain. *I* must have that shadrach.

"Mildred," I exclaimed, "will you not give me this paper-weight? Give it to me for my own?"

"What do you want to do with it?" she asked sarcastically. "Analyse it again?"

"Mildred," said I, "I did not give it to Janet. I gave it to Dr. Gilbert, and he must have given it to her. I know I had no right to give it away at all, but I did not believe that you would care; but now I beg that you will let me have it. Let me have it for my own. I assure you solemnly I will never give it away. It has caused trouble enough already."

"I don't exactly understand what you mean by trouble," she said, "but take it if you want it. You are perfectly welcome." And picking up her gloves and hat from the table she left me.

As I walked home my hatred of the wretched piece of metal in my hand increased with every step. I looked at it with disgust when I went to bed that night, and when my glance lighted upon it the next morning I involuntarily shrank from it, as if it had been an evil thing. Over and over again that day I asked myself why I should keep in my possession something which would make my regard for Mildred grow less and less; which would eventually make me care for her not at all? The very thought of not caring for Mildred sent a pang through my heart.

My feelings all prompted me to rid myself of what I looked upon as a calamitous talisman, but my reason interfered. If I still wished to marry Janet it was my duty to welcome indifference to Mildred.

In this mood I went out. to stroll, to think, to decide: and that I might be ready to act on my decision I put the shadrach into my pocket. Without exactly intending it I walked toward the Bronce place, and soon found myself on the edge of a pretty pond which lay at the foot of the garden. Here, in the shade of a tree, there stood a bench, and on this lay a book, an ivory paper-cutter in its leaves as marker.

I knew that Mildred had left that book on the bench; it was her habit to come to this place to read. As she had not taken the volume with her, it was probable that she intended soon to return. But then the sad thought came to me that if she saw me there she would not return. I picked up the book; I read the pages she had been reading. As I read I felt that I could think the very thoughts that she thought as she read. I was seized with a yearning to be with her, to read with her, to think with her. Never had my soul gone out to Mildred as at that moment, and yet, heavily dangling in my pocket, I carried—I could not bear to think of it. Seized by a sudden impulse, I put down the book; I drew out the shadrach, and, tearing off the silver band, I tossed the vile bit of metal into the pond.

"There!" I cried. "Go out of my possession, out of my sight! You shall work no charm on me. Let nature take its course, and let things happen as they may." Then, relieved from the weight on my heart and the weight in my pocket, I went home.

Nature did take its course, and in less than a fortnight from that day the engagement of Janet and Dr. Gilbert was announced. I had done nothing to prevent this, and the news did not disturb my peace of mind; but my relations with Mildred very much disturbed it. I had hoped that, released from the baleful influence of the shadrach, her friendly feelings toward me would return, and my passion for her had now grown so strong that I waited and watched, as a wrecked mariner waits and watches for the sight of a sail, for a sign that she had so far softened toward me that I might dare to speak to her of my love. But no such sign appeared.

I now seldom visited the Bronce house; no one of that family, once my best friends, seemed to care to see me. Evidently Mildred's feelings toward me had extended themselves to the rest of the household. This was not surprising, for her family had long been accustomed to think as Mildred thought.

One day I met Mr. Bronce at the post-office, and, some other gentlemen coming up, we began to talk of a proposed plan to introduce a system of water-works into the village, an improvement much desired by many of us.

"So far as I am concerned," said Mr. Bronce, "I am not now in need of anything of the sort. Since I set up my steam-pump I have supplied my house from the pond at the end of my garden with all the water we can possibly want for every purpose."

"Do you mean," asked one of the gentlemen, "that you get your drinking-water in that way?"

"Certainly," replied Mr. Bronce. "The basin of the pond is kept as clean and in as good order as any reservoir can be, and the water comes from an excellent, rapid-flowing spring. I want nothing better."

A chill ran through me as I listened. The shadrach was in that pond. Every drop of water which Mildred drank, which touched her, was influenced by that demoniacal paper-weight, which, without knowing what I was doing, I had thus bestowed upon the whole Bronce family.

When I went home I made diligent search for a stone which might be about the size and weight of the shadrach, and having repaired to a retired spot I practised tossing it as I had tossed the bit of metal into the pond. In each instance I measured the distance which I had thrown the stone, and was at last enabled to make a very fair estimate of the distance to which I had thrown the shadrach when I had buried it under the waters of the pond.

That night there was a half-moon, and between eleven and twelve o'clock, when everybody in our village might be supposed to be in bed and asleep, I made my way over the fields to the back of the Bronce place, taking with me a long fish-cord with a knot in it, showing the average distance to which I had thrown the practice stone. When I reached the pond I stood as nearly as possible in the place by the bench from which I had hurled the shadrach, and to this spot I pegged one end of the cord. I was attired in an old tennis suit, and, having removed my shoes and stockings, I entered the water, holding the roll of cord in my hand. This I slowly unwound as I advanced toward the middle of the pond, and when I reached the knot I stopped, with the water above my waist.

I had found the bottom of the pond very smooth, and free from weeds and mud, and I now began feeling about with my bare feet, as I moved from side to side, describing a small arc; but I discovered nothing more than an occasional pebble no larger than a walnut.

Letting out some more of the cord, I advanced a little farther into the centre of the pond, and slowly described another arc. The water was now nearly up to my armpits, but it was not cold, though if it had been I do not think I should have minded it in the ardour of my search. Suddenly I put my foot on something hard and as big as my fist, but in an instant it moved away from under my foot; it must have been a turtle. This occurrence made me shiver a little, but I did not swerve from my purpose, and, loosing the string a little more, I went farther into the pond. The water was now nearly up to my chin, and there was something weird, mystical, and awe-inspiring in standing thus in the depths of this silent water, my eyes so near its gently rippling surface, fantastically lighted by the setting moon, and tenanted by nobody knew what cold and slippery creatures. But from side to side I slowly moved, reaching out with my feet in every direction, hoping to touch the thing for which I sought.

Suddenly I set my right foot upon something hard and irregular. Nervously I felt it with my toes. I patted it with my bare sole. It was as big as the shadrach! It felt like the shadrach. In a few moments I was almost convinced that the direful paper-weight was beneath my foot.

Closing my eyes, and holding my breath, I stooped down into the water, and groped on the bottom with my hands. In some way I had moved while stooping, and at first I could find nothing. A sensation of dread came over me as I felt myself in the midst of the dark solemn water—around me, above me, everywhere,—almost suffocated, and apparently deserted even by the shadrach. But just as I felt that I could hold my breath no longer, my fingers touched the thing that had been under my foot, and, clutching it, I rose and thrust my head out of the water. I could do nothing until I had taken two or three long breaths; then, holding up the object in my hand to the light of the expiring moon, I saw that it was like the shadrach; so like, indeed, that I felt that it must be it.

Turning, I made my way out of the water as rapidly as possible, and, dropping on my knees on the ground, I tremblingly lighted the lantern which I had left on the bench, and turned its light on the thing I had found. There must be no mistake; if this was not the shadrach I would go in again. But there was no necessity for re-entering the pond; it *was* the shadrach.

With the extinguished lantern in one hand and the lump of mineral evil in the other, I hurried home. My wet clothes were sticky and chilly in the night air. Several times in my haste I stumbled over clods and briers, and my shoes, which I had not taken time to tie, flopped up and down as I ran. But I cared for none of these discomforts; the shadrach was in my power.

Crossing a wide field I heard, not far away, the tramping of hoofs, as of a horseman approaching at full speed. I stopped and looked in the direction of the sound. My eyes had now become so accustomed to the dim light that I could distinguish objects somewhat plainly, and I quickly perceived that the animal that was galloping toward me was a bull. I well knew what bull it was; this was Squire Starling's pasture-field, and that was his great Alderney bull, Ramping Sir John of Ramapo II.

I was well acquainted with that bull, renowned throughout the neighbourhood for his savage temper and his noble pedigree—son of Ramping Sir John of Ramapo I., whose sire was the Great Rodolphin, son of Prince Maximus of Granby, one of whose daughters averaged eighteen pounds of butter a week, and who himself had killed two men.

The bull, who had not perceived me when I crossed the field before, for I had then made my way with as little noise as possible, was now bent on punishing my intrusion upon his domains, and bellowed as he came on. I was in a position of great danger. With my flopping shoes it was impossible to escape by flight; I must stand and defend myself. I turned and faced the furious creature, who was not twenty feet distant, and then with all my strength I hurled the shadrach, which I held in my right hand, directly at his shaggy forehead. My ability to project a missile was considerable, for I had held, with credit, the position of pitcher in a base-ball nine, and as the shadrach struck the bull's head with a thud he stopped as if he had suddenly run against a wall.

I do not know that actual and violent contact with the physical organism of a recipient accelerates the influence of a shadrach upon the mental organism of said recipient, but I do know that the contact of my projectile with that bull's skull instantly cooled the animal's fury. For a few moments he stood and looked at me, and then his interest in me as a man and trespasser appeared to fade away; and, moving slowly from me, Ramping Sir John of Ramapo II. began to crop the grass.

I did not stop to look for the shadrach; I considered it safely disposed of. So long as Squire Starling used that field for a pasture, connoisseurs in mineral fragments would not be apt to wander through it, and when it should be ploughed the shadrach, to ordinary eyes no more than a common stone, would be buried beneath the sod. I awoke the next morning refreshed and happy, and none the worse for my wet walk.

"Now," I said to myself, "nature shall truly have her own way. If the uncanny comes into my life and that of those I love, it shall not be brought in by me."

About a week after this I dined with the Bronce family. They were very cordial, and it seemed to me the most natural thing in the world to be sitting at their table. After dinner Mildred and I walked together in the garden. It was a charming evening, and we sat down on the bench by the edge of the pond. I spoke to her of some passages in the book I had once seen there.

"Oh, have you read that?" she asked with interest.

"I have seen only two pages of it," I said, "and those I read in the volume you left on this bench, with a paper-cutter in it for a marker. I long to read more and talk with you of what I have read."

"Why, then, didn't you wait? You might have known that I would come back."

I did not tell her that I knew that because I was there she would not have come. But before I left the bench I discovered that hereafter, wherever I might be, she was willing to come and stay.

Early in the next spring Mildred and I were married, and on our wedding-trip we passed through a mining district in the mountains. Here we visited one of the great ironworks, and were both interested in witnessing the wonderful power of man, air, and fire over the stubborn king of metals.

"What is this substance?" asked Mildred of one of the officials who was conducting us through the works.

"That," said the man, "is what we call shad—"

"My dear," I cried, "we must hurry away this instant or we shall lose the train. Come; quick; there is not a moment for delay." And with a word of thanks to the guide I seized her hand and led her, almost running, into the open air.

Mildred was amazed.

"Never before," she exclaimed, "have I seen you in such a hurry. I thought the train we decided to take did not leave for an hour."

"I have changed my mind," I said, "and think it will be a great deal better for us to take the one which leaves in ten minutes."

THE WICKED EDITOR'S CHRISTMAS DREAM
by
Alice Mary Vince
1893

He was a very good editor, as Editors go, though some of them do not go very far; just a little given to promise where he never meant to perform, which after all is a frailty common to all mankind, and not exclusively confined to Editors, so he must not be judged too harshly. Besides, neither his faults or his virtues have anything to do with his dream. It was his Christmas dinner which brought about all that. He was never quite sure himself whether it was the goose, or the pudding, or the walnuts, possibly the punch. In my opinion the blame should be divided equally between the four, with perhaps a rather sharper reprimand to the punch. It happened in front of a great big Christmas fire in his own dining room, but he did not know that until it was all over. He thought he was in his sanctum at the office, and that the telephone bell was ringing. He never was accustomed to answer the summons quickly, and he did not answer it quickly now. It kept on persistently, and then he looked up and addressed the unoffending instrument as though it were a dilatory office boy. He was just going leisurely towards it when straight from it came something to meet him—something thin, and weird, and wavy—which he instantly recognised as the inevitable Christmas Ghost. He had a great dislike to all ghosts, but a particular aversion to the Christmas species. They were so moral, so improving, so bent on doing good. At other seasons of the year ghosts content themselves with tapping, creaking, and occasionally pulling the clothes off your bed, but at Christmas they always become priggish and apt to rake up things you would far sooner forget all about. The Editor saw that he was about to be bored, and he sighed deeply as asked:

"Will you kindly give your name? I do not think I have had the pleasure of meeting you before."

"No," said the Ghost, "this is my first edition. I have been allotted to wait upon you this evening and show you round bit."

"Thank you," said the Editor, "but the chief reporter generally attends to this sort of thing. You will find him in the other office. Good evening."

"Not so," said the Ghost. "It is to you I am sent, and you know that if I sought the chief reporter, you would make your escape by the back way. You see we know all about you."

The Ghost then moved all the best articles of furniture into one corner, and seated himself in the midst of them. "There is a spirit taking a snap shot of this interview," he explained, "and it will give better impression down below if one corner of your room is decently furnished."

"I see you are thoroughly up to date," said the Editor; "would you tell me the origin of the Christmas Ghost?"

"Dyspepsia," answered the Ghost, briefly.

"Why is he so much more respectable and tiresome than any of the other kind?"

"There is nothing like the liver," said the Ghost, "for awakening the conscience, and there is no season of the year when the liver is more likely to be out of order and the conscience correspondingly susceptible. We take advantage of this, and come to earth to administer our rebukes and suggest improvements."

"I suppose you follow the old rules—pictures of the past; present, and future," said the Editor.

"Yes, I work the old lines," replied the Ghost "though I flatter myself I have introduced a little variety into the business. Shall we start? You won't want a catalogue, shall you?"

The Editor groaned.

"You won't think it rude if I sit out the whole of the show," he said. I had an important engagement this evening and I have a singular repugnance to keeping anyone waiting."

"You shall go at half time," said the Ghost.

Then the room was darkened, and the Editor felt swiftly whirled through the air. He shut his eyes and opened them to find himself in a very strange place. He had, as it were, a bird's eyes view of a number of homes, all poorly furnished, and filled with men, women, and children, looking scantily fed and clad. In the centre of the place was a pyramid of used foolscap, dusty with age, at which the people gazed sadly. Some of them held closely-written sheets in their hands and seemed to be brooding over them despairingly.

"What is this?" asked the Editor.

"This," said the Ghost, "is the Abode of Dejected Men and Rejected Copy. You have largely helped in peopling this."

"Well," said the Editor, "there wasn't room for it all, you know, and I did my best."

"Not always," said the Ghost, in denouncing tones. "Read that."

He pointed to a manuscript over very which a very thin, pallid-looking man was leaning, and the Editor read it carefully. It was addressed to him and bore a date of some weeks ago, but he had never read it before.

"By Jove," he said, "that's uncommonly good. I'll use that on Friday."

"Too late," said the ghost monotonously, too late. Look into the man's face."

The Editor looked. It was the face of a corpse.

"That man died of want," said the Ghost.

The Editor shivered.

"Shall we move on?" he said. "This place is draughty and I have a slight cold on my chest.

There was another rush through the air, and then they stopped where there was perfect Pandemonium of movement and noise. All about were hung various copies of contents' bills of the Editor's own paper, and up and down ran boys shouting it out, and offering it for sale. The Editor was proud to see how the people rushed to buy it.

"It has an immense circulation," he said with a smile of satisfaction.

"Yes," said the Ghost, grimly. "It has—down here. Read that bill out to me."

"Horrible murder. Shocking disclosures at the Divorce Court. Suicide of a well-known tradesman. Full details in second edition," read the Editor as well as he could above the din of the boys shouting "Sposhul," and the stampede of the buyers' feet. "Yes, I remember that well. We got that murder before anybody."

"Do not boast," said the spirit, "Watch this boy and girl."

The Editor followed the direction of the pointing hand. Both boy and girl were reading the paper earnestly and attentively. The girl who was pretty and innocent looking, was gloating over the story of the Divorce, and the boy was drinking in every line of the Murder case.

"We shall see them again," said the Ghost.

On they went through the Babel and the Editor saw many strange sights as they passed along. Here and there he caught a glimpse of a prison cell, once he saw a gallows, and everywhere his paper was being read. When they got to the extreme end of the place the Ghost stopped.

"There are the two you saw just now," he said. The Editor looked but would not have recognised them. The girl had grown flaunting and bold, and the boy cunning and wizen-faced. He did not like the change.

"Am I answerable for this?" he asked.

"Yes," said the Ghost. "You and others are answerable for all this."

"But," remonstrated the Editor, "the realistic stuff sells so well now-a-day's, everyone goes in for it."

"Even so," said the Ghost, "and that girl is an outcast and that boy is going to the gallows. Have you had enough?"

"I should be glad to go," said the Editor, "If you have nothing pleasanter to show me."

"I was not sent to be pleasant," said the Ghost.

"I gathered that from the very first," said the Editor, for they had left the noisy regions and were ascending again.

"Is it all over?" he asked, for he seemed to be sitting in his office chair once more.

"Not quite," said the Ghost, "You are a little wavering in your politics, are you not?"

"I think you can hardly say that," said the Editor. "It's rather hard to please everybody, yon know."

"I understand," said the Ghost, "you are a wobbler. Feel the effects of that."

The Ghost made strange signals in the air, and the Editor instantly found himself seized and shaken roughly from side to side. On his right was a grim apparition all collar and hawk-like eyes, and on his left was one who wore an eye-glass of what seemed that dread moment to be forty horse-power.

"Who and what are these?" he gasped.

"The one to the right is known as the Grim Old Masterpiece, the other we call the Man of Parts. Have you decided between them?"

The Editor could only just shriek "Yes," so severe was the shaking, and then he freed himself with a tremendous effort. The fire was out, and he was in a cold perspiration.

"There was too much nutmeg in that punch," he said, as he lowered the gas and went to bed.

MUSTAPHA
by
S. Baring-Gould
1894

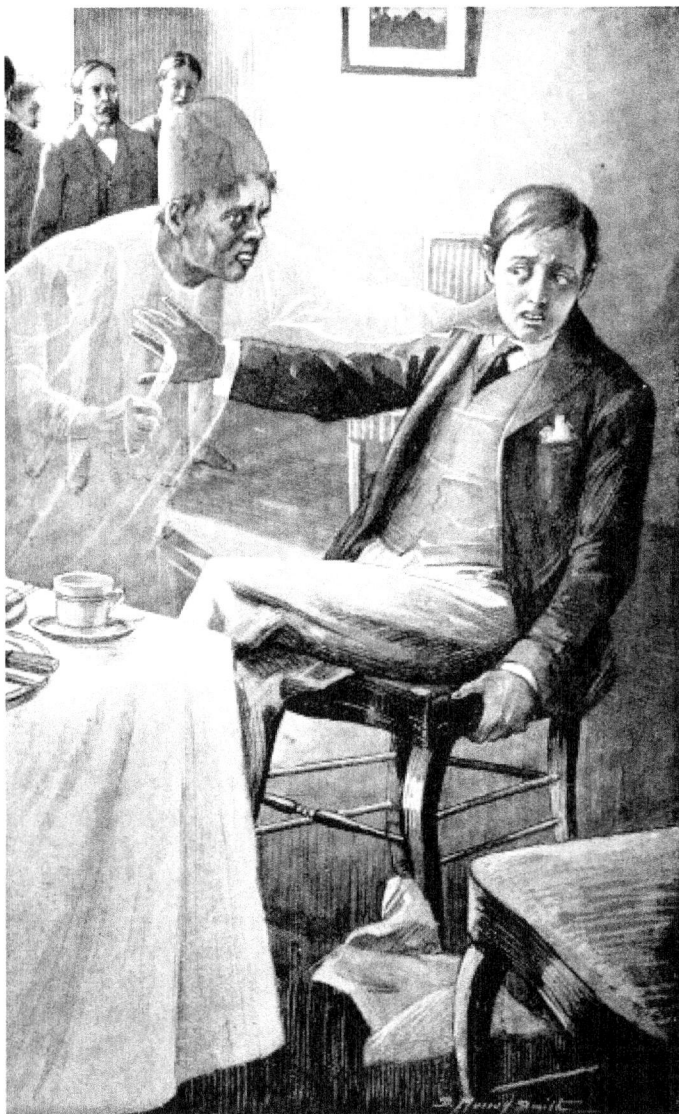

Illustrated by D. Murray Smith

I.

Among the many hangers-on at the Hotel de l'Europe at Luxor—donkey-boys, porters, guides, antiquity dealers—was one, a young man named Mustapha, who proved a general favourite.

I spent three winters at Luxor, partly for my health, partly for pleasure, mainly to make artistic studies, as I am by profession a painter. So I came to know Mustapha fairly well in three stages, during those three winters.

When first I made his acquaintance he was in the transition condition from boyhood to manhood. He had an intelligent face, with bright eyes, a skin soft as brown silk, with a velvety hue on it. His features were regular, and if his face was a little too round to quite satisfy an English artistic eye, yet this was a peculiarity to which one soon became accustomed. He was unflaggingly good-natured and obliging. A mongrel, no doubt, he was; Arab and native Egyptian blood were mingled in his veins. But the result was happy; he combined the patience and gentleness of the child of Mizraim with the energy and pluck of the son of the desert.

Mustapha had been a donkey-boy, but had risen a stage higher, and looked, as the object of his supreme ambition, to become some day a dragoman, and blaze like one of these gilded beetles in lace and chains, rings and weapons. To become a dragoman—one of the most obsequious of men till engaged, one of the veriest tyrants when engaged—to what higher could an Egyptian boy aspire?

To become a dragoman means to go in broadcloth and with gold chains when his fellows are half naked; to lounge and twist the moustache when his kinsfolk are toiling under the water-buckets; to be able to extort backsheesh from all the tradesmen to whom he can introduce a master; to do nothing himself and make others work for him; to be able to look to purchase two, three, even four wives when his father contented himself with one; to soar out of the region of native virtues into that of foreign vices; to be superior to all instilled prejudices against spirits and wine—that is the ideal set before young Egypt through contact with the English and the American tourist.

We all liked Mustapha. No one had a bad word to say of him. Some pious individuals rejoiced to see that he had broken with the

Koran, as if this were a first step towards taking up with the Bible. A free-thinking professor was glad to find that Mustapha had emancipated himself from some of those shackles which religion places on august, divine humanity, and that by getting drunk he gave pledge that he had risen into a sphere of pure emancipation, which eventuates in ideal perfection.

As I made my studies I engaged Mustapha to carry my easel and canvas, or camp-stool. I was glad to have him as a study, to make him stand by a wall or sit on a pillar that was prostrate, as artistic exigencies required. He was always ready to accompany me. There was an understanding between us that when a drove of tourists came to Luxor he might leave me for the day to pick up what he could then from the natural prey; but I found him not always keen to be off duty to me. Though he could get more from the occasional visitor than from me, he was above the ravenous appetite for backsheesh which consumed his fellows.

He who has much to do with the native Egyptian will have discovered that there are in him a fund of kindliness and a treasure of good qualities. He is delighted to be treated with humanity, pleased to be noticed, and ready to repay attention with touching gratitude. He is by no means as rapacious for backsheesh as the passing traveller supposes; he is shrewd to distinguish between man and man; likes this one, and will do anything for him unrewarded, and will do naught for another for any bribe.

The Egyptian is now in a transitional state. If it be quite true that the touch of England is restoring life to his crippled limbs, and the voice of England bidding him rise up and walk, there are occasions on which association with Englishmen is a disadvantage to him. Such an instance is that of poor, good Mustapha.

It was not my place to caution Mustapha against the pernicious influences to which he was subjected, and, to speak plainly, I did not know what line to adopt, on what ground to take my stand, if I did. He was breaking with the old life, and taking up with what was new, retaining of the old only what was bad in it, and acquiring of the new none of its good parts. Civilisation—European civilisation—is excellent, but cannot be swallowed at a gulp, nor does it wholly suit the oriental digestion.

That which impelled Mustapha still further in his course was the attitude assumed towards him by his own relatives and the natives of his own village. They were strict Moslems, and they regarded him as one on the highway to becoming a renegade. They treated him with mistrust, showed him aversion, and loaded him with reproaches. Mustapha had a high spirit, and he resented rebuke. Let his fellows grumble and objurgate, said he; they would cringe to him when he became a dragoman, with his pockets stuffed with piastres.

There was in our hotel, the second winter, a young fellow of the name of Jameson, a man with plenty of money, superficial good nature, little intellect, very conceited and egotistic, and this fellow was Mustapha's evil genius. It was Jameson's delight to encourage Mustapha in drinking and gambling. Time hung heavy on his hands. He cared nothing for hieroglyphics, scenery bored him, antiquities, art, had no charm for him. Natural history presented to him no attraction, and the only amusement level with his mental faculties was that of hoaxing natives, or breaking down their religious prejudices.

Matters were in this condition as regarded Mustapha, when an incident occurred during my second winter at Luxor that completely altered the tenor of Mustapha's life.

One night a fire broke out in the nearest village. It originated in a mud hovel belonging to a fellah; his wife had spilled some oil on the hearth, and the flames leaping up had caught the low thatch, which immediately burst into a blaze. A wind was blowing from the direction of the Arabian desert, and it carried the flames and ignited the thatch before it on other roofs; the conflagration spread, and the whole village was menaced with destruction. The greatest excitement and alarm prevailed. The inhabitants lost their heads. Men ran about rescuing from their hovels their only treasures—old sardine tins and empty marmalade pots; women wailed, children sobbed; no one made any attempt to stay the fire; and, above all, were heard the screams of the woman whose incaution had caused the mischief, and who was being beaten unmercifully by her husband.

The few English in the hotel came on the scene, and with their instinctive energy and system set to work to organise a corps and subdue the flames. The women and girls who were rescued from the menaced hovels, or plucked out of those already on fire, were in many cases unveiled, and so it came to pass that Mustapha, who, under English direction, was ablest and most vigorous in his efforts to stop the conflagration, met his fate in the shape of the daughter of Ibraim the Farrier.

By the light of the flames he saw her, and at once resolved to make that fair girl his wife.

No reasonable obstacle intervened, so thought Mustapha. He had amassed a sufficient sum to entitle him to buy a wife and set up a household of his own. A house consists of four mud walls and a low thatch, and housekeeping in an Egyptian house is as elementary and economical as the domestic architecture. The maintenance of a wife and family is not costly after the first outlay, which consists in indemnifying the father for the expense to which he has been put in rearing a daughter.

The ceremony of courting is also elementary, and the addresses of the suitor are not paid to the bride, but to her father, and not in person by the candidate, but by an intermediary.

Mustapha negotiated with a friend, a fellow hanger-on at the hotel, to open proceedings with the farrier. He was to represent to the worthy man that the suitor entertained the most ardent admiration for the virtues of Ibraim personally, that he was inspired with but one ambition, which was alliance with so distinguished a family as his. He was to assure the father of the damsel that Mustapha undertook to proclaim through Upper and Lower Egypt, in the ears of Egyptians, Arabs, and Europeans, that Ibraim was the most remarkable man that ever existed for solidity of judgment, excellence of parts, uprightness of dealing, nobility of sentiment, strictness in observance of the precepts of the Koran, and that finally Mustapha was anxious to indemnify this same paragon of genius and virtue for his condescension in having cared to breed and clothe and feed for several years a certain girl, his daughter, if Mustapha might have that daughter as his wife. Not that he cared for the daughter in herself, but as a means whereby he might have the honour of entering into alliance with one so distinguished and so esteemed of Allah as Ibraim the Farrier.

To the infinite surprise of the intermediary, and to the no less surprise and mortification of the suitor, Mustapha was refused. He was a bad Moslem. Ibraim would have no alliance with one who had turned his back on the Prophet and drunk bottled beer.

Till this moment Mustapha had not realised how great was the alienation between his fellows and himself—what a barrier he had set up between himself and the men of his own blood. The refusal of his suit struck the young man to the quick. He had known and played with the farrier's daughter in childhood, till she had come of age to veil her face; now that he had seen her in her ripe charms, his heart was deeply stirred and engaged. He entered into himself, and going to the mosque he there made a solemn vow that if he ever touched wine, ale, or spirits again he would cut his throat, and he sent word to Ibraim that he had done so, and begged that he would not dispose of his daughter and finally reject him till he had seen how that he who had turned in thought and manner of life from the Prophet would return with firm resolution to the right way.

II.

From this time Mustapha changed his conduct. He was obliging and attentive as before, ready to exert himself to do for me what I wanted, ready also to extort money from the ordinary tourist for doing nothing, to go with me and carry my tools when I went forth painting, and to joke and laugh with Jameson; but, unless he were unavoidably detained, he said his prayers five times daily in the mosque, and no inducement whatever would make him touch anything save sherbet, milk, or water.

Mustapha had no easy time of it. The strict Mohammedans mistrusted this sudden conversion, and believed that he was playing a part. Ibraim gave him no encouragement. His relatives maintained their reserve and stiffness towards him.

His companions, moreover, who were in the transitional stage, and those who had completely shaken off all faith in Allah and trust in the Prophet and respect for the Koran, were incensed at his desertion. He was ridiculed, insulted; he was waylaid and beaten. The young fellows mimicked him, the elder scoffed at him.

Jameson took his change to heart, and laid himself out to bring him out of his pot of scruples.

"Mustapha ain't any sport at all now," said he. "I'm hanged if he has another para from me." He offered him bribes in gold, he united with the others in ridicule, he turned his back on him, and refused to employ him. Nothing availed. Mustapha was respectful, courteous, obliging as before, but he had returned, he said, to the faith and rule of life in which he had been brought up, and he would never again leave it.

"I have sworn," said he, "that if I do I will cut my throat."

I had been, perhaps, negligent in cautioning the young fellow the first winter that I knew him against the harm likely to be done him by taking up with European habits contrary to his law and the feelings and prejudices of his people. Now, however, I had no hesitation in expressing to him the satisfaction I felt at the courageous and determined manner in which he had broken with acquired habits that could do him no good. For one thing, we were now better acquaintances, and I felt that as one who had known him for more than a few months in the winter, I had a good right to speak. And, again, it is always easier or pleasanter to praise than to reprimand.

One day when sketching I cut my pencil with a pruning-knife I happened to have in my pocket; my proper knife of many blades had been left behind by misadventure.

Mustapha noticed the knife and admired it, and asked if it had cost a great sum.

"Not at all," I answered. "I did not even buy it. It was given me. I ordered some flower seeds from a seeds-man, and when he sent me the consignment he included this knife in the case as a present. It is not worth more than a shilling in England."

He turned it about, with looks of admiration.

"It is just the sort that would suit me," he said. "I know your other knife with many blades. It is very fine, but it is too small. I do not want it to cut pencils. It has other things in it, a hook for taking stones from a horse's hoof, a pair of tweezers for removing hairs. I do not want such, but a knife such as this, with such a curve, is just the thing."

"Then you shall have it," said I. "You are welcome. It was for rough work only that I brought the knife to Egypt with me."

I finished a painting that winter that gave me real satisfaction. It was of the great court of the temple of Luxor by evening light, with the last red glare of the sun over the distant desert hills, and the eastern sky above of a purple depth. What colours I used! the intensest on my palette, and yet fell short of the effect.

The picture was in the Academy, was well hung, abominably represented in one of the illustrated guides to the galleries, as a blotch, by some sort of photographic process on gelatine; my picture sold, which concerned me most of all, and not only did it sell at a respectable figure, but it also brought me two or three orders for Egyptian pictures. So many English and Americans go up the Nile, and carry away with them pleasant reminiscences of the Land of the Pharaohs, that when in England they are fain to buy pictures which shall remind them of scenes in that land.

I returned to my hotel at Luxor in November, to spend there a third winter. The fellaheen about there saluted me as a friend with an affectionate delight, which I am quite certain was not assumed, as they got nothing out of me save kindly salutations. I had the Egyptian fever on me, which, when once acquired, is not to be shaken off—an enthusiasm for everything Egyptian, the antiquities, the history of the Pharaohs, the very desert, the brown Nile, the desolate hill ranges, the ever blue sky, the marvellous colorations at rise and set of sun, and last, but not least, the prosperity of the poor peasants.

I am quite certain that the very warmest welcome accorded to me was from Mustapha, and almost the first words he said to me on my meeting him again were: "I have been very good. I say my prayers. I drink no wine, and Ibraim will give me his daughter in the second Iomada—what you call January."

"Not before, Mustapha?"

"No, sir; he says I must be tried for one whole year, and he is right."

"Then soon after Christmas you will be happy!"

"I have got a house and made it ready. Yes. After Christmas there will be one very happy man—one very, very happy man in Egypt, and that will be your humble servant, Mustapha."

III.

We were a pleasant party at Luxor, this third winter, not numerous, but for the most part of congenial tastes. For the most part we were keen on hieroglyphics, we admired Queen Hatasou and we hated Rameses II. We could distinguish the artistic work of one dynasty from that of another. We were learned on cartouches, and flourished our knowledge before the tourists dropping in.

One of those staying in the hotel was an Oxford don, very good company, interested in everything, and able to talk well on everything—I mean everything more or less remotely connected with Egypt. Another was a young fellow who had been an attaché at Berlin, but was out of health—nothing organic the matter with his lungs, but they were weak. He was keen on the political situation, and very anti-Gallican, as every man who has been in Egypt naturally is, who is not a Frenchman.

There was also staying in the hotel an American lady, fresh and delightful, whose mind and conversation twinkled like frost crystals in the sun, a woman full of good-humour, of the most generous sympathies, and so droll that she kept us ever amused.

And, alas! Jameson was back again, not entering into any of our pursuits, not understanding our little jokes, not at all content to be there. He grumbled at the food—and, indeed, that might have been better; at the monotony of the life at Luxor, at his London doctor for putting the veto on Cairo because of its drainage, or rather the absence of all drainage. I really think we did our utmost to draw Jameson into our circle, to amuse him, to interest him in something; but one by one we gave him up, and the last to do this was the little American lady.

From the outset he had attacked Mustapha, and endeavoured to persuade him to shake off his "squeamish nonsense," as Jameson called his resolve. "I'll tell you what it is, old fellow," he said, "life isn't worth living without good liquor, and as for that blessed Prophet of yours, he showed he was a fool when he put a bar on drinks."

But as Mustapha was not pliable he gave him up. "He's become just as great a bore as that old Rameses," said he. "I'm sick of the whole concern, and I don't think anything of fresh dates, that you fellows make such a fuss about. As for that stupid old Nile—there ain't a fish worth eating comes out of it. And those old Egyptians were arrant humbugs. I haven't seen a lotus since I came here, and they made such a fuss about them too."

The little American lady was not weary of asking questions relative to English home life, and especially to country-house living and amusements.

"Oh, my dear!" said she, "I would give my ears to spend a Christmas in the fine old fashion in a good ancient manor-house in the country."

"There is nothing remarkable in that," said an English lady.

"Not to you, maybe; but there would be to us. What we read of and make pictures of in our fancies, that is what you live. Your facts are our fairy tales. Look at your hunting."

"That, if you like, is fun," threw in Jameson. "But I don't myself think anything save Luxor can be a bigger bore than country-house life at Christmas time—when all the boys are back from school."

"With us," said the little American, "our sportsmen dress in pink like yours—the whole thing—and canter after a bag of anise seed that is trailed before them."

"Why do they not import foxes?"

"Because a fox would not keep to the road. Our farmers object pretty freely to trespass; so the hunting must of necessity be done on the highway, and the game is but a bag of anise seed. I would like to see an English meet and a run."

This subject was thrashed out after having been prolonged unduly for the sake of Jameson.

"Oh, dear me!" said the Yankee lady. "If but that chef could be persuaded to give us plum-puddings for Christmas, I would try to think I was in England."

"Plum-pudding is exploded," said Jameson. "Only children ask for it now. A good trifle or a tipsy-cake is much more to my taste; but this hanged cook here can give us nothing but his blooming custard pudding and burnt sugar."

"I do not think it would be wise to let him attempt a plum-pudding," said the English lady. "But if we can persuade him to permit me I will mix and make the pudding, and then he cannot go far wrong in the boiling and dishing up."

"That is the only thing wanting to make me perfectly happy," said the American. "I'll confront monsieur. I am sure I can talk him into a good humour, and we shall have our plum-pudding."

No one has yet been found, I do believe, who could resist that little woman. She carried everything before her. The cook placed himself and all his culinary apparatus at her feet. We took part in the stoning of the raisins, and the washing of the currants, even the chopping of the suet; we stirred the pudding, threw in sixpence apiece, and a ring, and then it was tied up in a cloth, and set aside to be boiled. Christmas Day came, and the English chaplain preached us a practical sermon on "Goodwill towards men." That was his text, and his sermon was but a swelling out of the words just as rice is swelled to thrice its size by boiling.

We dined. There was an attempt at roast beef—it was more like baked leather. The event of the dinner was to be the bringing in and eating of the plum-pudding.

Surely all would be perfect. We could answer for the materials and the mixing. The English lady could guarantee the boiling. She had seen the plum-pudding "on the boil," and had given strict injunctions as to the length of time during which it was to boil.

But, alas! the pudding was not right when brought on the table. It was not enveloped in lambent blue flame—it was not crackling in the burning brandy. It was sent in dry, and the brandy arrived separate in a white sauce-boat, hot indeed, and sugared, but not on fire.

There ensued outcries of disappointment. Attempts were made to redress the mistake by setting fire to the brandy in a spoon, but the spoon was cold. The flame would not catch, and finally, with a sigh, we had to take our plum-pudding as served.

"I say, chaplain!" exclaimed Jameson, "practice is better than precept, is it not?"

"To be sure it is."

"You gave us a deuced good sermon. It was short, as it ought to be; but I'll go better on it, I'll practise where you preached, and have larks, too!"

Then Jameson started from table with a plate of plum-pudding in one hand and the sauce-boat in the other. "By Jove!" he said, "I'll teach these fellows to open their eyes. I'll show them that we know how to feed. We can't turn out scarabs and cartouches in England, that are no good to anyone, but we can produce the finest roast beef in the world, and do a thing or two in puddings."

And he left the room.

We paid no heed to anything Jameson said or did. We were rather relieved that he was out of the room, and did not concern ourselves about the "larks" he promised himself, and which we were quite certain would be as insipid as were the quails of the Israelites.

In ten minutes he was back, laughing and red in the face. "I've had splitting fun," he said. "You should have been there."

"Where, Jameson?"

"Why, outside. There were a lot of old moolahs and other hoky-pokies sitting and contemplating the setting sun and all that sort of thing, and I gave Mustapha the pudding. I told him I wished him to try our great national English dish, on which her Majesty the Queen dines daily. Well, he ate and enjoyed it, by George. Then I said, 'Old fellow, it's uncommonly dry, so you must take the sauce to it.' He asked if it was only sauce—flour and water. 'It's sauce, by Jove,' said I, 'a little sugar to it; no bar on the sugar, Musty.' So I put the boat to his lips and gave him a pull. By George, you should have seen his face! It was just thundering fun. 'I've done you at last, old Musty,' I said. 'It is best cognac.' He gave me such a look! He'd have eaten me, I believe—and he walked away. It was just splitting fun. I wish you had been there to see it."

I went out after dinner, to take my usual stroll along the river-bank, and to watch the evening lights die away on the columns and obelisk. On my return I saw at once that something had happened which had produced commotion among the servants of the hotel. I had reached the salon before I inquired what was the matter.

The boy who was taking the coffee round said: "Mustapha is dead. He cut his throat at the door of the mosque. He could not help himself. He had broken his vow."

I looked at Jameson without a word. Indeed, I could not speak; I was choking. The little American lady was trembling, the English lady crying. The gentlemen stood silent in the windows, not speaking a word.

Jameson's colour changed. He was honestly distressed, uneasy, and tried to cover his confusion with bravado and a jest.

"After all," he said, "it is only a nigger the less."

"Nigger!" said the American lady. "He was no nigger, but an Egyptian."

"Oh! I don't pretend to distinguish between your blacks and whity-browns any more than I do between your cartouches," returned Jameson.

"He was no black," said the American lady, standing up. "But I do mean to say that I consider you an utterly unredeemed black——"

"My dear, don't," said the Englishwoman, drawing the other down. "It's no good. The thing is done. He meant no harm."

IV.

I could not sleep. My blood was in a boil. I felt that I could not speak to Jameson again. He would have to leave Luxor. That was tacitly understood among us. Coventry was the place to which he would be consigned.

I tried to finish in a little sketch I had made in my notebook when I was in my room, but my hand shook, and I was constrained to lay my pencil aside. Then I took up an Egyptian grammar, but could not fix my mind on study. The hotel was very still. Everyone had gone to bed at an early hour that night, disinclined for conversation. No one was moving. There was a lamp in the passage; it was partly turned down. Jameson's room was next to mine. I heard him stir as he undressed, and talk to himself. Then he was quiet. I wound up my watch, and emptying my pocket, put my purse under the pillow. I was not in the least heavy with sleep. If I did go to bed I should not be able to close my eyes. But then—if I sat up I could do nothing.

I was about leisurely to undress, when I heard a sharp cry, or exclamation of mingled pain and alarm, from the adjoining room. In another moment there was a rap at my door. I opened, and Jameson came in. He was in his nightshirt, and looking agitated and frightened.

"Look here, old fellow," said he in a shaking voice, "there is Musty in my room. He has been hiding there, and just as I dropped asleep he ran that—knife of yours into my throat."

"My knife?"

"Yes—that pruning-knife you gave him, you know. Look here—I must have the place sewn up. Do go for a doctor, there's a good chap,"

"Where is the place?"

"Here on my right gill."

Jameson turned his head to the left, and I raised the lamp. There was no wound of any sort there. I told him so.

"Oh, yes! That's fine—I tell you I felt his knife go in."

"Nonsense, you were dreaming."

"Dreaming! Not I. I saw Musty as distinctly as I now see you."

"This is a delusion, Jameson," I replied. "The poor fellow is dead."

"Oh, that's very fine," said Jameson. "It is not the first of April, and I don't believe the yarns that you've been spinning. You tried to make believe he was dead, but I know he is not. He has got into my room, and he made a dig at my throat with your pruning-knife."

"I'll go into your room with you."

"Do so. But he's gone by this time. Trust him to cut and run."

I followed Jameson, and looked about. There was no trace of anyone beside himself having been in the room. Moreover, there was no place but the nut-wood wardrobe in the bedroom in which anyone could have secreted himself I opened this and showed that it was empty.

After a while I pacified Jameson, and induced him to go to bed again, and then I left his room. I did not now attempt to court sleep. I wrote letters with a hand not the steadiest, and did my accounts.

As the hour approached midnight I was again startled by a cry from the adjoining room, and in another moment Jameson was at my door.

"That blooming fellow Musty is in my room still," said he. "He has been at my throat again."

"Nonsense," I said. "You are labouring under hallucinations. You locked your door."

"Oh, by Jove, yes—of course I did; but, hang it, in this hole, neither doors nor windows fit, and the locks are no good, and the bolts nowhere. He got in again somehow, and if I had not started up the moment I felt the knife, he'd have done for me. He would, by George. I wish I had a revolver."

I went into Jameson's room. Again he insisted on my looking at his throat.

"It's very good of you to say there is no wound," said he. "But you won't gull me with words. I felt his knife in my windpipe, and if I had not jumped out of bed——"

"You locked your door. No one could enter. Look in the glass, there is not even a scratch. This is pure imagination."

"I'll tell you what, old fellow, I won't sleep in that room again. Change with me, there's a charitable buffer. If you don't believe in Musty, Musty won't hurt you, maybe—anyhow you can try if he's solid or a phantom. Blow me if the knife felt like a phantom."

"I do not quite see my way to changing rooms," I replied; "but this I will do for you. If you like to go to bed again in your own apartment, I will sit up with you till morning."

"All right," answered Jameson. "And if Musty comes in again, let out at him and do not spare him. Swear that."

I accompanied Jameson once more to his bedroom. Little as I liked the man, I could not deny him my presence and assistance at this time. It was obvious that his nerves were shaken by what had occurred, and he felt his relation to Mustapha much more than he cared to show. The thought that he had been the cause of the poor fellow's death preyed on his mind, never strong, and now it was upset with imaginary terrors.

I gave up letter writing, and brought my Baedeker's *Upper Egypt* into Jameson's room, one of the best of all guide-books, and one crammed with information. I seated myself near the light, and with my back to the bed, on which the young man had once more flung himself

"I say," said Jameson, raising his head, "is it too late for a brandy-and-soda?"

"Everyone is in bed."

"What lazy dogs they are. One never can get anything one wants here."

"Well, try to go to sleep."

He tossed from side to side for some time, but after a while, either he was quiet, or I was engrossed in my Baedeker, and I heard nothing till a clock struck twelve. At the last stroke I heard a snort and then a gasp and a cry from the bed. I started up, and looked round. Jameson was slipping out with his feet onto the floor.

"Confound you!" said he angrily, "you are a fine watch, you are, to let Mustapha steal in on tiptoe whilst you are cartouching and all that sort of rubbish. He was at me again, and if I had not been sharp he'd have cut my throat. I won't go to bed any more!"

"Well, sit up. But I assure you no one has been here."

"That's fine. How can you tell? You had your back to me, and these devils of fellows steal about like cats. You can't hear them till they are at you."

It was of no use arguing with Jameson, so I let him have his way.

"I can feel all the three places in my throat where he ran the knife in," said he. "And—don't you notice?—I speak with difficulty."

So we sat up together the rest of the night. He became more reasonable as dawn came on, and inclined to admit that he had been a prey to fancies. The day passed very much as did others—Jameson was dull and sulky. After déjeuner he sat on at table when the ladies had risen and retired, and the gentlemen had formed in knots at the window, discussing what was to be done in the afternoon.

Suddenly Jameson, whose head had begun to nod, started up with an oath and threw down his chair.

"You fellows!" he said, "you are all in league against me. You let that Mustapha come in without a word, and try to stick his knife into me."

"He has not been here."

"It's a plant. You are combined to bully me and drive me away. You don't like me. You have engaged Mustapha to murder me. This is the fourth time he has tried to cut my throat, and in the *salle à manger*, too, with you all standing round. You ought to be ashamed to call yourselves Englishmen. I'll go to Cairo. I'll complain."

It really seemed that the feeble brain of Jameson was affected. The Oxford don undertook to sit up in the room the following night.

The young man was fagged and sleep-weary, but no sooner did his eyes close, and clouds form about his head, than he was brought to wakefulness again by the same fancy or dream. The Oxford don had more trouble with him on the second night than I had on the first, for his lapses into sleep were more frequent, and each such lapse was succeeded by a start and a panic.

The next day he was worse, and we felt that he could no longer be left alone. The third night the attaché sat up to watch him.

Jameson had now sunk into a sullen mood. He would not speak, except to himself, and then only to grumble.

During the night, without being aware of it, the young attaché, who had taken a couple of magazines with him to read, fell asleep. When he went off he did not know. He woke just before dawn, and in a spasm of terror and self-reproach saw that Jameson's chair was empty.

Jameson was not on his bed. He could not be found in the hotel.

At dawn he was found—dead, at the door of the mosque, with his throat cut.

A CHRISTMAS GHOST STORY
by
Percy Andreae
1895

Illustrated by Charles H. Heydemann

I was miserable. What a fool I had been. Why had I come here? Why hadn't I refused this invitation like a man, and spent my Christmas in my chambers, or with my old maiden aunt in Drearington, or anywhere—anywhere but just here, where I knew I should be so unspeakably miserable?

You need not sneer and snigger, my doughty reader. You've been in love yourself, don't tell me, and if you haven't you ought to have been, and if you have you ought to know better, and, once more, if you haven't, then don't read my story, but leave it to your betters.

I shall never forget that New Year's Eve at Mount Edgmont, for the simple reason that I had never felt more miserable in my life. Mount Edgmont, as the reader probably knows, is the principal seat of the Duke of Teignmouth, and one of the oldest family estates in England. Reginald de L'Isle, the Duke of Teignmouth's only son, and I had been chums at Eton. Evelyn de L'Isle, the Duke of Teignmouth's only daughter and Reggy's younger sister—the sweetest girl that ever breathed—had in former days been—well, a sort of chum of mine too, when I used to spend part of my holidays with Reggy at Mount Edgmont. I was an orphan, by name Ralph Moreton. My family was a fairly good one, but unfortunately nothing to compare with the de L'Isles, who belonged to the very highest of the land. I had a fair position in the Civil Service, and a private income of about four hundred a year—all very pleasant to a man of ordinary aspirations, but terribly inadequate to one whose friends are heirs to dukedoms and baronies, and who has the misfortune to lose his heart to one of the richest and proudest heiresses in England.

Evelyn de L'Isle had always liked me, I knew, and perhaps—if I had ventured to push myself—this liking might have ripened later on into something deeper. But how would it have ended? I knew the Duke of Teignmouth and his family pride and prejudice only too well. He was as kind-hearted a man in his way as one could ever wish to meet, but still he never let you forget that he was the grand seigneur, and that there was a certain limit beyond which no advance was possible with him. As for Lady Evelyn herself, what she would have said or done, had she known of my hopeless passion, I never ventured to consider. We had always been staunch friends, and even after my schooldays were over, and we met as full-grown mortals in London society and on other occasions, she never dropped the old cordial tone towards me. But the moment I felt whither I was drifting I exerted all my power of will and drew back—alas! to no purpose, so far as my happiness was concerned. I had told myself that I was a fool, and yet grew more miserable from day today. I had sworn I would never set foot again in Mount Edgmont or any other possession of the Duke of Teignmouth's, and kept my oath for two years, at the risk of mortally offending my best friend, Reginald de L'Isle. I had even eschewed society, and refused invitations to houses where I knew I should meet Evelyn; in short, I had accomplished unheard of sacrifices in my heroic resolve to conquer a hopeless passion—and yet here I was at last again under her own father's roof, more miserable than ever, and worse than all, I knew I had given grave offence to Lady Evelyn herself, who had noticed my reticent manner towards her, and not knowing its cause, had naturally attributed it to coldness, unfriendliness, or heaven knows what.

To increase my martyrdom, I had now learned, nay, seen with my own eyes, that I had a rival in the field—as if that made any difference, indeed. And yet I had reasons, other than those of mere jealousy, to brood despairingly over this fatal circumstance. Lord Bertie Goring, who seemed to be generally recognised as the successful suitor for Evelyn de L'Isle's hand, was an old Etonian like Reggy and myself. He was what is commonly known among young men as "a good sort after all," a term which is admittedly an apologetic one, and implies a "notwithstanding" with a more or less long tail behind it. Thus I was well aware that Bertie Goring was an inveterate gambler, a hard drinker, and generally a fast liver in every sense of the term. To see Evelyn smile upon this man, who was confoundedly good-looking too, and to know that the match between her and him was practically as settled as such things can be without the actual ratification of the contracting parties themselves—why, goodness me, need I dilate any further on all it meant for me?

On that New Year's Eve there was a grand costume ball at Mount Edgmont. I had danced once with Evelyn, and had been refused a second dance rather coldly and haughtily. Thereupon I had placed myself—fool as I was in a position where I could see and watch the progress of Bertie Goring's courtship. There were about two hundred guests at the ball, thirty of whom—and I amongst the number—were staying at the castle. As the night wore on I could bear the hateful strain no longer, and taking a suitable opportunity, I slipped away from the gay throng downstairs, and betook myself to the smoking-room in the eastern tower, where I passed a quarter of an hour or so in giving expression to the sentiments recorded in the first paragraph of this story.

Solitude is wonderfully solacing to a sick heart, and this room was so remote from the bustle and gaiety I had left, that I might have fancied myself hundreds of miles away from the scene of my sufferings. Knowing that none of my fellow-guests were likely to find their way through the intricate passages and corridors to this rarely visited wing of the immense mansion, I abandoned myself unreservedly to the thoughts that were tormenting me, and sat for a long while, with my arms spread on the table and my face buried in them—in an attitude, in short, which foolish people with my complaint are wont to assume on such occasions.

After a while the stillness of the place, which was only dimly lighted by one lamp with red glass hanging from the centre of the ceiling, began to tell upon my feelings, but in a curious way. While it calmed me in one respect, it seemed to impart to me a sense of unrest which I should find it difficult to explain. It struck me of a sudden that I should be missed at the ball, and that my retirement to this secluded corner of the castle would appear strange. As this thought occurred to me, I raised my head with the intention of going back and fighting out my trouble resolutely and with a calm front. There was nothing I dreaded so much, indeed, as to see the real state of my mind exposed to other eyes.

To my consternation, however, I found when I looked up that I was no longer the only occupant of the room. I blushed as I thought of the position in which I had been discovered, but the next instant I started up with an exclamation of absolute dismay, for, incredible though it seemed, my first impression was that the person sitting on the opposite side of the table, with his eyes fixed upon me with a steady, earnest gaze, was no other than the Duke of Teignmouth himself. Yet it was impossible. I remembered having seen the Duke downstairs in the costume of a Spanish grandee, while this personage was dressed like an English cavalier of the sixteenth century. The likeness, nevertheless, was so startling that it fairly took my breath away, and I stood for a considerable while staring open-mouthed at the motionless figure in front of me. Who could it be? And how could he have entered the room without my observing him? That he was not one of the more intimate guests of the evening was certain, else I should have known him, and yet for a stranger to the house to have found his way unaided through all those labyrinthine corridors to this lonesome spot appeared next to impossible.

All these reflections passed through my mind quite slowly, and an uncanny sensation followed in their wake, for, while I thus stared and reflected, my companion never once took his eyes off my face, but sat there rigid like a figure in wax, save for that steady, piercing gaze I have mentioned, which gave his countenance something life-like and real.

At last I could stand the oppressive silence no longer. After all, we could not remain sitting opposite one another trying to stare each other out of countenance for the rest of the night.

"That is a marvellous get-up of yours," I ventured to remark at last, by way of opening up a conversation. My own costume was that of a Spanish toreador. "I wonder I never noticed you downstairs."

But in lieu of a reply, my strange companion merely inclined his head very gravely, without, however, removing his eyes from my face, then rose from his chair, stood for a moment drawn up to his full height, which was very imposing, and then, again without turning his head away from me, glided slowly and perfectly noiselessly out of the room.

The effect of all this upon me was so thrilling that I felt a shiver pass through my body from the crown of my head to the soles of my feet, and in my agitation I started up, overthrowing my chair, and seized by an irresistible impulse, rushed to the door and out into the passage in pursuit of my strange visitant. The passage led to a winding staircase which descended to the eastern wing of the castle, upon which the tower was built. At the top of this staircase I saw the strange figure, with its head still turned towards me as before, waiting apparently in anticipation of my following it.

I am not of a timid disposition in ordinary parlance, but in this instance I have no hesitation in admitting that a sensation of absolute fear crept over me, and I stood for a moment irresolute whether to advance or go back to the room I had left. But before I could make up my mind either way, the figure moved on again, descending the stairs in the same gliding, noiseless fashion in which it had passed out of the smoking-room, and, obeying the same impulse as before, I moved on likewise, now, however, rather led than pursuing.

I thought I knew the ins and outs of Mount Edgmont perfectly, having spent many a summer and winter vacation during my schooldays in exploring every nook and corner of the magnificent old castle with Reggy. But it became evident to me now that I had a guide whose knowledge of its intricacies was far superior to my own. We passed swiftly through a maze of doors and rooms and corridors, for the most part dark or very sparely lighted, now turning abruptly into some passage which apparently led to nowhere in particular, now mounting or descending staircases the locality of which I was already far too bewildered to remember. Presently I could distinguish the strains of the dance-music and the hum of the guests in the distance, and knew that we were approaching the scene of the festivity. Was my strange companion going to mix boldly with the gay throng below? For a moment it shot across my mind that the whole thing might be some practical joke perpetrated at my expense by Reggy himself, who was rather addicted to this questionable species of fun. But I was soon undeceived. Of a sudden my guide halted at the end of a wide corridor, and, as if his movements and mine were in some way interdependent, I, too, came to an abrupt standstill.

Where we were I knew not, for I had entirely lost my sense of locality, but I could see that six or seven paces ahead of me, where the figure remained stationary, there was a door which stood slightly ajar, letting a flood of light into the passage. As I stood and gazed, the somewhat grim features of the figure, which I could plainly distinguish in the light from the half-open door, relaxed into a kindly smile, as if inviting me to advance. Hesitating no longer, I rushed forward precipitately, but too late—before I reached the spot the figure had vanished. Without considering what I was doing, I pushed open the door through which I felt certain it had passed, and burst into the room, determined at any cost to follow and gain speech of my strange acquaintance. But the sight that met my view here made me start back in confusion. The room, fairly sized and luxuriously furnished, was lighted up by a profusion of taper-candles. At the further end was a huge mirror, reaching almost to the ceiling, and in front of it, tranquilly engaged in fastening a fresh rose in her hair, stood Evelyn de L'Isle.

She turned round with a little start as I entered.

"Mr. Moreton!'" she exclaimed, in a tone of surprise.

"I—I beg your pardon," I stammered, greatly embarrassed, "I thought—I mean, I followed—surely he entered here."

And I looked round the room dumbfounded. There was no trace of any one else there.

"He Who?" she asked, following my astonished glance.

I felt dreadfully foolish. What was I to say? I had committed an unpardonable breach of good manners. This was Lady Evelyn's boudoir, as I now recognised, and I had burst in upon her in this rude and unceremonious fashion, like some crazed being. There was nothing for it but to confess my folly, and make such excuses for my-self as I could.

"Lady Evelyn," I said, "I hardly know how to explain; but—but I believe I have seen a ghost."

She turned pale.

"A ghost?" she said, tremulously. "What was it like?"

I told her of my adventure, to which she listened at first gravely. But as I proceeded she turned her head away, and toyed nervously with the lace of her dress. It struck me that she looked confused, and a chance glance at the reflection of her face in the mirror showed me that it was covered with blushes. I cannot describe the sensation the discovery produced in me. Had I been fooled after all, and did she know it? I scarcely dared to pursue the thought, and after I had finished my story I waited in silence for her to speak.

The pause that ensued was painfully embarrassing to me, but presently she turned her face, and looked at me with a curiously arch expression.

"You say you went alone to the smoking-room in the tower?" she asked.

"Yes," I answered.

"And stayed there quite alone for nearly half an hour?"

Again I answered affirmatively.

"Why?" she asked, with a brevity which disconcerted me not a little.

"I hardly know," I replied, trying to look innocent. "I felt a little out of sorts, and went there to have a few minutes' quiet."

The answer seemed to satisfy her, and she remained silent for a moment.

"Lady Evelyn," I said, "if I have been made the subject of a practical joke, I would take it as a favour if you would tell me so."

"A practical joke?" she said reflectively. "No, I think not." Then breaking off with a little embarrassed laugh, she asked: "You are quite sure the figure you saw smiled at you?"

"Distinctly," I answered; and thinking it best to treat the matter lightly, I added: "On the whole I must acknowledge that the ghost, if it was one, behaved most amiably."

"It does not always do so," she said. "But I am glad it was pleasant—for your sake," she added, as if with an afterthought, and again I saw a deep blush tinge her cheeks, which made me feel uncomfortably suspicious of having been tricked.

"Perhaps as you are here, Mr. Moreton," she continued, before I could speak, "you won't mind taking me down to the ball-room, unless you wish to resume your solitary musings in the smoking-room."

There was something so provokingly roguish in these words, and yet her manner in expressing them was so embarrassed and timid, that I felt at a loss for an answer. I gave her my arm, and we made our way in silence through the corridor which I had traversed only a few moments before, and which I now saw led to the picture-gallery adjoining the grand staircase. There were a few couples roaming about the gallery as we crossed it and at the opposite side I recognised Bertie Goring wandering from niche to niche with a disconsolate air.

Lady Evelyn saw him too, and, stopping suddenly, turned back

as if to pass out of the gallery by another door. It was evident that she wished to elude him—a circumstance that made my heart leap with a wicked joy. But the manoeuvre came too late, and in another moment he overtook us, and claimed her as his partner.

I bowed silently, and Lady Evelyn transferred her arm from me to him. As she did so, however, she remarked, drawing forth her dancing card:

"Let me see, our next dance is the second after this, I think, Mr. Moreton. You will find me near the fountain in the conservatory."

Saying which, she deliberately drew her pencil through the name standing against the dance in question on her card, and left me standing in a transport of surprise and pleasure.

How long I remained in that attitude I can't say, but I was aroused presently by a well-known voice at my elbow, saying:

"Well, Moreton, you look quite awestruck. What has happened?"

It was the Duke himself, Evelyn's father. Recollecting myself instantly, I put on a laughing face, and replied:

"You will hardly believe it, sir, but I've just seen a ghost."

The effect of my words was an unexpected one.

"What do you mean, Moreton?' his Grace said, almost sternly. "I trust you are joking."

"If it is a joke, sir," I answered, rather nettled by his curt tone, "it is certainly not of my making."

And I related my adventure, discreetly omitting, however, to mention the fact of its having terminated with my intrusion into Lady Evelyn's boudoir.

The Duke listened with a frown that grew deeper as I proceeded. When I had finished, he looked at me for a moment keenly; then, turning sharply on his heel, he said:

"Have the goodness to follow me, Mr. Moreton."

I obeyed silently, and he led me round the great gallery, stopping at last before a huge painting set in an ancient framing, which did not hang on the wall like the others, but was let into the stonework like a frieze. Pointing to it, he said:

"Was the person you saw anything like that?"

"The very man, by Jove," I exclaimed, forgetting all formality in my surprise at the likeness, which was indeed striking.

I saw the Duke start slightly, and give me a look of displeasure.

"I beg, then," he said coldly, "that you will forget what you have seen, Mr. Moreton, and above all that you will not speak about it to any one, whether it be a member of my family or not. It is not agreeable to me that my guests should meet with adventures of this description under my roof."

With these words he left me, considerably perplexed. This was turning the tables with a vengeance, I thought. After all, it was not I who had sought the ghost's acquaintance, it was the ghost who had sought mine, and why this fact should call his Grace's wrath down upon my head, I was at a loss to conceive.

I consoled myself, however, with the thought of Lady Evelyn and her spontaneous concession of the dance she had refused me at the commencement of the evening, and soon forgot all about this little incident.

As soon as the appointed time arrived I hastened to the conservatory, where I found Lady Evelyn already awaiting me.

She rose as I approached, and placing her arm in mine, suggested that we should sit out the dance. There was a shyness in her manner, so unlike her, and yet a certain assurance withal that made my very heartstrings quiver. I remembered having had a similar sensation two years before, when I was first seized with my mad infatuation, and withdrew to save myself from the misery of a passion which I felt to be hopeless. Ah, how ill-bred and churlish and yet here she must have thought me! I was again at her side, as madly in love as ever.

"Mr. Moreton," she said, as we moved on, "I wanted to ask you not to tell any one about—about what happened to you an hour ago. If you don't mind, I should prefer that it remained between you and me."

"But I have already told his Grace, Lady Evelyn," I said, with some dismay. "Had I only known——"

"My father?" she exclaimed. "How very unfortunate. And did he—did he seem surprised?"

"I think he was annoyed, Lady Evelyn. My adventure appeared to displease him greatly, though it must be admitted that it was not of my seeking."

"Perhaps he thinks differently," she answered.

Her tone seemed to imply that she herself was inclined to think

differently, which only tended to increase my surprise. But before I could ask her for an explanation, our short *tête-d-tête* was brought to a premature end by the sudden appearance of the Duke himself. He approached us hurriedly from a side-entrance, and addressing his daughter, told her somewhat peremptorily that she was wanted in the ball-room.

"I am sorry I must ask you to resign Lady Evelyn to me, Mr. Moreton," he said, turning to me with the same look of haughty displeasure which his face had worn when he parted from me in the picture-gallery. "Some of our guests are leaving, and my daughter has to perform her duties as hostess."

And without waiting for me to reply, he gave his arm to Lady Evelyn, and led her away. I stood utterly perplexed, the more so as I thought I noticed an abashed look on Lady Evelyn's face, as she left the conservatory on her father's arm. What was the meaning of it all? What had I done to incur the anger of one who, ever since I was a boy, had always treated me with almost fatherly kindness, and had liked me too, for Reggy had often told me so?

I began to feel myself the victim of some extraordinary mystery. But if this unpleasant incident caused me trouble, what now followed affected me far more deeply.

I saw no more of Lady Evelyn that night. But the next day, and the day after, I could not but feel that my presence at Mount Edgmont had become distasteful to its proprietor. His manner towards me was as cold and distant as was compatible with the politeness of a host, and, what annoyed and puzzled me more than anything else, he seemed to be incessantly on the watch to prevent any meeting between me and Lady Evelyn. To increase my sense of discomfort, my old friend and school-fellow Reggy, who was usually heartiness itself towards me, grew of a sudden constrained and embarrassed, like one who has something weighing upon him and cannot sum up courage to come out with it.

Such a state of affairs was unendurable to me for any length of time, and at last I made up my mind to leave Mount Edgmont. When I told Reggy that I found myself obliged to return to town on the following day, a look of relief came into his face. Then he suddenly placed his hand on my shoulder, and said:

"Ralph, old fellow, why did you never tell me about this?"

"About what?" I asked, surprised at his sudden burst of feeling.

"I mean, about this unfortunate attachment."

"Attachment? What are you talking about?"

Reggy looked at me with a quiet smile.

"Ralph, my boy," he said, "I can't tell you how sorry I am. If she were in my giving, you should have her, that's all I can say. But you know the governor's strong notions on the subject."

If he had struck me a sudden blow with his clenched hand, it could not have staggered me more than his words did.

"How do you know——" I stammered.

"The governor told me himself," he said.

"The Duke?" I exclaimed. "Impossible. Why, not even Evelyn herself dreams—"

The look of comic compassion with which he received my words made me redden with shame. I saw it all instantly. My secret had been betrayed, was perhaps the common property of the guests assembled at Mount Edgmont. By what means it had become so, I knew not, nor dared consider. But the idea itself was maddening, above all on account of Evelyn herself, for—great powers—what a confounded fool she must think me. I could not trust myself to say any more to Reggy, and left him in a frame of mind which I will leave the reader to imagine.

How I passed the remainder of that day I don't remember. I only know that I sought an interview with the Duke, and informed him of my intention to depart on the morrow. Nothing else passed between us, but his manner was unusually kind, and I think he felt sorry for me. Lady Evelyn did not appear downstairs at all that day. She was indisposed, it was said, but my own belief was that she preferred not to meet me again. To add to my mortification, I learned that Lord Bertie Goring had been closeted with the Duke for nearly an hour that morning, and had presumably made his formal proposal for the hand of Lady Evelyn.

At last the night came, and I was able to escape from the company which had become a veritable torment to me. Ah, what a night it proved! The room I occupied was situated in the left wing of the castle, which was of comparatively modern build. Although I had retired to rest early, it was some time past midnight before I fell into a troubled sleep. There was one dream in particular which haunted me, recurring again and again with incessant repetition. I was trying to escape from Mount Edgmont by night, and could not. The figure I had seen in the room in the tower a few evenings ago was always at my side, and led me astray in the corridors of the castle, leaving me at last standing at the door of Lady Evelyn's boudoir, where I entered to find her, as I had found her that evening, fastening a fresh rose in her hair before the mirror. Then the vision vanished, and the dream and the unsuccessful flight began afresh, until at last I shrieked aloud in my anguish, and awoke.

For an instant I still imagined I was dreaming, for there, not three paces from my bed, standing in the moonlight which shone through the window-casement into the room, I saw that strange figure once more, its eyes now fixed upon me with a stern, angry look.

As I started up, it raised both arms aloft, and shook them menacingly. With a loud cry I sprang out of bed, and rushed at the spectre; but before I reached the spot, it was gone.

At that moment I heard a succession of cries, which seemed to come from someone beneath my window, and almost simultaneously there was a sharp rapping at my door, and I heard a voice outside call to me to open.

Utterly bewildered, I unlocked the door, only to start back again with an exclamation of astonishment. The person who now entered hurriedly, and with signs of extreme agitation on his face, was no other than the Duke of Teignmouth himself.

"Where is Lord Bertie?" he asked. "His room is empty. Great God, if it should be true——"

"Goring?" I exclaimed. "What has happened to him?"

"I fear he has met with foul play, Moreton" the old Duke said with a white face. "I am not usually affected by dreams—but this one was fearful, I saw—hark, what is that?" he broke off, as cries beneath my window sounded again louder than before.

I rushed to the casement, flung it open, and looked out. The next moment I fell back laughing.

In the snow, just underneath my window, hammering with all his might against the door which led from this wing of the castle on to the terrace, stood Lord Bertie. He was—I blush to say it—in his night-shirt. How he had got there, heaven knew. But I did not stop to think or explain. Seizing the lighted candle which the Duke held in his hand, I hurried out of the room, followed by his Grace himself, and passing quickly through the corridor and down the staircase, unbolted the door, and let the unfortunate fellow in.

At the sight of the Duke he looked somewhat confused, but his pale face showed that he was suffering more from fright than embarrassment.

"How the deuce did you get out there, Goring?" I cried. "You must have climbed out of window. This door here was locked and bolted."

It was some time before he could find speech to explain.

"I've had the most extraordinary experience," he stuttered at last—"woke up about half an hour ago almost strangled by some masquerading fellow who had got into my room somehow. When I tried to seize him, he was out of the door like a shot, and I after him. He led me a regular dance, upstairs and downstairs, till at last he disappeared out of this door, and I, like a fool, followed. When I got outside, he was no more to be seen, and when I wanted to get back again, I found the door wouldn't open," he added viciously.

The Duke listened in silence, but his face was very grave, and he glanced at me with a curious look of interest, which emboldened me to relate my own second adventure with the ghost that night. He said nothing, save to request Goring and myself to keep the matter quiet. But when we had lighted Goring, all shivering and quaking with cold, to his room, the Duke stopped for a moment at my door, and said:

"I should like to see you to morrow again for a few minutes, before you go, Ralph. Good night."

And with these words he left me. "Ralph, Ralph," I kept repeating to myself, as I pondered over his speech. The old Duke had not called me by my Christian name since I was at school at Eton.

The next morning at ten o'clock I presented myself in the Duke's study with a heavy heart. On my way there I had passed the conservatory, where I had seen Lady Evelyn walking with Bertie Goring, who, by the way, was afflicted with an awful cold, and by her embarrassed air and his animated manner I had little difficulty in guessing the nature of their interview.

"Sit down, Moreton," said his Grace, when I entered. "There are one or two things I wish to say to you. In the first place, I thought it might interest you to know that Lord Bertie Goring is at this moment offering his hand to Lady Evelyn."

I bowed silently. I was only too well aware of the fact.

"It is Goring's own wish to have his answer direct from her," he continued. "You probably know what it will be, Moreton."

"Your Grace," I stammered, half ashamed and half angry at what I thought a cruel and unbecoming jest.

"Well, well," he said, "Evelyn has told me that her affections have been engaged elsewhere since several years, and though I may frankly tell you that under ordinary conditions I could never have consented to such a match—not that I have any objection to your personal character, my dear boy——"

I started up electrified, nearly knocking down my chair in my amazement.

"There are certain circumstances," the Duke went on, "which I dare not ignore, and which lead me to believe that you will make Evelyn a good husband. Stay," he continued, in a lower voice, seeing my movement of delirious joy, "there is one other matter which I wish to tell you about, and which may perhaps explain a good deal that has seemed incomprehensible to you. Three hundred years ago, Moreton, an ancestor of mine, gave his only daughter away in marriage to a rich but profligate and brutal nobleman. Her husband ill-treated her, and she died broken-hearted, for she had loved a better man. Her father challenged his own son-in-law to mortal combat, and killed him, after which he shut himself up in this very castle Mount Edgmont, and died two years later, overwhelmed with shame and remorse. This is a matter of common historical knowledge. What is less commonly known is that ever since that time no aspirant to the hand of a daughter of the de L'Isles has escaped a visitation from the spectre of that most unhappy of fathers, who signifies his approval or disapproval of the intended alliance in an unmistakable manner; and woe to him who disregards it. The figure you saw and followed on that night of the ball was the ghost of my unfortunate ancestor. Had you frankly told me the end of your adventure, which I only learned yesterday from Evelyn's lips, you might have been spared the mortification you have undergone."

He rose as he spoke the last words, and laid his hand kindly upon my shoulder. Then he touched a bell on his table, and ordered the servant who entered to tell Lady Evelyn that he wished to have a few moments' conversation with her.

What I said and did I haven't the slightest recollection. I only know that when Lady Evelyn entered her father's study a few minutes later, she found me there alone, and stood blushing and confused on the threshold.

What thereupon took place, however, I remember with a distinctness that will never fade, but I fear it would scarcely sound new to any one, except perhaps the doughty reader whom I apostrophised at the commencement of my story, and him, or her, as the case may be,

it would presumably not interest at all.

Besides, one must draw the line somewhere, even in a ghost story. Considering that I had never made love to Lady Evelyn, it may seem strange to say that not thirty seconds after she entered the room all trace of embarrassment had vanished both from her face and mine. But then—what else but a strange sequel could be expected to so strange a wooing?

THE OLD PORTRAIT
by
Hume Nisbet
1896

Old-fashioned frames are a hobby of mine. I am always on the prowl amongst the framers and dealers in curiosities for something quaint and unique in picture frames. I don't care much for what is inside them, for being a painter it is my fancy to get the frames first and then paint a picture which I think suits their probable history and design. In this way I get some curious and I think also some original ideas.

One day in December, about a week before Christmas, I picked up a fine but dilapidated specimen of wood-carving in a shop near Soho. The gilding had been worn nearly away, and three of the corners broken off; yet as there was one of the corners still left, I hoped to be able to repair the others from it. As for the canvas inside this frame, it was so smothered with dirt and time stains that I could only distinguish it had been a very badly painted likeness of some sort, of some commonplace person, daubed in by a poor pot-boiling painter to fill the second-hand frame which his patron may have picked up cheaply as I had done after him; but as the frame was alright I took the spoiled canvas along with it, thinking it might come in handy.

For the next few days my hands were full of work of one kind and another, so that it was only on Christmas Eve that I found myself at liberty to examine my purchase which had been lying with its face to the wall since I had brought it to my studio.

Having nothing to do on this night, and not in the mood to go out, I got my picture and frame from the corner, and laying them upon the table, with a sponge, basin of water, and some soap, I began to wash so that I might see them the better. They were in a terrible mess, and I think I used the best part of a packet of soap-powder and had to change the water about a dozen times before the pattern began to show up on the frame, and the portrait within it asserted its awful crudeness, vile drawing, and intense vulgarity. It was the bloated, piggish visage of a publican clearly, with a plentiful supply of jewellery displayed, as is usual with such masterpieces, where the features are not considered of so much importance as a strict fidelity in the depicting of such articles as watch-guard and seals, finger rings, and breast pins; these were all there, as natural and hard as reality.

The frame delighted me, and the picture satisfied me that I had not cheated the dealer with my price, and I was looking at the monstrosity as the gaslight beat full upon it, and wondering how the owner could be pleased with himself as thus depicted, when something about the background attracted my attention—a slight marking underneath the thin coating as if the portrait had been painted over some other subject.

It was not much certainly, yet enough to make me rush over to my cupboard, where I kept my spirits of wine and turpentine, with which, and a plentiful supply of rags, I began to demolish the publican ruthlessly in the vague hope that I might find something worth looking at underneath.

A slow process that was, as well as a delicate one, so that it was close upon midnight before the gold cable rings and vermilion visage disappeared and another picture loomed up before me; then giving it the final wash over, I wiped it dry, and set it in a good light on my easel, while I filled and lit my pipe, and then sat down to look at it.

What had I liberated from that vile prison of crude paint? For I did not require to set it up to know that this bungler of the brush had covered and defiled a work as far beyond his comprehension as the clouds are from the caterpillar.

The bust and head of a young woman of uncertain age, merged within a gloom of rich accessories painted as only a master hand can paint who is above asserting his knowledge, and who has learnt to cover his technique. It was as perfect and natural in its sombre yet quiet dignity as if it had come from the brush of Moroni.

A face and neck perfectly colourless in their pallid whiteness, with the shadows so artfully managed that they could not be seen, and for this quality would have delighted the strong minded Queen Bess.

At first as I looked I saw in the centre of a vague darkness a dim patch of grey gloom that drifted into the shadow. Then the greyness appeared to grow lighter as I sat from it, and leaned back in my chair until the features stole out softly, and became clear and definite, while the figure stood out from the background as if tangible, although, having washed it, I knew that it had been smoothly painted.

An intent face, with delicate nose, well-shaped, although bloodless, lips, and eyes like dark caverns without a spark of light in them. The hair loosely about the head and oval cheeks, massive, silky-textured, jet black, and lustreless, which hid the upper portion of her brow, with the ears, and fell in straight indefinite waves over the left breast, leaving the right portion of the transparent neck exposed.

The dress and background were symphonies of ebony, yet full of subtle colouring and masterly feeling; a dress of rich brocaded velvet with a back ground that represented vast receding space, wondrously suggestive and awe-inspiring.

I noticed that the pallid lips were parted slightly, and showed a glimpse of the upper front teeth, which added to the intent expression of the face. A short upper tip, which, curled upward, with the underlip full and sensuous, or rather, if colour had been in it, would have been so.

It was an eerie looking face that I had resurrected on this midnight hour of Christmas Eve; in its passive pallidity it looked as if the blood had been drained from the body, and that I was gazing upon an open-eyed corpse.

The frame, also, I noticed for the first time, in its details appeared to have been designed with the intention of carrying out the idea of life in death; what had before looked like scroll-work of flowers and fruit were loathsome snake-like worms twined amongst charnel-house bones which they half covered in a decorative fashion; a hideous design in spite of its exquisite workmanship, that made me shudder and wish that I had left the cleaning to be done by daylight.

I am not at all of a nervous temperament, and would have laughed had anyone told me that I was afraid, and yet, as I sat here alone, with that portrait opposite to me in this solitary studio, away from all human contact; for none of the other studios were tenanted on this night, and the janitor had gone on his holiday; I wished that I had spent my evening in a more congenial manner, for in spite of a good fire in the stove and the brilliant gas, that intent face and those haunting eyes were exercising a strange influence upon me.

I heard the clocks from the different steeples chime out the last hour of the day, one after the other, like echoes taking up the refrain and dying away in the distance, and still I sat spellbound, looking at that weird picture, with my neglected pipe in my hand, and a strange lassitude creeping over me.

It was the eyes which fixed me now with the unfathomable depths and absorbing intensity. They gave out no light, but seemed to draw my soul into them, and with it my life and strength as I lay inert before them, until overpowered I lost consciousness and dreamt.

I thought that the frame was still on the easel with the canvas, but the woman had stepped from them and was approaching me with a floating motion, leaving behind her a vault filled with coffins, some of them shut down whilst others lay or stood upright and open, showing the grizzly contents in their decaying and stained cerements.

I could only see her head and shoulders with the sombre drapery of the upper portion and the inky wealth of hair hanging round.

She was with me now, that pallid face touching my face and those cold bloodless lips glued to mine with a close lingering kiss, while the soft black hair covered me like a cloud and thrilled me through and through with a delicious thrill that, whilst it made me grow faint, intoxicated me with delight.

As I breathed she seemed to absorb it quickly into herself, giving me back nothing, getting stronger as I was becoming weaker, while the warmth of my contact passed into her and made her palpitate with vitality.

And all at once the horror of approaching death seized upon me, and with a frantic effort I flung her from me and started up from my chair dazed for a moment and uncertain where I was, then consciousness returned and I looked round wildly.

The gas was still blazing brightly, while the fire burned ruddy in the stove. By the timepiece on the mantel I could see that it was half-past twelve.

The picture and frame were still on the easel, only as I looked at them the portrait had changed, a hectic flush was on the cheeks while the eyes glittered with life and the sensuous lips were red and ripe-looking with a drop of blood still upon the nether one. In a frenzy of horror I seized my scraping knife and slashed out the vampire picture, then tearing the mutilated fragments out I crammed them into my stove and watched them frizzle with savage delight.

I have that frame still, but I have not yet had courage to paint a suitable subject for it.

WOLVERDEN TOWER
by
Grant Allen
1899

Maisie Llewelyn had never been asked to Wolverden before; therefore, she was not a little elated at Mrs. West's invitation. For Wolverden Hall, one of the loveliest Elizabethan manor-houses in the Weald of Kent, had been bought and fitted up in appropriate style (the phrase is the upholsterer's) by Colonel West, the famous millionaire from South Australia. The Colonel had lavished upon it untold wealth, fleeced from the backs of ten thousand sheep and an equal number of his fellow-countrymen; and Wolverden was now, if not the most beautiful, at least the most opulent country-house within easy reach of London.

Mrs. West was waiting at the station to meet Maisie. The house was full of Christmas guests already, it is true; but Mrs. West was a model of stately, old-fashioned courtesy: she would not have omitted meeting one among the number on any less excuse than a royal command to appear at Windsor. She kissed Maisie on both cheeks—she had always been fond of Maisie—and, leaving two haughty young aristocrats (in powdered hair and blue-and-gold livery) to hunt up her luggage by the light of nature, sailed forth with her through the door to the obsequious carriage.

The drive up the avenue to Wolverden Hall Maisie found quite delicious. Even in their leafless winter condition the great limes looked so noble; and the ivy-covered hall at the end, with its mullioned windows, its Inigo Jones porch, and its creeper-clad gables, was as picturesque a building as the ideals one sees in Mr. Abbey's sketches. If only Arthur Hume had been one of the party now, Maisie's joy would have been complete. But what was the use of thinking so much about Arthur Hume, when she didn't even know whether Arthur Hume cared for her?

A tall, slim girl, Maisie Llewelyn, with rich black hair, and ethereal features, as became a descendant of Llewelyn ap Iorwerth. The sort of girl we none of us would have called anything more than "interesting" till Rossetti and Burne-Jones found eyes for us to see that the type is beautiful with a deeper beauty than that of your obvious pink-and-white prettiness. Her eyes, in particular, had a lustrous depth that was almost superhuman, and her fingers and nails were strangely transparent in their waxen softness.

"You won't mind my having put you in a ground-floor room in the new wing, my dear, will you?" Mrs West inquired, as she led

Maisie personally to the quarters chosen for her. "You see, we're so unusually full, because of these tableaux!"

Maisie gazed round the ground-floor room in the new wing with eyes of mute wonder. If this was the kind of lodging for which Mrs. West thought it necessary to apologise, Maisie wondered of what sort were those better rooms which she gave to the guests she delighted to honour. It was a large and exquisitely decorated chamber, with the softest and deepest Oriental carpet Maisie's feet had ever felt, and the daintiest curtains her eyes had ever lighted upon. True, it opened by French windows on to what was nominally the ground in front; but as the Italian terrace, with its formal balustrade and its great stone balls, was raised several feet above the level of the sloping garden below, the room was really on the first floor for all practical purposes. Indeed, Maisie rather liked the unwonted sense of space and freedom which was given by this easy access to the world without; and, as the windows were secured by great shutters and fasteners, she had no counter-balancing fear lest a nightly burglar should attempt to carry off her little pearl necklet or her amethyst brooch, instead of directing his whole attention to Mrs. West's famous diamond tiara.

She moved naturally to the window. She was fond of nature. The view it disclosed over the Weald at her feet was wide and varied. Misty range lay behind misty range, in a faint December haze, receding and receding, till away to the south, half hidden by vapour, the Sussex downs loomed vague in the distance. The village church, as happens so often in the case of old lordly manors, stood within the grounds of the Hall, and close by the house. It had been built, her hostess said, in the days of the Edwards, but had portions of an older Saxon edifice still enclosed in the chancel. The one eyesore in the view was its new white tower, recently restored (or rather, rebuilt), which contrasted most painfully with the mellow grey stone and mouldering corbels of the nave and transept.

"What a pity it's been so spoiled!" Maisie exclaimed, looking across at the tower. Coming straight as she did from a Merioneth rectory, she took an ancestral interest in all that concerned churches.

"Oh, my dear!" Mrs. West cried, "*please* don't say that, I beg of you, to the Colonel. If you were to murmur 'spoiled' to him you'd wreck his digestion. He's spent ever so much money over securing the foundations and reproducing the sculpture on the old tower we took down, and it breaks his dear heart when anybody disapproves of it. For *some* people, you know, are so absurdly opposed to reasonable restoration."

"Oh, but this isn't even restoration, you know," Maisie said, with the frankness of twenty, and the specialist interest of an antiquary's daughter. "This is pure reconstruction."

"Perhaps so," Mrs. West answered. "But if you think so, my dear, don't breathe it at Wolverden."

A fire, of ostentatiously wealthy dimensions, and of the best glowing coal burned bright on the hearth, but the day was mild, and hardly more than autumnal. Maisie found the room quite unpleasantly hot. She opened the windows and stepped out on the terrace. Mrs. West followed her. They paced up and down the broad gravelled platform for a while—Maisie had not yet taken off her travelling-cloak and hat—and then strolled half unconsciously towards the gate of the church. The churchyard, to hide the tombstones of which the parapet had been erected, was full of quaint old monuments, with broken-nosed cherubs, some of them dating from a comparatively early period. The porch, with its sculptured niches deprived of their saints by puritan hands, was still rich and beautiful in its carved detail. On the seat inside an old woman was sitting. She did not rise as the lady of the manor approached, but went on mumbling and muttering inarticulately to herself in a sulky undertone. Still, Maisie was aware, none the less, that the moment she came near a strange light gleamed suddenly in the old woman's eyes, and that her glance was fixed upon her. A faint thrill of recognition seemed to pass like a flash through her palsied body. Maisie knew not why, but she was dimly afraid of the old woman's gaze upon her.

"It's a lovely old church!" Maisie said, looking up at the trefoil finials on the porch—"all, except the tower."

"We *had* to reconstruct it," Mrs. West answered apologetically. Mrs. West's general attitude in life was apologetic, as though she felt she had no right to so much more money than her fellow-creatures. "It would have fallen if we hadn't done something to buttress it up. It was really in a most dangerous and critical condition."

"Lies! lies! lies!" the old woman burst out suddenly, though in a strange, low tone, as if speaking to herself. "It would not have fallen—they knew it would not. It could not have fallen. It would never have fallen if they had not destroyed it. And even then—I was there when they pulled it down—each stone clung to each, with arms and legs and hands and claws, till they burst them asunder by main force with their new-fangled stuff—I don't know what they call it—dynamite, or something. It was all of it done for one man's vainglory!"

"Come away, dear," Mrs. West whispered. But Maisie loitered.

"Wolverden Tower was fasted thrice," the old woman continued, in a sing-song quaver. "It was fasted thrice with souls of maids against every assault of man or devil. It was fasted at the foundation against earthquake and ruin. It was fasted at the top against thunder and lightning. It was fasted in the middle against storm and battle. And there it would have stood for a thousand years if a wicked man had not raised a vainglorious hand against it. For that's what the rhyme says—

"Fasted thrice with souls of men.
 Stands the tower of Wolverden;
 Fasted thrice with maidens' blood.
 A thousand years of fire and flood
 Shall see it stand as erst it stood."

She paused a moment, then, raising one skinny hand towards the brand-new stone, she went on in the same voice, but with malignant fervour?

"A thousand years the tower shall stand
 Till ill assailed by evil hand;
 By evil hand in evil hour.
 Fasted thrice with warlock's power.
 Shall fall the stanes of Wulfhere's tower."

She tottered off as she ended, and took her seat on the edge of a depressed vault in the churchyard close by, still eyeing Maisie Llewellyn with a weird and curious glance, almost like the look which a famishing man casts upon the food in a shop-window.

"Who is she?" Maisie asked, shrinking away in undefined terror.

"Oh, old Bessie," Mrs. West answered, looking more apologetic (for the parish) than ever. "She's always hanging about here. She has nothing else to do, and she's an outdoor pauper. You see, that's the worst of having the church in one's grounds, which is otherwise picturesque and romantic and baronial; the road to it's public; you must admit all the world; and old Bessie *will* come here. The servants are afraid of her. They say she's a witch. She has the evil eye, and she drives girls to suicide. But they cross her hand with silver all the same, and she tells them their fortunes—gives them each a butler. She's full of dreadful stories about Wolverden Church—stories to make your blood run cold, my dear, compact with old superstitions and murders, and so forth. And they're true, too, that's the worst of them. She's quite a character. Mr. Blaydes, the antiquary, is really attached to her; he says she's now the sole living repository of the traditional folklore and history of the parish. But I don't care for it myself. It 'gars one greet,' as we say in Scotland. Too much burying alive in it, don't you know, my dear, to quite suit *my* fancy."

They turned back as she spoke towards the carved wooden lych-gate, one of the oldest and most exquisite of its class in England. When they reached the vault by whose doors old Bessie was seated, Maisie turned once more to gaze at the pointed lancet windows of the Early English choir, and the still more ancient dog-tooth ornament of the ruined Norman Lady Chapel.

"How solidly it's built!" she exclaimed, looking up at the arches which alone survived the fury of the Puritan. "It really looks as if it would last for ever."

Old Bessie had bent her head, and seemed to be whispering something at the door of the vault. But at the sound she raised her eyes, and, turning her wizened face towards the lady of the manor, mumbled through her few remaining fang-like teeth an old local saying, "Bradbury for length, Wolverden for strength, and Church Hatton for beauty!"

"Three brothers builded churches three;
And fasted thrice each church shall be:
Fasted thrice with maidens' blood.

To make them safe from fire and flood;
Fasted thrice with souls of men.
Hatton, Bradbury, Wolverden!"

"Come away," Maisie said, shuddering. "I'm afraid of that woman. Why was she whispering at the doors of the vault down there? I don't like the look of her."

"My dear," Mrs. West answered, in no less terrified a tone, "I will confess I don't like the look of her myself. I wish she'd leave the place. I've tried to make her. The Colonel offered her fifty pounds down and a nice cottage in Surrey if only she'd go—she frightens me so much; but she wouldn't hear of it. She said she must stop by the bodies of her dead—that's her style, don't you see: a sort of modern ghoul, a degenerate vampire—and from the bodies of her dead in Wolverden Church no living soul should ever move her."

II

For dinner Maisie wore her white satin Empire dress, high-waisted, low-necked, and cut in the bodice with a certain baby-like simplicity of style which exactly suited her strange and uncanny type of beauty. She was very much admired. She felt it, and it pleased her. The young man who took her in, a subaltern of engineers, had no eyes for any one else; while old Admiral Wade, who sat opposite her with a plain and skinny dowager, made her positively uncomfortable by the persistent way in which he stared at her simple pearl necklet.

After dinner, the tableaux. They had been designed and managed by a famous Royal Academician, and were mostly got up by the members of the house-party. But two or three actresses from London had been specially invited to help in a few of the more mythological scenes; for, indeed, Mrs. West had prepared the entire entertainment with that topsy-turvy conscientiousness and scrupulous sense of responsibility to society which pervaded her view of millionaire morality. Having once decided to offer the county a set of tableaux, she felt that millionaire morality absolutely demanded of her the sacrifice of three weeks' time and several hundred pounds' money in order to discharge her obligations to the county with becoming magnificence.

The first tableau, Maisie learned from the gorgeous programme, was "Jephthah's Daughter." The subject was represented at the pathetic moment when the doomed virgin goes forth from her father's house with her attendant maidens to bewail her virginity for two months upon the mountains, before the fulfilment of the awful vow which bound her father to offer her up for a burnt offering. Maisie thought it too solemn and tragic a scene for a festive occasion. But the famous R.A. had a taste for such themes, and his grouping was certainly most effectively dramatic.

"A perfect symphony in white and grey," said Mr. Wills, the art critic.

"How awfully affecting!" said most of the young girls.

"Reminds me a little too much, my dear, of old Bessie's stories," Mrs. West whispered low, leaning from her seat across two rows to Maisie.

A piano stood a little on one side of the platform, just in front of the curtain. The intervals between the pieces were filled up with songs, which, however, had been evidently arranged in keeping with the solemn and half-mystical tone of the tableaux. It is the habit of amateurs to take a long time in getting their scenes in order, so the interposition of the music was a happy thought as far as its prime intention went. But Maisie wondered they could not have chosen some livelier song for Christmas Eve than "Oh, Mary, go and call the cattle home, and call the cattle home, and call the cattle home, across the sands of Dee." Her own name was Mary when she signed it officially, and the sad lilt of the last line, "But never home came she," rang unpleasantly in her ear through the rest of the evening.

The second tableau was the "Sacrifice of Iphigenia." It was admirably rendered. The cold and dignified father, standing, apparently unmoved, by the pyre; the cruel faces of the attendant priests; the shrinking form of the immolated princess; the mere blank curiosity and inquiring interest of the helmeted heroes looking on, to whom this slaughter of a virgin victim was but an ordinary incident of the Achean religion. All these had been arranged by the Academical director with consummate skill and pictorial cleverness. But the group that attracted Maisie most among the components of the scene was that of the attendant maidens, more conspicuous here in their flowing white chitons than even they had been when posed as companions of the beautiful and ill-fated Hebrew victim. Two in particular excited her close attention—two very graceful and spiritual-looking girls, in long white robes of no particular age or country, who stood at the very end near the right edge of the picture. "How lovely they are, the two last on the right!" Maisie whispered to her neighbour—an Oxford undergraduate with a budding moustache. "I do so admire them!"

"Do you?" he answered, fondling the moustache with one dubious finger. "Well, now, do you know, I don't think I do. They're rather coarse-looking. And besides, I don't quite like the way they've got their hair done up in bunches; too fashionable, isn't it?—too much of the present day—I don't care to see a girl in a Greek costume, with her coiffure so evidently turned out by Truefitt's!"

"Oh, I don't mean those two," Maisie answered, a little shocked he should think she had picked out such meretricious faces; "I mean the two beyond them again—the two with their hair so simply and sweetly done—the ethereal-looking dark girls."

The undergraduate opened his mouth, and stared at her in blank amazement for a moment. "Well, I don't see——" he began, and broke off suddenly. Something in Maisie's eye seemed to give him pause. He fondled his moustache, hesitated and was silent.

"How nice to have read the Greek and know what it all means!" Maisie went on, after a minute. "It's a human sacrifice, of course; but, please, what is the story?"

The undergraduate hummed and hawed. "Well, it's in Euripides, you know," he said, trying to look impressive, "and—er—and I haven't taken up Euripides for my next examination. But I *think* it's like this. Iphigenia was a daughter of Agamemnon's, don't you know, and he had offended Artemis or somebody—some other Goddess; and he vowed to offer up to her the most beautiful thing that should be born that year, by way of reparation—just like Jephthah. Well, Iphigenia was considered the most beautiful product of the particular twelvemonth—don't look at me like that, please! you—you make me nervous—and so, when the young woman grew up—well, I don't quite recollect the ins and outs of the details, but it's a human sacrifice business, don't you see; and they're just going to kill her, though I *believe* a hind was finally substituted for the girl, like the ram for Isaac; but I must confess I've a very vague recollection of it." He rose from his seat uneasily. "I'm afraid," he went on, shuffling about for an excuse to move, "these chairs are too close. I seem to be incommoding you."

He moved away with a furtive air. At the end of the tableau one or two of the characters who were not needed in succeeding pieces came down from the stage and joined the body of spectators, as they often do, in their character-dresses—a good opportunity, in point of fact, for retaining through the evening the advantages conferred by theatrical costume, rouge, and pearl-powder. Among them the two girls Maisie had admired so much glided quietly toward her and took the two vacant seats on either side, one of which had just been quitted by the awkward undergraduate. They were not only beautiful in face and figure, on a closer view, but Maisie found them from the first extremely sympathetic. They burst into talk with her, frankly and at once, with charming ease and grace of manner. They were ladies in the grain, in instinct and breeding. The taller of the two, whom the other addressed as Yolande, seemed particularly pleasing. The very name charmed Maisie. She was friends with them at once. They both possessed a certain nameless attraction that constitutes in itself the best possible introduction. Maisie hesitated to ask them whence they came, but it was clear from their talk they knew Wolverden intimately.

After a minute the piano struck up once more. A famous Scotch vocalist, in a diamond necklet and a dress to match, took her place on the stage, just in front of the footlights. As chance would have it, she began singing the song Maisie most of all hated. It was Scott's ballad of 'Proud Maisie,' set to music by Carlo Ludovici—

'Proud Maisie is in the wood.
Walking so early;
Sweet Robin sits on the bush.
Singing so rarely.

"Tell me, thou bonny bird.

When shall I marry me?"
"When six braw gentlemen
Kirkward shall carry ye."
"Who makes the bridal bed.
Birdie, say truly?"
"The grey-headed sexton
That delves the grave duly.

"The glow-worm o'er grave and stone
Shall light thee steady;
The owl from the steeple sing.
'Welcome, Proud lady.'"

Maisie listened to the song with grave discomfort. She had never liked it, and to-night it appalled her. She did not know that just at that moment Mrs. West was whispering in a perfect fever of apology to a lady by her side, "Oh dear! oh dear! what a dreadful thing of me ever to have permitted that song to be sung here to-night! It was horribly thoughtless! Why, now I remember, Miss Llewelyn's name, you know, is Maisie! And there she is listening to it with a face like a sheet! I shall never forgive myself!"

The tall, dark girl by Maisie's side, whom the other called Yolande, leaned across to her sympathetically. "You don't like that song?" she said, with just a tinge of reproach in her voice as she said it.

"I hate it!" Maisie answered, trying hard to compose herself.

"Why so?" the tall, dark girl asked, in a tone of calm and singular sweetness. "It is sad, perhaps; but it's lovely—and natural!"

"My own name is Maisie," her new friend replied, with an ill-repressed shudder. "And somehow that song pursues me through life I seem always to hear the horrid ring of the words, 'When six braw gentlemen kirkward shall carry ye.' I wish to Heaven my people had never called me Maisie!"

"And yet *why*?" the tall, dark girl asked again, with a sad, mysterious air. "Why this clinging to life—this terror of death? this inexplicable attachment to a world of misery? And with such eyes as yours, too! Your eyes are like mine!" which was a compliment, certainly, for the dark girl's own pair were strangely deep and lustrous. "People with eyes such as those, that can look into futurity, ought not surely to shrink from a mere gate like death! For death is but a gate—the gate of life in its fullest beauty. It is written over the door, 'Mors Janua Vitae'"

"What door?" Maisie asked, for she remembered having read those selfsame words, and tried in vain to translate them, that very day, though the meaning was now clear to her.

The answer electrified her: "The gate of the vault in Wolverden churchyard."

She said it very low, but with pregnant expression.

"Oh, how dreadful!" Maisie exclaimed, drawing back. The tall, dark girl half frightened her.

"Not at all," the girl answered. "This life is so short, so vain, so transitory! And beyond it is peace—eternal peace—the calm of rest—the joy of the spirit."

"You come to anchor at last," her companion added.

"But if—one has somebody one would not wish to leave behind?" Maisie suggested timidly.

"He will follow before long," the dark girl replied with quiet decision, interpreting rightly the sex of the indefinite substantive. "Time passes so quickly. And if time passes quickly in time, how much more, then, in eternity!"

"Hush, Yolande," the other dark girl put in, with a warning glance; "there's a new tableau coming. Let me see, is this 'The Death of Ophelia'? No, that's number four; this is number three, 'The Martyrdom of St. Agnes.'"

III

"My dear," Mrs. West said, positively oozing apology, when she met Maisie in the supper-room, "I'm afraid you've been left in a corner by yourself almost all the evening!"

"Oh dear, no," Maisie answered with a quiet smile. "I had that Oxford undergraduate at my elbow at first; and afterwards those two nice girls, with the flowing white dresses and the beautiful eyes, came and sat beside me. What's their name, I wonder?"

"Which girls?" Mrs. West asked, with a little surprise in her tone, for her impression was rather that Maisie had been sitting between two empty chairs for the greater part of the evening, muttering at times to herself in the most uncanny way, but not talking to anybody.

Maisie glanced round the room in search of her new friends, and for some time could not see them. At last, she observed them in a remote alcove, drinking red wine by themselves out of Venetian-glass beakers. "Those two," she said, pointing towards them. "They're such charming girls! Can you tell me who they are? I've quite taken a fancy to them."

Mrs. West gazed at them for a second—or rather, at the recess towards which Maisie pointed—and then turned to Maisie with much the same oddly embarrassed look and manner as the undergraduate's. "Oh, *those*!" she said slowly, peering through and through her, Maisie thought. "Those—must be some of the professionals from London. At any rate—I'm not sure which you mean—over there by the curtain, in the Moorish nook, you say—well, I can't tell you their names! So they *must* be professionals."

She went off with a singularly frightened manner. Maisie noticed it and wondered at it. But it made no great or lasting impression.

When the party broke up, about midnight or a little later, Maisie went along the corridor to her own bedroom. At the end, by the door, the two other girls happened to be standing, apparently gossiping.

"Oh, you've not gone home yet?" Maisie said, as she passed, to Yolande.

"No, we're stopping here," the dark girl with the speaking eyes answered.

Maisie paused for a second. Then an impulse burst over her. "Will you come and see my room? she asked, a little timidly.

"Shall we go, Hedda?" Yolande said, with an inquiring glance at her companion.

Her friend nodded assent. Maisie opened the door, and ushered them into her bedroom.

The ostentatiously opulent fire was still burning brightly, the electric light flooded the room with its brilliancy, the curtains were drawn, and the shutters fastened. For a while the three girls sat together by the hearth and gossiped quietly. Maisie liked her new friends—their voices were so gentle, soft, and sympathetic, while for face and figure they might have sat as models to Burne-Jones or Botticelli. Their dresses, too, took her delicate Welsh fancy; they were so dainty, yet so simple. The soft silk fell in natural folds and dimples. The only ornaments they wore were two curious brooches of very antique workmanship—as Maisie supposed— somewhat Celtic in design, and enamelled in blood-red on a gold background. Each carried a flower laid loosely in her bosom. Yolande's was an orchid with long, floating streamers, in colour and shape recalling some Southern lizard; dark purple spots dappled its lip and petals. Hedda's was a flower of a sort Maisie had never before seen—the stem spotted like a viper's skin, green flecked with russet-brown, and uncanny to look upon; on either side, great twisted spirals of red-and-blue blossoms, each curled after the fashion of a scorpion's tail, very strange and lurid. Something weird and witch-like about flowers and dresses rather attracted Maisie; they affected her with the half-repellent fascination of a snake for a bird; she felt such blossoms were fit for incantations and sorceries. But a lily-of-the-valley in Yolande's dark hair gave a sense of purity which assorted better with the girl's exquisitely calm and nun-like beauty.

After a while Hedda rose. "This air is close," she said. "It ought to be warm outside to-night, if one may judge by the sunset. May I open the window?"

"Oh, certainly, if you like," Maisie answered, a vague foreboding now struggling within her against innate politeness.

Hedda drew back the curtains and unfastened the shutters. It was a moonlit evening. The breeze hardly stirred the bare boughs of the silver birches. A sprinkling of soft snow on the terrace and the hills just whitened the ground. The moon lighted it up, falling full upon the Hall; the church and tower below stood silhouetted in dark against a cloudless expanse of starry sky in the background. Hedda opened the window. Cool, fresh air blew in, very soft and genial, in spite of the snow and the lateness of the season. "What a glorious night!" she said, looking up at Orion overhead. "Shall we stroll out for a while in it?"

If the suggestion had not thus been thrust upon her from outside, it would never have occurred to Maisie to walk abroad in a strange place, in evening dress, on a winter's night, with snow whitening the ground; but Hedda's voice sounded so sweetly persuasive, and the idea itself seemed so natural now she had once proposed it, that

Maisie followed her two new friends on to the moonlit terrace without a moment's hesitation.

They paced once or twice up and down the gravelled walks. Strange to say, though a sprinkling of dry snow powdered the ground under foot, the air itself was soft and balmy. Stranger still, Maisie noticed, almost without noticing it, that though they walked three abreast, only one pair of footprints—her own—lay impressed on the snow in a long trail when they turned at either end and re-paced the platform. Yolande and Hedda must step lightly indeed; or perhaps her own feet might be warmer or thinner shod, so as to melt the light layer of snow more readily.

The girls slipped their arms through hers. A little thrill coursed through her. Then, after three or four turns up and down the terrace, Yolande led the way quietly down the broad flight of steps in the direction of the church on the lower level. In that bright, broad moonlight Maisie went with them undeterred; the Hall was still alive with the glare of electric lights in bedroom windows; and the presence of the other girls, both wholly free from any signs of fear, took off all sense of terror or loneliness. They strolled on into the churchyard. Maisie's eyes were now fixed on the new white tower, which merged in the silhouette against the starry sky into much the same grey and indefinite hue as the older parts of the building. Before she quite knew where she was, she found herself at the head of the worn stone steps which led into the vault by whose doors she had seen old Bessie sitting. In the pallid moonlight, with the aid of the greenish reflection from the snow, she could just read the words inscribed over the portal, the words that Yolande had repeated in the drawing-room, "Mors Janua Vitae'"

Yolande moved down one step. Maisie drew back for the first time with a faint access of alarm. "You're—you're not *going down* there!" she exclaimed, catching her breath for a second.

"Yes, I am," her new friend answered in a calmly quiet voice. "Why not? We live here."

"You live here?" Maisie echoed, freeing her arms by a sudden movement and standing away from her mysterious friends with a tremulous shudder.

"Yes, we live here," Hedda broke in, without the slightest emotion. She said it in a voice of perfect calm, as one might say it of any house in a street in London.

Maisie was far less terrified than she might have imagined beforehand would be the case under such unexpected conditions. The two girls were so simple, so natural, so strangely like herself, that she could not say she was really afraid of them. She shrank, it is true, from the nature of the door at which they stood, but she received the unearthly announcement that they lived there with scarcely more than a slight tremor of surprise and astonishment.

"You will come in with us?" Hedda said in a gently enticing tone. "We went into your bedroom."

Maisie hardly liked to say no. They seemed so anxious to show her their home. With trembling feet she moved down the first step, and then the second. Yolande kept ever one pace in front of her. As Maisie reached the third step, the two girls, as if moved by one design, took her wrists in their hands, not unkindly, but coaxingly. They reached the actual doors of the vault itself—two heavy bronze valves, meeting in the centre. Each bore a ring for a handle, pierced through a Gorgon's head embossed upon the surface. Yolande pushed them with her hand. They yielded instantly to her light touch, and opened inward. Yolande, still in front, passed from the glow of the moon to the gloom of the vault, which a ray of moonlight just descended obliquely. As she passed, for a second, a weird sight met Maisie's eyes. Her face and hands and dress became momentarily self-luminous—but through them, as they glowed, she could descry within every bone and joint of her living skeleton, dimly shadowed in dark through the luminous haze that marked her body.

Maisie drew back once more, terrified. Yet her terror was not quite what one could describe as fear: it was rather a vague sense of the profoundly mystical. "I can't! I can't!" she cried, with an appealing glance. "Hedda! Yolande! I cannot go with you."

Hedda held her hand tight, and almost seemed to force her. But Yolande, in front, like a mother with her child, turned round with a grave smile. "No, no," she said reprovingly. "Let her come if she will, Hedda, of her own accord, not otherwise. The tower demands a willing victim."

Her hand on Maisie's wrist was strong but persuasive. It drew her without exercising the faintest compulsion. "Will you come with us, dear?" she said, in that winning silvery tone which had captivated Maisie's fancy from the very first moment they spoke together. Maisie gazed into her eyes. They were deep and tender. A strange resolution seemed to nerve her for the effort. "Yes, yes—I—will—come—with you," she answered slowly.

Hedda on one side, Yolande on the other, now went before her, holding her wrists in their grasp, but rather enticing than drawing her. As each reached the gloom, the same luminous appearance which Maisie had noticed before spread over their bodies, and the same weird skeleton shape showed faintly through their limbs in darker shadow. Maisie crossed the threshold with a convulsive gasp. As she crossed it she looked down at her own dress and body. They were semi-transparent, like the others', though not quite so self-luminous; the framework of her limbs appeared within in less certain outline, yet quite dark and distinguishable.

The doors swung to of themselves behind her. Those three stood alone in the vault of Wolverden.

Alone, for a minute or two; and then, as her eyes grew accustomed to the grey dusk of the interior, Maisie began to perceive that the vault opened out into a large and beautiful hall or crypt, dimly lighted at first, but becoming each moment more vaguely clear and more dreamily definite. Gradually she could make out great rock-hewn pillars, Romanesque in their outline or dimly Oriental, like the sculptured columns in the caves of Ellora, supporting a roof of vague and uncertain dimensions, more or less strangely dome-shaped. The effect on the whole was like that of the second impression produced by some dim cathedral, such as Chartres or Milan, after the eyes have grown accustomed to the mellow light from the stained-glass windows, and have recovered from the blinding glare of the outer sunlight. But the architecture, if one may call it so, was more mosque-like and magical. She turned to her companions. Yolande and Hedda stood still by her side; their bodies were now self-luminous to a greater degree than even at the threshold; but the terrible transparency had disappeared altogether; they were once more but beautiful though strangely transfigured and more than mortal women.

Then Maisie understood in her own soul, dimly, the meaning of those mystic words written over the portal. Mors Janua Vitae" Death is the gate of life; and also the interpretation of that awful vision of death dwelling within them as they crossed the threshold; for through that gate they had passed to this underground palace.

Her two guides still held her hands, one on either side. But they seemed rather to lead her on now, seductively and resistlessly, than to draw or compel her. As she moved in through the hall, with its endless vistas of shadowy pillars, seen now behind, now in dim perspective, she was gradually aware that many other people crowded its aisles and corridors. Slowly they took shape as forms more or less clad, mysterious, varied, and of many ages. Some of them wore flowing robes, half mediaeval in shape, like the two friends who had brought her there. They looked like the saints on a stained-glass window. Others were girt merely with a light and floating Coan sash; while some stood dimly nude in the darker recesses of the temple or palace. All leaned eagerly forward with one mind as she approached, and regarded her with deep and sympathetic interest. A few of them murmured words—mere cabalistic sounds which at first she could not understand; but as she moved further into the hall, and saw at each step more clearly into the gloom, they began to have a meaning for her. Before long, she was aware that she understood the mute tumult of voices at once by some internal instinct. The Shades addressed her; she answered them. She knew by intuition what tongue they spoke; it was the Language of the Dead; and, by passing that portal with her two companions, she had herself become enabled both to speak and understand it.

A soft and flowing tongue, this speech of the Nether World—all vowels it seemed, without distinguishable consonants; yet dimly recalling every other tongue, and compounded, as it were, of what was common to all of them. It flowed from those shadowy lips as clouds issue inchoate from a mountain valley; it was formless, uncertain, vague, but yet beautiful. She hardly knew, indeed, as it fell upon her senses, if it were sound or perfume.

Through this tenuous world Maisie moved as in a dream, her two companions still cheering and guiding her. When they reached an inner shrine or chantry of the temple she was dimly conscious of more terrible forms pervading the background than any of those that had yet appeared to her. This was a more austere and antique apartment than the rest; a shadowy cloister, prehistoric in its severity; it recalled to her mind something indefinitely intermediate between the huge unwrought trilithons of Stonehenge and the massive granite pillars of Philae and Luxor. At the further end of the sanctuary a sort of Sphinx looked down on her, smiling mysteriously. At its base, on a rude megalithic throne, in solitary state, a High Priest was seated. He bore in his hand a wand or sceptre. All round, a strange court of half-unseen acolytes and shadowy hierophants stood attentive They were girt, as she fancied, in what looked like leopards' skins, or in the fells of some earlier prehistoric lion. These wore sabre-shaped teeth suspended by a string round their dusky necks; others had ornaments of uncut amber, or hatchets of jade threaded as collars on a cord of sinew. A few, more barbaric than savage in type, flaunted torques of gold as armlets and necklets.

The High Priest rose slowly and held out his two hands, just level with his head, the palms turned outward. "You have brought a willing victim as Guardian of the Tower?" he asked, in that mystic tongue, of Yolande and Hedda.

"We have brought a willing victim," the two girls answered.

The High Priest gazed at her. His glance was piercing. Maisie trembled less with fear than with a sense of strangeness, such as a neophyte might feel on being first presented at some courtly pageant. "You come of your own accord?" the Priest inquired of her in solemn accents.

"I come of my own accord," Maisie answered, with an inner consciousness that she was bearing her part in some immemorial ritual. Ancestral memories seemed to stir within her.

"It is well," the Priest murmured. Then he turned to her guides. "She is of royal lineage?" he inquired, taking his wand in his hand again.

"She is a Llewelyn," Yolande answered, "of royal lineage, and of the race that, after your own, earliest bore sway in this land of Britain. She has in her veins the blood of Arthur, of Ambrosius, and of Vortigern."

"It is well," the Priest said again. "I know these princes." Then he turned to Maisie. "This is the ritual of those who build," he said, in a very deep voice. "It has been the ritual of those who build from the days of the builders of Lokmariaker and Avebury. Every building man makes shall have its human soul, the soul of a virgin to guard and protect it. Three souls it requires as a living talisman against chance and change. One soul is the soul of the human victim slain beneath the foundation-stone; she is the guardian spirit against earthquake and ruin. One soul is the soul of the human victim slain when the building is half built up; she is the guardian spirit against battle and tempest. One soul is the soul of the human victim who flings herself of her own free will off tower or gable when the building is complete; she is the guardian spirit against thunder and lightning. Unless a building be duly fasted with these three, how can it hope to stand against the hostile powers of fire and flood and storm and earthquake?"

An assessor at his side, unnoticed till then, took up the parable. He had a stern Roman face, and bore a shadowy suit of Roman armour. "In times of old," he said, with iron austerity, "all men knew well these rules of building. They built in solid stone to endure for ever: the works they erected have lasted to this day, in this land and others. So built we the amphitheatres of Rome and Verona; so built we the walls of Lincoln, York, and London. In the blood of a king's son laid we the foundation-stone: in the blood of a king's son laid we the coping-stone: in the blood of a maiden of royal line fasted we the bastions against fire and lightning. But in these latter days, since faith grows dim, men build with burnt brick and rubble of plaster; no foundation spirit or guardian soul do they give to their bridges, their walls, or their towers: so bridges break, and walls fall in, and towers crumble, and the art and mystery of building aright have perished from among you."

He ceased. The High Priest held out his wand and spoke again. "We are the Assembly of Dead Builders and Dead Victims," he said, "for this mark of Wolverden; all of whom have built or been built upon in this holy site of immemorial sanctity. We are the stones of a living fabric. Before this place was a Christian church, it was a temple of Woden. And before it was a temple of Woden, it was a shrine of Hercules. And before it was a shrine of Hercules, it was a grove of Nodens. And before it was a grove of Nodens, it was a Stone Circle of the Host of Heaven. And before it was a Stone Circle of the Host of Heaven, it was the grave and tumulus and underground palace of Me, who am the earliest builder of all in this place; and my name in my ancient tongue is Wolf, and I laid and hallowed it. And after me, Wolf, and my namesake Wulfhere, was this barrow called Ad Lupum and Wolverden. And all these that are here with me have built and been built upon in this holy site for all generations. And you are the last who come to join us."

Maisie felt a cold thrill course down her spine as he spoke these words; but courage did not fail her. She was dimly aware that those who offer themselves as victims for service must offer themselves willingly; for the gods demand a voluntary victim; no beast can be slain unless it nod assent; and none can be made a guardian spirit who takes not the post upon him of his own free will. She turned meekly to Hedda. "Who are you?" she asked, trembling.

"I am Hedda," the girl answered, in the same soft sweet voice and winning tone as before; "Hedda, the daughter of Gorm, the chief of the Northmen who settled in East Anglia. And I was a worshipper of Thor and Odin. And when my father, Gorm, fought against Alfred, King of Wessex, was I taken prisoner. And Wulfhere, the Kenting, was then building the first church and tower of Wolverden. And they baptized me, and shrived me, and I consented of my own free will to be built under the foundation-stone. And there my body lies built up to this day; and *I* am the guardian spirit against earthquake and ruin."

"And who are you?" Maisie asked, turning again to Yolande.

"I am Yolande Fitz-Aylwin," the tall dark girl answered; "a royal maiden too, sprung from the blood of Henry Plantagenet. And when Roland Fitz-Stephen was building anew the choir and chancel of Wulfhere's minster, I chose to be immured in the fabric of the wall, for love of the Church and all holy saints; and there my body lies built up to this day; and *I* am the guardian against battle and tempest."

Maisie held her friend's hand tight. Her voice hardly trembled. "And I?" she asked once more. "What fate for me? Tell me!"

"Your task is easier far," Yolande answered gently. "For *you* shall be the guardian of the new tower against thunder and lightning. Now, those who guard against earthquake and battle are buried alive under the foundation-stone or in the wall of the building; there they die a slow death of starvation and choking. But those who guard against thunder and lightning cast themselves alive of their own free will from the battlements of the tower, and die in the air before they reach the ground; so their fate is the easiest and the lightest of all who would serve mankind; and thenceforth they live with us here in our palace."

Maisie clung to her hand still tighter. "Must I do it?" she asked, pleading.

"It is not *must*," Yolande replied in the same caressing tone, yet with a calmness as of one in whom earthly desires and earthly passions are quenched for ever. "It is as you choose yourself. None but a willing victim may be a guardian spirit. This glorious privilege comes but to the purest and best amongst us. Yet what better end can you ask for your soul than to dwell here in our midst as our comrade for ever, where all is peace, and to preserve the tower whose guardian you are from evil assaults of lightning and thunderbolt?"

Maisie flung her arms round her friend's neck. "But—I am afraid," she murmured. Why she should even wish to consent she knew not, yet the strange serene peace in these strange girls' eyes made her mysteriously in love with them and with the fate they offered her. They seemed to move like the stars in their orbits. "How shall I leap from the top?" she cried. "How shall I have courage to mount the stairs alone, and fling myself off from the lonely battlement?"

Yolande unwound her arms with a gentle forbearance. She coaxed her as one coaxes an unwilling child. "You will not be alone," she said, with a tender pressure. "We will all go with you. We will help you and encourage you. We will sing our sweet songs of life-in-death to you. Why should you draw back? All we have faced it in ten thousand ages, and we tell you with one voice, you need not fear it. 'Tis life you should fear—life, with its dangers, its toils, its heartbreakings. Here we dwell for ever in unbroken peace. Come, come, and join us!"

She held out her arms with an enticing gesture. Maisie sprang into them, sobbing. "Yes, I will come," she cried in an access of hysterical fervour. "These are the arms of Death—I embrace them. These are the lips of Death—I kiss them. Yolande, Yolande, I will do as you ask me!"

The tall dark girl in the luminous white robe stooped down and kissed her twice on the forehead in return. Then she looked at the High Priest. "We are ready," she murmured in a low, grave voice.

"The Victim consents. The Virgin will die. Lead on to the tower. We are ready! We are ready!"

IV

From the recesses of the temple—if temple it were—from the inmost shrines of the shrouded cavern, unearthly music began to sound of itself; with wild modulation, on strange reeds and tabors. It swept through the aisles like a rushing wind on an Æolian harp; at times it wailed with a voice like a woman's; at times it rose loud in an organ-note of triumph; at times it sank low into a pensive and melancholy flute-like symphony. It waxed and waned; it swelled and died away again; but no man saw how or whence it proceeded. Wizard echoes issued from the crannies and vents in the invisible walls; they sighed from the ghostly interspaces of the pillars; they keened and moaned from the vast overhanging dome of the palace. Gradually the song shaped itself by weird stages into a processional measure. At its sound the High Priest rose slowly from his immemorial seat on the mighty cromlech which formed his throne. The Shades in leopards' skins ranged themselves in bodiless rows on either hand; the ghostly wearers of the sabre-toothed lions' fangs followed like ministrants in the footsteps of their hierarch.

Hedda and Yolande took their places in the procession. Maisie stood between the two, with hair floating on the air; she looked like a novice who goes up to take the veil, accompanied and cheered by two elder sisters.

The ghostly pageant began to move. Unseen music followed it with fitful gusts of melody. They passed down the main corridor, between shadowy Doric or Ionic pillars which grew dimmer and ever dimmer again in the distance as they approached, with slow steps, the earthward portal.

At the gate, the High Priest pushed against the valves with his hand. They opened *outward*.

He passed into the moonlight. The attendants thronged after him. As each wild figure crossed the threshold the same strange sight as before met Maisie's eyes. For a second of time each ghostly body became self-luminous, as with some curious phosphorescence; and through each, at the moment of passing the portal, the dim outline of a skeleton loomed briefly visible. Next instant it had clothed itself as with earthly members.

Maisie reached the outer air. As she did so, she gasped. For a second, its chilliness and freshness almost choked her. She was conscious now that the atmosphere of the vault, though pleasant in its way, and warm and dry, had been loaded with fumes as of burning incense, and with somnolent vapours of poppy and mandragora. Its drowsy ether had cast her into a lethargy. But after the first minute in the outer world, the keen night air revived her. Snow lay still on the ground a little deeper than when she first came out, and the moon rode lower; otherwise, all was as before, save that only one or two lights still burned here and there in the great house on the terrace. Among them she could recognise her own room, on the ground floor in the new wing, by its open window.

The procession made its way across the churchyard towards the tower. As it wound among the graves an owl hooted. All at once Maisie remembered the lines that had so chilled her a few short hours before in the drawing-room—

"The glow-worm o'er grave and stone
Shall light thee steady;
The owl from the steeple sing.
'Welcome, proud lady!'"

But, marvellous to relate, they no longer alarmed her. She felt rather that a friend was welcoming her home; she clung to Yolande's hand with a gentle pressure.

As they passed in front of the porch, with its ancient yew-tree, a stealthy figure glided out like a ghost from the darkling shadow. It was a woman, bent and bowed, with quivering limbs that shook half palsied. Maisie recognised old Bessie. "I knew she would come!" the old hag muttered between her toothless jaws. "I knew Wolverden Tower would yet be duly fasted!"

She put herself, as of right, at the head of the procession. They moved on to the tower, rather gliding than walking. Old Bessie drew a rusty key from her pocket, and fitted it with a twist into the brand-new lock. "What turned the old will turn the new," she murmured, looking round and grinning. Maisie shrank from her as she shrank from not one of the Dead; but she followed on still into the ringers' room at the base of the tower.

Thence a staircase in the corner led up to the summit. The High Priest mounted the stair, chanting a mystic refrain, whose runic sounds were no longer intelligible to Maisie. As she reached the outer air, the Tongue of the Dead seemed to have become a mere blank of mingled odours and murmurs to her. It was like a summer breeze, sighing through warm and resinous pinewoods. But Yolande and Hedda spoke to her yet, to cheer her, in the language of the living. She recognised that as *revenants* they were still in touch with the upper air and the world of the embodied.

They tempted her up the stair with encouraging fingers. Maisie followed them like a child, in implicit confidence. The steps wound round and round, spirally, and the staircase was dim; but a supernatural light seemed to fill the tower, diffused from the bodies or souls of its occupants. At the head of all, the High Priest still chanted as he went his unearthly litany; magic sounds of chimes seemed to swim in unison with his tune as they mounted. Were those floating notes material or spiritual? They passed the belfry; no tongue of metal wagged; but the rims of the great bells resounded and reverberated to the ghostly symphony with sympathetic music. Still they passed on and on, upward and upward. They reached the ladder that alone gave access to the final story. Dust and cobwebs already clung to it. Once more Maisie drew back. It was dark overhead and the luminous haze began to fail them. Her friends held her hands with the same kindly persuasive touch as ever. "I cannot!" she cried, shrinking away from the tall, steep ladder. "Oh, Yolande, I cannot!"

"Yes, dear," Yolande whispered in a soothing voice. "You can. It is but ten steps, and I will hold your hand tight. Be brave and mount them!"

The sweet voice encouraged her. It was like heavenly music. She knew not why she should submit, or, rather, consent; but none the less she consented. Some spell seemed cast over her. With tremulous feet, scarcely realising what she did, she mounted the ladder and went up four steps of it.

Then she turned and looked down again. Old Bessie's wrinkled face met her frightened eyes. It was smiling horribly. She shrank back once more, terrified. "I can't do it," she cried, "if that woman comes up! I'm not afraid of you, dear,"—she pressed Yolande's hand,— "but she, she is too terrible!"

Hedda looked back and raised a warning finger. "Let the woman stop below," she said; "she savours too much of the evil world. We must do nothing to frighten the willing victim."

The High Priest by this time, with his ghostly fingers, had opened the trap-door that gave access to the summit. A ray of moonlight slanted through the aperture. The breeze blew down with it. Once more Maisie felt the stimulating and reviving effect of the open air. Vivified by its freshness, she struggled up to the top, passed out through the trap, and found herself standing on the open platform at the summit of the tower.

The moon had not yet quite set. The light on the snow shone pale green and mysterious. For miles and miles around she could just make out, by its aid, the dim contour of the downs, with their thin white mantle, in the solemn silence. Range behind range rose faintly shimmering. The chant had now ceased; the High Priest and his acolytes were mingling strange herbs in a mazar-bowl or chalice. Stray perfumes of myrrh and of cardamoms were wafted towards her. The men in leopards' skins burnt smouldering sticks of spikenard. Then Yolande led the postulant forward again, and placed her close up to the new white parapet. Stone heads of virgins smiled on her from the angles. She must front the east," Hedda said in a tone of authority: and Yolande turned her face towards the rising sun accordingly. Then she opened her lips and spoke in a very solemn voice. "From this new-built tower you fling yourself," she said, or rather intoned, "that you may serve mankind, and all the powers that be, as its guardian spirit against thunder and lightning. Judged a virgin, pure and unsullied in deed and word and thought, of royal race and ancient lineage—a Cymry of the Cymry—you are found worthy to be intrusted with this charge and this honour. Take care that never shall dart or thunderbolt assault this tower, as She that is below you takes care to preserve it from earthquake and ruin, and She that is midway takes care to preserve it from battle and tempest. This is your charge. See well that you keep it."

She took her by both hands. "Mary Llewelyn," she said, "you willing victim, step on to the battlement."

Maisie knew not why, but with very little shrinking she stepped as she was told, by the aid of a wooden footstool, on to the eastward-looking parapet. There, in her loose white robe, with her arms spread abroad, and her hair flying free, she poised herself for a second, as if about to shake out some unseen wings and throw herself on the air like a swift or a swallow.

"Mary Llewelyn," Yolande said once more, in a still deeper tone, with ineffable earnestness, "cast yourself down, a willing sacrifice, for the service of man, and the security of this tower against thunderbolt and lightning."

Maisie stretched her arms wider, and leaned forward in act to leap, from the edge of the parapet, on to the snow-clad churchyard.

V

One second more and the sacrifice would have been complete. But before she could launch herself from the tower, she felt suddenly a hand laid upon her shoulder from behind to restrain her. Even in her existing state of nervous exaltation she was aware at once that it was the hand of a living and solid mortal, not that of a soul or guardian spirit. It lay heavier upon her than Hedda's or Yolande's. It seemed to clog and burden her. With a violent effort she strove to shake herself free, and carry out her now fixed intention of self-immolation, for the safety of the tower. But the hand was too strong for her. She could not shake it off. It gripped and held her.

She yielded, and, reeling, fell back with a gasp on to the platform of the tower. At the selfsame moment a strange terror and commotion seemed to seize all at once on the assembled spirits. A weird cry rang voiceless through the shadowy company. Maisie heard it as in a dream, very dim and distant. It was thin as a bat's note; almost inaudible to the ear, yet perceived by the brain or at least by the spirit. It was a cry of alarm, of fright, of warning. With one accord, all the host of phantoms rushed hurriedly forward to the battlements and pinnacles. The ghostly High Priest went first, with his wand held downward; the men in leopards' skins and other assistants followed in confusion. Theirs was a reckless rout. They flung themselves from the top, like fugitives from a cliff, and floated fast through the air on invisible pinions. Hedda and

Yolande, ambassadresses and intermediaries with the upper air, were the last to fly from the living presence. They clasped her hand silently, and looked deep into her eyes. There was something in that calm yet regretful look that seemed to say, "Farewell! We have tried in vain to save you, sister, from the terrors of living."

The horde of spirits floated away on the air, as in a witches' Sabbath, to the vault whence it issued. The doors swung on their rusty hinges, and closed behind them. Maisie stood alone with the hand that grasped her on the tower.

The shock of the grasp, and the sudden departure of the ghostly band in such wild dismay, threw Maisie for a while into a state of semi-unconsciousness. Her head reeled round; her brain swam faintly. She clutched for support at the parapet of the tower. But the hand that held her sustained her still. She felt herself gently drawn down with quiet mastery, and laid on the stone floor close by the trap-door that led to the ladder.

The next thing of which she could feel sure was the voice of the Oxford undergraduate. He was distinctly frightened and not a little tremulous. "I think," he said very softly, laying her head on his lap, you had better rest a while, Miss Llewelyn, before you try to get down again. I hope I didn't catch you and disturb you too hastily. But one step more, and you would have been over the edge. I really couldn't help it."

"Let me go," Maisie moaned, trying to raise herself again, but feeling too faint and ill to make the necessary effort to recover the power of motion. "I want to go with them! I *want* to join them!"

"Some of the others will be up before long," the undergraduate said, supporting her head in his hands; "and they'll help me to get you down again. Mr. Yates is in the belfry. Meanwhile, if I were you, I'd lie quite still, and take a drop or two of this brandy."

He held it to her lips. Maisie drank a mouthful, hardly knowing what she did. Then she lay quiet where he placed her for some minutes. How they lifted her down and conveyed her to her bed she scarcely knew. She was dazed and terrified. She could only remember afterward that three or four gentlemen in roughly huddled clothes had carried or handed her down the ladder between them. The spiral stair and all the rest were a blank to her.

VI

When she next awoke she was lying in her bed in the same room at the Hall, with Mrs. West by her side, leaning over her tenderly.

Maisie looked up through her closed eyes and just saw the motherly face and grey hair bending above her. Then voices came to her from the mist, vaguely: "Yesterday was so hot for the time of year, you see!" "Very unusual weather, of course, for Christmas." "But a thunderstorm! So strange! I put it down to that. The electrical disturbance must have affected the poor child's head." Then it dawned upon her that the conversation she heard was passing between Mrs. West and a doctor.

She raised herself suddenly and wildly on her arms. The bed faced the windows. She looked out and beheld—the tower of Wolverden church, rent from top to bottom with a mighty rent, while half its height lay tossed in fragments on the ground in the churchyard.

"What is it?" she cried wildly, with a flush as of shame.

"Hush, hush!" the doctor said. "Don't trouble! Don't look at it!"

"Was it? after I came down?" Maisie moaned in vague terror.

The doctor nodded. "An hour after you were brought down," he said, "a thunderstorm broke over it. The lightning struck and shattered the tower. They had not yet put up the lightning-conductor. It was to have been done on Boxing Day."

A weird remorse possessed Maisie's soul. "My fault!" she cried, starting up. "My fault, my fault! I have neglected my duty!"

"Don't talk," the doctor answered, looking hard at her. "It is always dangerous to be too suddenly aroused from these curious overwrought sleeps and trances."

"And old Bessie?" Maisie exclaimed, trembling with an eerie presentiment.

The doctor glanced at Mrs. West. "How did she know?" he whispered. Then he turned to Maisie. "You may as well be told the truth as suspect it," he said slowly. "Old Bessie must have been watching there. She was crushed and half buried beneath the falling tower."

"One more question, Mrs. West," Maisie murmured, growing faint with an access of supernatural fear. "Those two nice girls who sat on the chairs at each side of me through the tableaux, are they hurt? Were they in it?"

Mrs. West soothed her hand. "My dear child," she said gravely, with quiet emphasis, "there were no other girls. This is mere hallucination. You sat alone by yourself through the whole of the evening."

THE BLUE ROOM
by
Lettice Galbraith
1897

It happened twice in my time. It will never happen again, they say, since Miss Erristoun (Mrs. Arthur, that is now), and Mr. Calder-Maxwell between them found out the secret of the haunted room, and laid the ghost; for ghost it was, though at the time Mr. Maxwell gave it another name, Latin, I fancy, but all I can remember about it now is that it somehow reminded me of poultry-rearing. I am the housekeeper at Mertoun Towers, as my aunt was before me, and her aunt before her, and first of all my great-grandmother, who was a distant cousin of the Laird, and had married the chaplain, but being left penniless at her husband's death, was thankful to accept the post which has ever since been occupied by one of her descendants. It gives us a sort of standing with the servants, being, as it were, related to the family; and Sir Archibald and my Lady have always acknowledged the connection, and treated us with more freedom than would be accorded to ordinary dependants.

Mertoun has been my home from the time I was eighteen. Something occurred then of which, since it has nothing to do with this story, I need only say that it wiped out for ever any idea of marriage on my part, and I came to the Towers to be trained under my aunt's vigilant eye for the duties in which I was one day to succeed her.

Of course I knew there was a story about the blue tapestry room. Everyone knew that, though the old Laird had given strict orders that the subject should not be discussed among the servants, and always discouraged any allusion to it on the part of his family and guests. But there is a strange fascination about everything connected with the supernatural, and orders or no orders, people, whether gentle or simple, will try to gratify their curiosity; so a good deal of surreptitious talk went on both in the drawing-room and the servants' hall, and hardly a guest came to the house but would pay a visit to the Blue Room and ask all manner of questions about the ghost. The odd part of the business was that no one knew what the ghost was supposed to be, or even if there were any ghost at all. I tried hard to get my aunt to tell me some details of the legend, but she always reminded me of Sir Archibald's orders, and added that the tale most likely started with the superstitious fancy of people who lived long ago and were very ignorant, because a certain Lady Barbara Mertoun had died in that room.

I reminded her that people must have died, at some time or other, in pretty nearly every room in the house, and no one had thought of calling them haunted, or hinting that it was unsafe to sleep there.

She answered that Sir Archibald himself had used the Blue Room, and one or two other gentlemen, who had passed the night there for a wager, and they had neither seen nor heard anything unusual. For her part, she added, she did not hold with people wasting their time thinking of such folly, when they had much better be giving their minds to their proper business.

Somehow her professions of incredulity did not ring true, and I wasn't satisfied, though I gave up asking questions. But if I said nothing, I thought the more, and often when my duties took me to the Blue Room I would wonder why, if nothing had happened there, and there was no real mystery, the room was never used; it had not even a mattress on the fine carved bedstead, which was only covered by a sheet to keep it from the dust. And then I would steal into the portrait gallery to look at the great picture of the Lady Barbara, who had died in the full bloom of her youth, no one knew why, for she was just found one morning stiff and cold, stretched across that fine bed under the blue tapestried canopy.

She must have been a beautiful woman, with her great black eyes and splendid auburn hair, though I doubt her beauty was all on the outside, for she had belonged to the gayest set of the Court, which was none too respectable in those days, if half the tales one hears of it are true; and indeed a modest lady would hardly have been painted in such a dress, all slipping off her shoulders, and so thin that one can see right through the stuff. There must have been something queer about her too, for they do say her father-in-law, who was known as the wicked Lord Mertoun, would not have her buried with the rest of the family; but that might have been his spite, because he was angry that she had no child, and her husband, who was but a sickly sort of man, dying of consumption but a month later, there was no direct heir; so that with the old Lord the title became extinct, and the estates passed to the Protestant branch of the family, of which the present Sir Archibald Mertoun is the head. Be that as it may, Lady Barbara lies by herself in the churchyard, near the lych-gate, under a grand marble tomb indeed, but all alone, while her husband's coffin has its place beside those of his brothers who died before him, among their ancestors and descendants in the great vault under the chancel.

I often used to think about her, and wonder why she died, and how; and then It happened and the mystery grew deeper than ever.

There was a family-gathering that Christmas, I remember, the first Christmas for many years that had been kept at Mertoun, and we had been very busy arranging the rooms for the different guests, for on New Year's Eve there was a ball in the neighbourhood, to which Lady Mertoun was taking a large party, and for that night, at least, the house was as full as it would hold.

I was in the linen-room, helping to sort the sheets and pillow-covers for the different beds, when my Lady came in with an open letter in her hand.

She began to talk to my aunt in a low voice, explaining something which seemed to have put her out, for when I returned from carrying a pile of linen to the head-housemaid I heard her say: "It is too annoying to upset all one's arrangements at the last moment. Why couldn't she have left the girl at home and brought another maid, who could be squeezed in somewhere without any trouble?"

I gathered that one of the visitors, Lady Grayburn, had written that she was bringing her companion, and as she had left her maid, who was ill, at home, she wanted the young lady to have a bedroom adjoining hers, so that she might be at hand to give any help that was required. The request seemed a trifling matter enough in itself, but it just so happened that there really was no room at liberty. Every bedroom on the first corridor was occupied, with the exception of the Blue Room, which, as ill-luck would have it, chanced to be next to that arranged for Lady Grayburn.

My aunt made several suggestions, but none of them seemed quite practicable, and at last my Lady broke out: "Well, it cannot be helped; you must put Miss Wood in the Blue Room. It is only for one night, and she won't know anything about that silly story."

"Oh, my Lady!" my aunt cried, and I knew by her tone that she had not spoken the truth when she professed to think so lightly of the ghost.

"I can't help it," her Ladyship answered: "beside I don't believe there is anything really wrong with the room. Sir Archibald has slept there, and he found no cause for complaint."

"But a woman, a young woman," my aunt urged; "indeed I wouldn't run such a risk, my Lady; let me put one of the gentlemen in there, and Miss Wood can have the first room in the west corridor."

"And what use would she be to Lady Grayburn out there?" said her Ladyship. "Don't be foolish, my good Marris. Unlock the door between the two rooms; Miss Wood can leave it open if she feels nervous; but I shall not say a word about that foolish superstition, and I shall be very much annoyed if any one else does so."

She spoke as if that settled the question, but my aunt wasn't easy. "The Laird," she murmured; "what will he say to a lady being put to sleep there?"

"Sir Archibald does not interfere in household arrangements. Have the Blue Room made ready for Miss Wood at once. *I* will take the responsibility,—if there is any."

On that her Ladyship went away, and there was nothing for it but to carry out her orders. The Blue Room was prepared, a great fire lighted, and when I went round last thing to see all was in order for the visitor's arrival, I couldn't but think how handsome and comfortable it looked. There were candles burning brightly on the toilet-table and chimney-piece, and a fine blaze of logs on the wide hearth. I saw nothing had been overlooked, and was closing the door when my eyes fell in the bed. It was crumpled just as if someone had thrown themselves across it, and I was vexed that the housemaids should have been so careless, especially with the smart new quilt. I went round, and patted up the feathers, and smoothed the counterpane, just as the carriages drove under the window.

By and by Lady Grayburn and Miss Wood came up-stairs, and knowing they had brought no maid, I went to assist in the unpacking. I was a long time in her Ladyship's room, and when I'd settled her I tapped at the next door and offered to help Miss Wood. Lady Grayburn followed me almost immediately to inquire the whereabouts of some keys. She spoke very sharply, I thought, to her companion, who seemed a timid, delicate slip of a girl, with nothing noticeable about her except her hair, which was lovely, pale golden, and heaped in thick coils all round her small head.

"You will certainly be late," Lady Grayburn said. "What an age you have been, and you have not half finished unpacking yet." The young lady murmured something about there being so little time. "You have had time to sprawl on the bed instead of getting ready," was the retort, and as Miss Wood meekly denied the imputation, I looked over my shoulder at the bed, and saw there the same strange indentation I had noticed before. It made my heart beat faster, for without any reason at all I felt certain that crease must have something to do with Lady Barbara.

Miss Wood didn't go to the ball. She had supper in the schoolroom with the young ladies' governess, and as I heard from one of the maids that she was to sit up for Lady Grayburn, I took her some wine and sandwiches about twelve o'clock. She stayed in the schoolroom, with a book, till the first party came home soon after two. I'd been round the rooms with the housemaid to see the fires were kept up, and I wasn't surprised to find that queer crease back on the bed again; indeed, I sort of expected it. I said nothing to the maid, who didn't seem to have noticed anything out of the way, but I told my aunt, and though she answered sharply that I was talking nonsense, she turned quite pale, and I heard her mutter something under breath that sounded like "God help her!"

I slept badly that night, for, do what I would, the thought of that poor young lady alone in the Blue Room kept me awake and restless. I was nervous, I suppose, and once, just as I was dropping off, I started up, fancying I'd heard a scream. I opened my door and listened, but there wasn't a sound, and after waiting a bit I crept back to bed, and lay there shivering till I fell asleep.

The household wasn't astir as early as usual. Every one was tired after the late night, and tea wasn't to be sent to the ladies till half-past nine. My aunt said nothing about the ghost, but I noticed she was fidgety, and asked almost first thing if anyone had been to Miss Wood's room. I was telling her that Martha, one of the housemaids, had just taken up the tray, when the girl came running in with a scared, white face. "For pity's sake, Mrs. Marris," she cried, "come to the Blue Room; something awful has happened!"

My aunt stopped to ask no questions. She ran straight up-stairs, and as I followed I heard her muttering to herself, "I knew it, I knew it. Oh Lord! what will my Lady feel like now?"

If I live to be a hundred I shall never forget that poor girl's face. It was just as if she'd been frozen with terror. Her eyes were wide open and fixed, and her little hands clenched in the coverlet on each side of her as she lay across the bed in the very place where that crease had been.

Of course the whole house was aroused. Sir Archibald sent one of the grooms post-haste for the doctor, but he could do nothing when he came; Miss Wood had been dead for at least five hours.

It was a sad business. All the visitors went away as soon as possible, except Lady Grayburn, who was obliged to stay for the inquest.

In his evidence the doctor stated death was due to failure of heart's action, occasioned possibly by some sudden shock; and though the jury did not say so in their verdict, it was an open secret that they blamed her Ladyship for permitting Miss Wood to sleep in the haunted room. No one could have reproached her more bitterly than she did herself, poor lady; and if she had done wrong she certainly suffered for it, for she never recovered from the shock of that dreadful morning, and became more or less of an invalid till her death five years later.

All this happened in 184__. It was fifty years before another woman slept in the Blue Room, and fifty years had brought with them many changes. The old Laird was gathered to his fathers, and his son, the present Sir Archibald, reigned in his stead; his sons were grown men, and Mr. Charles, the eldest, married, with a fine little boy of his own. My aunt had been dead many a year, and I was an old woman, though active and able as ever to keep the maids up to their work. They take more looking after now, I think, than in the old days before there was so much talk of education, and when young women who took service thought less of dress and more of dusting. Not but what education is a fine thing in its proper place, that is, for gentlefolk. If Miss Erristoun, now, hadn't been the clever, strong-minded young lady she is, she'd never have cleared the Blue Room of its terrible secret, and lived to make Mr. Arthur the happiest man alive.

He'd taken a great deal of notice of her when she first came in the summer to visit Mrs. Charles, and I wasn't surprised to find she was one of the guests for the opening of the shooting-season. It wasn't a regular house-party (for Sir Archibald and Lady Mertoun were away), but just half-a-dozen young ladies, friends of Mrs. Charles, who was but a girl herself, and as many gentlemen that Mr. Charles and Mr. Arthur had invited. And very gay they were, what with lunches at the covert-side, and tennis-parties, and little dances got up at a few hours' notice, and sometimes of an evening they'd play hide-and-seek all over the house just as if they'd been so many children.

It surprised me at first to see Miss Erristoun, who was said to be so learned, and had held her own with all the gentlemen at Cambridge, playing with the rest like any ordinary young lady; but she seemed to enjoy the fun as much as any one, and was always first in any amusement that was planned. I didn't wonder at Mr. Arthur's fancying her, for she was a handsome girl, tall and finely made, and carried herself like a princess. She had a wonderful head of hair, too, so long, her maid told me, it touched the ground as she sat on a chair to have it brushed. Everybody seemed to take to her, but I soon noticed it was Mr. Arthur or Mr. Calder-Maxwell she liked best to be with.

Mr. Maxwell is a Professor now, and a great man at Oxford; but then he was just an undergraduate the same as Mr. Arthur, though more studious, for he'd spend hours in the library poring over those old books full of queer black characters, that they say the wicked Lord Mertoun collected in the time of King Charles the Second. Now and then Miss Erristoun would stay indoors to help him, and it was something they found out in their studies that gave them the clue to the secret of the Blue Room.

For a long time after Miss Wood's death all mention of the ghost was strictly forbidden. Neither the Laird nor her Ladyship could bear the slightest allusion to the subject, and the Blue Room was kept locked, except when it had to be cleaned and aired. But as the years went by the edge of the tragedy wore off, and by degrees it grew to be just a story that people talked about in much the same way as they had done when I first came to the Towers; and if many believed in the mystery and speculated as to what the ghost could be, there were others who didn't hesitate to declare Miss Wood's dying in that room was a mere coincidence, and had nothing to do with supernatural agency. Miss Erristoun was one of those who held most strongly to this theory. She didn't believe a bit in ghosts, and said straight out that there wasn't any of the tales told of haunted houses which could not be traced to natural causes, if people had courage and science enough to investigate them thoroughly.

It had been very wet all that day, and the gentlemen had stayed indoors, and nothing would serve Mrs. Charles but they should all have an old-fashioned tea in my room and "talk ghosts," as she called it. They made me tell them all I knew about the Blue Room, and it was then, when every one was discussing the story and speculating as to what the ghost could be, that Miss Erristoun spoke up. "The poor girl had heart-complaint," she finished by saying, "and she would have died the same way in any other room."

"But what about the other people who have slept there?" someone objected.

"They did not die. Old Sir Archibald came to no harm, neither did Mr. Hawksworth, nor the other man. They were healthy, and had plenty of pluck, so they saw nothing."

"They were not women," put in Mrs. Charles; "you see the ghost only appears to the weaker sex."

"The proves the story to be a mere legend," Miss Erristoun said with decision. "First it was reported that everyone who slept in the room died. Then one or two men did sleep there, and remained alive; so the tale had to be modified, and since one woman could be proved to have died suddenly there, the fatality was represented as attaching to women only. If a girl with a sound constitution and good nerve were once to spend the night in that room, your charming family spectre would be discredited for ever."

There was a perfect chorus of dissent. None of the ladies could agree, and most of the gentlemen doubted whether any woman's nerve would stand the ordeal. The more they argued the more Miss Erristoun persisted in her view, till at last Mrs. Charles got vexed, and cried: "Well, it is one thing to talk about it and another to do it. Confess now, Edith, you daren't sleep in that room yourself."

"I dare and I will," she answered directly. "I don't believe in ghosts, and I am ready to stand the test. I will sleep in the Blue Room to-night, if you like, and tomorrow morning you will have to confess that whatever there may be against the haunted chamber, it is not a ghost."

I think Mrs. Charles was sorry she'd spoken then, for they all took Miss Erristoun up, and the gentlemen were for laying wagers as to whether she'd see anything or not. When it was too late she tried to laugh aside her challenge as absurd, but Miss Erristoun wouldn't be put off. She said she meant to see the thing through, and if she wasn't allowed to have a bed made up, she'd carry in her blankets and pillows, and camp out on the floor.

The others were all laughing and disputing together, but I saw Mr. Maxwell look at her very curiously. Then he drew Mr. Arthur aside, and began to talk in an undertone. I couldn't hear what he said, but Mr. Arthur answered quite short:

"It's the maddest thing I ever heard of, and I won't allow it for a moment."

"She will not ask your permission perhaps," Mr. Maxwell retorted. Then he turned to Mrs. Charles, and inquired how long it was since the Blue Room had been used, and if it was kept aired. I could speak to that, and when he'd heard that there was no bedding there, but that fires were kept up regularly, he said he meant to have the first refusal of the ghost, and if he saw nothing it would be time enough for Miss Erristoun to take her turn.

Mr. Maxwell had a kind of knack of settling things, and somehow with his quiet manner always seemed to get his own way. Just before dinner he came to me with Mrs. Charles, and said it was all right, I was to get the room made ready quietly, not for all the servants to know, and he was going to sleep there.

I heard next morning that he came down to breakfast as usual. He'd had an excellent night, he said, and never slept better.

It was wet again that morning, raining "cats and dogs," but Mr. Arthur went out in it all. He'd almost quarrelled with Miss Erristoun, and was furious with Mr. Maxwell for encouraging her in her idea of testing the ghost-theory, as they called it. Those two were together in the library most of the day, and Mrs. Charles was chaffing Miss Erristoun as they went up-stairs to dress, and asking her if she found the demons interesting. Yes, she said, but there was a page missing in the most exciting part of the book. They could not make head or tail of the context for some time, and then Mr. Maxwell discovered that a leaf had been cut out. They talked of nothing else all through dinner, the butler told me, and Miss Erristoun seemed so taken up with her studies, I hoped she'd forgotten about the haunted room. But she wasn't one of the sort to forget. Later in the evening I came across her standing with Mr. Arthur in the corridor. He was talking very earnestly, and I saw her shrug her shoulders and just look up at him and smile, in a sort of way that meant she wasn't going to give in. I was slipping quietly by, for I didn't want to disturb them, when Mr. Maxwell came out of the billiard-room. "It's our game," he said; "won't you come and play the tie?"

"I'm quite ready," Miss Erristoun answered, and was turning away, when Mr. Arthur laid his hand on her arm. "Promise me, first," he urged, "promise me that much, at least."

"How tiresome you are!" she said quite pettishly. "Very well then, I promise; and now please, don't worry me any more."

Mr. Arthur watched her go back to the billiard-room with his friend, and he gave a sort of groan. Then he caught sight of me and came along the passage. "She won't give it up," he said, and his face was quite white. "I've done all I can; I'd have telegraphed to my father, but I don't know where they'll stay in Paris, and anyway there'd be no time to get an answer. Mrs. Marris, she's going to sleep in that d—— room, and if anything happens to her—I——"he broke off short, and threw himself on to the window-seat, hiding his face in his folded arms.

I could have cried for sympathy with his trouble. Mr. Arthur has always been a favourite of mine, and I felt downright angry with Miss Erristoun for making him so miserable just out of a bit of bravado.

"I think they are all mad," he went on presently. "Charley ought to have stopped the whole thing at once, but Kate and the others have talked him round. He professes to believe there's no danger, and Maxwell has got his head full of some rubbish he has found in those beastly books on Demonology, and he's backing her up. She won't listen to a word I say. She told me point-blank she'd never speak to me again if I interfered. She doesn't care a hand for me; I know that now, but I can't help it; I—I'd give my life for her."

I did my best to comfort him, saying Miss Erristoun wouldn't come to any harm; bit it wasn't a bit of use, for I didn't believe in my own assurances. I felt nothing but ill could come of such tempting of Providence, and I seemed to see that other poor girl's terrible face as it had looked when we found her dead in that wicked room. However, it is a true saying that "a wilful woman will have her way," and we could do nothing to prevent Miss Erristoun's risking her life; but I made up my mind to one thing, whatever other people might do, *I* wasn't going to bed that night.

I'd been getting the winter-hangings into order, and the upholstress had used the little boudoir at the end of the long corridor for her work. I made up the fire, brought in a fresh lamp, and when the house was quiet, I crept down and settled myself there to watch. It wasn't ten yards from the door of the Blue Room, and over the thick carpet I could pass without making a sound, and listen at the keyhole. Miss Erristoun had promised Mr. Arthur she would not lock her door; it was the one concession he'd been able to obtain from her. The ladies went to their rooms about eleven, but Miss Erristoun stayed talking to Mrs. Charles for nearly an hour while her maid was brushing her hair. I saw her go to the Blue Room, and by and by Louise left her, and all was quiet. It must have been half-past one before I thought I heard something moving outside. I opened the door and looked out, and there was Mr. Arthur standing in the passage. He gave a start when he saw me. "You are sitting up," he said, coming into the room; "then you do believe there is evil work on hand to-night? The others have goon to bed, but I can't rest; it's no use my trying to sleep. I meant to stay in the smoking-room, but it is so far away; I couldn't hear there even if she called for help. I've listened at the door; there isn't a sound. Can't you go in and see if it's all right? Oh, Marris, if she should——"

I knew what he meant, but I wasn't going to admit *that* possible,—yet. "I can't go into a lady's room without any reason," I said; "but I've been to the door every few minutes for the last hour and more. It wasn't till half-past twelve that Miss Erristoun stopped moving about, and I don't believe, Mr. Arthur, that God will let harm come to her, without giving those that care for her some warning. I mean to keep on listening, and if there's the least hint of anything wrong, why I'll got to her at once, and you are at hand to help."

I talked to him a bit more till he seemed more reasonable, and then we sat there waiting, hardly speaking a word except when, from time to time, I went outside to listen. The house was deathly quiet; there was something terrible, I thought, in the stillness; not a sign of life anywhere save just in the little boudoir, where Mr. Arthur paced up and down, or sat with a strained look on his face, watching the door.

As three o'clock struck, I went out again. There is a window in the corridor, angle for angle with the boudoir-door. As I passed, some one stepped from behind the curtains and a voice whispered: "Don't be frightened Mrs. Marris; it is only me, Calder-Maxwell. Mr. Arthur is there, isn't he?" He pushed open the boudoir door. "May I come in?" he said softly. "I guessed you'd be about, Mertoun. I'm not at all afraid myself, but if there is anything in that little legend, it is as well for some of us to be on hand. It was a good idea of yours to get Mrs. Marris to keep watch with you."

Mr. Arthur looked at him as black as thunder. "If you didn't *know* there was something in it," he said, "you wouldn't be here now; and knowing that, you're nothing less than a blackguard for egging that girl on to risk her life, for the sake of trying to prove your insane theories. You are no friend of mine after this, and I'll never willingly see you or speak to you again."

I was fairly frightened at his words, and for how Mr. Maxwell might take them; but he just smiled, and lighted a cigarette, quite cool and quiet.

"I'm not going to quarrel with you, old chap," he said. "You're a bit on the strain to-night, and when a man has nerves he mustn't be held responsible for all his words." Then he turned to me. "You're a sensible woman, Mrs. Marris, and a brave one too, I fancy. If I stay here with Mr. Arthur, will you keep close outside Miss Erristoun's door? She may talk in her sleep quietly; that's of no consequence; but if she should cry out, go in at once, *at once*, you understand; we shall hear you, and follow immediately."

At that Mr. Arthur was on his feet. "You know more than you pretend," he cried. "You slept in that room last night. By Heaven, if you've played any trick on her I'll——"

Mr. Maxwell held the door open. "Will you go please, Mrs. Marris?" he said in his quiet way. "Mertoun, don't be a d—— fool."

I went as he told me, and I give you my word I was all ears, for I felt certain Mr. Maxwell knew more than we did, and that he expected something to happen.

It seemed like hours, though I know now it could not have been more than a quarter of that time, before I could be positive someone was moving behind that closed door.

At first I thought it was only my own heart, which was beating against my ribs like a hammer; but soon I could distinguish footsteps, and a sort of murmur like someone speaking continuously, but very low. Then a voice (it was Miss Erristoun's this time) said, "No, it is impossible; I am dreaming, I must be dreaming." There was a kind of rustling as though she were moving quickly across the floor. I had my fingers on the handle, but I seemed as if I'd lost power to stir; I could only wait for what might come next.

Suddenly she began to say something out loud. I could not make out the words, which didn't sound like English, but almost directly she stopped short. "I can't remember any more," she cried in a troubled tone. "What shall I do? I can't— —" There was a pause. Then——"No, *no!*" she shrieked. "Oh Arthur, Arthur!"

At that my strength came back to me, and I flung open the door.

There was a night-lamp burning on the table, and the room was quite light. Miss Erristoun was standing by the bed; she seemed to have backed up against it; her hands were down at her sides, her fingers clutching at the quilt. Her face was white as a sheet, and her eyes staring wide with terror, as well they might,—I know I never had such a shock in my life, for if it was my last word, I swear there was a man standing close in front of her. He turned and looked at me as I opened the door, and I saw his face as plain as I did here. He was young and very handsome, and his eyes shone like an animal's when you see them in the dark.

"Arthur!" Miss Erristoun gasped again, and I saw she was fainting. I sprang forward, and caught her by the shoulders just as she was falling back on the bed. It was all over in a second. Mr. Arthur had her in his arms, and when I looked up there were only us four in the room, for Mr. Maxwell had followed on Mr. Arthur's heels, and was kneeling beside me with his fingers on Miss Erristoun's pulse. "It's only a faint," he said, "she'll come round directly. Better take her out of this at once; here's a dressing gown." He threw the wrapper round her, and would have helped to raise her, but Mr. Arthur needed no assistance. He lifted Miss Erristoun as if she'd been a baby, and carried her straight to the boudoir. He laid her on the couch and knelt beside her, chafing her hands. "Get the brandy out of the smoking room, Maxwell," he said. "Mrs. Marris, have you any salts handy?"

I always carry a bottle in my pocket, so I gave it to him, before I ran after Mr. Maxwell, who had lighted a candle, and was going for the brandy. "Shall I wake Mr. Charles and the servants?" I cried. "He'll be hiding somewhere, but he hasn't had time to get out of the house yet."

He looked as if he thought I was crazed. "He—who?" he asked.

"The man," I said; "there was a man in Miss Erristoun's room. I'll call up Soames and Robert."

"You'll do nothing of the sort," he said sharply. "There was no man in that room."

"There was," I retorted, "for I saw him; and a great powerful man too. Someone ought to go for the police before he has time to get off."

Mr. Maxwell was always an odd sort of gentleman, but I didn't know what to make of the way he behaved then. He just leaned against the wall, and laughed till the tears came into his eyes.

"It is no laughing matter that I can see," I told him quite short, for I was angry at his treating the matter so lightly; "and I consider it no more than my duty to let Mr. Charles know that there's a burglar on the premises."

He grew grave at once then. "I beg your pardon, Mrs. Marris," he said seriously, "but I couldn't help smiling at the idea of the police. The vicar would be more to the point, all things considered. You really must not think of rousing the household; it might do Miss Erristoun a great injury, and could in no case be of the slightest use. Don't you understand? It was not a man at all you saw, it was an—well, it was what haunts the Blue Room."

Then he ran downstairs leaving me fairly dazed, for I'd made so sure what I'd seen was a real man, that I'd clean forgotten all about the ghost.

Miss Erristoun wasn't long regaining consciousness. She swallowed the brandy we gave her like a lamb, and sat up bravely, though she started at every sound and kept her hand in Mr. Arthur's like a frightened child. It was strange, seeing how independent and stand-off she'd been with him before, but she seemed all the sweeter for the change. It was as if they'd come to an understanding without any words; and indeed, he must have known she had cared for him all along, when she called out his name in her terror.

As soon as she'd recovered herself a little, Mr. Maxwell began asking questions. Mr. Arthur would have stopped him, but he insisted that it was of the greatest importance to hear everything while the impression was fresh; and when she had got over the first effort, Miss Erristoun seemed to find relief in telling her experience. She sat there with one hand in Mr. Arthur's while she spoke, and Mr. Maxwell wrote down what she said in his pocket-book.

She told us she went to bed quite easy, for she wasn't the least nervous, and being tired she soon dropped off to sleep. Then she had a sort of dream, I suppose, for she thought she was in the same room, only differently furnished, all but the bed. She described exactly how everything was arranged. She had the strangest feeling too, that she was not herself but someone else, and that she was going to do something,—something that must be done, though she was frightened to death, all the time, and kept stopping to listen at the inner door, expecting someone would hear her moving about and call out for her to go to them. That in itself was queer, for there was nobody sleeping in the adjoining room. In her dream, she went on to say, she saw a curious little silver brazier, one that stands in a cabinet in the picture-gallery (a fine example of *cinque cento* work, I think I've heard my Lady call it), and this she remembered holding in her hands a long time, before she set it on a little table beside the bed. Now the bed in the Blue Room is very handsome, richly carved on the cornice and frame, and especially on the posts, which are a foot square at the base and covered with relief-work in a design of fruit and flowers. Miss Erristoun said she went to the left-hand post at the foot, and after passing her hand over the carving, she seemed to touch a spring in one of the centre flowers, and the panel fell outwards like a lid, disclosing a secret cupboard out of which she took some papers and a box. She seemed to know what to do with the papers, though she couldn't tell us what was written on them; and she had a distinct recollection of taking a pastille from the box, and lighting it in the silver brazier. The smoke curled up and seem to fill the whole room with a heavy perfume, and the next thing she remembered was that she awoke to find herself standing in the middle of the floor, and,—what I had seen when I opened the door was there.

She turned quite white when she came to that part of the story, and shuddered. "I couldn't believe it," she said; "I tried to think I was still dreaming, but I wasn't, I wasn't. It was real, and it was there, and,—oh, it was horrible!"

She hid her face against Mr. Arthur's shoulder. Mr. Maxwell sat, pencil in hand, staring at her. "I was right then," he said. "I felt sure I was; but it seemed incredible."

"It is incredible," said Miss Erristoun; "but it is true, frightfully true. When I realized that I was awake, that it was actually real, I tried to remember the charge, you know, out of the office of exorcism, but I couldn't get through it. The words went out of my head; I felt my will-power failing; I was paralysed, as though I could make no effort to help myself and then,—then I—," she looked at Mr. Arthur and blushed all over her face and neck. "I thought of you, and I called,—I had a feeling that you would save me."

Mr. Arthur made no more ado about us than if we'd been a couple of dummies. He just put his arms round her and kissed her, while Mr. Maxwell and I looked the other way.

After a bit, Mr. Maxwell said: "One more question, please; what was it like?"

She answered after thinking for a minute. "It was like a man, tall and very handsome. I have an impression that its eyes were blue and very bright." Mr. Maxwell looked at me inquiringly, and I nodded. "And dressed?" he asked. She began to laugh almost hysterically. "It sounds too insane for words, but I think,—I am almost positive it wore ordinary evening dress."

"It is impossible," Mr. Arthur cried. "You were dreaming the whole time, that proves it."

"It doesn't," Mr. Maxwell contradicted. "They usually appeared in the costume of the day. You'll find that stated particularly both by Scott and Glanvil; Sprenger gives an instance too. Besides, Mrs. Marris thought it was a burglar, which argues that the,—the manifestation was objective, and presented no striking peculiarity in the way of clothing."

"What?" Miss Erristoun exclaimed. "You saw it too?" I told her exactly what I had seen. My description tallied with hers in everything, but the white shirt and tie, which from my position at the door I naturally should not be able to see.

Mr. Maxwell snapped the elastic round his note-book. For a long time he sat silently staring at the fire. "It is almost past belief," he said at last, speaking half to himself, "that such a thing could happen at the end of the nineteenth century, in these scientific rationalistic times that we think such a lot about, we, who look down from our superior intellectual height on the benighted superstitions of the Middle Ages." He gave an odd little laugh. "I'd like to get to the bottom of this business. I have a theory, and in the interest of psychical research and common humanity, I'd like to work it out. Miss Erristoun, you ought, I know, to have rest and quiet, and it is almost morning; but will you grant me one request. Before you are overwhelmed with questions, before you are made to relate your experience till the impression of to-night's adventure loses edge and clearness, will you go with Mertoun and myself to the Blue Room, and try to find the secret panel?"

"She shall never set foot inside that door again," Mr. Arthur began hotly, but Miss Erristoun laid a restraining hand on his arm.

"Wait a moment, dear," she said gently; "let us hear Mr. Maxwell's reasons. Do you think," she went on, "that my dream had a foundation in fact; that something connected with that dreadful thing is really concealed about the room?"

"I think," he answered, "that you hold the clue to the mystery, and I believe, could you repeat the action of your dream, and open the secret panel, you might remove for ever the legacy of one woman's reckless folly. Only if it is to be done at all, it must be soon, before the impression has had time to fade."

"It shall be done now," she answered; "I am quite myself again. Feel my pulse; my nerves are perfectly steady."

Mr. Arthur broke out into angry protestations. She had gone through more than enough for one night, he said, and he wouldn't have her health sacrificed to Maxwell's whims.

I have always thought Miss Erristoun handsome, but never, not even on her wedding-day, did she look so beautiful as then when she stood up in her heavy white wrapper, with all her splendid hair loose on her shoulders.

"Listen," she said; "if God gives us a plain work to do, we must do it at any cost. Last night I didn't believe in anything I could not understand. I was so full of pride in my own courage and common-sense, that I wasn't afraid to sleep in that room and prove the ghost was all superstitious nonsense. I have learned there are forces of which I know nothing, and against which my strength was utter weakness. God took care of me, and sent help in time; and if He has opened a way by which I may save other women from the danger I escaped, I should be worse than ungrateful were I to shirk the task. Bring the lamp Mr. Maxwell, and let us do what we can." Then she put both hands on Mr. Arthur's shoulders. "Why are you troubled?" she said sweetly. "You will be with me, and how can I be afraid?"

It never strikes me as strange now that burglaries and things can go on in a big house at night, and not a soul one whit the wiser. There were five people sleeping in the rooms on that corridor while we tramped up and down without disturbing one of them. Not but what we went as quietly as we could, for Mr. Maxwell made it clear that the less was known about the actual facts, the better. He went first, carrying the lamp, and we followed. Miss Erristoun shivered as her eyes fell on the bed, across which that dreadful crease showed plain, and I knew she was thinking of what might have been, had help not been at hand.

Just for a minute she faltered, then she went bravely on, and began feeling over the carved woodwork for the spring of the secret panel. Mr. Maxwell held the lamp close, but there was nothing to show any difference between that bit of carving and the other three posts. For full ten minutes she tried, and so did the gentlemen, and it seemed as though the dream would turn out a delusion after all, when all at once Miss Erristoun cried, "I have found it," and with a little jerk, the square of wood fell forward, and there was the cupboard just as she had described it to us.

It was Mr. Maxwell who took out the things, for Mr. Arthur wouldn't let Miss Erristoun touch them. There were a roll of papers and a little silver box. At the sight of the box she gave a sort of cry; "That is it," she said, and covered her face with her hands.

Mr Maxwell lifted the lid, and emptied out two or three pastilles. Then he unfolded the papers, and before he had fairly glanced at the sheet of parchment covered with queer black characters, he cried, "I knew it, I knew it! It is the missing leaf." He seemed quite wild with excitement. "Come along," he said.

"Bring the light, Mertoun; I always said it was no ghost, and now the whole thing is as clear as daylight. You see," he went on, as we gathered round the table in the boudoir, "so much depended on there being an heir. That was the chief cause of the endless quarrels between old Lord Mertoun and Barbara. He had never approved of the marriage, and was for ever reproaching the poor woman with having failed in the first duty of an only son's wife. His will shows that he did not leave her a farthing in event of her husband dying without issue. Then the feud with the Protestant branch of the family was very bitter, and the Sir Archibald of that day had three boys, he having married (about the same time as his cousin) Lady Mary Sarum, who had been Barbara's rival at Court and whom Barbara very naturally hated. So when the doctors pronounced Dennis Mertoun to be dying of consumption, his wife got desperate and had recourse to black magic. It is well known that the old man's collection of works on Demonology was the most complete in Europe. Lady Barbara must have had access to the books, and it was she who cut out this leaf. Probably Lord Mertoun discovered the theft and drew his own conclusions. That would account for his refusal to admit her body to the family vault. The Mertouns were staunch Romanists, and it is one of the deadly sins, you know, meddling with sorcery. Well Barbara contrived to procure the pastilles, and she worked out the spell according to the directions given here, and then,—Good God! Mertoun, what have you done?"

For before any one could interfere to check him, Mr. Arthur had swept the papers, box, pastilles, and all off the table and flung them into the fire. The thick parchment curled and shrivelled on the hot coals, and a queer, faint smell like incense spread heavily through the room. Mr. Arthur stepped to the window and threw the casement open. Day was breaking, and a sweet fresh wind swept in from the east which was all rosy with the glow of the rising sun.

"It is a nasty story," he said; "and if there be any truth in it, for the credit of the family and the name of a dead woman, let it rest for ever. We will keep our own counsel about to-night's work. It is enough for others to know that the spell of the Blue Room is broken, since a brave, pure-minded girl has dared to face its unknown mystery and has laid the ghost."

Mr. Calder-Maxwell considered a moment. "I believe you are right," he said, presently, with an air of resignation. "I agree to your proposition, and I surrender my chance of world-wide celebrity among the votaries of Psychical Research; but I *do* wish, Mertoun, you would call things by their proper names. It was *not* a ghost. It was an———"

But as I said, all I can remember now of the word he used is, that it somehow put me in mind of poultry-rearing.

NOTE.—The reader will observe that the worthy Mrs. Marris, though no student of Sprenger, unconsciously discerned the root-affinity of the *incubator* of the hen-yard and the *incubus* of the MALLEUS MALEFICARUM.

GHOSTS WHO BECAME FAMOUS,
A CHRISTMAS FANTASY
by
Carolyn Wells
1900

Illustrated by Bernard Jacob Rosenmeyer

When I first spoke to Gertrude about going down to our sea-shore cottage to spend Christmas, she treated the idea with scorn. This pleased me, for I knew that she would soon be enthusiastically approving my suggestion, if, indeed, she were not offering it as her own.

I was not surprised, therefore, to hear her, a few days later, telling a neighbor that, just for the novelty of the thing, we were going to spend the Christmas season at Beachhurst.

"We haven't quite decided," she continued, "but *I* think it would be great fun, and little Frederick would enjoy it so much. If my husband will only consent, I think we shall surely go."

I graciously allowed myself to be persuaded to consent to my own plan, and then Gertrude invited a house-party of a few friends to spend the holidays with us.

The "Woodpile," as we called our seaside home, was newly built that year, and as it was one of the finest cottages on the New Jersey coast, we were justly proud of it, and enjoyed the prospect of entertaining our friends with a novel and pleasing hospitality.

We arrived at the Woodpile two days before Christmas, and as we wished to conform to our time-honored custom of having our Christmas tree exhibited on Christmas eve, there was much to be done.

However, as the servants were capable, though not very willing, and the guests were willing, though not very capable, we soon had the machinery in motion for a jolly old-fashioned Christmas. The first evening we made rope-greens and holly-wreaths, and decorated the house with a determined enthusiasm that accomplished wonders.

Indeed, I never remember working so hard in all my life. I cut and tied and hammered and nailed, and ran up and down step-ladders, until I was so tired that when at last I found myself in bed I fell asleep at once.

From this deep sleep I awoke suddenly and with a jump.

The room was dark, save for a tiny spark of night-light. I looked and listened, but could see or hear nothing alarming; yet I felt an irresistible impulse to rise and go down-stairs.

And when I say impulse, I do not mean merely a mental inclination, but an impelling force which seemed to move me physically, in defiance of my own volition.

I was not frightened, I had no thought of fire or burglars; I simply rose and put on my bath-robe and slippers because I could not help it.

For the same reason, I went out into the hall, down the stairs, and into the parlor. This was a large apartment, which was already decorated in holiday fashion, and where we were to stand the Christmas tree on the morrow.

As I entered, I was surprised to notice the chill air of the room.

The Woodpile was amply provided with heating appliances, for when we built it we had thought of an occasional winter visit; but the parlor seemed filled with a wet, icy atmosphere which hung about in clouds and gave something the effect of a frozen wash-day.

Still acting involuntarily, I crossed the room, though I grew colder with every step, and sat down in an arm-chair near the fireplace.

There was no fire on the hearth, but I did not select my seat with a view to warming myself, but because I was unable to resist the power that pushed me into that particular chair.

As I sat there, I was cold, extremely cold, but not shivering; the calm iciness of the atmosphere seemed to imbue my whole being, and I sat, silent and immovable, with a half-conscious sense of admiring my own magnificent inanition.

Then the thought came into my mind that I was about to see a ghost.

Even this did not startle me. Although possessed of a natural fear of the supernatural, yet at that time I did not really believe in ghosts, and, anyway, I was very sure "I would rather see than be one."

So when the misty, frosty air gradually settled into a distinct though semi-transparent shape, I knew at once that I was in the presence of a ghost.

I was not frightened; indeed, as the cold seemed to intensify with this condensation, a fleeting idea passed through my mind that a ghost would be a fine thing for refrigerating purposes.

And then, as I looked with interest upon his ghostship, there seemed something familiar about him.

I was sure I had never seen a ghost before, yet that tall, commanding figure walking toward me with a stately and solemn step seemed somehow like an old acquaintance. I gazed at the ghost more curiously.

He wore a complete suit of armor, of an antique make that appealed strongly to my collecting instincts, and my fingers fairly itched for his wonderful helmet.

His face was that of an oldish man, yet his flowing, dark beard was only partially silvered, and his expression, though a trifle sad, seemed to betoken a strong, noble nature.

He made me think of Henry Irving, although he was not at all like him, and, besides, so far as I knew, Irving was not yet dead.

Undoubtedly he was a ghost, and a ghost of no small importance, and after waiting a suitable time for him to speak, I concluded to open a conversation myself. For there suddenly flashed across my mind one of the rules laid down for ghosts in Lewis Carroll's "Phantasmagoria," and which was doubtless meant for just such an occasion as this:

Wait for the Victim to commence:
No Ghost of any common sense
Begins a conversation.

But while I was considering in what terms to address a strange ghost, and what degree of welcome to offer him,—for the same instructions further say:

All Ghosts instinctively detest
The Man that fails to treat his guest
With proper cordiality, —

the apparition stalked a few steps nearer to me, and announced in a deep, hollow voice:

"I am thy father's spirit,
Doomed for a certain time to walk the night."

And then I recognized my visitor. Of course he was not my father's spirit at all, but the Ghost of Hamlet's Father, and that was why he was associated in my mind with Henry Irving.

"Hamlet," I cried, "king, father, royal Dane, my! but I'm glad to see you!"

I had not intended to speak in this colloquial way, but I had always felt a warm sympathy for the old gentleman, and somehow it broke through my icy calm.

Perhaps it broke through his also, for he stopped stalking, and stood regarding me with a countenance more in sorrow than in anger. Then he said:

"For this assurance, thanks. I would that I
Might say the same to you. But of a truth
Your presence here, at this especial time,
Hinders my dearest plans."

"No! Is that so?" said I, much concerned. "But I'm only here for a week, or ten days at most; can't your plans wait that long?"

"Not so; on Christmas eve—to-morrow night—
I do expect that there will join me here
A dozen of my fellows—fellow-ghosts,
Doomed for a certain time to walk the night."

"Oho!" said I, "I see; you have made my house a rendezvous for
Christmas eve, because you thought it would be otherwise vacant."

"'T is so, my friend; and lend thy serious hearing
To what I shall unfold. In vain I've sought
In the Old World a castle or a church,
A ruined abbey or an ancient tower,
Where I and some few spirits of my choice
Might congregate, unnoticed and alone.
But futile all my search. If here or there
We stealthily assembled, lo, there came
A horde of squeaking, gibbering, sheeted dead,
Intruding on our would-be privacy.
At my wits' end, I thought, there's one last chance;
Mayhap, across the sea, the newer world,
With less of legend and tradition,
May offer us a haven, where, in peace
And unmolested, we may work our will."

"Yes, yes, I see," cried I; "you came here thinking the Jersey
coast the farthest possible remove from a ghost-haunted
atmosphere. But what is your work? What are you contemplating
that excludes your fellow-ghosts?"

"But soft! methinks I scent the morning air.
Brief let me be; and yet I ever was
Rambling and slow of speech. I will call up
A comrade spirit; he shall tell thee all.
Ho, Marley's Ghost, appear!"

"Marley's Ghost!" I exclaimed. Surprise and delight had now entirely melted my icy calm, and I rose to shake hands cordially with Marley's Ghost as with an old friend.

The hand-shaking gave me a peculiar sensation, for though I could see his hand grasp my own and jog up and down with it, yet I felt nothing but a handful of ice-cold air, like an evaporated snowball.

All my life I had been familiar with Marley's Ghost, and now he stood before me: the same face; the very same Marley in his pigtail, usual waistcoat, tights, and boots, with his chain clasped about his middle. His body was transparent, so that, looking through his waistcoat, I could see the two buttons on his coat behind. His chain clanked delightfully as he crossed the floor, and when he sat down in an arm-chair and wrung his hands and gave a frightful cry, I realized afresh that this was truly Marley's Ghost that I had known and loved for years. I insist that I was not in the least frightened, but still it was a bit horrifying when Marley's Ghost took off the bandage that was round his head, and his lower jaw dropped down upon his breast. But I remembered that this was a habit of this particular spirit, and, unheeding the Carroll theory, I waited for him to speak.

"It is extremely awkward, my dear sir." he said, "to object to a man's presence in his own house, but I will explain our predicament in a few words, and perhaps you can aid us in some way."

"My services are at your disposal," said I, for just at that moment it seemed to me that to assist Marley's Ghost and the Ghost of Hamlet's Father was the only aim of my life.

"We are about to organize a club," went on the spirit of Jacob Marley, "of Ghosts Who Became Famous. Now, you will readily see that such a club should be kept very select and none admitted to membership except those who are unquestionably famous."

"And myriads there be,"

broke in the Ghost of Hamlet's Father,

"whose natural gifts

Are poor to these of mine; and yet they come

With pomp and circumstance-to join our ranks."

"I sympathize with you," I said, and sincerely, "for I know how difficult it is to keep undesirable members out of a club; and, without question, you two gentlemen, as the most famous ghosts of all time, are qualified to judge an applicant's claims."

"That is true," said Marley's Ghost; "but though we are the most famed, others also have won lasting recognition. But they are few. It would surprise you to know how few ghosts have become really famous. However, such ones as we have invited to be charter members of our club will arrive here at midnight, in charge of Captain Vanderdecken, on the good ship *The Flying Dutchman*. Of course you understand that when we selected this house and this room for our meeting it was on the supposition that you would spend Christmas in your city home, and this house would be unoccupied, as it has been all winter."

"It is indeed awkward," said I, "for though I would gladly leave to-morrow, and take my family, yet I can't ask my guests to go away so suddenly. But stay; I have an idea. You don't want this room until midnight. Suppose I defer our Christmas tree until Christmas morning. Then if I can make everybody go to bed before midnight the coast will be clear for you."

My spectral guests were delighted with this plan, and, as an expression of their gratitude, invited me to be present at the club meeting.

This was exactly what I wanted, and I accepted their invitation with pleasure.

"You are sure you can arrange matters so as to have this room vacated by midnight?" said Marley's Ghost, anxiously.

"I am sure of it," said I, for I resolved that I would do so, even if I were obliged forcibly to eject my guests.

"Swear!" said the Ghost of Hamlet's Father, in his stagy way.

"I swear it," I said earnestly.

As there were no cocks to crow, down at the sea-shore, I wondered if my guests would know when to depart; but even as I wondered, they disappeared slowly, like a dissolving view, and I was left alone.

I returned to my bed, and lay there, thinking how I should persuade Gertrude to consent to deferring the Christmas celebration as I wished.

But it was not difficult. She readily agreed that the tree would much better be exhibited on Christmas morning, for then our baby boy could enjoy it in its first glory, a pleasure which would be denied him at night.

On Christmas eve, then, I hurried every one off to bed well before midnight; and when the clock struck twelve, I arose, earnestly hoping that every one else in the house was asleep.

I softly descended the stairs, feeling again that impelling force, but by no means inclined to resist it.

When I entered the parlor, where the gaily trimmed tree stood in one corner, it was quite dark, save for the semi-luminous presence of several ghosts.

I at once recognized the Ghost of Hamlet's Father, who was stalking up and down.

Marley's Ghost was talking to three other spirits, whom I knew at once for the Ghost of Christmas Past, the Ghost of Christmas Present, and the Ghost of Christmas Yet to Come.

The Ghost of Hamlet's Father seemed too preoccupied to pay much attention to me, but Marley's Ghost was exceedingly polite, and told me who the various phantoms were.

"That," said he, pointing to a tall, gloomy specter, "is Banquo's Ghost; and this"—indicating another, in huntsman's garb—"is Herne the Hunter."

Cesar's Ghost I recognized for myself, and the noble figure, in its Roman drapery, must have thrilled Brutus when it appeared to him before the battle of Philippi.

The Headless Horseman seemed to be one of the most important ghosts, and the Hessian trooper looked especially weird, as he carried his head under his arm, and often carelessly left it lying around on a chair or table.

The Skeleton in Armor rattled about with a good deal of dignity. He wasn't as ghostly-looking as the others, but he was quite as ghastly.

One absurd and ridiculous-looking little specter was capering about with a saucy grin on his round, Brownie-like face. He was especially white, vapory, and wavy, and I knew him at once for the Phantom in Lewis Carroll's "Phantasmagoria." He skipped up and down the room and perched on chair-backs or table-tops, and continually instructed the more dignified specters concerning certain Maxims of Behavior, although very little heed was paid to his chatter.

Suddenly eleven spirits entered at once.

"Who are they?" I whispered to Marley's Ghost.

"Those are the various ghosts," he replied, "which appeared to King Richard III when he was in his tent in Bosworth Field. Of course you recognize the Tower Princes."

"Yes," said I, looking at the misty shapes of two beautiful children, who were like and yet unlike the familiar picture of them.

Queen Anne, too, I knew, and King Henry VI; but Buckingham, Clarence, and the others were to me simply picturesque phantoms, and I did not know which was which.

Marley's Ghost answered my questions politely, but I could see his attention was otherwise attracted, and he was covertly listening to a controversy which was going on between the Ghost of Hamlet's Father and the Headless Horseman.

"What is the trouble?" said I. "The trouble is," replied Marley's Ghost, "that there are three ghosts who want to belong to the club, and Hamlet doesn't want them. He thinks they aren't sufficiently famous; and as, when the club is formed, Hamlet will doubtless be elected president, of course his opinion must be considered. But the Headless Horseman thinks these doubtful members should come in."

"Who are they?" I asked.

"There they stand," said Marley's Ghost, pointing to three phantom figures that stood apart from the rest.

Two seemed to be companions—a tall, erect man, with close-curling red hair and queer red whiskers, and a woman in black, pale, and with a dreadful face.

The other ghost stood alone, and seemed rather morose and dejected, though apparently the spirit of a well-to-do gentleman.

"Those two together," said Marley's Ghost, "are Peter Quint and Miss Jessel."

"And who are they?" said I.

"Ah, you don't know!" said Marley's Ghost, with an air of satisfaction. "That strengthens my opinion that they are not famous; and yet they claim that they are well known in literary circles. They are characters in Henry James's 'The Two Magics.'"

"Never read it," said I; "but of course they're not famous at all, compared with you and old Hamlet."

"No," said Marley's Ghost, and he might be pardoned for clanking his chain a little ostentatiously, "but then, of course, they're younger. A hundred years hence, perhaps—"

"Yes," said I, "perhaps. And now, who is the dissatisfied-looking gentleman near them?"

"That," said Marley's Ghost, "is Tomlinson."

"Ah," said I, "Kipling's Tomlinson. I know him."

"Yes? And do you call him famous?"

"It's so hard to say," I answered. "To my mind, he is worthy of fame, but many readers do not agree with me. And he, too, is young."

"Yes," said Marley's Ghost, "but I was famous when very young. Why, the ghosts of Nell Cook and the Drummer of Salisbury Plain in the 'Ingoldsby Legends,' or even Gilbert's Phantom Curate, are better known than they."

"Yes," said I, thoughtfully, "or the extremely up-to-date ghosts of Frank R. Stockton, John Kendrick Bangs, and F. Marion Crawford."

The discussion became more general, and soon all the ghosts were arguing the question of "What is fame?" Peter Quint loudly asserted his claims on the ground that his author was the most famous of living novelists. "That may be," said Marley's Ghost, "but I am personally acquainted with a living gentleman who says he never read 'The Two Magics.'"

"Pooh!" said the Ghost of Peter Quint, "fame does not necessarily imply popularity. Because it was not one of the six best-selling books is no reason why the book I am in should not be considered famous. My author would scorn to be popular, but all the world calls him famous. Therefore I am famous."

Some ghosts differed with him in this opinion, but they let the question pass, saying that it mattered not about one's author, but certainly Peter Quint and Miss Jessel could by no means be considered famous characters.

"'Infamous' would describe them better," growled the Headless Horseman. He was sitting near me at the time, but as his head was lying on a window-seat across the room, the voice came from there, and the effect was extremely weird.

Tomlinson's principal claim was also on his author's reputation, and Marley's Ghost sagaciously opined that "after a hundred years he too, perhaps—"

Most of the ghosts were slow of thought and deliberate of speech, and the consequence was that they hadn't begun to organize their club, but were still mulling over the question of "What makes one famous?" when I heard footsteps in the room above, and knew that Gertrude had arisen.

Then I heard other footsteps of a childish, pattering nature, and I realized that my son and heir was already awake and would soon descend in search of his promised Christmas tree. Here was a predicament. If Gertrude or Baby Frederick should see these ghostly visitors they would faint and yell respectively. But how could I induce the club to adjourn?

I explained my difficulty to the Ghost of Queen Anne, who, being a woman, might have sympathy for Gertrude and the child.

But she only said, with an air of finality:

"Ghosts never depart until cockcrow."

At this I was in despair, for, as I have said, there were no cocks at Beachhurst. The situation was desperate. Already I could hear Gertrude and little Frederick on the stairs.

I thought of appealing to the Ghost of Hamlet's Father, but he was in the midst of a resounding speech in blank verse, and I felt sure he would not even notice me. Marley's Ghost was talking to the Skeleton in Armor, and by the clanking chains and the rattling bones I knew they were having a fierce argument, and I could not hope to gain their attention. The footsteps sounded farther down the stairs.

In despair, I cast my eyes at the tree, intended to give my son so much pleasure, and on it I happened to see a mechanical rooster. With a sudden inspiration I seized the toy and wound it up, and a loud and very natural crow was the result.

There was a swishing sound, a final clanking and rattling, and in an instant every ghost had disappeared.

To make assurance doubly sure, I wound up the rooster again, and when my wife and baby appeared on the scene, I greeted them with "A Merry Christmas!"

A GHOST-CHILD
by
Bernard Capes
1906

In making this confession public, I am aware that I am giving a butterfly to be broken on a wheel. There is so much of delicacy in its subject, that the mere resolve to handle it at all might seem to imply a lack of the sensitiveness necessary to its understanding; and it is certain that the more reverent the touch, the more irresistible will figure its opportunity to the common scepticism which is bondslave to its five senses. Moreover one cannot, in the reason of things, write to publish for Aristarchus alone; but the gauntlet of Grub Street must be run in any bid for truth and sincerity.

On the other hand, to withhold from evidence, in these days of what one may call a zetetic psychology, anything which may appear elucidatory, however exquisitely and rarely, of our spiritual relationships, must be pronounced, I think, a sin against the Holy Ghost.

All in all, therefore, I decide to give, with every passage to personal identification safeguarded, the story of a possession, or visitation, which is signified in the title to my narrative.

Tryphena was the sole orphaned representative of an obscure but gentle family which had lived for generations in the east of England. The spirit of the fens, of the long grey marshes, whose shores are the neutral ground of two elements, slumbered in her eyes. Looking into them, one seemed to see little beds of tiny green mosses luminous under water, or stirred by the movement of microscopic life in their midst. Secrets, one felt, were shadowed in their depths, too frail and sweet for understanding. The pretty love-fancy of babies seen in the eyes of maidens, was in hers to be interpreted into the very cosmic dust of sea-urchins, sparkling like chrysoberyls. Her soul looked out through them, as if they were the windows of a water-nursery.

She was always a child among children, in heart and knowledge most innocent, until Jason came and stood in her field of vision. Then spirit of the neutral ground as she was, inclining to earth or water with the sway of the tides, she came wondering and dripping, as it were, to land, and took up her abode for final choice among the daughters of the earth. She knew her woman's estate, in fact, and the irresistible attraction of all completed perfections to the light that burns to destroy them.

Tryphena was not only an orphan, but an heiress. Her considerable estate was administered by her guardian, Jason's father, a widower, who was possessed of this single adored child. The fruits of parental infatuation had come early to ripen on the seedling. The boy was self-willed and perverse, the more so as he was naturally of a hot-hearted disposition. Violence and remorse would sway him in alternate moods, and be made, each in its turn, a self-indulgence. He took a delight in crossing his father's wishes, and no less in atoning for his gracelessness with moving demonstrations of affection.

Foremost of the old man's most cherished projects was, very naturally, a union between the two young people. He planned, manoeuvred, spoke for it with all his heart of love and eloquence.

And, indeed, it seemed at last as if his hopes were to be crowned. Jason, returning from a lengthy voyage (for his enterprising spirit had early decided for the sea, and he was a naval officer), saw, and was struck amazed before, the transformed vision of his old child-play-fellow. She was an opened flower whom he had left a green bud—a thing so rare and flawless that it seemed a sacrilege for earthly passions to converse of her. Familiarity, however, and some sense of reciprocal attraction, quickly dethroned that eucharist. Tryphena could blush, could thrill, could solicit, in the sweet ways of innocent womanhood. She loved him dearly, wholly, it was plain—had found the realisation of her old formless dreams in this wondrous birth of a desire for one, in whose new-impassioned eves she had known herself reflected hitherto only for the most patronised of small gossips. And, for her part, fearless as nature, she made no secret of her love.

She was absorbed in, a captive to, Jason from that moment and for ever.

He responded. What man, however perverse, could have resisted, on first appeal, the attraction of such beauty, the flower of a radiant soul? The two were betrothed; the old man's cup of happiness was brimmed.

Then came clouds and a cold wind, chilling the garden of Hesperis. Jason was always one of those who, possessing classic noses, will cut them off, on easy provocation, to spite their faces.

He was so proudly independent, to himself, that he resented the least assumption of proprietorship in him on the part of other people—even of those who had the best claim to his love and submission. This pride was an obsession. It stultified the real good in him, which was considerable. Apart from it, he was a good, warm-tempered fellow, hasty but affectionate. Under its dominion, he would have broken his own heart on an imaginary grievance.

He found one, it is to be supposed, in the privileges assumed by love; in its exacting claims upon him; perhaps in its little unreasoning jealousies. He distorted these into an implied conceit of authority over him on the part of an heiress who was condescending to his meaner fortunes.

The suggestion was quite base and without warrant; but pride has no balance. No doubt, moreover, the rather childish self-depreciations of the old man, his father, in his attitude towards a match he had so fondly desired, helped to aggravate this feeling. The upshot was that, when within a few months of the date which was to make his union with Tryphena eternal, Jason broke away from a restraint which his pride pictured to him as intolerable, and went on a yachting expedition with a friend.

Then, at once, and with characteristic violence, came the reaction. He wrote, impetuously, frenziedly, from a distant port, claiming himself Tryphena's, and Tryphena his, for ever and ever and ever. They were man and wife before God. He had behaved like an insensate brute, and he was at that moment starting to speed to her side, to beg her forgiveness and the return of her love.

He had no need to play the suitor afresh. She had never doubted or questioned their mutual bondage, and would have died a maid for his sake. Something of sweet exultation only seemed to quicken and leap in her body, that her faith in her dear love was vindicated.

But the joy came near to upset the reason of the old man, already tottering to its dotage; and what followed destroyed it utterly.

The yacht, flying home, was lost at sea, and Jason was drowned.

I once saw Tryphena about this time. She lived with her near mindless charge, lonely, in an old grey house upon the borders of a salt mere, and had little but the unearthly cries of seabirds to answer to the questions of her widowed heart. She worked, sweet in charity, among the marsh folk, a beautiful unearthly presence; and was especially to be found where infants and the troubles of child-bearing women called for her help and sympathy. She was a wife herself, she would say quaintly; and some day perhaps, by grace of the good spirits of the sea, would be a mother. None thought to cross her statement, put with so sweet a sanity; and, indeed, I have often noticed that the neighbourhood of great waters breeds in souls a mysticism which is remote from the very understanding of land-dwellers.

How I saw her was thus:—I was fishing, on a day of chill calm, in a dinghy off the flat coast.

The stillness of the morning had tempted me some distance from the village where I was staying. Presently a sense of bad sport and healthy famine 'plumped' in me, so to speak, for luncheon, and I looked about for a spot picturesque enough to add a zest to sandwiches, whisky, and tobacco. Close by, a little creek or estuary ran up into a mere, between which and the sea lay a cluster of low sand-hills; and thither I pulled. The spot, when I reached it, was calm, chill desolation manifest—lifeless water and lifeless sand, with no traffic between them but the dead interchange of salt. Low sedges, at first, and behind them low woods were mirrored in the water at a distance, with an interval between me and them of sheeted glass; and right across this shining pool ran a dim, half-drowned causeway—the sea-path, it appeared, to and from a lonely house which I could just distinguish squatting among trees. It was Tryphena's house.

Now, paddling dispiritedly, I turned a cold dune, and saw a mermaid before me. At least, that was my instant impression. The creature sat coiled on the strand, combing her hair—that was certain, for I saw the gold-green tresses of it whisked by her action into rainbow threads. It appeared as certain that her upper half was flesh and her lower fish; and it was only on my nearer approach that this latter resolved itself into a pale green skirt, roped, owing to her posture, about her limbs, and the hem fanned out at her feet into a tail fin. Thus also her bosom, which had appeared naked, became a bodice, as near to her flesh in colour and texture as a smock is to a lady's-smock, which some call a cuckoo-flower.

It was plain enough now; yet the illusion for the moment had quite startled me.

As I came near, she paused in her strange business to canvass me. It was Tryphena herself, as after-inquiry informed me. I have never seen so lovely a creature. Her eyes, as they regarded me passing, were something to haunt a dream: so great in tragedy— not fathomless, but all in motion near their surfaces, it seemed, with green and rooted sorrows. They were the eyes, I thought, of an Undine late-humanised, late awakened to the rapturous and troubled knowledge of the woman's burden. Her forehead was most fair, and the glistening thatch divided on it like a golden cloud revealing the face of a wondering angel.

I passed, and a sand-heap stole my vision foot by foot. The vision was gone when I returned. I have reason to believe it was vouchsafed me within a few months of the coming of the ghost-child.

On the morning succeeding the night of the day on which Jason and Tryphena were to have been married, the girl came down from her bedroom with an extraordinary expression of still rapture on her face. After breakfast she took the old man into her confidence. She was childish still; her manner quite youthfully thrilling; but now there was a newborn wonder in it that hovered on the pink of shame.

'Father! I have been under the deep waters and found him. He came to me last night in my dreams—so sobbing, so impassioned—to assure me that he had never really ceased to love me, though he had near broken his own heart pretending it. Poor boy! poor ghost! What could I do but take him to my arms? And all night he lay there, blest and forgiven, till in the morning he melted away with a sigh that woke me; and it seemed to me that I came up dripping from the sea.'

'My boy! He has come back!' chuckled the old man. 'What have you done with him, Tryphena?'

'I will hold him tighter the next time,' she said.

But the spirit of Jason visited her dreams no more.

That was in March. In the Christmas following, when the mere was locked in stillness, and the wan reflection of snow mingled on the ceiling with the red dance of firelight, one morning the old man came hurrying and panting to Tryphena's door.

'Tryphena! Come down quickly! My boy, my Jason, has come back! It was a lie that they told us about his being lost at sea!'

Her heart leapt like a candle-flame! What new delusion of the old man's was this? She hurried over her dressing and descended. A garrulous old voice mingled with a childish treble in the breakfast-room. Hardly breathing, she turned the handle of the door, and saw Jason before her.

But it was Jason, the prattling babe of her first knowledge; Jason, the flaxen-headed, apple-cheeked cherub of the nursery; Jason, the confiding, the merry, the loving, before pride had come to warp his innocence. She fell on her knees to the child, and with a burst of ecstasy caught him to her heart.

She asked no question of the old man as to when or whence this apparition had come, or why he was here. For some reason she dared not. She accepted him as some waif, whom an accidental likeness had made glorious to their hungering hearts. As for the father, he was utterly satisfied and content. He had heard a knock at the door, he said, and had opened it and found this. The child was naked, and his pink, wet body glazed with ice. Yet he seemed insensible to the killing cold. It was Jason—that was enough. There is no date nor time for imbecility. Its phantoms spring from the clash of ancient memories. This was just as actually his child as—more so, in fact, than—the grown young figure which, for all its manhood, had dissolved into the mist of waters. He was more familiar with, more confident of it, after all. It had come back to be unquestioningly dependent on him; and that was likest the real Jason, flesh of his flesh.

'Who are you, darling?' said Tryphena.

'I am Jason,' answered the child.

She wept, and fondled him rapturously.

'And who am I?' she asked. 'If you are Jason, you must know what to call me.'

'I know,' he said; 'but I mustn't, unless you ask me.'

'I won't,' she answered, with a burst of weeping. 'It is Christmas Day, dearest, when the miracle of a little child was wrought. I will ask you nothing but to stay and bless our desolate home.'

He nodded, laughing.

'I will stay, until you ask me.'

They found some little old robes of the baby Jason, put away in lavender, and dressed him in them. All day he laughed and prattled; yet it was strange that, talk as he might, he never once referred to matters familiar to the childhood of the lost sailor.

In the early afternoon he asked to be taken out—seawards, that was his wish. Tryphena clothed him warmly, and, taking his little hand, led him away. They left the old man sleeping peacefully.

He was never to wake again.

As they crossed the narrow causeway, snow, thick and silent, began to fall. Tryphena was not afraid, for herself or the child. A rapture upheld her; a sense of some compelling happiness, which she knew before long must take shape on her lips.

They reached the seaward dunes—mere ghosts of foothold in that smoke of flakes. The lap of vast waters seemed all around them, hollow and mysterious. The sound flooded Tryphena's ears, drowning her senses. She cried out, and stopped.

'Before they go,' she screamed—'before they go, tell me what you were to call me!' The child sprang a little distance, and stood facing her. Already his lower limbs seemed dissolving in the mists.

'I was to call you mother!' he cried, with a smile and toss of his hand.

Even as he spoke, his pretty features wavered and vanished. The snow broke into him, or he became part with it. Where he had been, a gleam of iridescent dust seemed to show one moment before it sank and was extinguished in the falling cloud. Then there was only the snow, heaping an eternal chaos with nothingness.

Tryphena made this confession, on a Christmas Eve night, to one who was a believer in dreams. The next morning she was seen to cross the causeway, and thereafter was never seen again. But she left the sweetest memory behind her, for human charity, and an elf-life gift of loveliness.

AFTERWARD
by
Edith Wharton
1910

Illustrated by E. L. Blumenschein
Half tone plate engraved by H. Davidson

I

"Oh, there *is* one, of course, but you'll never know it."

The assertion, laughingly flung out six months earlier in a bright June garden, came back to Mary Boyne with a sharp perception of its latent significance as she stood, in the December dusk, waiting for the lamps to be brought into the library.

The words had been spoken by their friend Alida Stair, as they sat at tea on her lawn at Pangbourne, in reference to the very house of which the library in question was the central, the pivotal "feature." Mary Boyne and her husband, in quest of a country place in one of the southern or southwestern counties, had, on their arrival in England, carried their problem straight to Alida Stair, who had successfully solved it in her own case; but it was not until they had rejected, almost capriciously, several practical and judicious suggestions that she threw it out: "Well, there's Lyng, in Dorsetshire. It belongs to Hugo's cousins, and you can get it for a song."

The reason she gave for its being obtainable on these terms—its remoteness from a station, its lack of electric light, hot-water pipes, and other vulgar necessities—were exactly those pleading in its favour with two romantic Americans perversely in search of the economic drawbacks which were associated, in their tradition, with unusual architectural felicities.

"I should never believe I was living in an old house unless I was thoroughly uncomfortable," Ned Boyne, the more extravagant of the two, had jocosely insisted; "the least hint of 'convenience' would make me think it had been bought out of an exhibition, with the pieces numbered, and set up again." And they had proceeded to enumerate, with humorous precision, their various suspicions and exactions, refusing to believe that the house their cousin recommended was *really* Tudor till they learned it had no heating system, or that the village church was literally in the grounds till she assured them of the deplorable uncertainty of the water-supply.

"It's too uncomfortable to be true!" Edward Boyne had continued to exult as the avowal of each disadvantage was successively wrung from her; but he had cut short his rhapsody to ask, with a sudden relapse to distrust: "And the ghost? You've been concealing from us the fact that there is no ghost!"

Mary, at the moment, had laughed with him, yet almost with her laugh, being possessed of several sets of independent perceptions, had noted a sudden flatness of tone in Alida's answering hilarity.

"Oh, Dorsetshire's full of ghosts, you know."

"Yes, yes; but that won't do. I don't want to have to drive ten miles to see somebody else's ghost. I want one of my own on the premises. *Is* there a ghost at Lyng?"

His rejoinder had made Alida laugh again, and it was then that she had flung back tantalisingly: "Oh, there *is* one, of course, but you'll never know it."

"Never know it?" Boyne pulled her up. "But what in the world constitutes a ghost except the fact of its being known for one?"

"I can't say. But that's the story."

"That there's a ghost, but that nobody knows it's a ghost?"

"Well—not till afterward, at any rate."

"Till afterward?"

"Not till long, long afterward."

"But if it's once been identified as an unearthly visitant, why hasn't its *signalement* been handed down in the family? How has it managed to preserve its incognito?"

Alida could only shake her head. "Don't ask me. But it has."

"And then suddenly——" Mary spoke up as if from some cavernous depth of divination—"suddenly, long afterward, one says to one's self, '*That was it?*'"

She was oddly startled at the sepulchral sound with which her question fell on the banter of the other two, and she saw the shadow of the same surprise flit across Alida's clear pupils. "I suppose so. One just has to wait."

"Oh, hang waiting!" Ned broke in. "Life's too short for a ghost who can only be enjoyed in retrospect. Can't we do better than that, Mary?"

But it turned out that in the event they were not destined to, for within three months of their conversation with Mrs. Stair they were established at Lyng, and the life they had yearned for to the point of planning it out in all its daily details had actually begun for them.

It was to sit, in the thick December dusk, by just such a wide-hooded fireplace, under just such black oak rafters, with the sense that beyond the mullioned panes the downs were darkening to a deeper solitude: it was for the ultimate indulgence in such sensations that Mary Boyne had endured for nearly fourteen years the soul-deadening ugliness of the Middle West, and that Boyne had ground on doggedly at his engineering till, with a suddenness that still made her blink, the prodigious windfall of the Blue Star Mine had put them at a stroke in possession of life and the leisure to taste it. They had never for a moment meant their new state to be one of idleness; but they meant to give themselves only to harmonious activities. She had her vision of painting and gardening (against a background of grey walls), he dreamed of the production of his long-planned book on the "Economic Basis of Culture"; and with such absorbing work ahead no existence could be too sequestered; they could not get far enough from the world, or plunge deep enough into the past.

Dorsetshire had attracted them from the first by a semblance of remoteness out of all proportion to its geographical position. But to the Boynes it was one of the ever-recurring wonders of the whole incredibly compressed island—a nest of counties, as they put it—that for the production of its effects so little of a given quality went so far: that so few miles made a distance, and so short a distance a difference.

"It's that," Ned had once enthusiastically explained, "that gives such depth to their effects, such relief to their least contrasts. They've been able to lay the butter so thick on every exquisite mouthful."

The butter had certainly been laid on thick at Lyng: the old grey house, hidden under a shoulder of the downs, had almost all the finer marks of commerce with a protracted past. The mere fact that it was neither large nor exceptional made it, to the Boynes, abound the more completely in its special charm—the charm of having been for centuries a deep dim reservoir of life. The life had probably not been of the most vivid order: for long periods, no doubt, it had fallen as noiselessly into the past as the quiet drizzle of autumn fell, hour after hour, into the fish-pond between the yews; but these back-waters of existence sometimes breed, in their sluggish depths, strange acuities of emotion, and Mary Boyne had felt from the first the occasional brush of an intenser memory.

The feeling had never been stronger than on the December afternoon when, waiting in the library for the belated lamps, she rose from her seat and stood among the shadows of the hearth. Her husband had gone off, after luncheon, for one of his long tramps on the downs. She had noticed of late that he preferred to go alone; and, in the tried security of their personal relations, had been driven to conclude that his book was bothering him, and that he needed the afternoons to turn over in solitude the problems left from the morning's work. Certainly the book was not going as smoothly as she had imagined it would, and there were lines of perplexity between his eyes such as had never been there in his engineering days. He had often, then, looked fagged to the verge of illness, but the native demon of "worry" had never branded his brow. Yet the few pages he had so far read to her—the introduction, and a summary of the opening chapter—showed a firm hold on his subject, and an increasing confidence in his powers.

The fact threw her into deeper perplexity, since, now that he had done with "business" and its disturbing contingencies, the one other possible element of anxiety was eliminated. Unless it were his health, then? But physically he had gained since they had come to Dorsetshire, grown robuster, ruddier, and fresher-eyed. It was only within a week that she had felt in him the undefinable change that made her restless in his absence, and as tongue-tied in his presence as though it were *she* who had a secret to keep from him!

The thought that there *was* a secret somewhere between them struck her with a sudden smart rap of wonder, and she looked about her down the long room.

"Can it be the house?" she mused.

The room itself might have been full of secrets. They seemed to be piling themselves up, as evening fell, like the layers and layers of velvet shadow dropping from the low ceiling, the rows of books, the smoke-blurred sculpture of the hooded hearth.

"Why, of course—the house is haunted!" she reflected.

The ghost—Alida's imperceptible ghost—after figuring largely in the banter of their first month or two at Lyng, had been gradually discarded as too ineffectual for imaginative use. Mary had, indeed, as became the tenant of a haunted house, made the customary inquiries among her few rural neighbours, but, beyond a vague, "They dü say so, Ma'am," the villagers had nothing to impart. The elusive spectre had apparently never had sufficient identity for a legend to crystallise about it, and after a time the Boynes had laughingly set the matter down to their profit-and-loss account, agreeing that Lyng was one of the few houses good enough in itself to dispense with supernatural enhancements.

"And I suppose, poor, ineffectual demon, that's why it beats its beautiful wings in vain in the void," Mary had laughingly concluded.

"Or, rather," Ned answered, in the same strain, "why, amid so much that's ghostly, it can never affirm its separate existence as *the* ghost." And thereupon their invisible housemate had finally dropped out of their references, which were numerous enough to make them promptly unaware of the loss.

Now, as she stood on the hearth, the subject of their earlier curiosity revived in her with a new sense of its meaning—a sense gradually acquired through close daily contact with the scene of the lurking mystery. It was the house itself, of course, that possessed the ghost-seeing faculty, that communed visually but secretly with its own past; and if one could only get into close enough communion with the house, one might surprise its secret, and acquire the ghost-sight on one's own account. Perhaps, in his long solitary hours in this very room, where she never trespassed till the afternoon, her husband *had* acquired it already, and was silently carrying the weight of whatever it had revealed to him. Mary was too well versed in the code of the spectral world not to know that one could not talk about the ghosts one saw: to do so was almost as great a breach of taste as to name a lady in a club. But this explanation did not really satisfy her. "What, after all, except for the fun of the *frisson*," she reflected, "would he really care for any of their old ghosts?" And thence she was thrown back once more on the fundamental dilemma: the fact that one's greater or less susceptibility to spectral influences had no particular bearing on the case, since, when one *did* see a ghost at Lyng, one did not know it.

"Not till long afterward," Alida Stair had said. Well, supposing Ned *had* seen one when they first came, and had known only within the last week what had happened to him? More and more under the spell of the hour, she threw back her thoughts to the early days of their tenancy, but at first only to recall a gay confusion of unpacking, settling, arranging of books, and calling to each other from remote corners of the house as treasure after treasure of their habitation revealed itself to them. It was in this particular connection that she presently recalled a certain soft afternoon of the previous October, when, passing from the first rapturous flurry of exploration to a detailed inspection of the old house, she had pressed (like a novel heroine) a panel that opened on a narrow flight of stairs leading to an unsuspected flat ledge of the roof—the roof which, from below, seemed to slope away on all sides too abruptly for any but practised feet to scale.

The view from this hidden coign was enchanting, and she had flown down to snatch Ned from his papers and give him the freedom of her discovery. She remembered still how, standing on the narrow ledge, he had passed his arm about her while their gaze flew to the long, tossed horizon-line of the downs, and then dropped contentedly back to trace the arabesque of yew hedges about the fish-pond, and the shadow of the cedar on the lawn.

"And now the other way," he had said, gently turning her about within his arm; and closely pressed to him, she had absorbed, like some long, satisfying draft, the picture of the grey-walled court, the squat lions on the gates, and the lime-avenue reaching up to the highroad under the downs.

It was just then, while they gazed and held each other, that she had felt his arm relax, and heard a sharp "Hullo!" that made her turn to glance at him.

Distinctly, yes, she now recalled she had seen, as she glanced, a shadow of anxiety, of perplexity, rather, fall across his face; and, following his eyes, had beheld the figure of a man—a man in loose, greyish clothes, as it appeared to her—who was sauntering down the lime-avenue to the court with the tentative gait of a stranger seeking his way. Her short-sighted eyes had given her but a blurred impression of slightness and greyness, with something foreign, or at least unlocal, in the cut of the figure or its dress; but her husband had apparently seen more—seen enough to make him push past her with a sharp "Wait!" and dash down the twisting stairs without pausing to give her a hand.

A slight tendency to dizziness obliged her, after a provisional clutch at the chimney against which they had been leaning, to follow him first more cautiously; and when she had reached the attic landing she paused again, for a less definite reason, leaning over the oak banister to strain her eyes through the silence of the brown, sun-flecked depths. She lingered there till, somewhere in those depths, she heard the closing of a door; then, mechanically impelled, she went down the shallow flights of steps till she reached the lower hall.

The front door stood open on the sunlight of the court, and hall and court were empty. The library door was open, too, and after listening in vain for any sound of voices within, she quickly crossed the threshold, and found her husband alone, vaguely fingering the papers on his desk.

He looked up, as if surprised at her entrance, but the shadow of anxiety had passed from his face, leaving it even, as she fancied, a little brighter and clearer than usual.

"What was it? Who was it?" she asked.

"Who?" he repeated, with the surprise still all on his side.

"The man we saw coming toward the house."

He seemed to reflect. "The man? Why, I thought I saw Peters; I dashed after him to say a word about the stable drains, but he had disappeared before I could get down."

"Disappeared? But he seemed to be walking so slowly when we saw him."

Boyne shrugged his shoulders. "So I thought; but he must have got up steam in the interval. What do you say to our trying a scramble up Meldon Steep before sunset?"

That was all. At the time the occurrence had been less than nothing, had, indeed, been immediately obliterated by the magic of their first vision from Meldon Steep, a height which they had dreamed of climbing ever since they had first seen its bare spine heaving itself above the low roof of Lyng. Doubtless it was the mere fact of the other incident's having occurred on the very day of their ascent to Meldon that had kept it stored away in the unconscious fold of association from which it now emerged; for in itself it had no mark of the portentous. At the moment there could have been nothing more natural than that Ned should dash himself from the roof in the pursuit of dilatory tradesmen. It was the period when they were always on the watch for one or the other of the specialists employed about the place; always lying in wait for them, and dashing out at them with questions, reproaches, or reminders. And certainly in the distance the grey figure had looked like Peters.

Yet now, as she reviewed the rapid scene, she felt her husband's explanation of it to have been invalidated by the look of anxiety on his face. Why had the familiar appearance of Peters made him anxious? Why, above all, if it was of such prime necessity to confer with that authority on the subject of the stable drains, had the failure to find him produced such a look of relief? Mary could not say that any one of these considerations had occurred to her at the time, yet, from the promptness with which they now marshalled themselves at her summons, she had a sudden sense that they must all along have been there, waiting their hour.

II

WEARY with her thoughts, she moved toward the window. The library was now completely dark, and she was surprised to see how much faint light the outer world still held.

As she peered out into it across the court, a figure shaped itself in the tapering perspective of bare lines: it looked a mere blot of deeper grey in the greyness, and for an instant, as it moved toward her, her heart thumped to the thought, "It's the ghost!"

She had time, in that long instant, to feel suddenly that the man of whom, two months earlier, she had a brief distant vision from the roof was now, at his predestined hour, about to reveal himself as *not* having been Peters; and her spirit sank under the impending fear of the disclosure. But almost with the next tick of the clock the ambiguous figure, gaining substance and character, showed itself even to her weak sight as her husband's; and she turned away to meet him, as he entered, with the confession of her folly.

"It's really too absurd," she laughed out from the threshold, "but I never *can* remember!"

"Remember what?" Boyne questioned as they drew together.

"That when one sees the Lyng ghost one never knows it."

Her hand was on his sleeve, and he kept it there, but with no response in his gesture or in the lines of his fagged, preoccupied face.

"Did you think you'd seen it?" he asked, after an appreciable interval.

"Why, I actually took *you* for it, my dear, in my mad determination to spot it!"

"Me—just now?" His arm dropped away, and he turned from her with a faint echo of her laugh. "Really, dearest, you'd better give it up, if that's the best you can do."

"Yes, I give it up—I give it up. Have *you?*" she asked, turning round on him abruptly.

The parlour-maid had entered with letters and a lamp, and the light struck up into Boyne's face as he bent above the tray she presented.

"Have *you?*" Mary perversely insisted, when the servant had disappeared on her errand of illumination.

"Have I what?" he rejoined absently, the light bringing out the sharp stamp of worry between his brows as he turned over the letters.

"Given up trying to see the ghost." Her heart beat a little at the experiment she was making.

Her husband, laying his letters aside, moved away into the shadow of the hearth.

"I never tried," he said, tearing open the wrapper of a newspaper.

"Well, of course," Mary persisted, "the exasperating thing is that there's no use trying, since one can't be sure till so long afterward."

He was unfolding the paper as if he had hardly heard her; but after a pause, during which the sheets rustled spasmodically between his hands, he lifted his head to say abruptly, "Have you any idea *how long?*"

Mary had sunk into a low chair beside the fireplace. From her seat she looked up, startled, at her husband's profile, which was darkly projected against the circle of lamplight.

"No; none. Have *you?*" she retorted, repeating her former phrase with an added keenness of intention.

Boyne crumpled the paper into a bunch, and then inconsequently turned back with it toward the lamp.

"Lord, no! I only meant," he explained, with a faint tinge of impatience, "is there any legend, any tradition, as to that?"

"Not that I know of," she answered; but the impulse to add, "What makes you ask?" was checked by the reappearance of the parlour-maid with tea and a second lamp.

With the dispersal of shadows, and the repetition of the daily domestic office, Mary Boyne felt herself less oppressed by that sense of something mutely imminent which had darkened her solitary afternoon. For a few moments she gave herself silently to the details of her task, and when she looked up from it she was struck to the point of bewilderment by the change in her husband's face. He had seated himself near the farther lamp, and was absorbed in the perusal of his letters; but was it something he had found in them, or merely the shifting of her own point of view, that had restored his features to their normal aspect? The longer she looked, the more definitely the change affirmed itself. The lines of tension had vanished, and such traces of fatigue as lingered were of the kind easily attributable to steady mental effort. He glanced up, as if drawn by her gaze, and met her eyes with a smile.

"I'm dying for my tea, you know; and here's a letter for you," he said.

She took the letter he held out in exchange for the cup she proffered him, and, returning to her seat, broke the seal with the languid gesture of the reader whose interests are all enclosed in the circle of one cherished presence.

Her next conscious motion was that of starting to her feet, the letter falling to them as she rose, while she held out to her husband a long newspaper clipping.

"Ned! What's this? What does it mean?"

He had risen at the same instant, almost as if hearing her cry before she uttered it; and for a perceptible space of time he and she studied each other, like adversaries watching for an advantage, across the space between her chair and his desk.

"What's what? You fairly made me jump!" Boyne said at length, moving toward her with a sudden, half-exasperated laugh. The shadow of apprehension was on his face again, not now a look of fixed foreboding, but a shifting vigilance of lips and eyes that gave her the sense of his feeling himself invisibly surrounded.

Her hand shook so that she could hardly give him the clipping.

"This article—from the *Waukesha Sentinel*—that a man named Elwell has brought suit against you—that there was something wrong about the Blue Star Mine. I can't understand more than half."

They continued to face each other as she spoke, and to her astonishment, she saw that her words had the almost immediate effect of dissipating the strained watchfulness of his look.

"Oh, *that!*" He glanced down the printed slip, and then folded it with the gesture of one who handles something harmless and familiar. "What's the matter with you this afternoon, Mary? I thought you'd got bad news."

She stood before him with her undefinable terror subsiding slowly under the reassuring touch of his composure.

"You knew about this, then—it's all right?"

"Certainly I knew about it; and it's all right."

"But what *is* it? I don't understand. What does this man accuse you of?"

"Oh, pretty nearly every crime in the calendar." Boyne had tossed the clipping down, and thrown himself comfortably into an arm-chair near the fire. "Do you want to hear the story? It's not particularly interesting—just a squabble over interests in the Blue Star."

"But who is this Elwell? I don't know the name."

"Oh, he's a fellow I put into it—gave him a hand up. I told you all about him at the time."

"I daresay. I must have forgotten." Vainly she strained back among her memories. "But if you helped him, why does he make this return?"

"Oh, probably some shyster lawyer got hold of him and talked him over. It's all rather technical and complicated. I thought that kind of thing bored you."

His wife felt a sting of compunction. Theoretically, she deprecated the American wife's detachment from her husband's professional interests, but in practice she had always found it difficult to fix her attention on Boyne's report of the transactions in which his varied interests involved him. Besides, she had felt from the first that, in a community where the amenities of living could be obtained only at the cost of efforts as arduous as her husband's professional labours, such brief leisure as they could command should be used as an escape from immediate preoccupations, a flight to the life they always dreamed of living. Once or twice, now that this new life had actually drawn its magic circle about them, she had asked herself if she had done right; but hitherto such conjectures had been no more than the retrospective excursions of an active fancy. Now, for the first time, it startled her a little to find how little she knew of the material foundation on which her happiness was built.

She glanced again at her husband, and was reassured by the composure of his face; yet she felt the need of more definite grounds for her reassurance.

"But doesn't this suit worry you? Why have you never spoken to me about it?"

He answered both questions at once: "I didn't speak of it at first because it *did* worry me—annoyed me, rather. But it's all ancient history now. Your correspondent must have got hold of a back number of the '*Sentinel*.'"

She felt a quick thrill of relief. "You mean it's over? He's lost his case?"

There was a just perceptible delay in Boyne's reply. "The suit's been withdrawn—that's all."

But she persisted, as if to exonerate herself from the inward charge of being too easily put off. "Withdrawn because he saw he had no chance?"

"Oh, he had no chance," Boyne answered.

She was still struggling with a dimly felt perplexity at the back of her thoughts.

"How long ago was it withdrawn?"

He paused, as if with a slight return of his former uncertainty. "I've just had the news now; but I've been expecting it."

"Just now—in one of your letters?"

"Yes; in one of my letters."

She made no answer, and was aware only, after a short interval of waiting, that he had risen, and strolling across the room, had placed himself on the sofa at her side. She felt him, as he did so, pass an arm about her, she felt his hand seek hers and clasp it, and turning slowly, drawn by the warmth of his cheek, she met the smiling clearness of his eyes.

"It's all right—it's all right?" she questioned, through the flood of her dissolving doubts; and "I give you my word it never was righter!" he laughed back at her, holding her close.

III

ONE of the strangest things she was afterward to recall out of all the next day's strangeness was the sudden and complete recovery of her sense of security.

It was in the air when she woke in her low-ceilinged, dusky room; it accompanied her down-stairs to the breakfast-table, flashed out at her from the fire, and re-duplicated itself brightly from the flanks of the urn and the sturdy flutings of the Georgian teapot. It was as if, in some roundabout way, all her diffused fears of the previous day, with their moment of sharp concentration about the newspaper article—as if this dim questioning of the future, and startled return upon the past,—had between them liquidated the arrears of some haunting moral obligation. If she had indeed been careless of her husband's affairs, it was, her new state seemed to prove, because her faith in him instinctively justified such carelessness; and his right to her faith had overwhelmingly affirmed itself in the very face of menace and suspicion. She had never seen him more untroubled, more naturally and unconsciously in possession of himself, than after the cross-examination to which she had subjected him: it was almost as if he had been aware of her lurking doubts, and had wanted the air cleared as much as she did.

It was as clear, thank Heaven! as the bright outer light that surprised her almost with a touch of summer when she issued from the house for her daily round of the gardens. She had left Boyne at his desk, indulging herself, as she passed the library door, by a last peep at his quiet face, where he bent, pipe in his mouth, above his papers, and now she had her own morning's task to perform. The task involved on such charmed winter days almost as much delighted loitering about the different quarters of her demesne as if spring were already at work on shrubs and borders. There were such endless possibilities still before her, such opportunities to bring out the latent graces of the old place, without a single irreverent touch of alteration, that the winter months were all too short to plan what spring and autumn executed. And her recovered sense of safety gave, on this particular morning, a peculiar zest to her progress through the sweet, still place. She went first to the kitchen-garden, where the espaliered pear-trees drew complicated patterns on the walls, and pigeons were fluttering and preening about the silvery-slated roof of their cot. There was something wrong about the piping of the hot-house, and she was expecting an authority from Dorchester, who was to drive out between trains and make a diagnosis of the boiler. But when she dipped into the damp heat of the greenhouses, among the spiced scents and waxy pinks and reds of old-fashioned exotics—even the flora of Lyng was in the note!—she learned that the great man had not arrived, and the day being too rare to waste in an artificial atmosphere, she came out again and paced slowly along the springy turf of the bowling-green to the gardens behind the house. At their farther end rose a grass terrace, commanding, over the fish-pond and the yew hedges, a view of the long house-front, with its twisted chimney-stacks and the blue roof angles all drenched in the pale gold moisture of the air.

Seen thus, across the level tracery of the gardens, it sent her, from its open windows and hospitably smoking chimneys, the look of some warm human presence, of a mind slowly ripened on a sunny wall of experience. She had never before had so deep a sense of her intimacy with it, such a conviction that its secrets were all beneficent, kept, as they said to children, "for one's good," so complete a trust in its power to gather up her life and Ned's into the harmonious pattern of the long, long story it sat there weaving in the sun.

She heard steps behind her, and turned, expecting to see the gardener, accompanied by the engineer from Dorchester. But only one figure was in sight, that of a youngish, slightly built man, who, for reasons she could not on the spot have specified, did not remotely resemble her preconceived notion of an authority on hot-house boilers. The new-comer, on seeing her, lifted his hat, and paused with the air of a gentleman—perhaps a traveller—desirous of having it immediately known that his intrusion is involuntary. Lyng occasionally attracted the more cultivated traveller, and Mary half-expected to see the stranger dissemble a camera, or justify his presence by producing it. But he made no gesture of any sort, and after a moment she asked, in a tone responding to the courteous deprecation of his attitude: "Is there any one you wish to see?"

"I came to see Mr. Boyne," he replied. His intonation, rather than his accent, was faintly American, and Mary, at the familiar note, looked at him more closely. The brim of his soft felt hat cast a shade on his face, which, thus obscured, wore to her short-sighted gaze a look of seriousness, as of a person arriving "on business," and civilly but firmly aware of his rights.

Past experience had made Mary equally sensible to such claims; but she was jealous of her husband's morning hours, and doubtful of his having given any one the right to intrude on them.

"Have you an appointment with Mr. Boyne?" she asked.

He hesitated, as if unprepared for the question.

"Not exactly an appointment," he replied.

"Then I'm afraid, this being his working-time that he can't receive you now. Will you give me a message, or come back later?"

The visitor, again lifting his hat, briefly replied that he would come back later, and walked away as if to regain the front of the house. As his figure receded down the walk between the yew hedges, Mary saw him pause and look up an instant at the peaceful house-front bathed in faint winter sunshine; and it struck her, with a tardy touch of compunction, that it would have been more humane to ask if he had come from a distance, and to offer, in that case, to inquire if her husband could receive him. But as the thought occurred to her he passed out of sight behind a pyramidal yew, and at the same moment her attention was distracted by the approach of the gardener, attended by the bearded pepper-and-salt figure of the boiler-maker from Dorchester.

The encounter with this authority led to such far-reaching issues that they resulted in his finding it expedient to ignore his train, and beguiled Mary into spending the remainder of the morning in absorbed confabulation among the green-houses. She was startled to find when the colloquy ended, that it was nearly luncheon-time, and she half expected, as she hurried back to the house, to see her husband coming out to meet her. But she found no one in the court but an under-gardener raking the gravel, and the hall, when she entered it, was so silent that she guessed Boyne to be still at work behind the closed door of the library.

Not wishing to disturb him, she turned into the drawing-room, and there, at her writing-table, lost herself in renewed calculations of the outlay to which the morning's conference had committed her. The fact that she could permit herself such follies had not yet lost its novelty; and somehow, in contrast to the vague apprehensions of the previous days, it now seemed an element of her recovered security, of the sense that, as Ned had said, things in general had never been "righter."

She was still luxuriating in a lavish play of figures when the parlour-maid, from the threshold, roused her with a dubiously worded inquiry as to the expediency of serving luncheon. It was one of their jokes that Trimmle announced luncheon as if she were divulging a state secret, and Mary, intent upon her papers, merely murmured an absent-minded assent.

She felt Trimmle wavering doubtfully on the threshold, as if in rebuke of such unconsidered assent; then her retreating steps sounded down the passage, and Mary, pushing away her papers, crossed the hall, and went to the library door. It was still closed, and she wavered in her turn, disliking to disturb her husband, yet anxious that he should not exceed his normal measure of work. As she stood there, balancing her impulses, the esoteric Trimmle returned with the announcement of luncheon, and Mary, thus impelled, opened the library door.

Boyne was not at his desk, and she peered about her, expecting to discover him at the book-shelves, somewhere down the length of the room; but her call brought no response, and gradually it became clear to her that he was not in the library.

She turned back to the parlour-maid.

"Mr. Boyne must be up-stairs. Please tell him that luncheon is ready."

The parlour-maid appeared to hesitate between the obvious duty of obeying orders and an equally obvious conviction of the foolishness of the injunction laid upon her. The struggle resulted in her saying doubtfully, "If you please, Madam, Mr. Boyne's not up-stairs."

"Not in his room? Are you sure?"

"I'm sure, Madam."

Mary consulted the clock. "Where is he, then?"

"He's gone out," Trimmle announced, with the superior air of one who has respectfully waited for the question that a well-ordered mind would have first propounded.

Mary's previous conjecture had been right, then. Boyne must have gone to the gardens to meet her, and since she had missed him, it was clear that he had taken the shorter way by the south door, instead of going round to the court. She crossed the hall to the glass portal opening directly on the yew garden, but the parlour-maid, after another moment of inner conflict, decided to bring out: "Please, Madam, Mr. Boyne didn't go that way."

Mary turned back. "Where *did* he go? And when?"

"He went out of the front door, up the drive, Madam." It was a matter of principle with Trimmle never to answer more than one question at a time.

"Up the drive? At this hour?" Mary went to the door herself, and glanced across the court through the long tunnel of bare limes. But its perspective was as empty as when she had scanned it on entering the house.

"Did Mr. Boyne leave no message?" she asked.

Trimmle seemed to surrender herself to a last struggle with the forces of chaos.

"No, Madam. He just went out with the gentleman."

"The gentleman? What gentleman?" Mary wheeled about, as if to front this new factor.

"The gentleman who called, Madam," said Trimmle, resignedly.

"When did a gentleman call? Do explain yourself, Trimmle!"

Only the fact that Mary was very hungry, and that she wanted to consult her husband about the greenhouses, would have caused her to lay so unusual an injunction on her attendant; and even now she was detached enough to note in Trimmle's eye the dawning defiance of the respectful subordinate who has been pressed too hard.

"I couldn't exactly say the hour, Madam, because I didn't let the gentleman in," she replied, with the air of discreetly ignoring the irregularity of her mistress's course.

"You didn't let him in?"

"No, Madam. When the bell rang I was dressing, and Agnes—"

"Go and ask Agnes, then," Mary interjected. Trimmle still wore her look of patient magnanimity. "Agnes would not know, Madam, for she had unfortunately burnt her hand in trying the wick of the new lamp from town——" Trimmle, as Mary was aware, had always been opposed to the new lamp—"and so Mrs. Dockett sent the kitchen-maid instead."

Mary looked again at the clock. "It's after two! Go and ask the kitchen-maid if Mr. Boyne left any word."

She went into luncheon without waiting, and Trimmle presently brought her there the kitchen-maid's statement that the gentleman had called about one o'clock, that Mr. Boyne had gone out with him without leaving any message. The kitchen-maid did not even know the caller's name, for he had written it on a slip of paper, which he had folded and handed to her, with the injunction to deliver it at once to Mr. Boyne.

Mary finished her luncheon, still wondering, and when it was over, and Trimmle had brought the coffee to the drawing-room, her wonder had deepened to a first faint tinge of disquietude. It was unlike Boyne to absent himself without explanation at so unwonted an hour, and the difficulty of identifying the visitor whose summons he had apparently obeyed made his disappearance the more unaccountable. Mary Boyne's experience as the wife of a busy engineer, subject to sudden calls and compelled to keep irregular hours, had trained her to the philosophic acceptance of surprises; but since Boyne's withdrawal from business he had adopted a Benedictine regularity of life. As if to make up for the dispersed and agitated years, with their "stand-up" lunches and dinners rattled down to the joltings of the dining-car, he cultivated the last refinements of punctuality and monotony, discouraging his wife's fancy for the unexpected, and declaring that to a delicate taste there were infinite gradations of pleasure in the fixed recurrences of habit.

Still, since no life can completely defend itself from the unforeseen, it was evident that all Boyne's precautions would sooner or later prove unavailable, and Mary concluded that he had cut short a tiresome visit by walking with his caller to the station, or at least accompanying him for part of the way.

This conclusion relieved her from farther preoccupation, and she went out herself to take up her conference with the gardener. Thence she walked to the village post-office, a mile or so away; and when she turned toward home, the early twilight was setting in.

She had taken a foot-path across the downs, and as Boyne, meanwhile, had probably returned from the station by the highroad, there was little likelihood of their meeting on the way. She felt sure, however, of his having reached the house before her; so sure that, when she entered it herself, without even pausing to inquire of Trimmle, she made directly for the library. But the library was still empty, and with an unwonted exactness of visual memory she immediately observed that the papers on her husband's desk lay precisely as they had lain when she had gone in to call him to luncheon.

Then of a sudden she was seized by a vague dread of the unknown. She had closed the door behind her on entering, and as she stood alone in the long, silent, shadowy room, her dread seemed to take shape and sound, to be there audibly breathing and lurking among the shadows. Her short-sighted eyes strained through them, half-discerning an actual presence, something aloof, that watched and knew; and in the recoil from that intangible propinquity she threw herself suddenly on the bell-rope and gave it a desperate pull.

The long, quavering summons brought Trimmle in precipitately with a lamp, and Mary breathed again at this sobering reappearance of the usual.

"You may bring tea if Mr. Boyne is in," she said, to justify her ring.

"Very well, Madam. But Mr. Boyne is not in," said Trimmle, putting down the lamp.

"Not in? You mean he's come back and gone out again?"

"No, Madam. He's never been back."

The dread stirred again, and Mary knew that now it had her fast.

"Not since he went out with—the gentleman?"

"Not since he went out with the gentleman."

"But who *was* the gentleman?" Mary gasped out, with the sharp note of some one trying to be heard through a confusion of meaningless noises.

"That I couldn't say, Madam." Trimmle, standing there by the lamp, seemed suddenly to grow less round and rosy, as though eclipsed by the same creeping shade of apprehension.

"But the kitchen-maid knows—wasn't it the kitchen-maid who let him in?"

"She doesn't know either, Madam, for he wrote his name on a folded paper."

Mary, through her agitation, was aware that they were both designating the unknown visitor by a vague pronoun, instead of the conventional formula which, till then, had kept their allusions within the bounds of custom. And at the same moment her mind caught at the suggestion of the folded paper.

"But he must have a name! Where is the paper?"

She moved to the desk, and began to turn over the documents that littered it. The first that caught her eye was an unfinished letter in her husband's hand, with his pen lying across it, as though dropped there at a sudden summons.

"My dear Parvis,"—who was Parvis?—"I have just received your letter announcing Elwell's death, and while I suppose there is now no farther risk of trouble, it might be safer—"

She tossed the sheet aside, and continued her search; but no folded paper was discoverable among the letters and pages of manuscript which had been swept together in a promiscuous heap, as if by a hurried or a startled gesture.

"But the kitchen-maid *saw* him. Send her here," she commanded, wondering at her dullness in not thinking sooner of so simple a solution.

Trimmle, at the behest, vanished in a flash, as if thankful to be out of the room, and when she reappeared, conducting the agitated underling, Mary had regained her self-possession, and had her questions ready.

The gentleman was a stranger, yes—that she understood. But what had he said? And, above all, what had he looked like? The first question was easily enough answered, for the disconcerting reason that he had said so little—had merely asked for Mr. Boyne, and, scribbling something on a bit of paper, had requested that it should at once be carried in to him.

"Then you don't know what he wrote? You're not sure it *was* his name?"

The kitchen-maid was not sure, but supposed it was, since he had written it in answer to her inquiry as to whom she should announce.

"And when you carried the paper in to Mr. Boyne, what did he say?"

The kitchen-maid did not think that Mr. Boyne had said anything, but she could not be sure, for just as she had handed him the paper and he was opening it, she had become aware that the visitor had followed her into the library, and she had slipped out, leaving the two gentlemen together.

"But then, if you left them in the library, how do you know that they went out of the house?"

This question plunged the witness into momentary inarticulateness, from which she was rescued by Trimmle, who, by means of ingenious circumlocutions, elicited the statement that before she could cross the hall to the back passage she had heard the gentlemen behind her, and had seen them go out of the front door together.

"Then, if you saw the gentleman twice, you must be able to tell me what he looked like."

But with this final challenge to her powers of expression it became clear that the limit of the kitchen-maid's endurance had been reached. The obligation of going to the front door to "show in" a visitor was in itself so subversive of the fundamental order of things that it had thrown her faculties into hopeless disarray, and she could only stammer out, after various panting efforts at evocation, "His hat, mum, was different-like, as you might say—"

"Different? How different?" Mary flashed out, her own mind, in the same instant, leaping back to an image left on it that morning, and then lost under layers of subsequent impressions.

"His hat had a wide brim, you mean? and his face was pale—a youngish face?" Mary pressed her, with a white-lipped intensity of interrogation. But if the kitchen-maid found any adequate answer to this challenge, it was swept away for her listener down the rushing current of her own convictions. The stranger—the stranger in the garden! Why had Mary not thought of him before? She needed no one now to tell her that it was he who had called for her husband and gone away with him. But who was he, and why had Boyne obeyed his call?

IV

It leaped out at her suddenly, like a grin out of the dark, that they had often called England so little—"such a confoundedly hard place to get lost in."

A confoundedly hard place to get lost in! That had been her husband's phrase. And now, with the whole machinery of official investigation sweeping its flash-lights from shore to shore, and across the dividing straits; now, with Boyne's name blazing from the walls of every town and village, his portrait (how that wrung her!) hawked up and down the country like the image of a hunted criminal; now the little compact populous island, so policed, surveyed and administered, revealed itself as a Sphinx-like guardian of abysmal mysteries, staring back into his wife's anguished eyes as if with the malicious joy of knowing something they would never know!

In the fortnight since Boyne's disappearance there had been no word of him, no trace of his movements. Even the usual misleading reports that raise expectancy in tortured bosoms had been few and fleeting. No one but the bewildered kitchen-maid had seen him leave the house, and no one else had seen "the gentleman" who accompanied him. All inquiries in the neighbourhood failed to elicit the memory of a stranger's presence that day in the neighbourhood of Lyng. And no one had met Edward Boyne, either alone or in company, in any of the neighbouring villages, or on the road across the downs, or at either of the local railway-stations. The sunny English noon had swallowed him as completely as if he had gone out into Cimmerian night.

Mary, while every external means of investigation was working at its highest pressure, had ransacked her husband's papers for any trace of antecedent complications, of entanglements or obligations unknown to her, that might throw a faint ray into the darkness. But if any such had existed in the background of Boyne's life, they had disappeared as completely as the slip of paper on which the visitor had written his name. There remained no possible thread of guidance except—if it were indeed an exception—the letter which Boyne had apparently been in the act of writing when he received his mysterious summons. That letter, read and reread by his wife, and submitted by her to the police, yielded little enough for conjecture to feed on.

"I have just heard of Elwell's death, and while I suppose there is now no farther risk of trouble, it might be safer——" That was all. The "risk of trouble" was easily explained by the newspaper clipping which had apprised Mary of the suit brought against her husband by one of his associates in the Blue Star enterprise. The only new information conveyed in the letter was the fact of its showing Boyne, when he wrote it, to be still apprehensive of the results of the suit, though he had assured his wife that it had been withdrawn, and though the letter itself declared that the plaintiff was dead. It took several weeks of exhaustive cabling to fix the identity of the "Parvis" to whom the fragmentary communication was addressed, but even after these inquiries had shown him to be a Waukesha lawyer, no new facts concerning the Elwell suit were elicited. He appeared to have had no direct concern in it, but to have been conversant with the facts merely as an acquaintance, and possible intermediary; and he declared himself unable to divine with what object Boyne intended to seek his assistance.

This negative information, sole fruit of the first fortnight's search, was not increased by a jot during the slow weeks that followed. Mary knew that the investigations were still being carried on, but she had a vague sense of their gradually slackening, as the actual march of time seemed to slacken. It was as though the days, flying horror-struck from the shrouded image of the one inscrutable day, gained assurance as the distance lengthened, till at last they fell back into their normal gait. And so with the human imaginations at work on the dark event. No doubt it occupied them still, but week by week and hour by hour it grew less absorbing, took up less space, was slowly but inevitably crowded out of the foreground of consciousness by the new problems perpetually bubbling up from the vaporous caldron of human experience.

Even Mary Boyne's consciousness gradually felt the same lowering of velocity. It still swayed with the incessant oscillations of conjecture; but they were slower, more rhythmical in their beat. There were moments of overwhelming lassitude when, like the victim of some poison which leaves the brain clear, but holds the body motionless, she saw herself domesticated with the Horror, accepting its perpetual presence as one of the fixed conditions of life.

These moments lengthened into hours and days, till she passed into a phase of stolid acquiescence. She watched the familiar routine of life with the incurious eye of a savage on whom the meaningless processes of civilization make but the faintest impression. She had come to regard herself as part of the routine, a spoke of the wheel, revolving with its motion; she felt almost like the furniture of the room in which she sat, an insensate object to be dusted and pushed about with the chairs and tables. And this deepening apathy held her fast at Lyng, in spite of the entreaties of friends and the usual medical recommendation of "change." Her friends supposed that her refusal to move was inspired by the belief that her husband would one day return to the spot from which he had vanished, and a beautiful legend grew up about this imaginary state of waiting. But in reality she had no such belief: the depths of anguish enclosing her were no longer lighted by flashes of hope. She was sure that Boyne would never come back, that he had gone out of her sight as completely as if Death itself had waited that day on the threshold. She had even renounced, one by one, the various theories as to his disappearance which had been advanced by the press, the police, and her own agonised imagination. In sheer lassitude her mind turned from these alternatives of horror, and sank back into the blank fact that he was gone.

No, she would never know what had become of him—no one would ever know. But the house *knew;* the library in which she spent her long, lonely evenings knew. For it was here that the last scene had been enacted, here that the stranger had come, and spoken the word which had caused Boyne to rise and follow him. The floor she trod had felt his tread; the books on the shelves had seen his face; and there were moments when the intense consciousness of the old, dusky walls seemed about to break out into some audible revelation of their secret. But the revelation never came, and she knew it would never come. Lyng was not one of the garrulous old houses that betray the secrets entrusted to them. Its very legend proved that it had always been the mute accomplice, the incorruptible custodian, of the mysteries it had surprised. And Mary Boyne,

sitting face to face with its silence, felt the futility of seeking to break it by any human means.

V

"I don't say it *wasn't* straight, yet don't say it *was* straight. It was business."

Mary, at the words, lifted her head with a start, and looked intently at the speaker.

When, half an hour before, a card with "Mr. Parvis" on it had been brought up to her, she had been immediately aware that the name had been a part of her consciousness ever since she had read it at the head of Boyne's unfinished letter. In the library she had found awaiting her a small neutral-tinted man with a bald head and gold eye-glasses, and it sent a strange tremor through her to know that this was the person to whom her husband's last known thought had been directed.

Parvis, civilly, but without vain preamble,—in the manner of a man who has his watch in his hand—had set forth the object of his visit. He had "run over" to England on business, and finding himself in the neighbourhood of Dorchester, had not wished to leave it without paying his respects to Mrs. Boyne; without asking her, if the occasion offered, what she meant to do about Bob Elwell's family.

The words touched the spring of some obscure dread in Mary's bosom. Did her visitor, after all, know what Boyne had meant by his unfinished phrase? She asked for an elucidation of his question, and noticed at once that he seemed surprised at her continued ignorance of the subject. Was it possible that she really knew as little as she said?

"I know nothing—you must tell me," she faltered out; and her visitor thereupon proceeded to unfold his story. It threw, even to her confused perceptions, and imperfectly initiated vision, a lurid glare on the whole hazy episode of the Blue Star Mine. Her husband had made his money in that brilliant speculation at the cost of "getting ahead" of some one less alert to seize the chance; the victim of his ingenuity was young Robert Elwell, who had "put him on" to the Blue Star scheme.

Parvis, at Mary's first startled cry, had thrown her a sobering glance through his impartial glasses.

"Bob Elwell wasn't smart enough, that's all; if he had been, he might have turned round and served Boyne the same way. It's the kind of thing that happens every day in business. I guess it's what the scientists call the survival of the fittest," said Mr. Parvis, evidently pleased with the aptness of his analogy.

Mary felt a physical shrinking from the next question she tried to frame; it was as though the words on her lips had a taste that nauseated her.

"But then—you accuse my husband of doing something dishonourable?"

Mr. Parvis surveyed the question dispassionately. "Oh, no, I don't. I don't even say it wasn't straight." He glanced up and down the long lines of books, as if one of them might have supplied him with the definition he sought. "I don't say it *wasn't* straight, and yet I don't say it *was* straight. It was business." After all, no definition in his category could be more comprehensive than that.

Mary sat staring at him with a look of terror. He seemed to her like the indifferent, implacable emissary of some dark, formless power.

"But Mr. Elwell's lawyers apparently did not take your view, since I suppose the suit was withdrawn by their advice."

"Oh, yes, they knew he hadn't a leg to stand on, technically. It was when they advised him to withdraw the suit that he got desperate. You see, he'd borrowed most of the money he lost in the Blue Star, and he was up a tree. That's why he shot himself when they told him he had no show."

The horror was sweeping over Mary in great, deafening waves.

"He shot himself? He killed himself because of *that?*"

"Well, he didn't kill himself, exactly. He dragged on two months before he died." Parvis emitted the statement as unemotionally as a gramophone grinding out its "record."

"You mean that he tried to kill himself, and failed? And tried again?"

"Oh, he didn't have to *try* again," said Parvis, grimly.

They sat opposite each other in silence, he swinging his eye-glass thoughtfully about his finger, she, motionless, her arms stretched along her knees in an attitude of rigid tension.

"But if you knew all this," she began at length, hardly able to force her voice above a whisper, "how is it that when I wrote you at the time of my husband's disappearance you said you didn't understand his letter?"

Parvis received this without perceptible embarrassment. "Why, I didn't understand it—strictly speaking. And it wasn't the time to talk about it, if I had. The Elwell business was settled when the suit was withdrawn. Nothing I could have told you would have helped you to find your husband."

Mary continued to scrutinize him. "Then why are you telling me now?"

Still Parvis did not hesitate. "Well, to begin with, I supposed you knew more than you appear to—I mean about the circumstances of Elwell's death. And then people are talking of it now; the whole matter's been raked up again. And I thought, if you didn't know, you ought to."

She remained silent, and he continued: "You see, it's only come out lately what a bad state Elwell's affairs were in. His wife's a proud woman, and she fought on as long as she could, going out to work, and taking sewing at home, when she got too sick— something with the heart, I believe. But she had his bedridden mother to look after, and the children, and she broke down under it, and finally had to ask for help. That attracted attention to the case, and the papers took it up, and a subscription was started. Everybody out there liked Bob Elwell, and most of the prominent names in the place are down on the list, and people began to wonder why—"

Parvis broke off to fumble in an inner pocket. "Here," he continued, "here's an account of the whole thing from the 'Sentinel'—a little sensational, of course. But I guess you'd better look it over."

He held out a newspaper to Mary, who unfolded it slowly, remembering, as she did so, the evening when, in that same room, the perusal of a clipping from the "Sentinel" had first shaken the depths of her security.

As she opened the paper, her eyes, shrinking from the glaring head-lines, "Widow of Boyne's Victim Forced to Appeal for Aid," ran down the column of text to two portraits inserted in it. The first was her husband's, taken from a photograph made the year they had come to England. It was the picture of him that she liked best, the one that stood on the writing-table up-stairs in her bedroom. As the eyes in the photograph met hers, she felt it would be impossible to read what was said of him, and closed her lids with the sharpness of the pain.

"I thought if you felt disposed to put your name down—" she heard Parvis continue.

She opened her eyes with an effort, and they fell on the other portrait. It was that of a youngish man, slightly built, with features somewhat blurred by the shadow of a projecting hat-brim. Where had she seen that outline before? She stared at it confusedly, her heart hammering in her throat and ears. Then she gave a cry.

"This is the man—the man who came for my husband!"

She heard Parvis start to his feet, and was dimly aware that she had slipped backward into the corner of the sofa, and that he was bending above her in alarm. With an intense effort she straightened herself, and reached out for the paper, which she had dropped.

"It's the man! I should know him anywhere!" she cried in a voice that sounded in her own ears like a scream.

Parvis's voice seemed to come to her from far off, down endless, fog-muffled windings.

"Mrs. Boyne, you're not very well. Shall I call somebody? Shall I get a glass of water?"

"No, no, no!" She threw herself toward him, her hand frantically clenching the newspaper. "I tell you, it's the man! I *know* him! He spoke to me in the garden!"

Parvis took the journal from her, directing his glasses to the portrait. "It can't be, Mrs. Boyne. It's Robert Elwell."

"Robert Elwell?" Her white stare seemed to travel into space. "Then it was Robert Elwell who came for him."

"Came for Boyne? The day he went away?" Parvis's voice dropped as hers rose. He bent over, laying a fraternal hand on her, as if to coax her gently back into her seat. "Why, Elwell was dead! Don't you remember?"

Mary sat with her eyes fixed on the picture, unconscious of what he was saying.

"Don't you remember Boyne's unfinished letter to me—the one you found on his desk that day? It was written just after he'd heard of Elwell's death." She noticed an odd shake in Parvis's unemotional voice. "Surely you remember that!" he urged her.

Yes, she remembered: that was the profoundest horror of it. Elwell had died the day before her husband's disappearance; and this was Elwell's portrait; and it was the portrait of the man who had spoken to her in the garden. She lifted her head and looked slowly about the library. The library could have borne witness that it was also the portrait of the man who had come in that day to call Boyne from his unfinished letter. Through the misty surgings of her brain she heard the faint boom of half-forgotten words—words spoken by Alida Stair on the lawn at Pangbourne before Boyne and his wife had ever seen the house at Lyng, or had imagined that they might one day live there.

"This was the man who spoke to me," she repeated.

She looked again at Parvis. He was trying to conceal his disturbance under what he imagined to be an expression of indulgent commiseration; but the edges of his lips were blue. "He thinks me mad; but I'm not mad," she reflected; and suddenly there flashed upon her a way of justifying her strange affirmation.

She sat quiet, controlling the quiver of her lips, and waiting till she could trust her voice to keep its habitual level; then she said, looking straight at Parvis: "Will you answer me one question, please? When was it that Robert Elwell tried to kill himself?"

"When—when?" Parvis stammered.

"Yes; the date. Please try to remember."

She saw that he was growing still more afraid of her. "I have a reason," she insisted.

"Yes, yes. Only I can't remember. About two months before, I should say."

"I want the date," she repeated.

Parvis picked up the newspaper. "We might see here," he said, still humouring her. He ran his eyes down the page. "Here it is. Last October—the——"

She caught the words from him. "The 20th, wasn't it?" With a sharp look at her, he verified. "Yes, the 20th. Then you *did* know?"

"I know now." Her white stare continued to travel past him. "Sunday, the 20th—that was the day he came first."

Parvis's voice was almost inaudible. "Came *here* first?"

"Yes."

"You saw him twice, then?"

"Yes, twice." She breathed it at him. "He came first on the 20th of October. I remember the date because it was the day we went up Meldon Steep for the first time." She felt a faint gasp of inward laughter at the thought that but for that she might have forgotten.

Parvis continued to scrutinise her, as if trying to intercept her gaze.

"We saw him from the roof," she went on. "He came down the lime-avenue toward the house. He was dressed just as he is in that picture. My husband saw him first. He was frightened, and ran down ahead of me; but there was no one there. He had vanished."

"Elwell had vanished?" Parvis faltered.

"Yes." Their two whispers seemed to grope for each other. "I couldn't think what had happened. I see now. He *tried* to come then; but he wasn't dead enough—he couldn't reach us. He had to wait for two months; and then he came back again—and Ned went with him."

She nodded at Parvis with the look of triumph of a child who has successfully worked out a difficult puzzle. But suddenly she lifted her hands with a desperate gesture, pressing them to her bursting temples.

"Oh, my God! I sent him to Ned—I told him where to go! I sent him to this room!" she screamed out.

She felt the walls of books rush toward her, like inward falling ruins; and she heard Parvis, a long way off, as if through the ruins, crying to her, and struggling to get at her. But she was numb to his touch, she did not know what he was saying. Through the tumult she heard but one clear note, the voice of Alida Stair, speaking on the lawn at Pangbourne.

"You won't know till afterward," it said. "You won't know till long, long afterward."

" 'You won't Know till afterward' it said.
'You won't know till long, long afterward.' "

BONE TO BONE
by
E. G. Swain
1912

William Whitehead, Fellow of Emmanuel College, in the University of Cambridge, became Vicar of Stoneground in the year 1731. The annals of his incumbency were doubtless short and simple: they have not survived. In his day were no newspapers to collect gossip, no Parish Magazines to record the simple events of parochial life. One event, however, of greater moment then than now, is recorded in two places. Vicar Whitehead failed in health after 23 years of work, and journeyed to Bath in what his monument calls "the vain hope of being restored." The duration of his visit is unknown; it is reasonable to suppose that he made his journey in the summer, it is certain that by the month of November his physician told him to lay aside all hope of recovery.

Then it was that the thoughts of the patient turned to the comfortable straggling vicarage he had left at Stoneground, in which he had hoped to end his days. He prayed that his successor might be as happy there as he had been himself. Setting his affairs in order, as became one who had but a short time to live, he executed a will, bequeathing to the Vicars of Stoneground, for ever, the close of ground he had recently purchased because it lay next the vicarage garden. And by a codicil, he added to the bequest his library of books. Within a few days, William Whitehead was gathered to his fathers.

A mural tablet in the north aisle of the church, records, in Latin, his services and his bequests, his two marriages, and his fruitless journey to Bath. The house he loved, but never again saw, was taken down 40 years later, and re-built by Vicar James Devie. The garden, with Vicar Whitehead's "close of ground" and other adjacent lands, was opened out and planted, somewhat before 1850, by Vicar Robert Towerson. The aspect of everything has changed. But in a convenient chamber on the first floor of the present vicarage the library of Vicar Whitehead stands very much as he used it and loved it, and as he bequeathed it to his successors "for ever."

The books there are arranged as he arranged and ticketed them. Little slips of paper, sometimes bearing interesting fragments of writing, still mark his places. His marginal comments still give life to pages from which all other interest has faded, and he would have but a dull imagination who could sit in the chamber amidst these books without ever being carried back 180 years into the past, to the time when the newest of them left the printer's hands.

Of those into whose possession the books have come, some have doubtless loved them more, and some less; some, perhaps, have left them severely alone. But neither those who loved them, nor those who loved them not, have lost them, and they passed, some century and a half after William Whitehead's death, into the hands of Mr. Batchel, who loved them as a father loves his children. He lived alone, and had few domestic cares to distract his mind. He was able, therefore, to enjoy to the full what Vicar Whitehead had enjoyed so long before him. During many a long summer evening would he sit poring over long-forgotten books; and since the chamber, otherwise called the library, faced the south, he could also spend sunny winter mornings there without discomfort. Writing at a small table, or reading as he stood at a tall desk, he would browse amongst the books like an ox in a pleasant pasture.

There were other times also, at which Mr. Batchel would use the books. Not being a sound sleeper (for book-loving men seldom are), he elected to use as a bedroom one of the two chambers which opened at either side into the library. The arrangement enabled him to beguile many a sleepless hour amongst the books, and in view of these nocturnal visits he kept a candle standing in a sconce above the desk, and matches always ready to his hand.

There was one disadvantage in this close proximity of his bed to the library. Owing, apparently, to some defect in the fittings of the room, which, having no mechanical tastes, Mr. Batchel had never investigated, there could be heard, in the stillness of the night, exactly such sounds as might arise from a person moving about amongst the books. Visitors using the other adjacent room would often remark at breakfast, that they had heard their host in the library at one or two o'clock in the morning, when, in fact, he had not left his bed. Invariably Mr. Batchel allowed them to suppose that he had been where they thought him. He disliked idle controversy, and was unwilling to afford an opening for supernatural talk. Knowing well enough the sounds by which his guests had been deceived, he wanted no other explanation of them than his own, though it was of too vague a character to count as an explanation. He conjectured that the window-sashes, or the doors, or "something," were defective, and was too phlegmatic and too unpractical to make any investigation. The matter gave him no concern.

Persons whose sleep is uncertain are apt to have their worst nights when they would like their best. The consciousness of a special need for rest seems to bring enough mental disturbance to forbid it. So on Christmas Eve, in the year 1907, Mr. Batchel, who would have liked to sleep well, in view of the labours of Christmas Day, lay hopelessly wide awake. He exhausted all the known devices for courting sleep, and, at the end, found himself wider awake than ever. A brilliant moon shone into his room, for he hated window-blinds. There was a light wind blowing, and the sounds in the library were more than usually suggestive of a person moving about. He almost determined to have the sashes "seen to," although he could seldom be induced to have anything "seen to." He disliked changes, even for the better, and would submit to great inconvenience rather than have things altered with which he had become familiar.

As he revolved these matters in his mind, he heard the clocks strike the hour of midnight, and having now lost all hope of falling asleep, he rose from his bed, got into a large dressing gown which hung in readiness for such occasions, and passed into the library, with the intention of reading himself sleepy, if he could.

The moon, by this time, had passed out of the south, and the library seemed all the darker by contrast with the moonlit chamber he had left. He could see nothing but two blue-grey rectangles formed by the windows against the sky, the furniture of the room being altogether invisible. Groping along to where the table stood, Mr. Batchel felt over its surface for the matches which usually lay there; he found, however, that the table was cleared of everything. He raised his right hand, therefore, in order to feel his way to a shelf where the matches were sometimes mislaid, and at that moment, whilst his hand was in mid-air, the matchbox was gently put into it!

Such an incident could hardly fail to disturb even a phlegmatic person, and Mr. Batchel cried "Who's this?" somewhat nervously. There was no answer. He struck a match, looked hastily round the room, and found it empty, as usual. There was everything, that is to say, that he was accustomed to see, but no other person than himself.

It is not quite accurate, however, to say that everything was in its usual state. Upon the tall desk lay a quarto volume that he had certainly not placed there. It was his quite invariable practice to replace his books upon the shelves after using them, and what we may call his library habits were precise and methodical. A book out of place like this, was not only an offence against good order, but a sign that his privacy had been intruded upon. With some surprise, therefore, he lit the candle standing ready in the sconce, and proceeded to examine the book, not sorry, in the disturbed condition in which he was, to have an occupation found for him.

The book proved to be one with which he was unfamiliar, and this made it certain that some other hand than his had removed it from its place. Its title was "The Compleat Gard'ner" of M. de la Quintinye made English by John Evelyn Esquire. It was not a work in which Mr. Batchel felt any great interest. It consisted of divers reflections on various parts of husbandry, doubtless entertaining enough, but too deliberate and discursive for practical purposes. He had certainly never used the book, and growing restless now in mind, said to himself that some boy having the freedom of the house, had taken it down from its place in the hope of finding pictures.

But even whilst he made this explanation he felt its weakness. To begin with, the desk was too high for a boy. The improbability that any boy would place a book there was equalled by the improbability that he would leave it there. To discover its uninviting character would be the work only of a moment, and no boy would have brought it so far from its shelf.

Mr. Batchel had, however, come to read, and habit was too strong with him to be wholly set aside. Leaving "The Compleat Gard'ner" on the desk, he turned round to the shelves to find some more congenial reading.

Hardly had he done this when he was startled by a sharp rap upon the desk behind him, followed by a rustling of paper. He turned quickly about and saw the quarto lying open. In obedience to the instinct of the moment, he at once sought a natural cause for what he saw. Only a wind, and that of the strongest, could have opened the book, and laid back its heavy cover; and though he accepted, for a brief moment, that explanation, he was too candid to retain it longer. The wind out of doors was very light. The window sash was closed and latched, and, to decide the matter finally, the book had its back, and not its edges, turned towards the only quarter from which a wind could strike.

Mr. Batchel approached the desk again and stood over the book. With increasing perturbation of mind (for he still thought of the matchbox) he looked upon the open page. Without much reason beyond that he felt constrained to do something, he read the words of the half completed sentence at the turn of the page—

"at dead of night he left the house and passed into the solitude of the garden."

But he read no more, nor did he give himself the trouble of discovering whose midnight wandering was being described, although the habit was singularly like one of his own. He was in no condition for reading, and turning his back upon the volume he slowly paced the length of the chamber, "wondering at that which had come to pass."

He reached the opposite end of the chamber and was in the act of turning, when again he heard the rustling of paper, and by the time he had faced round, saw the leaves of the book again turning over. In a moment the volume lay at rest, open in another place, and there was no further movement as he approached it. To make sure that he had not been deceived, he read again the words as they entered the page. The author was following a not uncommon practise of the time, and throwing common speech into forms suggested by Holy Writ: "So dig," it said, "that ye may obtain."

This passage, which to Mr. Batchel seemed reprehensible in its levity, excited at once his interest and his disapproval. He was prepared to read more, but this time was not allowed. Before his eye could pass beyond the passage already cited, the leaves of the book slowly turned again, and presented but a termination of five words and a colophon.

The words were, "to the North, an Ilex." These three passages, in which he saw no meaning and no connection, began to entangle themselves together in Mr. Batchel's mind. He found himself repeating them in different orders, now beginning with one, and now with another. Any further attempt at reading he felt to be impossible, and he was in no mind for any more experiences of the unaccountable. Sleep was, of course, further from him than ever, if that were conceivable. What he did, therefore, was to blow out the candle, to return to his moonlit bedroom, and put on more clothing, and then to pass downstairs with the object of going out of doors.

It was not unusual with Mr. Batchel to walk about his garden at night-time. This form of exercise had often, after a wakeful hour, sent him back to his bed refreshed and ready for sleep. The convenient access to the garden at such times lay through his study, whose French windows opened on to a short flight of steps, and upon these he now paused for a moment to admire the snow-like appearance of the lawns, bathed as they were in the moonlight. As he paused, he heard the city clocks strike the half-hour after midnight, and he could not forbear repeating aloud

"At dead of night he left the house, and passed into the solitude of the garden."

It was solitary enough. At intervals the screech of an owl, and now and then the noise of a train, seemed to emphasise the solitude by drawing attention to it and then leaving it in possession of the night. Mr. Batchel found himself wondering and conjecturing what Vicar Whitehead, who had acquired the close of land to secure quiet and privacy for garden, would have thought of the railways to the west and north. He turned his face northwards, whence a whistle had just sounded, and saw a tree beautifully outlined against the sky. His breath caught at the sight. Not because the tree was unfamiliar. Mr. Batchel knew all his trees. But what he had seen was "to the north, an Ilex."

Mr. Batchel knew not what to make of it all. He had walked into the garden hundreds of times and as often seen the Ilex, but the words out of the "Compleat Gard'ner" seemed to be pursuing him in a way that made him almost afraid. His temperament, however, as has been said already, was phlegmatic. It was commonly said, and Mr. Batchel approved the verdict, whilst he condemned its inexactness, that "his nerves were made of fiddle-string," so he braced himself afresh and set upon his walk round the silent garden, which he was accustomed to begin in a northerly direction, and was now too proud to change. He usually passed the Ilex at the beginning of his perambulation, and so would pass it now.

He did not pass it. A small discovery, as he reached it, annoyed and disturbed him. His gardener, as careful and punctilious as himself, never failed to house all his tools at the end of a day's work. Yet there, under the Ilex, standing upright in moonlight brilliant enough to cast a shadow of it, was a spade.

Mr. Batchel's second thought was one of relief. After his extraordinary experiences in the library (he hardly knew now whether they had been real or not) something quite commonplace would act sedatively, and he determined to carry the spade to the tool-house.

The soil was quite dry, and the surface even a little frozen, so Mr. Batchel left the path, walked up to the spade, and would have drawn it towards him. But it was as if he had made the attempt upon the trunk of the Ilex itself. The spade would not be moved. Then, first with one hand, and then with both, he tried to raise it, and still it stood firm. Mr. Batchel, of course, attributed this to the frost, slight as it was. Wondering at the spade's being there, and annoyed at its being frozen, he was about to leave it and continue his walk, when the remaining words of the "Compleat Gard'ner" seemed rather to utter themselves, than to await his will—

"So dig, that ye may obtain."

Mr. Batchel's power of independent action now deserted him. He took the spade, which no longer resisted, and began to dig. "Five spadefuls and no more," he said aloud. "This is all foolishness."

Four spadefuls of earth he then raised and spread out before him in the moonlight. There was nothing unusual to be seen. Nor did Mr. Batchel decide what he would look for, whether coins, jewels, documents in canisters, or weapons. In point of fact, he dug against what he deemed his better judgment, and expected nothing. He spread before him the fifth and last spadeful of earth, not quite without result, but with no result that was at all sensational. The earth contained a bone. Mr. Batchel's knowledge of anatomy was sufficient to show him that it was a human bone. He identified it, even by moonlight, as the *radius*, a bone of the forearm, as he removed the earth from it, with his thumb.

Such a discovery might be thought worthy of more than the very ordinary interest Mr. Batchel showed. As a matter of fact, the presence of a human bone was easily to be accounted for. Recent excavations within the church had caused the upturning of numberless bones, which had been collected and reverently buried. But an earth-stained bone is also easily overlooked, and this *radius* had obviously found its way into the garden with some of the earth brought out of the church.

Mr. Batchel was glad, rather than regretful at this termination to his adventure. He was once more provided with something to do. The re-interment of such bones as this had been his constant care, and he decided at once to restore the bone to consecrated earth. The time seemed opportune. The eyes of the curious were closed in sleep, he himself was still alert and wakeful. The spade remained by his side and the bone in his hand. So he betook himself, there and then, to the churchyard. By the still generous light of the moon, he found a place where the earth yielded to his spade, and within a few minutes the bone was laid decently to earth, some 18 inches deep.

The city clocks struck one as he finished. The whole world seemed asleep, and Mr. Batchel slowly returned to the garden with his spade. As he hung it in its accustomed place he felt stealing over him the welcome desire to sleep. He walked quietly on to the house and ascended to his room. It was now dark: the moon had passed on and left the room in shadow. He lit a candle, and before undressing passed into the library. He had an irresistible curiosity to see the passages in John Evelyn's book which had so strangely adapted themselves to the events of the past hour.

In the library a last surprise awaited him. The desk upon which the book had lain was empty. "The Compleat Gard'ner" stood in its place on the shelf. And then Mr. Batchel knew that he had handled a bone of William Whitehead, and that in response to his own entreaty.

A GHOST STORY
by
Alice Hegan Rice
1913

It was Christmas Eve and the snow was coming down in the most proper and conventional way. The little Georgia town did not usually celebrate in such an orthodox fashion, but this year was a glorious exception.

Mr. Brent Worthington rose from his desk in the office of his big cotton mill, and went to the window, smiling complacently. In fact, he had been rather well pleased with himself and the world generally ever since his arrival from New York the day before.

For ten years now he had made this flying trip South during the holiday to have a look at his plant, and to hear a full report of the year's business. It was always more or less of a bore to leave his luxurious home on the Hudson for a week in hot Pullman cars, and in small, badly-kept Southern hotels, but this year the annoyance was doubled by the fact that Christmas day would find him away from his family.

A storm of protest had followed his decision to come. His wife had argued, and his four youngsters had implored, but with Worthington, business was business, and nothing was allowed to interfere. And, after all, he had his compensation.

All day he had been attending meetings, reading statistics and hearing reports, and the result amazed him. Since his active and effective efforts to defeat the child labor bill at the last session of the legislature, a new superintendent had been installed who had reduced the pay-roll almost by a third. In fact, during the past decade, the business had actually trebled!

As he stood at the window, his eyes swept with satisfaction the group of well-kept mills surrounded by well-kept grounds. At the right was a hospital, and at the left a night-school, equipped for the employees at his own expense. Let the sentimentalists who were raising such an out-cry against manufacturers come and have a look for themselves!

What a miracle, the past ten years had wrought in his fortunes! As he looked out through the gathering dusk he could see himself as he was when he first came to Georgia. Practically penniless, without friends or influence, but possessed of a shrewd, Phoenix-like quality that made him rise from each business failure, wiser, shrewder, more confident for the next venture. Step by step he had risen at first, then by bounds. A fortunate marriage with the woman of his heart had brought him capital with which to experiment, and by that time his experiments were based on wisdom and experience. He not only became chief owner of the Georgia mill, but a promoter of vast financial projects in the East as well. His name was already among the best known of the younger men in Wall Street.

Still smiling, he looked at his watch. It was yet two hours before his dinner engagement with his partner, so he decided instead of returning to the hotel at once, he would write some letters home.

Snapping on the electric light, he sat down at the roll-top desk and was soon absorbed in covering sheet after sheet of paper with his small, precise hand-writing. The mill and all about it was soon forgotten. He was back in his home on the Hudson, in the loving environment of his family. Every familiar detail of the great living room was present to him; the mellow light from shaded lamps and flaring logs; the soft rich tones of the hangings; the glints of brass and bronze; all the warmth and glow and harmony of a well-ordered home. He could imagine his tall, fair-haired wife with baby Elsie clinging to her skirts, moving about hanging the stockings, while Bob and Kitty sat on the hearth-rug, making holly wreaths, their faces rosy with anticipation, and little Billy romped and tumbled under everybody's feet.

Mr. Worthington at last gathered up the scattered pages of his letter, and moved into a big, comfortable chair before the fire to read over what he had written. Darkness had enveloped the world outside, and the big mill was very still and deserted save for the rising wind that whistled plaintively around the sharp corners of the big, bleak building.

Suddenly, as Mr. Worthington sat there just outside the circle of light from the green-shaded hanging bulb, he became conscious of a curious phenomenon. A strange stir was becoming manifest in the mill below, the muffled whirr of machinery was heard, and a sort of subdued activity was making itself felt. He rose unsteadily and went to the door. Everything was still and yet not still, he heard things in the silence as one sometimes sees things in the dark. Greatly puzzled, he tip-toed to the stair-way and looked down.

Hurrying through the passage below were troops of shadowy children, with old, anxious faces, each apparently bent on an important errand, and each hurrying, breathless, to accomplish it. Some were ragged and dirty, all were shivering. On and on they came, some short and stunted, some tall and aenemic, some wearing spectacles, some on crutches, all eager and anxious.

Worthington came cautiously down the steps and spoke to one of the girls:

"What are you doing here?" he asked. "We've come back," she whispered without looking up, "We always have to come back on Christmas Eve."

"What for?"

"I dunno. Factory laws I reckon. All the children that ever has worked here, whether they are dead or growed up has to come back on Christmas Eve. I must go on now 'er I'll git docked."

"But wait!" cried Worthington, "I must speak with you."

"I can't wait, Mister. The mill starts at half-past five every morning and we got to be there when the wheels start. I keep a-wakin' up all through the night to see if it ain't time to git up. There's the whistle!"

He heard no sound but the soft shuffling of the children's hurrying feet. Slipping unnoticed into the throng he followed the current. Through the weave-rooms, and card-rooms they went, seeking their old occupations. By far the greater number pushed on to the spinning room, and there fell to work sweeping, doffing, spinning as if every second counted.

Worthington moved about from one group to another, but nobody glanced at him or noticed him. Finally he paused before a very small girl who was rubbing her eyes with the back of her hand.

"What is the matter?" he asked.

She turned a squinting little face up to his. The eye-lids were heavy and inflamed.

"It's me eyes," she said, "they're sick. They don't hurt me none in here where its always kinder dark, but out doors most kills 'em."

"But you've no business being here at all!" protested Worthington, "you're too little."

A sly look came into her wizened face.

"I'm a' orphunt," she said, "a orphunt don't have to be but ten."

"But you aren't ten," urged Worthington, thinking of his own ten-year old Kitty, half a head taller than the little bent figure before him.

"I kin write me name," she said defiantly, "and I got a affydavid that I'm poverty-stricken. Gus Gullers' little sister ain't but eight either, and she got in."

Worthington turned away sickened. As he made his way toward the door he seemed to see the figure of a boy bending over a whirring wheel and at the same time snatching bites from a piece of bread he held in his hand.

"Why do you eat now?" he asked irritably, "why don't you wait for your noon hour?"

"What's the diffrunce?" the boy answered sullenly. "The machin-ery don't stop fer nothin' and I got to watch this here wheel from five-thirty in the mornin' 'til five-thirty in the afternoon. There ain't no time to eat."

"How much do you make?" asked Worthington, watching the hunks of bread that were being bolted at available moments.

"Forty cents a day," said the boy, "but often we can git a extry hour or two at night. I bin on fer two hours a night three times this week!"

"Why don't you go to the night school?" Worthington sternly demanded. "That's what I built it for, for boys like you. There's a good gymnasium. Don't any of you boys take advantage of it?"

A cynical smile came into the haggard face.

"Do we look like we need exercise? Time night comes my feet is so swoll I can't git my shoes off. Some nights I jus' leaves 'em on all night. No, we don't none of us use the gymnasium."

A cold blast of air swept through the rooms, and for a moment it seemed to blow all the shadowy forms away, but presently they were back again working harder than ever. Worthington saw near him a couple of boys, better dressed and apparently better fed than the others. To them he turned hopefully:

"You don't find the mill such a very bad place, do you?"

"You betcher we don't!" answered the elder child, a sophisticated lad of thirteen, with a quid of tobacco in his mouth. "You couldn't git me back in school fer nothin'. I'm makin' seventy-five a day, and I'm on me own hook. I don't have to answer to nobody. I ain't been home fer a week, go to a picture show ever' night I don't work, and sleep in the back of Griller's saloon. No slate pencils in mine!"

Worthington's heart sank. Something in the boy's bright, keen eyes reminded him of his Bob who led his classes in the best Prep School in New York State.

"Who are those babies coming through the hall?" he asked.

"Them's the Toters. They leave school 'bout eleven to pack the grub to the mills. Onct they gits here they hardly ever gits back. They hang around and sometime pick up a job. The boss, he don't mind, it gits 'em stuck on the mill, so's they want to quit school and start to work."

Worthington looked back over the spinning room and through the door into the weave room. Every nook and corner had filled with phantom shapes. Dozens and dozens of children were still pouring in, hurrying to accomplish a given task in a given time. Their backs were bent, their eyes were heavy, and the color was gone from their faces. And this, he thought, was Christmas Eve when even the ghost of a child should be happy!

Something touched his arm. It was not one of the childish wraiths he had been watching, but a flesh-and-blood mortal like himself, a poor old derelict of a woman, with deep-set, hopeless eyes staring out of a gaunt face, and strands of grey hair falling about her shoulders.

"Have you seen them?" she asked wildly.

"Who?"

"My childern. They say that all the childern that ever has worked in the mills comes back to their work on Christmas Eve. I never see mine ner hear 'em, but I comes every year just to be near if they should come."

"How many were there?" asked Worthington.

"Six, sir. I brought 'em here after their father died, 'cause I didn't know no other way. I started in at the mills myself when I was nine, and I never knowed nothin' else. I been workin' here off and on ever since. I can remember when I first started how eager and willin' I was. I couldn't wait fer the whistles to blow. And now Heaven just seems like a place where there ain't no whistles."

"And the children, were they willing to work here?"

"Oh yes, sir. Willin' and eager like me, at first. But they got tireder and tireder, 'til they died off one by one. And now there's just me left, left to go on doing the same thing I been doing eleven hours a day for nearly forty years, and ninety cents and a broken heart each night to show fer it all. Oh! I want my childern, my childern!"

Worthington felt a sudden spasm in his throat, and a burning under his lids. At the same moment came the sharp ring of the telephone. Instinctively he put out his hand and it closed on the receiver that stood on his office desk.

"Hello there!" came the cheery voice of his partner. "I've been trying to locate you. The turkey is getting cold. Aren't you coming to help us celebrate Christmas?"

"Sure," said Worthington, still somewhat dazed. "I'll be there in twenty minutes. But I say, Old Man, we'll have to cut out the after festivities. You see,—I—the truth is a most important matter has just come up at the mill, and I've got to thresh the whole business out with you before I take that mid-night train for New York."

THE SNOW
by
Hugh Walpole
1929

The second Mrs. Ryder was a young woman not easily frightened, but now she stood in the dusk of the passage leaning back against the wall, her hand on her heart, looking at the grey-faced window beyond which the snow was steadily falling against the lamplight.

The passage where she was led from the study to the dining-room, and the window looked out on to the little paved path that ran at the edge of the Cathedral green. As she stared down the passage she couldn't be sure whether the woman were there or no. How absurd of her! She knew the woman was not there. But if the woman was not, how was it that she could discern so clearly the old-fashioned grey cloak, the untidy grey hair and the sharp outline of the pale cheek and pointed chin? Yes, and more than that, the long sweep of the grey dress, falling in folds to the ground, the flash of a gold ring on the white hand. No. No. NO. This was madness. There was no one and nothing there. Hallucination . . .

Very faintly a voice seemed to come to her: 'I warned you. This is for the last time. . . .'

The nonsense! How far now was her imagination to carry her? Tiny sounds about the house, the running of a tap somewhere, a faint voice from the kitchen, these and something more had translated themselves into an imagined voice. 'The last time . . .'

But her terror was real. She was not normally frightened by anything. She was young and healthy and bold, fond of sport, hunting, shooting, taking any risk. Now she was truly *stiffened* with terror—she could not move, could not advance down the passage as she wanted to and find light, warmth, safety in the dining-room. All the time the snow fell steadily, stealthily, with its own secret purpose, maliciously, beyond the window in the pale glow of the lamplight.

Then unexpectedly there was noise from the hall, opening of doors, a rush of feet, a pause and then in clear beautiful voices the well-known strains of 'Good King Wenceslas.' It was the Cathedral choir boys on their regular Christmas round. This was Christmas Eve. They always came just at this hour on Christmas Eve.

With an intense, almost incredible relief she turned back into the hall. At the same moment her husband came out of the study.

They stood together smiling at the little group of mufflered, becoated boys who were singing, heart and soul in the job, so that the old house simply rang with their melody.

Reassured by the warmth and human company, she lost her terror. It had been her imagination. Of late she had been none too well. That was why she had been so irritable. Old Doctor Bernard was no good: he didn't understand her case at all. After Christmas she would go to London and have the very best advice . . .

Had she been well she could not, half an hour ago, have shown such miserable temper over nothing. She knew that it was over nothing and yet that knowledge did not make it any easier for her to restrain herself. After every bout of temper she told herself that there should never be another—and then Herbert said something irritating, one of his silly muddle-headed stupidities, and she was off again!

She could see now as she stood beside him at the bottom of the staircase, that he was still feeling it. She had certainly half an hour ago said some abominably rude personal things—things that she had not at all meant—and he had taken them in his meek, quiet way. Were he not so meek and quiet, did he only pay her back in her own coin, she would never lose her temper. Of that she was sure. But who wouldn't be irritated by that meekness and by the only reproachful thing that he ever said to her: 'Elinor understood me better, my dear '? To throw the first wife up against the second! Wasn't that the most tactless thing that a man could possibly do? And Elinor, that worn elderly woman, the very opposite of her own gay, bright, amusing self? That was why Herbert had loved her, because she was gay and bright and young. It was true that Elinor had been devoted, that she had been so utterly wrapped up in Herbert that she lived only for him. People were always recalling her devotion, which was sufficiently rude and tactless of them.

Well, she could not give anyone that kind of old-fashioned sugary devotion; it wasn't in her, and Herbert knew it by this time.

Nevertheless she loved Herbert in her own way, as he must know, know it so well that he ought to pay no attention to the bursts of temper. She wasn't well. She would see a doctor in London . . .

The little boys finished their carols, were properly rewarded, and tumbled like feathery birds out into the snow again. They went into the study, the two of them, and stood beside the big open log-fire. She put her hand up and stroked his thin beautiful cheek.

'I'm so sorry to have been cross just now, Bertie. I didn't mean half I said, you know.'

But he didn't, as he usually did, kiss her and tell her that it didn't matter. Looking straight in front of him, he answered:

'Well, Alice, I do wish you wouldn't. It hurts, horribly. It upsets me more than you think. And it's growing on you. You make me miserable. I don't know what to do about it. And it's all about nothing.'

Irritated at not receiving the usual commendation for her sweetness in making it up again, she withdrew a little and answered:

'Oh, all right. I've said I'm sorry. I can't do any more.'

'But tell me,' he insisted, 'I want to know. What makes you so angry, so suddenly?—and about nothing at all.'

She was about to let her anger rise, her anger at his obtuseness, obstinacy, when some fear checked her, a strange unanalysed fear, as though someone had whispered to her, 'Look out! This is the last time!'

'It's not altogether my own fault,' she answered, and left the room.

She stood in the cold hall, wondering where to go. She could feel the snow falling outside the house and shivered. She hated the snow, she hated the winter, this beastly, cold dark English winter that went on and on, only at last to change into a damp, soggy English spring.

It had been snowing all day. In Polchester it was unusual to have so heavy a snowfall. This was the hardest winter that they had known for many years.

When she urged Herbert to winter abroad—which he could quite easily do—he answered her impatiently; he had the strongest affection for this poky dead-and-alive Cathedral town. The Cathedral seemed to be precious to him; he wasn't happy if he didn't go and see it every day! She wouldn't wonder if he didn't think more of the Cathedral than he did of herself. Elinor had been the same; she had even written a little book about the Cathedral, about the Black Bishop's Tomb and the stained glass and the rest . . .

What was the Cathedral after all? Only a building!

She was standing in the drawing-room looking out over the dusky ghostly snow to the great hulk of the Cathedral that Herbert said was like a flying ship, but to herself was more like a crouching beast licking its lips over the miserable sinners that it was for ever devouring.

As she looked and shivered, feeling that in spite of herself her temper and misery were rising so that they threatened to choke her, it seemed to her that her bright and cheerful fire-lit drawing-room was suddenly open to the snow. It was exactly as though cracks had appeared everywhere, in the ceiling, the walls, the windows, and that through these cracks the snow was filtering, dribbling in little tracks of wet down the walls, already perhaps making pools of water on the carpet.

This was of course imagination, but it was a fact that the room was most dreadfully cold although a great fire was burning and it was the cosiest room in the house.

Then, turning, she saw the figure standing by the door. This time there could be no mistake. It was a grey shadow, and yet a shadow with form and outline—the untidy grey hair, the pale face like a moon-lit leaf, the long grey clothes, and something obstinate, vindictive, terribly menacing in its pose.

She moved and the figure was gone; there was nothing there and the room was warm again, quite hot in fact. But young Mrs. Ryder, who had never feared anything in all her life save the vanishing of her youth, was trembling so that she had to sit down, and even then her trembling did not cease. Her hand shook on the arm of her chair.

She had created this thing out of her imagination of Elinor's hatred of her and her own hatred of Elinor. It was true that they had never met, but who knew but that the spiritualists were right, and Elinor's spirit, jealous of Herbert's love for her, had been there driving them apart, forcing her to lose her temper and then hating her for losing it? Such things might be! But she had not much time for speculation. She was preoccupied with her fear. It was a definite, positive fear, the kind of fear that one has just before one goes under an operation. Someone or something was threatening her. She clung to her chair as though to leave it were to plunge into disaster. She looked around her everywhere; all the familiar things, the pictures, the books, the little tables, the piano were different now, isolated, strange, hostile, as though they had been won over by some enemy power.

She longed for Herbert to come and protect her; she felt most kindly to him. She would never lose her temper with him again— and at that same moment some cold voice seemed to whisper in her ear: 'You had better not. It will be for the last time.'

At length she found courage to rise, cross the room and go up to dress for dinner. In her bedroom courage came to her once more. It was certainly very cold, and the snow, as she could see when she looked between her curtains, was falling more heavily than ever, but she had a warm bath, sat in front of her fire and was sensible again.

For many months this odd sense that she was watched and accompanied by someone hostile to her had been growing. It was the stronger perhaps because of the things that Herbert told her about Elinor; she was the kind of woman, he said, who, once she loved anyone, would never relinquish her grasp; she was utterly faithful. He implied that her tenacious fidelity had been at times a little difficult.

'She always said,' he added once,'that she would watch over me until I rejoined her in the next world. Poor Elinor!' he sighed. 'She had a fine religious faith, stronger than mine, I fear.'

It was always after one of her tantrums that young Mrs. Ryder had been most conscious of this hallucination, this dreadful discomfort of feeling that someone was near you who hated you—but it was only during the last week that she began to fancy that she actually saw anyone, and with every day her sense of this figure had grown stronger.

It was, of course, only nerves, but it was one of those nervous afflictions that became tiresome indeed if you did not rid yourself of it. Mrs. Ryder, secure now in the warmth and intimacy of her bedroom, determined that henceforth everything should be sweetness and light. No more tempers! Those were the things that did her harm.

Even though Herbert were a little trying, was not that the case with every husband in the world? And was it not Christmas time? Peace and Good Will to men! Peace and Good Will to Herbert!

They sat down opposite to one another in the pretty little dining-room hung with Chinese woodcuts, the table gleaming and the amber curtains richly dark in the firelight.

But Herbert was not himself. He was still brooding, she supposed, over their quarrel of the afternoon. Weren't men children? Incredible the children that they were!

So when the maid was out of the room she went over to him, bent down and kissed his forehead.

'Darling . . . you're still cross, I can see you are. You mustn't be. Really you mustn't. It's Christmas time and, if I forgive you, you must forgive me.'

'You forgive me?' he asked, looking at her in his most aggravating way. 'What have you to forgive me for?'

Well, that was really too much. When she had taken all the steps, humbled her pride.

She went back to her seat, but for a while could not answer him because the maid was there. When they were alone again she said, summoning all her patience:

'Bertie dear, do you really think that there's anything to be gained by sulking like this? It isn't worthy of you. It isn't really.'

He answered her quietly.

'Sulking? No, that's not the right word. But I've got to keep quiet. If I don't I shall say something I'm sorry for.' Then, after a pause, in a low voice, as though to himself: 'These constant rows are awful.'

Her temper was rising again; another self that had nothing to do with her real self, a stranger to her and yet a very old familiar friend.

'Don't be so self-righteous,' she answered, her voice trembling a little. 'These quarrels are entirely my own fault, aren't they?'

'Elinor and I never quarrelled,' he said, so softly that she scarcely heard him.

'No! Because Elinor thought you perfect. She adored you. You've often told me. I don't think you perfect. I'm not perfect either. But we've both got faults. I'm not the only one to blame.'

'We'd better separate,' he said, suddenly looking up. 'We don't get on now. We used to. I don't know what's changed everything. But, as things are, we'd better separate.'

She looked at him and knew that she loved him more than ever, but because she loved him so much she wanted to hurt him, and because he had said that he thought he could get on without her she was so angry that she forgot all caution. Her love and her anger helped one another. The more angry she became the more she loved him.

'I know why you want to separate,' she said. 'It's because you're in love with someone else. ('How funny,' something inside her said. 'You don't mean a word of this.') You've treated me as you have, and then you leave me.'

'I'm not in love with anyone else,' he answered her steadily, 'and you know it. But we are so unhappy together that it's silly to go on . . . silly. . . . The whole thing has failed.'

There was so much unhappiness, so much bitterness, in his voice that she realised that at last she had truly gone too far. She had lost him.

She had not meant this. She was frightened and her fear made her so angry that she went across to him.

'Very well then . . . I'll tell everyone . . . what you've been. How you've treated me.'

'Not another scene,' he answered wearily. 'I can't stand any more. Let's wait. Tomorrow is Christmas Day . . .'

He was so unhappy that her anger with herself maddened her. She couldn't bear his sad, hopeless disappointment with herself, their life together, everything.

In a fury of blind temper she struck him; it was as though she were striking herself. He got up and without a word left the room. There was a pause, and then she heard the hall door close. He had left the house.

She stood there, slowly coming to her control again. When she lost her temper it was as though she sank under water. When it was all over she came once more to the surface of life, wondering where she'd been and what she had been doing. Now she stood there, bewildered, and then at once she was aware of two things, one that the room was bitterly cold and the other that someone was in the room with her.

This time she did not need to look around her. She did not turn at all, but only stared straight at the curtained windows, seeing them very carefully, as though she were summing them up for some future analysis, with their thick amber folds, gold rod, white lines—and beyond them the snow was falling.

She did not need to turn, but, with a shiver of terror, she was aware that that grey figure who had, all these last weeks, been approaching ever more closely, was almost at her very elbow. She heard quite clearly: 'I warned you. That was the last time.''

At the same moment Onslow the butler came in. Onslow was broad, fat and rubicund—a good faithful butler with a passion for church music. He was a bachelor and, it was said, disappointed of women. He had an old mother in Liverpool to whom he was greatly attached.

In a flash of consciousness she thought of all these things when he came in. She expected him also to see the grey figure at her side. But he was undisturbed, his ceremonial complacency clothed him securely.

'Mr. Fairfax has gone out,' she said firmly. Oh, surely he must see something, feel something.

'Yes, Madam!' Then, smiling rather grandly: 'It's snowing hard. Never seen it harder here. Shall I build up the fire in the drawing-room, Madam?'

'No, thank you. But Mr. Fairfax's study . . .'

'Yes, Madam. I only thought that as this room was so warm you might find it chilly in the drawing-room.'

This room warm, when she was shivering from head to foot; but holding herself lest he should see . . . She longed to keep him there, to implore him to remain; but in a moment he was gone, softly closing the door behind him.

Then a mad longing for flight seized her, and she could not move. She was rooted there to the floor, and even as, wildly trying to cry, to scream, to shriek the house down, she found that only a little whisper would come, she felt the cold touch of a hand on hers.

She did not turn her head: her whole personality, all her past life, her poor little courage, her miserable fortitude were summoned to meet this sense of approaching death which was as unmistakable as a certain smell, or the familiar ringing of a gong.

She had dreamt in nightmares of approaching death and it had always been like this, a fearful constriction of the heart, a paralysis of the limbs, a choking sense of disaster like an anaesthetic.

'You were warned,' something said to her again.

She knew that if she turned she would see Elinor's face, set, white, remorseless. The woman had always hated her, been vilely jealous of her, protecting her wretched Herbert.

A certain vindictiveness seemed to release her. She found that she could move, her limbs were free.

She passed to the door, ran down the passage, into the hall. Where would she be safe? She thought of the Cathedral, where to-night there was a carol service. She opened the hall door and just as she was, meeting the thick, involving, muffling snow, she ran out.

She started across the green towards the Cathedral door. Her thin black slippers sank in the snow. Snow was everywhere—in her hair, her eyes, her nostrils, her mouth, on her bare neck, between her breasts.

'Help! Help! Help!' she wanted to cry, but the snow choked her. Lights whirled about her. The Cathedral rose like a huge black eagle and flew towards her.

She fell forward, and even as she fell a hand, far colder than the snow, caught her neck. She lay struggling in the snow and as she struggled there two hands of an icy fleshless chill closed about her throat.

Her last knowledge was of the hard outline of a ring pressing into her neck. Then she lay still, her face in the snow, and the flakes eagerly, savagely, covered her.

ABOUT THE EDITOR

Andi Brooks is an Anglo-Irish writer and anthologist based in Tokyo. He began writing on vintage horror and science fiction films for UK and American magazines in the early 1990s. With Frank J. Dello Stritto, he co-authored *Vampire Over London: Bela Lugosi in Britain* (Cult Movies Press 2000), a critically acclaimed biography of the famous movie star who defined the portrayal of Dracula on both stage and screen. A greatly expanded second edition was published in 2015. In 2017, Andi received the *Rondo Hatton Classic Horror Award* for *Dracula and the It Girl*, an article recounting the short-lived love affair between Bela Lugosi and silent screen star Clara Bow. His short stories and poetry have been published in anthologies and magazines in the UK and Japan, and read on the *Kaidankai: Ghost and Supernatural Stories podcast.*

In 2020, he published *Ghostly Tales of Japan*, a collection of thirty original ghostly stories set throughout Japanese history. The book was published in French and Japanese editions in 2022.

In addition to writing fiction, Andi is a copywriter and feature writer for the men's fashion magazine, *The Rake Japan,* the curator of *The Bela Lugosi Blog*, and an electronic musician. Boasting ancestors who had regular congress with the spirit world, Andi has enjoyed a lifelong interest in the supernatural.

CHRISTMAS CLASSICS FROM KIKUI PRESS

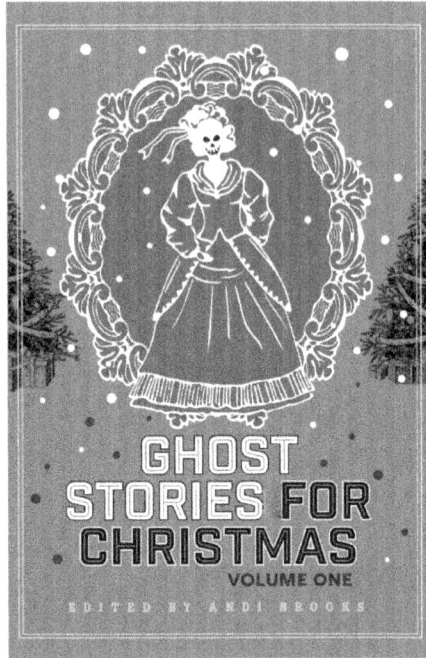

GHOST STORIES FOR CHRISTMAS VOLUME ONE

Embrace the spirits of Christmases past with this bumper illustrated anthology of festive tales from the golden age of the Christmas ghost story. This first volume in an annual series brings together an enthralling collection of Christmas ghost stories from the pens of writers both legendary and all-but-forgotten. Within its covers, you will find whimsical tales to bring a smile to your face, poignant tales to bring a tear to your eye, and blood-curdling tales to send a chill of festive fear coursing through your veins.

Turn the lights down low and snuggle up in your favourite corner to read these ghostly stories of Christmas long ago, but don't forget to keep one eye on the shadows closing in around you!

Available in paperback and Kindle editions from all Amazon marketplaces.

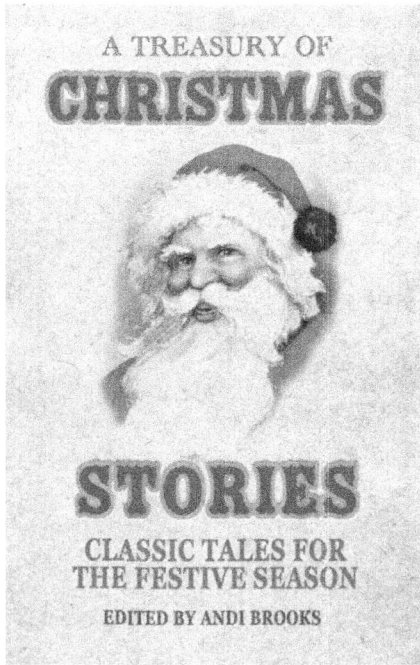

A TREASURY OF CHRISTMAS STORIES
Classic Tales for the Festive Season

Celebrate the most joyous time in the year-long calendar with this heart-warming illustrated collection of Christmas stories, poems, and newspaper articles from around the world. Capturing the timeless spirit of the season, *A Treasury of Christmas Stories* will become a cherished part of the festive season for you and your family for many Christmasses to come.

Featuring: The Elves and the Shoemaker, Account of a Visit From St. Nicolas, The Fir Tree, The Beggar Boy at Christ's Christmas Tree, The Snow Man, In the Workhouse-Christmas Day, Babouscka, A Christmas Dream and How it Came True, Christmas at Sea, Is There Really a Santa Claus, The House of the Seven Santas, The Gift of the Magi, The Adventure of the Blue Carbuncle, Christmas Every day, and more

Available in paperback and Kindle editions from all Amazon marketplaces.

BY ANDI BROOKS

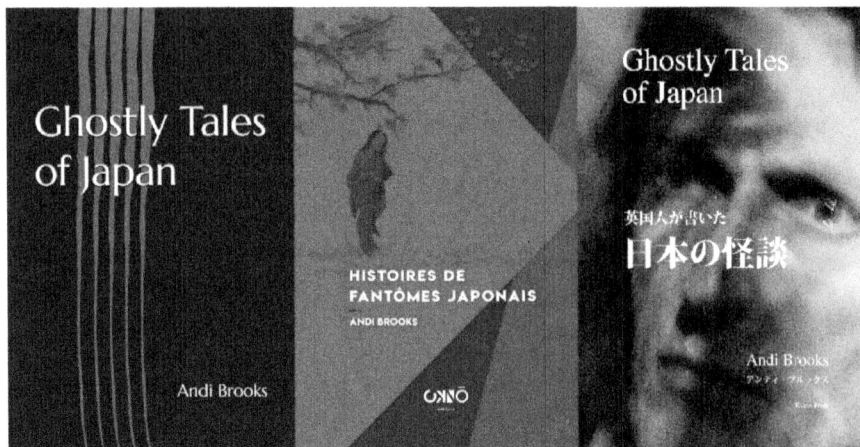

GHOSTLY TALES OF JAPAN

An eerie collection of stories, *Ghostly Tales of Japan* explores the mysterious side of a country where the supernatural is accepted as an everyday fact of life. From the ancient past to the present day, award-winning writer and long-term Tokyo resident Andi Brooks takes you on a journey into a realm of shadows separated from our own world by a gossamer-thin veil. By turns horrific, whimsical, and moving, the thirty original stories will make you question the reality of the world around you.

English Kindle, paperback and hardback editions published by *Kikui Press* (kikuipress@gmail.com). Available from all Amazon marketplaces. Ebook edition available from all major online book stores.

French grand format and poche paperback editions published by *OKNO-éditions*: www.oknofilmseditions.fr/okno-editions (contact@oknofilmseditions.fr).

Japanese paperback and Kindle editions published by *Kikui Press*.

Available from all Amazon marketplaces.

WITH FRANK J. DELLO STRITTO

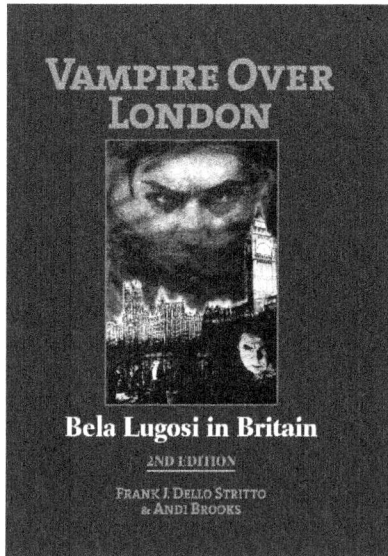

VAMPIRE OVER LONDON: BELA LUGOSI IN BRITAIN
(Expanded Second Edition)

The critically acclaimed updated and greatly expanded second edition biography of Hungarian-born actor Bela Lugosi is a compelling tale of a fading Hollywood legend's last stab at greatness. Retracing Lugosi's forgotten last tour of Dracula in austere post-war Britain, Frank J. Dello Stritto & Andi Brooks have unearthed previously unknown facts, interviewed Lugosi's co-workers who had never spoken publicly about their time with him, and located scores of people across Britain who saw Lugosi's last Dracula and still remember the thrill of seeing him perform. The authors also tell the behind-the-scenes stories of Lugosi's British films: Mystery of the Mary Celeste (1935), Dark Eyes of London (1939), and Mother Riley Meets the Vampire (1951). Vampire Over London tells, for the first time, the full story of Bela Lugosi in Britain. This deluxe hardback edition is available from *Cult Movies Press*: www.cultmoviespress.com

GHOST STORIES
FOR
CHRISTMAS
Volume Three

coming from

KIKUI PRESS

in

2024

Printed in Great Britain
by Amazon